D0399413

THIS WICKED WORLD

ALSO BY RICHARD LANGE

Dead Boys

THIS WICKED WORLD

A Novel

Richard Lange

LITTLE, BROWN AND COMPANY
New York Boston London

Little, Brown and Company
Hachette Book Group
237 Park Avenue, New York, NY 10017
Visit our website at www.HachetteBookGroup.com

First Edition: June 2009

Library of Congress Cataloging-in-Publication Data
Lange, Richard.
This wicked world : a novel / Richard Lange.—1st ed.
p. cm.
ISBN 978-0-316-01737-4
1. Bartenders—Fiction. 2. Murder—Investigation—California—Los Angeles—Fiction. 3. Los Angeles (Calif.)—Fiction. I. Title.
PS3612.A565T48 2009
813'.6—dc22 2009006620

10 9 8 7 6 5 4 3 2 1

RRD-IN

Printed in the United States of America

For Kim Turner

"There's a light within the light."

No hope.

See, that's what gives me guts.

—Minutemen, "It's Expected I'm Gone"

THIS WICKED WORLD

Prologue

Oscar awoke from a dream of heaven. Opening his eyes, he saw swollen clouds massed in a dark sky and realized that he was back on earth. No more glittering mansions, no more streets of gold.

He sat up on the bench in MacArthur Park, and the pain that roared through him drove tears into his eyes. His arms, his legs—there was no part of his body that didn't hurt. He was full of liquid fire that burned him from the inside out.

He lifted his shirt. The makeshift bandage he'd fashioned out of a blue cotton dress he'd found in a Dumpster had slipped out of place, exposing the worst of the bites on his stomach. The edges of the wound were black, and it oozed bloody pus. Afraid to look too closely, Oscar grimaced and slid the bandage back into position.

Struggling to his feet, he hobbled along the concrete path that led to the lake on the other side of the park, careful not to stumble, lest he attract the attention of the police who patrolled the area. He was feverish, dizzy. The shouts of a group of boys playing soccer were like nails being pounded into his throbbing head as he hurried into the dank, piss-smelling tunnel that passed under Wilshire Boulevard.

When he was midway through the passage, he turned to look over his shoulder, and there it was, the devil that had been following him all morning, silhouetted against the square of light at the entrance to the tunnel. Oscar could make out the creature's horns, its tail, its cloven hooves. He'd always known that the time would come when he'd have to pay for his sins, and he was ready, he would go without a fight, but not until he'd said good-bye to Maribel and the baby. Carlos would give him money to go to them. He had to find Carlos.

He came up out of the tunnel and walked next to the lake. A cold wind ruffled the surface of the black water, and an empty paper cup floating there spun round and round like something wounded. Oscar had seen fishermen pull tennis shoes from the murk, a sleeping bag, a rusty sword, and there were rumors of corpses resting on the bottom.

Near the boathouse a fat white duck quacked furiously as Oscar passed by.

"Farewell, my friend," Oscar said. He'd been talking to birds since he was a child in Guatemala. The other boys had called him Saint Francis. Spray from the fountain in the middle of the lake, a flickering plume of water twenty feet high, was like a cool hand on his cheek. He watched the tall palm trees that bordered the park hiss and strike like angry snakes.

At the frantic corner of Wilshire and Alvarado an old man preached the love of Jesus through a cheap megaphone that wreathed his words in static. "Jesus is love! Jesus is power! Jesus is life!" Juanito was there too, hawking counterfeit ID cards. He sat on a fire hydrant and whispered offers at passersby, his eyes constantly moving, alert for police or gangbangers who might try to shake him down. Oscar asked if he'd seen Carlos.

"You look like shit," Juanito said.

"*Callate, pendejo*. Just tell me where he is."

"Home Depot, with Francisco. Some white son of a bitch said he'd use them on a painting job today."

Oscar coughed. The pain buckled his knees, and purple spiders skittered across his eyeballs.

"Come to Jesus!" the old man with the megaphone yelled.

"Yes, come to Jesus," Oscar said to the devil.

Juanito hissed and shook his head. "You keep talking to yourself like that, and they're gonna lock you up."

Oscar crossed Alvarado and headed east on Wilshire. The delicious smell drifting out of a *pupuseria* stopped him in his tracks. He hadn't eaten in two days, couldn't keep anything down. When he opened the door, the dark-skinned fat woman behind the counter turned away from the portable television she was watching and looked at him. It was a tiny restaurant: two tables with plastic floral-print tablecloths, the specials handwritten on sheets of colored paper tacked to the walls.

"*Por favor,*" Oscar said. "Can you give a sick man something to eat?"

"Get out of here, you filthy drunk," the woman shouted. "This is a respectable place."

"*Por favor, señora.*"

The woman picked up the knife she'd been using to chop carrots and pointed it at Oscar.

"Out with you. Now!"

"Fuck you then, you old witch," Oscar said. He spit on the floor before hurrying outside.

A block later he stopped and leaned against the side of a building. He was racked by chills that rattled his teeth. God give me strength, he prayed. The devil trotted up the sidewalk toward him. It had a pointy black beard and carried a flaming sword. Oscar saw it best out of the corner of his eye. If he looked at the demon directly, it turned into an old man or a schoolgirl or a mailbox.

"I'm not afraid of you," Oscar shouted at the devil. "I'm ready to die." But who, he wondered, would take care of his animals when he was gone?

Carlos, Francisco, and a few others were sitting on a low cinderblock wall next to the driveway at Home Depot. As Oscar approached, a pickup pulled out of the parking lot, and the men swarmed around it, shouting, "Take me." "I speaking English." "How many?" The driver shook his head and left without hiring anyone.

"The fat queer."

"Seriously. He wanted someone to fuck him in the ass."

"Give me a hundred bucks, and I'll do it," Carlos said. He saw Oscar and shouted, "Look out! A zombie!"

Oscar stumbled over to the group and sank to the cold sidewalk, rested his back against the wall. Sweat rolled down his face and neck; his T-shirt was soaked with it.

"Man, I've got to tell you, you stink," Francisco said. "Last night it was so bad, it was like sleeping next to a dead pig."

Carlos punched him in the arm and said, "Have mercy. The boy's sick."

"Sure, fine, so change beds with me."

Waving Francisco quiet, Carlos crouched next to Oscar and asked him, "How is it today?"

Oscar shook his head, too exhausted to speak. He couldn't even open his eyes. A police car raced past, lights flashing, sirens blaring, and to Oscar it sounded like the end of the world.

"Have you eaten?" Carlos asked.

Again Oscar shook his head. Carlos moved closer to him, grabbed one of his arms, and draped it around his neck. "Francisco," he said, "let's carry him to McDonald's."

"What about the painting?"

"That *cabrón* isn't going to show up. A storm is coming. Get over here."

They helped Oscar walk across the parking lot to the restaurant and sat him in one of the plastic booths. Francisco left to meet a girl in the park, and Carlos joined the long line of customers waiting to order at the counter. Oscar watched the children in the restaurant's playground. One little boy had such a serious look on his face as he climbed and crawled and slid that Oscar almost laughed. He thought of his son, looked forward to holding him once more.

Carlos brought Oscar a cheeseburger and an orange juice. Oscar managed to choke down half of the sandwich before the nausea set in. When he reached for the juice, Carlos grabbed his hand and examined the bites there.

"These are infected," he said. "My father lost a foot that way. You've got to go to the clinic."

"They know that I'm hurt," Oscar replied. "They may be watching it."

"We'll sneak in the back, then. We'll put you in a disguise."

Oscar pulled his hand away and shook his head. "It's not important," he said. "The devil has come for me, and there's nothing I can do about it."

"You're delirious," Carlos said. "Your blood is full of poison. Please let me take you to see the doctor."

Oscar smiled, though it hurt his cracked lips to do so.

"You've always been a good friend, Carlos," he said. "Remember in Zunil, when we stole that burro from the trashman, and it kicked you in the ass? I tell you, I've never laughed so hard in my life."

"You were supposed to have control over all the animals, Saint Francis. What happened?"

Oscar watched an old man in a McDonald's uniform mop up a drink that had been spilled on the floor. Was this the better life the man had dreamed of?

"We should never have come here," he said.

"But we did," Carlos replied, "and now here we are."

Oscar pushed away the tray with the rest of the burger on it and sat up a little straighter. "Listen," he said, "I want to see Maribel and Alex. Could you give me money for the bus?"

"If you promise to go to the clinic when you return," Carlos said.

Oscar placed his hand over his heart. "I promise," he said.

Carlos passed him two dollar bills and a few quarters.

Oscar sipped from his drink, then said, "And will you feed my dog tonight?"

Oscar felt stronger when they got out into the fresh air, which was now heavy with the threat of rain. His head was clearer, and he could walk without stumbling. He and Carlos banged fists when they parted in front of Home Depot, and Oscar blinked back tears. He knew it was the last time they would see each other.

On his way back to Alvarado to catch a bus going south, he passed a botanica and decided to stop in. A bell rang when he entered. It was a small, dusty shop, cluttered with votive candles and incense and icons. A statue of San Simón, in a broad-brimmed hat, black suit, and red tie, sat on the counter between the Virgin of Guadalupe and a hooded Santa Muerte.

Oscar's mother had often visited Simón's shrine in Zunil to ask for things like luck in the lottery or a new kitchen table. Oscar always thought it was a bit silly, a comfort for superstitious housewives and old men. The Church didn't even recognize Simón after all. Today, though, Oscar was happy to see something that reminded him of home. Others had left offerings of tequila and cigars, but he had nothing to give. Nonetheless, he bowed his head and mumbled a quick prayer.

"Oh powerful San Simón, please help me and protect me from any dangers. Oh Judas Simón, I call you brother in my heart because you are everywhere and you are always with me."

The owner of the shop, a tall, skinny man in a long robe and feathered headdress, parted a curtain of beads and stepped through it.

"Can I help you, my son?" he asked.

"I was just speaking to San Simón."

"You seem troubled. Would you like to come in back for a cleansing? Only twenty dollars, and you will feel much better."

"I have no money, sir."

"No money?"

"I am a poor man."

"I see, but you must understand that you can't get something without giving something. Especially from San Simón."

"You smile when you say that?" Oscar snapped. "But you should be ashamed to be living in this world."

The owner scowled and pointed. "Your nose," he said.

Oscar raised his hand to his face, and his fingers came away covered with blood.

It was raining when he walked out. He squeezed his nostrils shut with the napkin the store owner had given him and tilted his head back to let the fat drops cool his face. The pain inside him had returned, more intense than ever, but he kept moving, afraid that if he stopped, he wouldn't get started again.

Los Angeles was not its haughty self in the rain. It was like a wet cat: humiliated, confused. People stepped gingerly on suddenly slippery sidewalks, looking like they'd been lied to. The gutters, clogged with garbage, overflowed, and water puddled in busy intersections.

Oscar waited for the bus with a mumbling loco and a couple of old ladies who shared an umbrella. The rain came down harder, the drops slamming into the pavement like suicides. Oscar zipped his jacket and pulled the hood over his head.

The bus arrived, a great hissing, snorting beast throwing up silver sheets of spray. Oscar climbed aboard and pushed his way to the back. It was too hot; there were too many people. He winced every time he brushed against someone, and his whole body was slick with rancid sweat. A few stops later a seat opened up, and he fell into it.

Raindrops chased one another across the window. Though it was only noon, it had grown so dark outside, all the cars had their lights on. Oscar began to have trouble breathing. It felt like someone was standing on his chest. For the first time he was frightened.

When he closed his eyes he saw heaven; when he opened them, the rain. The bus stopped, and the devil came through the doors. It walked down the aisle toward Oscar, pointed a bony finger at him. Oscar thought of Maribel and Alex, heaven and the rain.

"The Lord is with me," he shouted.

Lightning flashed, turning everyone into ghosts. The devil swung its fiery sword, and Oscar fell backward into a black pit, fell down and down and—oh, God, the thunder in his head.

1

JIMMY. HEY, JIMMY."

Jimmy Boone raises a hand to signal Robo to hold off, he's in the middle of taking an order, but Robo either doesn't see or doesn't care.

"You hear about that kid they found dead on the bus?" he says.

"Later, buddy, okay?" Boone replies. "I'm busy."

The big redhead he's serving can't decide what she wants, a cosmo or an appletini. "Which do you recommend?" she asks, sexing up her southern drawl. Another tourist cutting loose, getting crazy in Hollywood.

"Hard to say," Boone replies. "They're both popular."

Red slides her sunglasses down to the end of her nose, rests her elbows on the bar to give Boone a nice shot of her freckled cleavage, and says, "Let's put it this way: which'll get me fucked up fastest?"

"I'd go with the appletini."

The Tick Tock restaurant is on Hollywood Boulevard, a few blocks east of the Chinese Theater, and most of the patrons are out-of-towners looking for a little old-time glitz and glamour. The guidebooks tell how the place opened in 1910, was a hot spot throughout the thirties and forties, closed in 1972, becoming a notorious squat for runaway teens, then reopened in 2004, when the boulevard began to come back.

The new owner, an Israeli businessman named Weinberg, spent a fortune getting the place into shape. The bar, all the woodwork, is original, and they even replaced the dozens of clocks jammed into every nook and cranny that gave the restaurant its name.

The bar runs along one wall, separated from the dining room by a chest-high partition. Boone can see over it to the tables, where Joe Blow from Iowa and his brood eat their fifteen-dollar burgers. It's the perfect tourist trap: cheaper than Musso's, more authentic than Hooters, and every once in a while a C-list celebrity stops in, someone from *Survivor* or an eighties sitcom.

Red sips her drink and says, "This'll do just fine, sweet cheeks."

Sweet cheeks. Jesus.

Boone isn't looking to hook up with a customer. Nine times out of ten, it's nothing but trouble. Apparently, though, the customers haven't heard this statistic. It's gotten so bad lately that Boone has been thinking about taking the advice of an old pro who told him that a simple way to keep things professional is to pick up a cheap wedding band at a pawn shop and wear it when you're behind the bar. He wonders if Red would take that kind of hint.

"You an actor?" she asks.

"Nah. I'm a bartender," Boone replies. "Do you want to run a tab?"

"Sure," Red says and hands over a Gold Card. "I thought everyone in Hollywood was an actor."

"A lot of the girls working here take acting classes. Does that count?"

"I'm staying up the street, at the Renaissance, here for a medical supplies conference."

"Great hotel," Boone says, trying to figure out some way to be polite about moving on. Delia didn't show for her shift again, and thirsty customers are lined up all the way to the waitress station.

"Be nice to have a friendly tour guide," Red says.

"Talk to Robo, our doorman," Boone replies. "I bet he can help you out." He turns quickly to the guy standing next to Red and asks what he wants, and it's go-go time after that. Gonzalo, the bar back, handles the drinks for the dining room while Boone moves up and down the stick, pouring beers and blending margaritas, completely focused on keeping his orders straight and making sure tabs are settled.

He falls into a groove sometimes when he's slammed, and an hour will pass like nothing. It makes him think back to Corcoran, when a day could last a month, no matter how many goddamn games of dominoes or chess you played, trying to burn off your time.

Right when things are busiest, Simon, the owner's son, appears at the end of the bar. A little schmuck with curly black hair and a prominent mole on his cheek, he runs the place for his father. This entitles him to hit on all the waitresses when he isn't holed up in the office watching online porn and entertaining his "boys," the greasy pack of rich shitheads he rolls with. He's twenty-three, drives a Lexus, and recently boasted to Boone that he's popped eight cherries so far. The mere sight of the guy is enough to put Boone in a foul mood.

"See that dude?" Simon asks, pointing with his nose at a wigger in a baby blue warm-up suit who's been nursing a Southern Comfort and Coke and chatting up the other customers.

"Eminem?" Boone asks. The kid looks fourteen, but Boone checked his ID when he ordered, a Florida license that put him at twenty-two.

"Watch him," Simon says. "I think he's up to no good."

"You want Robo to walk him out?"

"What did I just say? I want you to watch him. Find out what his game is and call me."

Boone grits his teeth, being talked to like that by such a punk, but there's not much he can do about it. Employment opportunities are limited for ex-cons, and he needs the job.

"You got it, boss," he says, the words stinging his tongue like acid.

It isn't long before Boone hears the kid offer to sell ecstasy to a young couple who look ready to party. Money changes hands, the deal is done, and the wigger moves on to work another section of the bar.

Boone calls Simon in the office.

"The kid's selling X," he says.

"Okay. Now what I want you to do is take him out back, to the alley, and I'll meet you there."

"I'm a bartender, Simon, not security. You've got Robo for this kind of shit."

"Robo has enough to do. Get Gonzalo to watch the bar for a minute while you handle this."

Boone hangs up. Deep breaths from the stomach. He needs to get past the initial red-hot, "I want to kill every fucking thing" spasm and shove his anger into a cage, where he can gawk at it like it's a poor, dumb zoo animal. It's a trick a shrink taught him in the joint, but it's tough today. The tiger fights back with all its strength.

* * *

BOONE HAS EVERYTHING under control by the time he steps out from behind the bar. He's focused yet alert, his antennae extended. He feels like he used to when guarding a client at a crowded premiere, like a cocked and loaded pistol. It's good to be back in action, even if he is just rousting some goofball.

He swoops down on the wigger, who's bobbing his shaved head and mouthing the words to the old Beastie Boys song blasting out of the sound system. Putting his hand in the middle of the kid's back, Boone exerts just enough pressure to get him moving, all the while talking in a low, friendly voice, a big smile on his face.

"Hey, bro, how's it goin'? Having a good time? Buddy of mine wants to invite you to join our VIP club. Have you tried any of our drink specials?"

The idea is to fill his pea brain with so much noise that by the time he realizes what's up, he'll be out of the restaurant.

"We got three-buck Jager shots, kamikazes."

"Do I know you?" the kid asks as they pass the bathrooms. He stiffens and slows, starts to turn around. Too late. Boone grabs his wrist and twists his arm up between his shoulder blades as he shoves him through the back door and across the alley that runs behind the restaurant, pinning him face-first against a brick wall and kicking his ankles until he spreads his legs wide.

"What the fuck?" the wigger yells. "You best get offa me, motherfucker."

The stench of rotting garbage from a nearby Dumpster has Boone breathing through his mouth. Simon steps into the alley with a mean smile.

"Let me see him," he says.

Boone wraps an arm around the kid's throat and turns him to face Simon, who is careful to keep his distance. Spillover from a neon sign on the boulevard gives everything a spooky green glow and makes them all look like monsters.

"So you're a real pimp, huh? Big-time dope dealer," Simon says to the kid, getting all South Central via Beverly Hills.

"The fuck you talking about, dope dealer?" the kid replies.

"I got you on camera, dog, selling to my customers. The cops are on their way."

The wigger struggles a bit, and Boone tightens up on his windpipe to calm him. The kid's pulse taps frantically against the thin skin on the underside of Boone's forearm.

"What's your name, playa?" Simon asks.

"Virgil," the kid replies. "Folks call me V for Vendetta."

"What do you think this is, Virgil, the fucking ghetto? The fucking trailer park where you grew up? This is Hollywood, son, and I own this town."

"I didn't know," Virgil says, his voice rising into a whine. "Come on and let me go and you'll never see me again."

"Let you go. Right. How old are you?"

"Twenty-two."

"Bullshit. That mustache of yours looks like a motherfucking eyelash."

"Okay, eighteen."

"Eighteen? Oh, man, the booty bandits down at County are gonna be scrapping over you."

"Come on, dog."

Simon rubs his mole and pretends to think while Virgil trembles in Boone's choke hold, close to crying. Boone frowns at Simon and shakes his head to say, "That's enough," but Simon ignores him.

"Show me everything you got," Simon says.

"What?"

"The drugs, fool."

Virgil reaches into his pocket and brings out a plastic bag. Simon grabs it and empties it on top of a Dumpster.

"Shit, doc, you make house calls?" he says as he sorts through the contents. "We got some rock, some powder—what is it?"

"Crank."

"These pills?"

"Vicodin."

"Nice!"

Simon sweeps everything back into the bag and says, "You know what I have to do, right? I'm confiscating all this garbage and taking it off the street. We have to think about the children."

"Come on, dog," Virgil wails. "Why you want to rip me off?"

"Why you want to peddle drugs in my house? You're lucky I don't have my man here tear you a new asshole."

"Seriously, bro, somebody fronted me that stuff. I come back with nothing, I'm in deep shit."

"You're in deep shit right now, you idiot. What are you? Retarded? Let him go, Jimmy."

Finally, Boone thinks as he releases his grip and Virgil scurries out of reach. A couple of real criminal masterminds going head-to-head. Boone wants to smack them both. Virgil runs halfway down the alley, then stoops to pick up an empty beer bottle and turns back to face Boone and Simon.

"You stupid bitch," Simon says. "I'm giving you a pass. Take it and get the fuck out of here."

"I'm not kidding," Virgil says around a sob. "Give me my shit." Green tears crawl down his cheeks.

Simon takes a few steps toward him, and Virgil throws the

bottle, which shatters harmlessly in the shadows. He then runs to where the alley opens onto Cherokee, turns left, and disappears.

Simon is bent at the waist, laughing. "Now that was fucking funny," he says.

Boone snorts disgustedly and walks inside the restaurant. Danny Berkson, his lawyer, lined up this bartending gig for him when Boone was released from prison six months ago; worked out some kind of deal with Simon's dad, an old friend of his. Boone is grateful, but he isn't sure how much longer he'll be able to tolerate Simon. And this kind of crap, jacking dope dealers—if his parole officer got wind of it, she'd violate him for sure.

Simon catches up to him and pats him on the shoulder.

"You must have been an excellent bodyguard," he says with a nasty grin.

Boone doesn't respond.

"Too bad you fucked up, huh?"

"Too bad," Boone says. He thought the story of how he ended up here was going to stay between him, Berkson, and Weinberg, but now Simon knows too. Boone hopes that whatever shit Simon helps himself to from Virgil's stash is cut with rat poison.

CUSTOMERS ARE THREE deep at the bar when Boone returns. Gonzalo is getting it from all sides. Boone steps behind the stick and dives right in. After a few orders he finds his rhythm, and his troubles slide to the back of his mind. Work can be a blessing sometimes, when everything else lists toward rotten.

The crowd thins out at about eleven, when the restaurant stops serving and everyone moves on to one of the clubs in the neighborhood. Wait an hour in line, pay twenty bucks to some jerk-off with too much gel in his hair, and maybe you'll catch a glimpse of a drunk starlet's snatch.

This is Boone's favorite part of the night, the sudden quiet after all the hustle. It feels like a party has just ended, kind of mellow, kind of melancholy. He listens to the waitresses gossiping at the end of the bar as he polishes wineglasses. They're all ten years younger than him. How the hell does that happen?

Gonzalo is practicing tossing ice and catching it in a cup behind his back, some kind of Tom Cruise *Cocktail* move. He's saving up to open his own place in Mazatlán where he'll serve sweet, potent drinks with names like the Itchy Pussy and the Cum Shot to sorority girls on spring break. "You can come work for me," he told Boone the other day. Definitely an offer to consider.

Boone puts the Nirvana unplugged CD on the sound system and begins setting up for the day guy. Mr. King and Gina roll in for Mr. King's nightcap. Mr. King is dressed to the nines as usual, in an ascot and a dark blue jacket with brass buttons. He's eighty-two, a retired cameraman whose heyday was in the fifties and sixties. He's got those big, thick glasses, and his last few strands of white hair are combed straight back and lacquered across his spotted scalp. Gina, his fourth wife, is a mail-order bride from the Philippines. She's a plump little woman, maybe thirty years old. Looks more Spanish than Asian.

They live in a condo at the base of the hills and come in an hour before closing every night. In spite of the difference in their ages, they seem to get along just fine. Gina doesn't speak much English but always has a smile on her face, and the old man treats her with a gentleness Boone doesn't often see husbands display toward their wives.

Mr. King once told him that Filipino women are the best in the world. Loyal, loving, good cooks. "They smell kind of strange down there," he said, pointing at his crotch. "But you get used to it quick enough." Boone didn't tell him that he'd been with plenty of Olongapo whores when he was in the Marines and never once caught a whiff of anything funny.

"What can I get you tonight?" Boone asks. "The usual?"

"For Gina, a Sprite, but for me, it'll be a Blood and Sand," Mr. King replies.

"A Blood and Sand, huh? You're gonna have to help me with that one."

Mr. King leans back on his stool and rubs his hands together. He's on a mission to turn Boone into a proper bartender. That means once a week or so he forgoes his usual martini to order a drink nobody's heard of since Kennedy died, then guides Boone through the process of preparing it. Boone gets a kick out of the way he calls out the ingredients, playing teacher.

"First, you'll need a shaker filled with ice."

"Got it."

"Now an ounce of scotch—not the good stuff, something blended will do fine—and an ounce of orange juice."

Boone measures them out and pours them into the shaker.

"Then three-quarter ounces each of cherry brandy and sweet vermouth."

"I bet you sleep good tonight."

"Shake it, strain it into a martini glass, and I'll have mine with two cherries."

Boone slaps down a napkin and sets the drink in front of Mr. King, who sips it, his hand shaking a bit as he raises the glass, then nods approvingly and says, "Fantastic. Make yourself one, Jimmy."

Boone doesn't necessarily want a drink, but it's part of the routine: Mr. King always buys him one of whatever classic concoction he's having.

Boone has refilled the shaker with ice and added the scotch when Robo appears at the bar and motions him over. Robo stands six feet tall and weighs in at about 350 pounds. His enormous gut starts right below his chest and hangs over his belt, and there are thick rolls of fat on the back of his bald head. He couldn't run to save his life, but God be with you if he gets his hands on you. Boone once saw him dislocate a mouthy drunk's shoulder with a flick of his wrist, and he can fold half-dollars between his thumb and forefinger.

"Can you talk now?" Robo asks.

"Sure, man, shoot," Boone replies.

"You heard about that kid on the bus, right? The one with the dog bites?"

There was something about it on the news last week. A Guatemalan illegal turned up dead on an MTA bus. When they examined him they discovered that he was covered with dog bites that had gotten so infected, they'd killed him. The cops gave the picture from his bogus green card to the media, but nobody ever showed up to claim the body or to explain what had happened. A weird one, even for L.A.

"That was messed up," Boone says. "Did you know him?"

Robo snaps his head back, feigning indignation. "Why?" he asks. "Because all us beaners hang out together? No, man, I didn't know him, but it turns out my cousin, he knows someone who knows the kid's grandpa, who heard about my side work, the community outreach stuff..."

"Is that what you call it?"

Robo does hero-for-hire gigs for people who can't go to the police for this reason or that. He'll evict that crackhead who refuses to pay rent, convince that gangbanger he really doesn't want to date your daughter, or find out who your wife is screwing on her lunch break. Penny-ante strong-arm stuff and surveillance mostly. Half his customers pay him in trade—bodywork, haircuts. Even a fifty-gallon aquarium once.

"Seriously, *ese*, check it out," Robo says. "The grandpa wants to meet me tomorrow to talk business. I don't know what's going to go down, but he's got three hundred dollars to spend, and I'll give you fifty if you show up and pretend to be my cop buddy. All you got to do is wear a sport coat and sit there looking like you got a stick up your ass."

"Won't that scare him off?"

"Nah, nah. I'll tell him you're working under the table, that it don't matter that he's illegal or whatever. You'll make me look legit is all, like I got weight. I wouldn't ask you, but my regular white boy is fishing in Cabo."

Boone shrugs and throws up his hands. "I'd like to help you, man, but tomorrow's my day off, and I really need a day off."

Robo narrows his eyes, strokes his handlebar mustache. "You like that Olds I got for you?" he says. "Runs good, don't it? What'd I charge you for that again, for getting you that deal?"

"I'm just saying, I've got to stay out of trouble," Boone replies. "You know how it goes."

"There ain't gonna be no trouble, *ese*. I'll see to that."

Simon and his posse explode out of the back room and pass through the bar, laughing too loud and playing grab-ass. Simon stops, a little unsteady on his feet, and points at Robo.

"If you're in here, who's watching the door?"

"Just getting a drink of water, boss," Robo replies.

"And I told you I want you to wear a suit. Let's get that going next time you're on duty."

Robo tugs at his XXXL Raiders jersey and says, "Where'm I gonna find a suit that'll fit me?"

"That really ain't my problem, bro," Simon says. "Alls I know is, I can't have you looking like a thug."

"Denny's at Gower Gulch, eight a.m.," Robo hisses at Boone before following Simon and the others out the front door, saying, "Yo, we need to talk about a raise then, boss."

Boone finishes making the drink he started, shakes it, and pours it into a glass. OJ and scotch. Tastes pretty good. You wouldn't think it would, but it does.

He could say fuck it and stand Robo up tomorrow morning, but there's no denying that the '83 Cutlass the guy hooked him up with is a pretty decent five-hundred-dollar ride. He's had no real trouble with it yet, except that the battery won't hold a charge. It's hard for him to believe that he was driving a Porsche four years ago. Seems like he died since then and was born again into a different life.

Kurt Cobain is singing about the man who sold the world as Boone walks down to where Mr. King and Gina are sitting.

"This one's a winner," Boone says. He raises his glass. "Blood and Sand."

"After the Valentino picture," Mr. King says.

"How are you two doing tonight?"

Mr. King pats Gina's hand, and she smiles shyly. "It's our anniversary tomorrow. Two years," the old man says.

"Congratulations."

"What about you? Are you married?" Mr. King asks.

"I was," Boone replies. "It didn't work out."

"Well, don't give up. It's like the man said, 'Ever tried. Ever failed. No matter. Try again. Fail again. Fail better.' "

Boone raises his glass once more and says, "Hey, I like that."

The waitresses come out of the back room in their street clothes, all ready to go to a club. One of them cracks a joke, and the others laugh. Boone takes another sip of his drink, then moves off to help Gonzalo finish cleaning up.

2

FAIL BETTER. BOONE WAKES UP THINKING HE'S GOING TO take this as his motto, the most he can hope for. The previous night's dreams, more real than life a moment ago, slip away from him, and he lies in bed and listens to the birds' simple morning songs while waiting for dawn to chase the shadows into the corners.

He's in the midst of putting his day in order—the meeting at Denny's, the Laundromat, grocery shopping—when the past begins to circle like a persistent fly, demanding attention. As far as he's concerned, it does him no good to look backward when all he's going to do is beat himself up for the mistakes he's made. But sometimes, despite his best efforts, he's forced to contemplate the damage.

This time he goes back to when he was eighteen, right out of high school, and killing time in his hometown of Oildale, California, working pickup construction jobs and running with a hard crowd of wannabe bikers and gunslingers who were always half out of their heads on something, always zinging wildly between rage and black despair. He'd put in ten hours pounding nails in the merciless Central Valley sun, then spend the night drinking and doping with Chi Chi, McMartin, Frank, and the rest, doing his best to keep up.

Chi Chi was the ringleader. At twenty-three, he'd already

served time for robbery. He lived in a trailer next to an onion field at the edge of town, where the crew gathered every evening to listen to Metallica, drink whatever beer was on sale, and smoke bowl after bowl of dirt weed, and it was he who came up with the idea to break into Tony Rubio's cabinet shop.

Frank had worked for Tony for a while and remembered the combination to the lock on the door of the shop. They'd go in, steal as many tools as they could carry, pawn them in Bakersfield, then drive on to Magic Mountain to ride a new roller coaster and party at a motel with some girls Chi Chi knew from East L.A.

Boone had never stolen anything in his life, but, in a moment of drunken bravado, he volunteered for the job. Why the hell not? His mom was dying of lung cancer, his dad had split when he was a baby, and he didn't give two shits about anything. Also, his participation would give him some cred with the gang from Chi Chi's trailer.

He listened closely as the scheme was laid out: he and Chi Chi would go in and steal the tools, Little Jerry would act as lookout, and Frank would be playing pool at Shooters, so he'd have an alibi if the cops questioned him later.

The whole thing was so stupid it makes Boone wince even now. They didn't do any planning, didn't even bother to case the shop. The night it went down, they guzzled a twelve-pack of Pabst, parked the car by a canal, and set off through an orange grove to reach the shop, which was located in a Quonset hut next to Tony's house.

It was slow going beneath the trees. The stink of a nearby dairy came to them on a hot wind that rattled leaves and rearranged shadows, and Chi Chi stumbled in the dark and fell, spitting a curse.

They paused at the edge of the grove. The shop lay twenty-five yards away, across a dirt road, and beyond that was the house. It was after midnight, and all the lights were out. The full moon, small and bright overhead, cast a graveyard pall, and a dog barked somewhere in the distance.

Once they got Jerry settled in a spot where he could keep an eye on things, Boone and Chi Chi stepped out onto the road and sprinted for the shop. Chi Chi spun the combination into the lock, and the door creaked as it swung open. Boone's heart tossed in his chest. He glanced over his shoulder at the house. Nothing.

It was pitch dark in the windowless shop. Chi Chi fired up his disposable lighter and began pointing out the most valuable items. Within seconds, however, the lighter grew too hot for him to hold, and the flame died. Chi Chi let the lighter cool, then sparked it again, and Boone set about gathering as many tools as he could before Chi Chi's thumb began to cook.

They worked in short bursts of weak, watery light. The router and bits, the circular saw. The petty-cash box was right where Frank said it would be, in the bottom drawer of the desk. Everything went into two duffel bags they'd brought along to carry the loot.

Boone was grinning as they stepped outside. He couldn't believe they'd actually pulled the heist off. But then a powerful white beam scorched their eyes, and a voice shouted, "Hands on your heads, boys."

Turns out Tony had installed an alarm since he'd fired Frank, one that went off in the house if anyone entered the shop. He waited for them to come out, got the drop on them, then used his shotgun to herd them into the yard, where they knelt next to Jerry, who was being covered by Tony's wife and a .45. She'd spotted him pissing in the bushes, his stream shining in the moonlight. Approaching sirens cut the night's stillness to ribbons.

The judge offered Boone a choice of jail or the military, so two weeks later he said good-bye to his mom and caught the bus to the Marine Corps Recruit Depot in San Diego. He enjoyed his four years in the service. The physical training added a thick layer of muscle to his frame, and the complex web of rules and regulations was the first real discipline he'd ever known. Even being forced to show respect for the officers, no matter what species of asshole they were, was good for him, a valuable lesson in how to hold his tongue and play the game.

Plus, it was a hell of a lot of fun. He got to shoot powerful weapons, blow up stuff with his fellow devil dogs, and see some of the world—the Philippines, Korea, Japan. He learned a little Tagalog, a little Japanese; climbed Mount Fuji while on leave; and fell in mad, sad love with an Okinawan bar girl who called herself Sunshine.

He also discovered that he could fight. A soft-spoken black guy in his platoon, Carl Perry, had won a few amateur bouts back in Compton, and Boone spent hours in the gym with him, training, sparring, and soaking up his knowledge of boxing. When it came to technique, Boone was a bit of a brawler. The first few times he climbed into the ring, anger welled up in him after taking a few jabs from Carl, and he charged in, swinging wildly. After a while, though, he was able to channel that anger into powerful punches that often rocked the bigger man back on his heels.

"Damn, Jimmy," Carl said once. "You got zero style, but when you hit somebody, dude's gonna know it."

Boone returned to Oildale only once, near the end of his first year in the corps, to attend his mother's funeral. Cancer had finally brought her down. She'd done a lousy job raising him, always more wrapped up in whatever roughneck was helping with the rent and buying her wine than in her only child, but Boone was a Marine now, and brimming with notions of honor and duty. He put on his dress blues, helped carry the casket, and tossed a white rose into the grave when the preacher said it was time.

Afterward, he stopped by Shooters for a drink. Chi Chi was in the midst of a two-year bit for the cabinet-shop burglary, but Little Jerry was there, having got off with probation, and so were McMartin, Frank, and a couple others from the old gang. It started out fine. They bought Boone shots and told him again and again how sorry they were to hear about his mom's passing. A few hours of beer and tequila took their toll, however, and eventually Frank asked Boone if he wanted to hot rail some speed, and Jerry said he was a fucking stooge for choosing the military over prison.

Boone dropped Jerry with a short sharp right to the solar plexus and left him puking Cuervo on the floor of the bar as he walked out to his truck. He filled his tank, spit out the window, and drove all the way back to Pendleton without stopping.

Enough, Boone thinks. He rolls out of bed and pulls on cut-off sweatpants and a T-shirt and sets out for a run in the hills. He has a tough route and an easy one, and today he does the tough one, which is five miles round-trip and takes him up a fire road that gives him a tour-bus view of the Hollywood sign, hanging by its fingertips from a dusty, weedy hillside.

He hops in the shower when he gets back and is in the process of drying off when there's a knock at the front door. Stepping into the living room with a towel wrapped around his waist, he shouts, "Who is it?"

"It's just me, Amy Vitello, from apartment three."

The new girl. They met last week when she moved in. Boone manages the complex, eight Spanish-style bungalows set around a small palm-shaded courtyard, in exchange for reduced rent—another deal arranged by his lawyer. It's easy duty: watering the grass, unclogging sinks, collecting checks on the first of the month.

"Gimme a sec," he says.

Boone steps into a pair of jeans and buttons up a clean shirt, something off a hanger. Wiping the fog from the bathroom mirror with the edge of his hand, he smoothes his close-cropped black hair and checks his nostrils and the corners of his eyes. She's pretty, this Amy. He's not looking for a girlfriend, has nothing to offer one, but she's pretty.

"Sorry for bugging you so early," Amy says when he opens the door, "but I heard the shower running."

"Not a problem. What's up?"

"One of my windows won't close. It's jammed or something, and I've got to go to work."

"Let's check it out," Boone says.

He follows her across the courtyard. She's about five-five with long, dark hair pulled into a ponytail, very professional this morning in gray pinstriped slacks and a white blouse. He likes that she has some curves, a real figure. It sets her apart from the flocks of skinny minnies he sees in the bar every night.

"Don't look," she says over her shoulder as they walk into her place. "I'm still getting settled." Boxes are stacked everywhere, and a partially assembled wall unit from Ikea takes up most of the living room floor.

The problem window is in the bedroom, which is a little more pulled together. The queen-size bed is covered with an orange spread, and Amy's clothes are hung neatly in the closet. Boone tugs on the window, wiggles it, but it won't budge.

"These old double-hung things have a tensioned wire in the frame that gets tangled sometimes," he says. "I'll have to remove the sash to find out what's going on."

Amy pulls back her sleeve to glance at her watch and says, "I'm running superlate."

"Go ahead and split," Boone says. "I've got a key, and as soon as I get back from a meeting I have this morning, I'll sort it out."

"Is it okay to leave the window open until then?" Amy asks.

Boone jerks his thumb toward the front door and says, "Have you met Mrs. Hu, in number five?"

"The little old lady who peeks through the curtains every time I pass by?"

"She keeps her hearing aid cranked to where she picks up sounds only dogs can hear and carries a .38 in the pocket of her housecoat. You don't have to worry."

Amy has a cute laugh that seems like it might get away from her once in a while. It makes Boone smile.

He waits on the porch while she gathers her purse and jacket and a canvas shoulder bag stuffed with books and papers.

"Thanks for your help," she says as she locks the door.

"I'm just glad it was something I know how to fix. Makes me seem all manly and stuff."

She turns to look at him with a smirk in her green eyes. "And that's important, right?"

"Isn't it?" Boone replies. "I can never remember."

He starts back across the courtyard as Amy heads down the walkway to the street.

"Have a nice day," he calls after her, wishing instantly that he'd come up with something slicker.

"You too," she replies.

BOONE DRIVES INTO Gower Gulch a little before eight. The corner of Sunset and Gower got its name in the 1920s, when extras hoping to be cast in the silent Westerns being shot at nearby studios would gather there. In a nod to this, the shopping center that now occupies the space has been styled to look like an old frontier town, albeit a frontier town consisting of a sushi bar, a Starbucks, and a Walgreens. The Denny's takes up a corner of the parking lot.

Robo is wedged into a booth, talking to a waitress. "There's my homeboy now," he says when he sees Boone enter the restaurant. "Come on over here, dog."

The security-guard uniform Robo is wearing is too small for him, and his shirt is missing a button. He asks Boone if he wants coffee and orders it from the waitress when he says yes.

"You look good, man," he says. "I like that coat. That's definitely something a cop would wear."

"I bought it for job interviews," Boone says. "Haven't used it yet." He leans across the table to flick the badge on Robo's chest. "What are you supposed to be?"

"Don't give me no shit. I been working since you last saw me. I go from the Tick Tock to a prop house over here and guard it all night."

"Two jobs, huh?"

"Two? More like five or six. I do yards with my cousin, hang drywall. Man, I got babies to feed. Check it out." He struggles to pull his wallet from his back pocket, opens it, and flips through the photos there. "Maria is six, Junior is five, George is three, and Rosalie, the baby, is about a year. There's something wrong with her hips. We got medical bills up the ass. And George, see how he's cross-eyed?"—he points with a stubby finger—"He's gonna need an operation to fix that, special glasses. I'll tell you, bro, when I'm not sleeping, I'm working. That's just how it is."

The waitress delivers Boone's coffee. He stirs in some sugar.

"What about you?" Robo asks. "You got kids?"

"No," Boone says, tapping the spoon on the rim of his cup. "No kids."

THREE MONTHS AFTER Boone got out of the Marines he met Lila in a bar in Pacific Beach. Lila, oh, Lila. Blond hair, big fake titties, and a rich daddy—a former jarhead's wet dream. Boone moved into her oceanfront condo two days after they hooked up for the first time, in the backseat of her Beamer. A couple of weeks of drinking and fucking convinced them that what they had was something real, and they drove to Vegas and got hitched on the sly.

Rich daddy wasn't happy when he found out about the marriage. He called Boone into the office of his construction company, offered him five grand to get lost, said he respected Boone for turning him down, then asked, "How about ten?"

"What's your problem with me?" Boone wanted to know.

"Truthfully?" rich daddy said. "You're a good-for-nothing Okie, and I don't want your blood mixing with mine."

He cut off Lila's allowance, had them evicted from the condo. Fine. They'd make it on their own. Boone's job installing car stereos paid enough to rent a creaky one-bedroom apartment on the edge of downtown, and Lila signed up with a temp agency, though she never seemed to get any assignments.

Boone looked forward to Friday nights when they'd splurge on a couple of steaks, maybe invite some friends over to drink beer and listen to music. It wasn't a glamorous life, but they were paying their bills and having a few laughs. Lila got depressed at times, but a tall Jack and Coke usually snapped her out of it.

Then Boone came home one day and found her sprawled on the bed, weeping desolately. She'd just learned that she was pregnant. They'd talked about kids but had decided to wait until buying Huggies wouldn't mean missing a meal, so Boone was a little taken aback. Nonetheless, he tried to say the right things, telling Lila that babies come when they want to, that he could get another day at the shop, and that everything would be just fine. As he spoke, it was wild, but he actually began to believe his reassurances, and a strange, unexpected joy swelled inside him.

Lila, though, laughed through her tears and said, "Are you crazy? No way I'm having this baby." Boone remembered rich daddy's comment about his blood and felt like he'd been sucker punched.

Things changed after the abortion, or maybe they snapped into focus for the first time. Lila decided she needed to spend more time with her friends, so most nights Boone came home to an empty apartment, threw something in the microwave for dinner, and fell asleep in front of the TV, waking when Lila stumbled in at three or four in the morning. Whenever he wanted to do something with her, she was always too tired. On his days off he went to movies by himself or rode his bicycle to the border and back.

He was as lonely as he'd ever been. His marriage was falling apart, and he didn't know how to stop it. The one time he tried to talk to Lila about the chasm that had opened between them, she brushed him off, saying, "Is it really *that* serious?" and on a couple of occasions he caught her whispering to rich daddy on the phone.

Then one day she announced that she was going on a family trip to Maui, and Boone wasn't invited. He left for work that morning with a knot in his stomach and the feeling that if he spoke, he'd vomit. Their coldness, father's and daughter's, shocked him. They were the kind of people he'd always thought were better than that.

When he got home that evening, all of Lila's stuff was gone. She'd left him the thrift-store furniture, a note saying she was sorry, and a five-hundred-dollar check signed by rich daddy, which Boone tore to bits and flushed down the toilet. The divorce papers showed up a week later.

The marriage had been a stupid mistake, and he'd thought he was done making stupid mistakes after leaving Oildale. Suddenly unsure of his instincts, Boone proceeded cautiously for a long time afterward. Stripping his life to the bone, he retreated into routine, planning his days down to the minute.

During the week there was plenty to do, with work and keeping the apartment squared away, but the weekends were a little scarier, all that time to fill. He joined a kickboxing gym, pumped iron, and ran until his legs wouldn't carry him any farther. The idea was to keep moving forward, no matter what, like a locomotive on its track. On a good night he fell asleep as soon as his head hit the pillow.

Robo scratches his massive forearm. There's a faded tattoo there of two masks, comedy and tragedy, and the words "Smile now, cry later." *Cholo* stuff. Boone sips his coffee and fiddles with a jelly packet.

"Here he comes," Robo says under his breath, looking past Boone to the front door of the restaurant. "Get ready, Officer Whitey."

Robo raises his hand and shouts a greeting in Spanish. A little man, not more than five feet tall, approaches the table. He has dark skin and broad Indian features. Robo motions for him to sit next to Boone, but the man hesitates, eyes downcast. Robo explains that Boone is a police officer, a friend who can help them, and the guy finally removes his blue Dodgers cap and lowers himself into the booth, keeping to the edge of the seat.

Robo asks him if he wants coffee, and he says no. Boone's Spanish is pretty good, but the man speaks so softly, he's often drowned out by the clatter of plates and conversations at other tables. Boone struggles to follow what's being said, scowling alternately at the man and at Robo, whoever is speaking. That's about as much cop attitude as he can muster this early in the morning.

Señor Rosales is from the town of Zunil in Guatemala. He's been in the United States for thirty years and works as a janitor at a sweatshop downtown. The dead kid on the bus was his grandson, Oscar, who'd come to L.A. three years ago, after his father died in a car crash in Guatemala, to try to make some money to keep the family afloat.

Rosales and Oscar met for the first time when the boy arrived in town, Rosales having left Zunil long before the kid was born. Oscar looked so much like his father, Rosales's son, that at first Rosales thought he was talking to a phantom.

They got together for dinner, and Rosales gave Oscar a few leads on jobs, but after that they didn't see much of each other because both were working all the time. Then Oscar met a girl and had a baby with her and was even busier. The old man hadn't heard from his grandson in three months when he saw his picture in the newspaper and learned that he was dead.

Rosales hasn't been able to sleep since. His dreams are spiked with horrible scenes of Oscar dying alone and scared and in pain, far from home. How could something like this happen? Dog bites! Infection! To such a good boy. In the U.S. It's a mystery he can't live with, and he wants Robo to solve it, to uncover the chronology of Oscar's final days.

Robo leans back and strokes his mustache with his thumb and forefinger after Rosales makes his request, as if he's debating whether to take on the job. It's all an act, though, Boone's sure of it, because Robo has never turned down a job.

A girl with blue hair sitting in the next booth says, "I asked for cottage cheese instead of potatoes. Can I get cottage cheese?" The waitress refills Boone's and Robo's cups.

"Why didn't he claim the boy's body?" Boone asks Robo, interrupting his deliberation.

"*Qué?*" Robo says. "What?"

It bugs Boone that the old guy didn't make the trip to the morgue. He says, "Ask him why, if he cares so much, if it bothers him so much now, he didn't claim his grandson's body."

"*You* ask him," Robo replies.

Boone puts the question to the old man, and for the first time since sitting down, Rosales lifts his gaze from the tabletop. He glares at Boone briefly, fire in his bloodshot eyes, then turns to give his answer to Robo.

He says that, of course, Boone doesn't understand why he was afraid, because Boone is rich and white and doesn't know what it's like to get fucked with every time you turn around. He says that he's illegal and didn't want any trouble. He says that if they'd arrested him when he went to get the kid, where would he be then? He has a job, a house, and a woman who depends on him.

He pauses for a second, then adds, *And I drink, okay? I am not strong inside.*

He goes back to staring at the table, at his gnarled hands curled into fists there. His bottom lip quivers ever so slightly.

Robo shoots Boone a look like, "See what you did?" but Boone keeps his cop face on. It was a legitimate question. He realizes he's only here for window dressing, but Robo should find out what he's stepping in before he's knee-deep in it.

Robo tells Rosales that he'll help him out, but he'll need to hear anything the old man knows about Oscar's whereabouts before he died.

Rosales gives Robo a scrap of paper with an address on it for Oscar's girlfriend, the mother of Oscar's child. This is all he has, he says, but she might know something. Where he was working, people he associated with. Then he hands over an envelope stuffed with wrinkled tens and twenties, Robo's fee.

Robo tells him that he'll start the investigation immediately and report back to him with anything he comes up with. *God bless you,* Rosales says. He shakes hands with Robo but ignores Boone, then walks slowly to the door, leaving an air of such deep sadness behind that Boone and Robo sit in gloomy silence long after he's gone.

Finally, Robo says, "Want breakfast? It's on me."

"Nah, bro, I have to go," Boone replies.

"Come on. That Grand Slam is good. Bacon *and* sausage."

"One of my tenants has a broken window, and I promised to fix it."

Robo rubs the side of his shaved head and raises his eyebrows. "Okay, uh, check it out," he says. "Here's the real deal: my car's in the shop."

Boone knew he'd heard something coming. "No, Robo."

"Take you twenty minutes to drive me down to talk to the kid's baby momma. I'll be in and out in ten, then twenty minutes to get back. What's that? An hour?" Robo slides the money out of the envelope and counts out a few bills. "When's the last time you made fifty dollars in an hour?"

Boone bites his tongue. His base rate as a bodyguard was a thousand a day, but Robo doesn't need to know that. He looks at his watch, looks at the money. Tips have been lousy at the Tick Tock lately, his phone bill is due, and the way Rosales reacted when Boone asked about his grandson's body makes him feel like he owes the old man a little something.

"It's a hundred dollars," he says. "You haven't paid me yet for showing up here."

Robo peels a few more battered bills off the stack. "Eighty okay?"

"And I'll have that breakfast first."

3

Boone and Robo hit the last of rush-hour traffic as they drive south on the Harbor to talk to Oscar Rosales's girlfriend. It locks up coming out of downtown and stays tight all the way past USC. The city spreads out flat and gray on both sides of the freeway and seems to go on forever. An easy place to get lost, Boone thinks. Which is good if you're running from something, but hell if you're not.

The Cutlass's air-conditioning doesn't work, so they ride with the windows down. Robo punches in a classic rock station on the radio and sings along. "I dreamed I was in a Hollywood movie." Boone gives up trying to find the perfect lane, the one that's moving steadily. He just stays in the middle all the way to the Florence exit.

On Florence, they head west, cruising past grim, graffiti-covered liquor stores, muffler shops, and burger-and-burrito joints. Ten, fifteen years ago these neighborhoods were all black, but now the crumbling apartment buildings and sun-bleached stucco houses with bars on their doors and windows are filled mostly with Latinos.

"Holy shit. Florence and Normandie," Robo says as they roll through the intersection. "You remember the riots?"

"That was ninety-two, right?" Boone replies. "I was a senior in high school. We watched it on TV." And his mom said, "Look at those stupid niggers burning up their own shit." He leaves that part out.

"It was wild, *ese,*" Robo says. "The first day, when the verdict came down, I got home from this car wash I was working at and watched the brothers beat the shit out of that dude, that truck driver, on TV. I was like, 'What the fuck?' All kinds of craziness was jumping off, and the cops were too scared to go in and do anything about it.

"Then the next day they shut the car wash down and told us to go home because there was some kind of curfew. The shit was spreading out of South Central into the rest of the city. We could smell the smoke and see the fires from the roof of our apartment building.

"A bunch of *vatos* were hanging out on Whittier Boulevard, and me and my homie, Sneaky, walked over to see what was up. Guys were blasting their stereos, and girls were dancing. It was like a party. There were no cops anywhere, and everyone was screaming 'Fuck the police' and '*Viva la raza*' and all kinds of stupidness.

"Then someone chucked a bottle at a fire truck, and someone broke a window on a shoe store, and all of a sudden everybody lost it and was snatching shit and wrecking shit and trying to turn over cars.

"I followed some people into a market, and we started grabbing candy and cigarettes. I don't know what we were thinking. We *weren't* thinking. The owner, this Korean *pendejo* everybody in the neighborhood hated, yelled for us to stop, but nobody gave a fuck. Fools just kept crowding into the store and taking whatever they wanted.

"A couple of *vatos* jumped the counter and tried to open

the register, and the Korean came up with a piece and started shooting. Everybody panicked and rushed for the door. I was in back by the cooler, and you've never seen this fat boy run so fast.

"When I got outside I felt something wet on my face and thought I'd been winged. I didn't realize that one of the Korean's rounds had put holes in a couple of the cans in the twelve-pack I was carrying.

"Nobody got hurt, but a couple of locos still wanted to burn the store down. They didn't, though, because they were too chickenshit to go back. The owner stood in the doorway of the place with his pistol in his hand until the crowd finally broke up.

"The car wash stayed closed until Monday, and I lost a whole weekend of work. Something like sixty people got killed, and they had the National Guard in some neighborhoods, tanks and shit.

"It's weird, but I haven't looked at things the same since. I mean, one on one, everybody's cool, but crowds make me real nervous, just thinking about how people turned on each other like animals. *Mi abuelita* kept saying it was the devil out there, loose in the streets, and maybe she was right. You got a better explanation?"

THE ADDRESS ROSALES gave them on Seventy-fourth Street is a tiny pink Spanish-style house with a small yard and a couple of raggedy rose bushes, all surrounded by a low chain-link fence. Boone parks in front, and Robo hauls himself out of the Olds with a groan, buttons his uniform shirt over his gut, and tucks it into his pants. Leaning over to look in the window of the car, he says, "You want to come in with me? It's kinda hot out here."

"Am I on the clock?" Boone asks.

"Huh?"

"Do I have to wear the cop jacket?"

"Might as well, right? You brought it."

Might as well. Boone shakes his head at how stupid Robo is for trying to pretend that he hadn't been planning this all along. It *is* hotter than hell, though, and he has to piss after all that coffee, so he gets out of the car and leans in to grab his jacket off the backseat, where he stowed it when they left Denny's.

He follows Robo through a gate in the fence and up the concrete walk to the porch. There's a white plastic chair sitting there, and a dusty hummingbird feeder that looks like it hasn't been filled in years hangs from the eaves. The front door is open, but the house is dark beyond the heavy black security screen. Boone hears people speaking Spanish on a TV somewhere inside.

Robo bangs on the screen and calls out, "*Hola?*"

A young girl coalesces out of the murk with a baby perched on her hip. The girl's black hair is cut short, and she's wearing jeans and a white tank top with the word DIVA spelled out in rhinestones. The baby is naked except for a diaper.

"*Si?*" the girl says.

"Maribel *está aqui?*" Robo asks.

"*Soy* Maribel."

Robo tells her that he's a friend of Oscar's grandfather and would like to talk to her for a minute. She asks if he's police. *No, no, I'm too honest for that,* he says in Spanish. Maribel looks past him at Boone, and Robo adds, *Now him, he's not so honest, but he's working for me today.*

Maribel flashes a little smile, then says something over her shoulder to someone else in the room. Another girl appears with a key that Maribel uses to unlock the screen.

"Bet you a million she doesn't know he's dead," Boone whispers.

He and Robo step into the living room. It smells like baby powder and Pine-Sol. The sofa is covered with a colorful blanket, and there's an unmade bed in the dining room. A framed painting of Jesus hangs on one wall and a poster of Mickey and Minnie Mouse on another. A Mexican soap opera is playing on the TV.

An older woman in a bathrobe comes walking up the hallway from the back of the house. Her hair is wet, and she's wiping her hands on a towel. She stops short, startled, when she sees the men, and draws her robe tighter around herself.

What's happening? she asks.

They've come about Oscar, Maribel replies.

The woman's shoulders sag like she knows it's going to be bad news. She rattles off a stream of curses under her breath—*pinche* this and *pinche* that—then offers the men coffee. They say no, *gracias,* really, but she hustles off to the kitchen anyway.

Turns out the woman is Maribel's aunt, and the other girl is Maribel's cousin. The uncle also lives there, and the cousin's husband, but they're at work.

Maribel motions for Robo and Boone to sit on the couch. She drops into a torn recliner and uses a remote to mute the TV.

This is Oscar's son, Alex, she tells Robo. The baby grabs the thin gold chain and crucifix around her neck, and she has to pry them out of his little fingers. *Have you seen Oscar?*

Young lady, Robo says, *I don't know a gentle way to put this, but Oscar is dead.*

Maribel slumps in the recliner and raises one hand to her mouth. Her dark eyes fill with tears, but she doesn't break down. Her cousin, however, gasps and runs for the kitchen, shouting, "*Mamá! Mamá!*" This frightens little Alex, who begins to cry.

I'm sorry, Robo says. Boone looks down at the floor, out the window. It's as awful a moment as he's had in a while, everything laid bare like this.

The aunt and cousin return, both hysterical, and Robo has to calm them down before he can tell the story. How Oscar was found on the bus; how he died from infected dog bites; and how Oscar's grandfather hired him to find out what happened.

Maribel's face is blank, but her stoicism is betrayed by occasional sharp intakes of breath, stillborn sobs. Her aunt sits on the arm of the recliner and strokes the girl's hair as Robo explains to her that he needs her help to uncover the truth.

The baby wants down. Maribel props him against the coffee table. He bounces a few times to test his legs, then loses his balance and sits abruptly on the floor.

Just start at the beginning, Robo says. *Tell me everything.*

She says it was like a dream, some of it. She and Oscar met at a nightclub downtown. He was a good dancer. Looking at him you wouldn't think it—he was a little bowlegged, a little stocky—but he was naturally graceful. When he approached their table, Maribel's girlfriends all hoped he was coming to ask them, but she knew it was her he wanted.

His eyes could never keep a secret, she said. *Never.*

They danced to a few songs, and he bought her a Coke. He wasn't crude like the other boys, cracking dirty jokes and talking tough into their phones. He asked her about her life and actually listened when she told him about it. Then he told her about his.

He was washing dishes at a restaurant but wanted to get into construction. His father had died the year before, and Oscar was sending most of the money he made to his mother in Guatemala, to buy food for his little brother and sister and keep them in school. Eventually, he told Maribel, he'd move back to Zunil, where he'd build a big house and open a store that sold computers.

I said, "Oh, so you're a dreamer," Maribel recalls. *And he said to me, "Dreams are for children. A man makes plans."*

Maribel says she'd been lonely since coming from Guatemala herself the year before, and Boone guesses that South Central, with its razor wire, bulletproof Plexiglas, and dead lawns, wasn't what she'd pictured when she fantasized about California.

Shortly after she arrived, a gang of black boys surrounded her while she was on her way home from the market. They grabbed her breasts and ran off with the bread and eggs her aunt had sent her for. After that she rarely ventured out, except to help her aunt clean houses. She spent her days watching TV and writing letters to friends back home.

The night she met Oscar was the first time she'd been to a club in L.A., and she fell in love with him before he'd even asked if he could call her sometime. She was sixteen, he was nineteen, and they were made for each other. He took her to the beach, to Disneyland. He bought her a pair of sandals she admired at a swap meet and showed her how to play a few songs on the old guitar her uncle had lying around the house.

Her family liked him too. *Didn't you?* Maribel says to her aunt and cousin. Both nod and say, *Yes, yes.* They fed him, let him sleep on the couch rather than ride the bus home late at night.

And then Maribel found out that she was pregnant. She was scared when the doctor gave her the news, wondering how Oscar would react, but her heart was saved when he shouted with joy and said they'd been blessed by God. When she began to show, he'd put his mouth to her belly and whisper messages to the child, telling it to take its time, grow strong and healthy, and he cried when they found out it was a boy.

He promised her aunt and uncle that he'd marry Maribel as soon as he'd saved enough money to rent a place of their own. He was starting to get painting jobs, which paid a lot better than restaurant work, and two or three months were all he'd need. Until then, he said, he'd give them fifty dollars a week for Maribel's room and board.

And he did, Maribel's aunt interjects. *Every week, fifty dollars.*

The only problem, Maribel continues, was that he couldn't manage to put any money away, no matter how hard he worked. Between what he sent home to Guatemala and what he paid her aunt and uncle, he was still just getting by, even with the extra he earned collecting cans and newspapers during his off-hours.

He grew desperate when Alex was born. Someone passed him a few cartons of stolen cigarettes, and he peddled them in bars and on the street. Next it was Adidas sneakers, thirty-one pairs. Soon after, a policeman pulled him and a friend over in a hot car, and Oscar barely escaped, making a run for it while the cop drew his gun and shouted for him to stop.

Then one day he showed up with five hundred dollars and a bouquet of roses for Maribel and a big bag of toys for Alex. He said the money was an advance he'd received from a new boss.

The man owned a ranch in the desert, and he'd hired Oscar to look after his animals—chickens, goats, dogs. Oscar loved animals, and Maribel remembers that he was so excited about the job, he had to stop in the middle of telling her about it to catch his breath.

There was a downside, however: he would be staying in a trailer on the property, and it was so far away that he wouldn't be able to visit her and Alex very often. Houses were cheap out there, though, and the salary was good, and since he wouldn't be paying for an apartment and bus fare and everything else that gobbled up his money in the city, he'd soon have enough saved to rent a place and bring her and Alex to join him. They'd finally be married and live as a family.

Maribel was uneasy. So much could go wrong. But Oscar put his arms around her and the baby as the three of them lay together on a blanket under the lemon tree in the backyard of her aunt's house and said, "*Remember, Maribel, good things can happen as easily as bad. We forget that sometimes.*"

And I believed him, Maribel says, shaking her head.

He left the next morning—that was early in December—eager to start his new job. A week later he called to tell her that everything was fine; he was settling in. An envelope containing a couple of hundred-dollar bills arrived around Christmas. The note accompanying the money said that he was working hard and was sorry he couldn't get away for the holidays.

Then two months passed with no word. Maribel says she awoke every morning swollen with hope, thinking, *This is the day he will come back to me,* and went to bed every night ready to die.

Sometime in February the phone rang after midnight, and it

was Oscar on the other end. He sounded strange, frightened, as he apologized for not sending money, not calling, not visiting. He asked Maribel to put Alex up to the phone so he could tell him that he loved him, and he was crying when she got back on. "*You must forget me,*" he said. "*I've failed you. Find a better man.*"

One more envelope came, a hundred dollars inside, no note, and that was the last she'd heard from him.

Maribel's face is as expressionless at the end of her story as it was in the beginning, but her fingers are trembling.

Boone feels a tug and looks down to find Alex using his pant leg to pull himself to his feet. He stands with his hands on Boone's knee and gurgles up at him with a wet, baby-toothed grin. Boone smiles back, he can't help it, and tousles the boy's thick black hair. He thinks about Lila, about their baby. It was the right thing to do, he tells himself for the thousandth time.

Do you know the address of the ranch where he went to work? Robo asks Maribel.

She shakes her head.

How about where he was living before the ranch? Do you know that?

Maribel stands and walks to a purse sitting on a dresser in the dining room, roots around in it, and returns to the recliner with a bright pink address book. She pages through it and points to a listing. Robo copies the information into a small notebook.

Alex is still staring at Boone. He says, "Nunununununu."

Alex, don't bother him, Maribel's aunt snaps. She makes a move to scoop him up, but Boone waves her off. "It's okay," he says in English.

If you find out what happened, will you let us know? the aunt asks Robo.

Yes, ma'am. It will be my first call, he says.

Alex loses his balance and falls. He sits there whimpering until a stuffed monkey lying on the floor beside him catches his attention.

Robo and Boone stand.

I'm sorry, young lady, to be the one to give you this terrible news, Robo says to Maribel. *I'll pray for you, and my family will pray for you.*

"*Gracias, señor,*" she replies. The shaking in her hands has moved up into her shoulders. Her aunt follows Boone and Robo to the door. Boone steps quickly out of the gloom of the house and into the razor-sharp sunlight. He exhales loudly, then fills his lungs with fresh air, but the heaviness is still there.

The aunt locks the security screen behind Robo and Boone, and a wail from inside the house rattles the men's bones. It grows louder and louder before choking off in a strangled sob. Boone hurries for the car, angry at Robo, angry at himself. This isn't what he signed up for when he agreed to help out today. Not at all.

He and Robo sit sweating behind their sunglasses as they head back down Florence. It's hotter than usual for May. They pass an accident. A gardener's truck has T-boned a Honda. The police are there, an ambulance. Broken glass glitters on the asphalt, and it hurts to look at the sputtering glare of the flares routing traffic around the site.

Boone never got the chance to piss at Maribel's. He pulls into a gas station and walks inside. The Arab kid behind the counter tells him that the restroom is for customers only. Boone buys a bottle of Gatorade in order to get the key. He washes up when he's finished, but there are no paper towels in the dispenser. "Fuck!" he grunts, then wipes his hands on his pants. On his way back to the car he rolls the cold bottle across his forehead.

When they hit the freeway, Robo opens his notebook and runs his finger over the address Maribel gave him. "This is down by MacArthur Park," he says. "Tough neighborhood."

"Later," Boone replies.

"What do you mean later?"

"You're going to ask me to go with you, but I can't until later. I have things I've got to do today. Besides, it's better to show up at night anyway. You're more likely to catch whoever lives there at home."

Robo grins and pats Boone on the shoulder. "Look at you," he says. "Now you're even thinking like a cop."

All Boone is thinking is that little Alex is going to have questions about his daddy someday, and that Maribel should be able to give him some answers. That's the only reason he's decided to back Robo up tonight. Understanding why he's doing something so stupid doesn't make him feel any better about it, however.

"I can't believe you got me caught up in this," he says.

"Don't blame me, dog," Robo says. "You got a good heart."

"No, I don't. I don't. I'm a fucking chump."

Robo turns on the radio. There are commercials on the classic rock station, so he switches to oldies. "Earth Angel" is playing.

"This is my mom's song," Robo says.

"Fuck your mom," Boone replies.

"Fuck your mom too."

The downtown skyscrapers loom ahead, their upper stories poking through the thick yellow layer of putrid afternoon smog, and something's attracted a swarm of helicopters, police and news. Another bank robbery, another car chase. Boone punches the gas to pass a slow-moving pickup hauling a load of shopping carts. Some days, man, it's hard to remember why he was so eager to get out of prison.

4

EVERY TIME THE LASER HITS A NEW SPOT ON SPILLER'S NECK, it feels like a drop of hot bacon grease. He grits his teeth and clenches his fists but doesn't make a sound as the little Japanese nurse in the pink smock moves the device, which looks to Spiller like a fat penlight at the end of a robot arm, over the tattoo, busting up the ink so that his immune system can carry it off and dispose of it.

He still has his sleeve and the pieces on his chest and back, but the one on his neck was a favorite, a classic screaming skull with a rattlesnake coiled on top designed especially for him by Dago Bob, the baddest inkslinger in Chula Vista. What can he do though? His lawyer told him he'll have a much better chance of winning custody of Jenna if he doesn't show up in family court looking like a San Quentin shot caller, so everything that shows when he wears a dress shirt has to go.

And Spiller's in a hurry to get the job finished because he has to do something about the custody situation as soon as possible. Jenna's whore of a mother, Riley, is entering her in those baby beauty pageants every weekend, making her vamp around onstage in bathing suits and little cowgirl outfits for who knows what kind of drooling skeevs. The bitch even sent Spiller's mom a picture of three-year-old Jenna in full makeup—lipstick, eye shadow. If that's not abuse, Spiller doesn't know what is. It's like Riley's begging some sick fuck to molest his beautiful daughter.

That's what he gets for marrying a stripper. They're wrong in the head, all of them. Everybody warned him, said, "Just bang her and dump her ass," and that's what he'd planned to do, but only six weeks after they started hanging out she missed her period, and his life has been shit ever since.

This time next year, though, he'll have proved to the court what a filthy pig Riley is, and Jenna will be living with him full-time, a regular little girl again, no more body glitter and hair spray. Maybe she'll be able to forget what her mother made her do, or at least maybe she won't be messed up forever by it.

Ow! Ow! Ow! Fuck! The nurse moves the laser over the snake's fangs. This is Spiller's third treatment, and the doctor said it would take at least ten to get rid of the tattoo completely. At eight hundred dollars per session, Spiller's going to have to bump up his earning power a little, talk to Taggert about a bigger cut, or maybe do some freelance on the side. Stony Petrovich is always asking him to come along on jobs, and he's as good as they get, a real righteous, careful dude.

The nurse finally sits back, swings the laser out of the way, and removes her dark goggles.

"Are you okay?" she asks.

Spiller takes off his goggles. "Can't hurt steel," he replies.

"We'll see you again in eight weeks," the nurse says as she smears antibiotic cream on his neck. "The color is fading fast. We're making good progress."

"Can't you speed it up some?"

"We have to allow your body time to purge the ink between sessions."

The nurse places a gauze pad on the tattoo and tapes it down. She's so close, Spiller can smell her shampoo, something spicy. He's never had a thing for Asian chicks, but the feel of her cool fingers on his skin is kind of turning him on.

"Apply the ointment the doctor gave you twice a day for a week or so," she says. "Some scabbing may occur, but leave it alone. If you don't, you can cause scarring."

Yeah, yeah, yeah. Spiller has heard all this before. "So where's the weirdest place you've ever seen a tattoo?" he asks, flirting.

The nurse blushes, won't even look at him. "You'd be surprised," she says.

"Betcha I wouldn't."

The little bitch stops him cold then, saying, "Okay, Mr. Spiller, eight weeks," before picking up his folder and hurrying out of the room.

Too much man for her, that's all, Spiller thinks. He puts on his shirt and straightens his ponytail. After checking the door, he opens a few drawers in search of any drugs that might be lying around, but no luck.

In the waiting room is a *cholo* with XVIII tattooed across his forehead. Eighteenth Street. Spiller once shot a *vato* from that set in the heart in a beef over stolen credit cards. Might have been this idiot's brother.

"S'up, *ese*," Spiller says as he passes by, and he can feel the *vato* mad-dogging him, his eyes boring into his back, until the door closes behind him. Spiller chuckles all the way down in the elevator, thinking of homeboy wondering, "Who the fuck was that *cabrón*?"

THE EXPLORER IS parked in a loading zone, T.K. behind the wheel, his nose buried in one of his kung fu magazines. Spiller sneaks up on him and pounds on the tinted glass of the passenger-side window. T.K.'s head snaps back, and he reaches for his

Glock, which is tucked between the seat and the center console. He hisses when he sees that it's Spiller and rolls his eyes.

"You're a funny motherfucker all right," he says.

"Why so jumpy?" Spiller asks as he climbs into the truck. "Back on the pipe?"

This is a sore subject with T.K. While attending college in Kansas City, business school, he developed a nasty crack habit and ended up dropping out. Having studied various martial arts as a kid, he spent the next few years as a rock-smoking, fire-breathing, neck-breaking enforcer for local dope dealers and loan sharks, a complete animal serving up eternal woe to those who crossed his bosses. Eventually, he was saved by a jailhouse preacher and managed to quit dope, but any mention of those days still makes him squirm, and Spiller loves to make him squirm.

"Talkin' about being on the pipe," T.K. says. "Who lets some motherfucker named Dr. Tat B. Gone shoot a laser at him?"

"That's just the name of the business," Spiller replies. "It's a chain. They've got real doctors and nurses inside."

"So if you get cancer, you going to Dr. Tumor B. Gone?" T.K. switches to a TV announcer voice and says, " 'The cancer specialists. One eight hundred CHEMO. Call for a location near you.' "

"You been working on that the whole time I was in there?" Spiller asks.

T.K. starts the truck and turns the air conditioner on high. He's six foot three and sheathed in slabs of muscle. Not high yellow, exactly, but not superblack either. Half and half. Got his Chinese momma's eyes and his daddy's kinky hair. Spiller, at five four and one hundred and twenty pounds, with his pale, freckled skin, invisible eyebrows, and thinning red hair, always feels like a grub next to him.

He tried to convince Taggert to give him another partner, saying he and T.K. stood out too much as a team, saying, "For fuck's sake, when bullets fly and the cops work bystanders afterwards, who's not going to remember a pair like us?"

But all Taggert said was, "So you'll have to be smarter then, more strategic."

Spiller shakes a Camel from his pack and lights up.

"Roll down the goddamn window," T.K. barks.

Spiller hits the button, then touches the bandage on his neck, pressing it until it hurts.

A silver Rolls darts in front of them on its way to the left-turn lane. T.K. leans on the horn and throws up his hands. "They got the worst fucking drivers in the world here in Beverly Hills," he says as they cruise down Wilshire, past Tiffany and Barneys and Gucci. "All these old Mr. Magoo Jews with their handicapped passes."

Spiller is watching a man on the sidewalk—expensive suit, expensive shoes, sunglasses, phone stuck in his ear. He looks like he should be in a magazine ad, selling something. Probably some movie homo, some producer, never suffered a day in his life. Savage fantasies bloom in Spiller's mind. He makes the guy beg for his life, then shoves a gun past his perfect teeth and blows his smirky face off. No, no, he fucks the guy's movie-star girlfriend in front of him, cums on *the guy's* face, then guts both of them.

Spiller grimaces, shocked once again by his own daydreams, how they always end in bloody mayhem. If he ripped open someone else's head and looked inside, would he see the same things there? He doubts it. Something in him got broken along the way, or maybe he was born like this. He can never decide which, and in order to keep from obsessing about it until he's sick to his stomach, he picks up T.K.'s magazine and flips through it.

" 'The Black Hand,' 'The Way of the White Dragon,' " he scoffs. "Oh, look here, 'Seven Star Praying Mantis.' Man, this is such horseshit. I could beat any of these guys in a bar fight."

"Is that right?" T.K. replies, looking down his nose at Spiller, trying to come off laid back and superior.

"I mean, I know you're all into it," Spiller continues, "but you've got to admit kung fu's a racket like everything else. Look at these ads in here. It's all about selling crap to kids—cheap swords and ninja outfits."

"I had no idea you were an expert in martial arts," T.K. says.

"I'm not," Spiller says, "but I *am* an expert in bullshit."

Spiller's second stepfather, Jack, claimed to know karate, said he learned it in the army. He used it to beat up on Spiller's mom until Spiller, barely twelve years old, snuck up on him one day while he was napping on the couch and bashed him in the face with an aluminum baseball bat, breaking his jaw in three places.

Things didn't work out like they were supposed to though. Spiller's mom chose Jack over her son, packing Spiller off to Grandma's house, where he stayed for two long years, until Jack finally left Mom for a waitress at the bowling alley where he worked. Spiller has never forgiven his mother for this. In fact, on a few occasions it's taken everything in him not to lash out at her and get a little payback.

"Well, my system ain't horseshit; it's deadly," T.K. says.

"Your system? You got a system?"

"It's called 'Killer Instincts: Way of the Ghetto Warrior.'

It's a self-defense and fitness program combined. I took a little bit from all the disciplines and blended it with my own techniques."

Spiller raises his eyebrows and flicks the ash from his cigarette out the window. "What kind of techniques?" he asks. "I've seen you fight. You ain't nothing special."

"I've created unique combinations of punches, kicks, and blocks," T.K. says. "And then there's the Southside Sledgehammer, my patented move, which is guaranteed to stop anyone in their tracks."

Spiller laughs. "That I got to see," he says. "The Southside Sledgehammer. Is that what you used on those two Russians who beat you down and I had to jump in and save your ass?"

"You know what happened then," T.K. says, narrowing his eyes, getting hot. "You know I had the flu."

Spiller's phone rings. He shushes T.K. and answers.

"Are you done with your manicure?" Taggert rasps. Someone slashed his throat in Folsom, and it messed up his voice for good.

"You mean my doctor's appointment?" Spiller says. "Yeah, I am."

"Good, because I have a thing for you two. Some junky defaulted on a loan, and now I get his house. You guys are going to go over and help him move."

"We don't have to stop at U-Haul or anything, do we?" Spiller asks.

"Nope, the furniture's mine too," Taggert replies. "Just put his ass out on the street."

"Okeydokey, boss."

Spiller writes the directions Taggert gives him on a parking stub, then hangs up.

"We're going to Echo Park, over by Dodger Stadium," he

tells T.K. "Gotta toss some doper out of his house. Maybe you can use the Sledgehammer on him."

T.K. is back to being above it all. He raises his hand to indicate that he's about done with this subject and says, "Laugh now, motherfucker, but wait till the DVD comes out."

"Oh, now you've got a DVD too?"

"I met a producer down at the club who did videos for Busta and DMX, all those cats, and he's going to hook me up. It's going to be bigger than Tae Bo."

It cracks Spiller up how every nigger in L.A. is one miracle away from being a millionaire. He lights another Camel. They're stopped at a red light, and a little kid in the backseat of the car in the next lane is making goofy faces, staring at his reflection in the Explorer's tinted glass. Spiller thinks how he could put a bullet right through the brat's eye from here, open a fist-size hole in the back of his head, and spatter his brains all over everyone else in the car, really freak their asses out.

BOONE LETS HIMSELF into Amy Vitello's bungalow and walks back to the bedroom. He sets his red plastic toolbox on the floor and takes out a hammer and screwdriver. A few taps and a little prying, and he's able to remove the wooden stops from the window frame in one piece. The sash lifts out easily after that.

As he suspected, the wire that raises the sash is tangled on its spool. Luckily, he bought a few extra replacement units the last time a tenant had this problem, so he doesn't have to make a trip to Home Depot.

He removes the old spool from the frame, puts in a new one, attaches the wire to the sash, and reseats it. In less than half an hour the window slides up and down smoothly again.

On his way out Boone notices a collection of framed photos

on Amy's dresser. Even though he's pretty sure it's crossing the tenant/property-manager line, he pauses to look them over.

There's an old black-and-white with scalloped edges, probably Grandma and Grandpa, and a color one of a naked baby on a blanket, probably Amy. Everybody's smiling in the family portrait. Mom, Dad, a couple of brothers, a couple of sisters. It's easy to pick out Amy. She's ten or eleven, cute even in braces. There she is in a graduation gown; there she is in front of the Eiffel Tower; and—what's this?—there she is in a police uniform, LAPD, an official portrait.

Damn! It figures that the first woman he's had eyes for since getting out of prison is a cop. At least he found out now, before he did anything stupid. It's not like he was planning to make any big moves on her anyway. Let's be realistic: He's an ex-con surviving on tips and charity, a man who's blown every chance he's been given, whose life seems to be moving backward instead of forward. Now is not the time to be chasing a girl like Amy. He's got to hunker down and stick to the basics, like he did after Lila left him. Look what one moment of weakness, agreeing to help Robo out, led to: he'll be lucky if he doesn't get his ass shot off tonight.

In a dark mood, Boone stashes his toolbox in the little shed where he keeps the lawnmower and paint and plumber's snake and returns to his bungalow. He collects his dirty clothes and shoves them into his old seabag, then sets out on foot for the Laundromat in the minimall a couple blocks away.

The jacaranda trees are in bloom, and the sidewalk is covered with crushed purple blossoms. An old man pushes a paleta cart down Franklin, the tinkling of its little bell no match for the whoosh and roar of traffic in the street. He looks like Oscar's grandfather. Boone buys a mango popsicle from him and eats it on the way, his bag balanced on his shoulder.

At the Laundromat, Boone divides his clothes into two loads, one hot, one cold, whites and everything else. The only other person in the place is a fat homeless man who is standing around in a Hawaiian-print bathing suit while he waits for the rest of his clothes to dry.

"How you?" he asks Boone.

"I'm all right."

"You see that on the news about those bombs?"

"Sure did," Boone says, with no idea what the guy's talking about.

"Fucking bombs."

"Fucking bombs."

The Laundromat's air-conditioning is on the fritz, and Boone is sweating by the time he gets his washers going. His phone rings. Berkson, his lawyer. He steps outside to take the call, squeezing past the homeless guy's shopping cart, which is piled high with newspapers and aluminum cans.

"How's tricks?" Berkson asks. "The job? The apartment?"

"Good," Boone replies. "Everything's good. Weinberg's son, the kid who runs the restaurant, is a real tool, but I can deal."

"If he's giving you trouble, I can talk to his father."

"Nah, it's just that I thought my past was going to stay between me, you, and Weinberg."

"And so it has," Berkson says, sounding surprised to hear differently.

"Well, someone told Simon," Boone says. "He made a crack about it last night."

"Yeah?"

"Something about how I fucked up as a bodyguard."

"Ahh, Jimmy, I'm truly sorry," Berkson says. "You think you can trust someone. Weinberg promised, but we both know what that's worth. I'll talk to him this afternoon."

Boone tilts his head back, feels all the little bones in his neck pop. "No, no," he says. "Let it lie. It's irritating, but it won't kill me."

"There you go. That's the right attitude."

"I mean, the kid's right. I did fuck up."

"But you had honorable intentions, Jimmy, and that makes all the difference. Always remember that."

Boone adjusts his sunglasses and says, "That's sweet of you, Danny, but I'd rather forget the whole thing."

"If you figure out how to do that, let me know," Berkson replies. "I have a few things that need forgetting too. But, look, I gotta run now. Call me if you need anything."

"Will do, buddy."

A car alarm goes off, startling Boone and a couple of pigeons tearing into a half-eaten bag of potato chips sitting in the homeless guy's cart. The owner of the car, an Asian woman, runs out of the nail parlor next door, barefoot, caught in the middle of a pedicure. She aims her remote at the silver Mercedes and thumbs the button repeatedly until the screeching stops.

Boone steps back into the Laundromat. The homeless man is moving his head in time to a Muzak version of Elton John's "Daniel," a dreamy look on his face.

"How you?" he asks Boone.

"Not so great."

"You see the bombs on the news?"

Boone checks his watch. Four hours until he's supposed to pick Robo up at Denny's and accompany him to Oscar Rosales's last known address. Four hours to kick himself for looking for trouble again.

T.K. PARKS IN front of the hulking Craftsman-style house in Echo Park, a couple blocks up from the lake. The place looks to have been neglected for a long time. It slumps defeated in the perpetual shade of two shaggy firs, weighed down by the dusty ivy that covers one wall and is now spreading over the roof like a dark green claw. Most of the windows are boarded up, and the last of the paint is peeling away.

"Who'd you say we're putting out?" T.K. asks. "Herman Munster?"

Spiller shrugs and opens the door of the truck. He reaches into the glove box for his pretty little Hawg 9 and slips it under his belt at the small of his back while T.K. retrieves his gun from between the console and the seat.

"I don't see why Taggert's interested in this wreck, unless he's doing the neighbors a favor," T.K. says. "You know what a shithole like this does to property values?"

"Could be a principle thing," Spiller replies.

"Principle. Yeah, right."

The picket fence surrounding the property is also in bad shape. Most of the slats are missing, and the ones that remain are broken or barely hanging on. The gate lies rotting in the waist-high weeds that have taken over the yard.

Spiller and T.K. walk up the cracked concrete path to the sagging porch. An orange cat sunning itself there rolls to its feet, glares at the men, then disappears into the bushes. Spiller feels the first step give slightly under his weight, the wood spongy, almost eaten through by termites.

"See that?" T.K. points the toe of his shoe at the small black pellets scattered among the Thai takeout menus that litter the porch. "Rat shit."

Spiller stops in his tracks, the muscles in his legs freezing up. When he was a baby, a rat climbed into his crib and bit him in the face. His mom says it never happened, that he must have dreamed it, but Spiller can still feel the animal's teeth ripping into his cheek and smell its garbage-dump breath.

One step. Two. He forces himself to walk to the front door, a scream rattling against the back of his teeth.

VIRGIL DRAWS HARD on the bong, the water inside bubbling as he fills his lungs with smoke. He feels a cough coming on but holds back, because this is the good shit, the kush, and he doesn't want to waste a bit of it.

Eton is sitting in his ornate wood and velvet vampire chair, telling one of his punk rock stories. He looks like a vampire too: tall and thin with dyed black hair hanging to his shoulders, one blue eye and one green, and skin so pale Virgil can see his veins. He's wearing leather pants and a sleeveless New York Dolls T-shirt. Real old school.

"We played Randy's Rodeo in San Antonio, where the Pistols played when they toured in seventy-seven," Eton says. "These fucking cowboys, a whole gang of drunk shit-kickers, were waiting for us in the parking lot afterward, wanted to beat our asses. Black Ron, our drummer—he was a real big boy—pulled a machete out of his road case and chased them off, screaming like some kind of funky...funky...rhino on crack. Hey, did you ever see *Jacob's Ladder*? Now that's a trippy fucking flick."

Eton Dogfood. That's his punk name. Virgil doesn't know his real one. He played bass in The Despised back in the eighties, a hard-core band that made it onto a few compilations but never put out their own CD. Now he deals all kinds of dope, and DJs at clubs and private parties.

Eton inherited this crazy old house from his grandma. In fact, her room upstairs is exactly as it was on the day she died.

He took Virgil up to see it once, all the dusty old lady stuff still on the dresser, her robe laid out on the bed, a closet full of shoes. Fucking freaky shit.

The whole place is freaky. The windows that haven't been boarded over are covered with thick velvet drapes that keep the rooms dark all day, but not so dark that you can't make out the peeling wallpaper and the water stains on the ceiling. There are candles everywhere, and paintings in heavy frames: men in armor, angels, hunting scenes. And the smell. Virgil once explored an abandoned gold mine with his dad, and the house smells exactly like it, like bat piss and dirt and rotting wood.

Virgil exhales a cloud of pungent smoke, passes the bong to Eton, and settles back on the couch, which matches Eton's chair.

Virgil's older sister, Olivia, met Eton at a club in Hollywood where he was spinning records when she first moved out from Tampa years ago. They became good friends, and she ended up moving into this house for a while, cooking, doing dishes, and making dope deliveries to earn her keep. "Olivia is like a little sister to me," Eton told Virgil. "A little sister with a really great ass."

When Virgil rolled into town a month ago and needed a place to crash, Olivia called Eton from wherever the hell she's living now, the desert or wherever, and arranged for him to stay at the house. At first Virgil was creeped out by the whole scene—the cobwebs, the rustling in the walls at night. He also thought that Eton might be gay and worried that he'd try to get with him. But everything turned out cool.

The best part was how generous Eton was with his stash, even fronting Virgil some stuff so he could earn a little money. Virgil started hitting the clubs and moving product, and things had been going pretty good. He'd built up a little bank and was able to get high whenever he wanted. Until last night.

"Where were you again when you got ripped off?" Eton asks for the third time.

Virgil rubs his shaved head and feels his scalp move under his fingers. That kush is some sick smoke fo sho, he thinks.

"Some yuppie place on Hollywood Boulevard. Had all these clocks everywhere. The Tick Tock or some shit."

"And you're sure they were cops?"

"Alls I know is two big motherfuckers came up with badges, saying they were police and that they wanted to talk. They didn't look like no police to me, though, so I knocked one of them on his ass and was about out the door when the other one stuck a gun in my ear. They dragged me out to the alley behind the restaurant and jacked me for all the dope I had and all my money too." The money part's the biggest lie—he's still got over a hundred bucks—but what the fuck.

"I slid you three hundred dollars' worth of shit," Eton says.

"I know, bro, and I feel really bad about that," Virgil says. "But I'm gonna repay you, I swear. If I gotta go out and rob a bank, I swear to God I will. 'Cause you trusted me, and that's a serious fucking thing."

Eton stares at Virgil with those weird different-colored eyes of his, and Virgil wonders if he's finally going to go off on him for losing the drugs, but the guy just smiles and says, "Man, I gotta get out of this town." He reaches for the two-liter bottle of Diet Pepsi on the coffee table and refills his big green plastic glass. "Don't ever try heroin, okay?" he says after taking a sip. "Promise me that."

"I promise," Virgil says, once again not knowing where the hell dude is coming from or how he got there.

There's a knock at the front door.

Eton leans forward in his chair and cocks his head. "Am I expecting customers?" he asks himself. "What day is today?"

"Friday," Virgil says.

Eton stands and walks to the door, glass in hand. "Yeah," he calls out after pressing his ear to the thick wood.

"Open the fucking door. Delivery from Taggert."

Taggert. Virgil has heard that name before. Eton turns to him with a scared look on his face. "Dude," he whispers, "there's a..." but is interrupted by more knocking.

"Fuck," Eton says. He twists the deadbolt, and whoever is on the other side pushes the door open, knocking him off balance, and spilling his Pepsi. Virgil watches from the couch as two men step inside and slam the door shut. The whole house shakes. There's a big black one with Chinese eyes and a little white one with a ponytail and a bandage on his neck. Both are carrying guns.

"Are you the owner?" the black guy asks Eton.

"This is my house," Eton replies.

"Remember the money you borrowed from Taggert?"

Eton tugs on the neck of his T-shirt. "A friend set something up when I needed a little help, yeah," he says.

"When'd you pay him back?"

"I've been..."

"You didn't pay him back," the white guy yells. "That's the answer to that one."

Eton sidles away from the men, says, "You know what, you're really freaking me out."

"Hold it right there," the black guy says, extending his arm and pointing his gun at Eton's head.

Eton puts his hands up. "Relax, bro," he says as he lowers himself into his chair.

Virgil bounces one knee and chews on a knuckle. He wants

to tell these guys he doesn't know anything about anything and split before any shit goes down, but he's too afraid to speak up.

There's a crash in the kitchen, a dirty pot settling in the sink, and the white guy flinches, snaps his gun toward the sound. He's breathing funny and sweating like he just ran a mile.

"What's that?" he asks sharply. "Who's back there?"

"There's nobody else," Eton says.

"Probably a fucking rat, huh?"

"I don't know, man. Maybe. Now, look..."

"You look," the black guy says, taking a sudden step into the living room. "You've got five minutes to pack a bag. Taggert's tired of your excuses. He's foreclosing on this place."

"You too, twink," the white guy says to Virgil. "Hit the road."

"Wait," Eton says, his voice strangled into a pathetic whine. "Let me call my friend Olivia. You know her, right? She'll straighten this out."

Oh, yeah. Now Virgil remembers. Taggert is Olivia's boyfriend out there in the desert. She mentioned him on the phone once. Virgil is so nervous, though, he can't decide if this is good or bad for him.

"Nope. No calls, no bullshit," the black guy says. "Everything's been said and done."

The white guy darts over to Eton and jabs him in the chest with the barrel of his gun. "Pack! Your! Fucking! Bags!" he yells.

There's another noise, the old house popping in the heat like it sometimes does. The white guy backs off and looks up at the ceiling with bulging eyes, like he's afraid something might drop on him.

"This isn't happening like this," Eton says. "Not to my

nana's house." He stands, a chrome revolver clutched in his fist.

"Gun!" the black guy shouts.

He and the white guy open fire, the muzzle flashes shockingly bright in the dark room; the noise painful, each explosion like a hammer blow to Virgil's chest. Eton flops back into the chair with part of his skull blown away. Blood gushes black from half a dozen holes in his body. His mouth opens once, twice, gulping, desperate, and then his head slumps forward, and he's dead, dead, dead.

5

VIRGIL RAISES HIS HANDS OVER HIS HEAD AND CLAMPS HIS eyes shut. "Stop!" he yells. "I'm Olivia's brother. My sister is Taggert's girlfriend. Don't shoot me, sirs. Please don't shoot me."

"Shut the fuck up," the black guy says.

"Yes, sir."

Virgil opens his eyes and realizes he's not breathing, hasn't been since the shooting started. Sucking in too much air, he coughs. Through a gunsmoke haze he sees the two men standing over Eton's body, their pistols still trained on him, as if he might spring back to life and begin squeezing off rounds at any moment.

"What a stupid fucking play," the white guy says.

"Yeah, well, you're calling Taggert about it, not me," the black guy replies.

Virgil lowers his arms and notices that his Buccaneers jersey is spattered with a jelly of brain, bone, and hair. Vomit surges from his stomach into his mouth, and he barely manages to choke it back. "Sirs, I gotta get this shirt off or I'm gonna puke," he says.

Both men turn to look at him.

"That's fucking nasty," the white guy says.

"Go on," the black guy says.

Virgil lifts the jersey over his head and throws it across the room, sits there shivering in his wife beater. A gurgle rises from Eton's corpse, blood draining, settling. Virgil stares at the floor to avoid looking at the body and to avoid making eye contact with the black guy, who's now pointing his gun at him.

"What are you doing here?" the black guys asks.

"Dude was a friend of my sister, Olivia. Talk to her. She'll tell you."

"Don't get a tone with me."

"I'm not. I'm sorry."

The white guy lights a cigarette, then pulls a phone out of his pocket, flips it open, and punches in a number.

"Boss? Spiller. Things went all to hell here. Your man drew on us as we were explaining the situation, and me and T.K. had to put him down. Also, there's a witness, some kid who was staying here with the guy. He claims to be Olivia's brother."

Virgil leans forward on the couch and shouts, "I won't say nothing, Mr. Taggert. I swear!"

"Shush," T.K. hisses, raising a threatening finger.

"Right, her brother," Spiller says. "What's your name, kid?"

"Virgil. Virgil Cherry."

"Virgil," Spiller says into the phone. He listens for a long time, then says, "We can do that, sure. Whatever you think's best. Right. Okay. Good-bye."

Spiller slaps the phone shut, crams it into a pocket. He lifts his shirt to wipe the sweat off his face, and Virgil glimpses a large tattoo on his stomach, a naked devil woman with her legs spread wide.

"Let me guess," T.K. says. When he speaks again his voice is a hoarse growl: " 'You shit, you eat it.' "

Spiller shrugs and says, "He wants us to clean up as best we can and get out to the ranch pronto."

"We should just burn the place down," T.K. says in his own voice. "Do everybody a favor."

He walks over to where Eton flung his gun when he was shot, on the floor halfway across the room. He picks up the revolver and sets it on a table, next to a bowl of dusty wax fruit. "You know the drill," he says to Spiller. "Find something to wrap him in."

He then turns to Virgil on the couch. "Duct tape," he says. "Any around here?"

Virgil tears his dry tongue from the roof of his mouth. "Maybe in back? In the laundry room?" he says.

"Show me."

"You're not gonna kill me, are you?"

"You're not gonna give me a reason to, are you?"

"No, sir."

"Okay, then."

T.K. slips his gun into the waistband of his jeans, and Virgil leads him through the filthy kitchen to the laundry room. They find a roll of silver duct tape in a cupboard there, plastic garbage bags, a saw. When they return to the living room, Spiller is waiting with the polka-dotted shower curtain from the bathroom.

"While we're doing this, kid, you're gonna collect our shell casings," T.K. says. "How many'd you fire, Spiller?"

"Five."

"And I popped three. Get to it."

Virgil drops to his hands and knees and crawls over to where T.K. and Spiller were standing when Eton pulled the gun on them. He rests his cheek on the grimy hardwood floor and looks around. One casing. Two. Three. It's going to be a bitch to find all of them, dark as it is in here.

T.K. takes Eton's arms and Spiller his legs, and they lift him out of the chair and lay him on his back on the shower curtain. Working together, they roll up the corpse in the mildewed plastic. The duct tape screeches as Spiller unwinds it, and he curses under his breath as he wraps it around and around the grisly package.

T.K. is careful not to step in the blood puddled on the floor as he attacks the gore-soaked chair with the saw, breaking it down for easy disposal.

"Kid," he says to Virgil, "as soon as you get done, grab us some towels. As many as you can round up."

Six, seven, fuck it. This is fucking bananas. Virgil jumps up and runs to the closet where Eton's grandma's linen is stored. He's happy to do whatever T.K. says because it's a lot easier than thinking for himself at the moment.

After loading up with an armful of sheets and towels, he races back to the living room, where T.K. is now sliding pieces of the chair into one of the trash bags and Spiller has finished his makeshift shroud. Spiller grabs a towel, kneels, and begins sopping up blood from the floor.

"We need soap," he says. "Some kind of detergent. And a mop or a scrub brush."

Back to the kitchen. Virgil snatches a bottle of Lysol from under the sink. There's a mop and bucket next to the refrigerator. He fills the bucket with water, pours in the Lysol, and carries it into the living room.

The two men have cleaned up most of the blood by now. When a towel or sheet is soaked through, it's deposited into one of the trash bags. T.K. takes the mop, dips it in the bucket, and swishes it across the floor.

"Wouldn't my momma be proud," he says. "Her boy looking like a motherfucking janitor after almost two years of college. You guys need to check for spray. On that wall there, the furniture."

Virgil takes a towel from the pile on the floor and uses it to wipe drops of blood from a lamp, a picture frame. A chunk of something pink and meaty clinging to a vase makes him gag. Spiller stands beside him, scrubbing the wall like a madman.

"Pay attention," he barks. "You're missing shit everywhere."

After the last of the bloody towels has been tossed into a garbage bag, the bucket emptied, the sink rinsed thoroughly, Virgil stands quietly next to the couch, trying to catch up to himself. His ears still ring from the gunfire. He wonders if he could make it out the back door and over the fence before T.K. or Spiller could shoot him.

T.K. turns his way and points. "You're the lookout," he says. "Get your ass in front and let us know when it's clear to load the truck."

"Since when do we trust this doofus?" Spiller asks. His shirt and pants are speckled with blood, and the hair that has come loose from his ponytail is plastered to his forehead.

"He's cool," T.K. says. "He knows that if he fucks up, Taggert will cut off his sister's titties and set her out for the coyotes, right?"

"I ain't gonna fuck up," Virgil says. "Just let's get this over with."

He walks across the porch, through the yard, and out to the sidewalk on somebody else's legs. Run, you motherfucker, he thinks, run, but nothing happens. A gardener is mowing a lawn up the block, but otherwise the street is deserted. Virgil signals T.K. and Spiller to get started.

They bring out the body first, taped up in the shower curtain, and lay it gently in the cargo bay of a black Explorer parked in front of the house. Next come the garbage bags holding the bloody towels and chair parts.

Virgil accompanies the two men into the house for one last sweep. Spiller licks his thumb and wipes freckles of blood off a porcelain horse while T.K. picks up Eton's gun.

Virgil has retrieved the Nike gym bag containing his clothes and is waiting for permission to leave when T.K. says, "Give me those casings you picked up."

Virgil reaches into the pocket of his sweatpants, pulls them out, and hands them over. "I could only find seven," he says.

"What the hell?" Spiller says. "On your knees, dickless."

The three of them crawl around on the floor and sweep their hands under credenzas and couches in search of the last casing.

"I flush a rat, you're dead," Spiller says to Virgil.

It's T.K. who eventually finds it. The brass glints in a beam of sunlight that sneaks through a crack in the drapes at about this time every day. Virgil remembers how Eton used to say that it marked the start of happy hour.

The three men move out to the porch, and T.K. closes the door behind them. Something rustles the weeds in the yard, Eton's cat, Tigger. He glares at them, tail swishing back and forth.

"Well, fellas," Virgil says, already easing down the walk toward the street, one twitch away from a flat-out sprint. What to say next? Thanks for not killing me?

"Hold it, snowflake," T.K. says. "Taggert wants to meet you."

"Where?"

"None of your business."

"Why?"

Spiller crowds in on Virgil and pokes the barrel of his gun into his ribs. "Ask another question," he says.

"Okay, but I gotta ride shotgun," Virgil says. "I get carsick."

A big black crow sitting on a telephone wire caws loudly as the three of them walk out to the truck. T.K. drives and Spiller sits in back. Virgil slips on his sunglasses to hide the tears in his eyes as they pull away from the curb. He should never have left Tampa, where he had a couple of fine bitches, a decent crib. Had to come to Cali though. Had to try to hit it big. Motherfuckers are never satisfied with what they got, he thinks. Always "wanting" themselves right into the ground.

BOONE GETS ON the 101 at Sunset, and it takes him fifteen stop-and-go minutes to reach the Alvarado exit. He drives south on Alvarado toward Seventh, where he's supposed to meet Robo at a bar, the Tango Room, at 8:00 p.m. After circling MacArthur Park once, he lucks into a parking space under a streetlight. It's 7:45.

He sits in his car for a minute and watches a man and woman argue in front of the bank across the street. Tweakers, both of them, skull-faced scarecrows barely there in baggy clothes. The woman runs the fingers of one hand through her stringy blond hair over and over as she berates the man, who raises a fist as if to strike her, then suddenly turns and scuttles away.

It's hard to believe this area was once known as the Champs-Élysées of Los Angeles. Back when it was called Westlake Park, it was surrounded by fancy hotels, restaurants, and stores, a shady haven a few blocks from downtown, with flower vendors, ice-cream carts, and paddleboats on the lake. But then the rich people moved out and the poor people moved in, and the city let the neighborhood go to hell.

These days the bones of once-glamorous old stores and theaters house fast-food joints, botanicas, and three-for-ten-dollars T-shirt shops, and thousands of Central American immigrants are packed into rattrap apartment buildings on the surrounding streets. They share the park with dope peddlers and gangbangers and dream their own dreams of escaping to the suburbs.

Boone pulls his steering-wheel lock from under the seat and slides it into place before stepping out of the car and locking the door. Robo asked him to wear his cop coat again, but he decides not to put it on until they get to the address Maribel gave them for Oscar. No sense standing out more than he already does.

He tries carrying the coat draped over one arm, but that's not going to work. He looks like a waiter. He tosses it over his shoulder, thumb hooked in the collar. Too fruity. Finally, he clutches the jacket in one hand and sets off for the meeting.

He sticks to the sidewalk on the perimeter of the park rather than cutting across. It's a no-man's-land in there after dark, and he doesn't need the cops or the dealers thinking he's another clueless white boy here to score.

When he reaches Alvarado, he turns right. Mariachi music booms out of a swap meet situated in an old movie theater across the street, and the sidewalks are crowded with families avoiding their sweltering apartments in the nearby tenements.

A young girl pushes a stroller with one hand and tows a dawdling toddler with the other. An old couple walking arm in arm pause to examine the bootleg DVDs a vendor has displayed on a scrap of cardboard.

"ID, ID," chants a kid holding a beer can sheathed in a paper bag.

Boone shakes his head.

A preacher is going at it on the corner of Alvarado and Wilshire. He screams into a megaphone, stomps his feet, claps his hands. "*Jesús es amor! Jesús es poder! Jesús es vida!*" Boone accepts a tract from one of his helpers, an old woman in a black shawl, and shoves it into his pocket without looking at it.

At Seventh he crosses Alvarado and spots the Tango Room, a down-and-dirty little cantina next to a cell phone store. Everybody in the joint turns to eyeball him when he steps through the door, then quickly turns away. Green, white, and red pennants flutter in the breeze from the air-conditioning, and a soccer game plays on a couple of televisions, competing with the trumpets and tubas wheezing out of the jukebox.

Boone bellies up, calls for a Tecate. All the stools are taken, so he stands against the wall, his back to a Budweiser Cinco de Mayo poster, and watches a couple of guys in cowboy hats shoot pool.

He's a little uneasy. Robo promised this would be a friendly visit, not an all-out interrogation, but it seems to Boone that any time you're asking questions about a dead man, there's the potential for things to get rowdy. Robo said Boone had a good heart, but that's not it at all. What it is, Boone thinks, is once a shit magnet, always a shit magnet.

Robo rolls in right after eight dressed in his guard uniform. The bartender greets him with a shout of, "*Orale, jefe,*" and they do some kind of complicated handshake. Robo waves Boone over to join them.

"*Este cabrón es mi amigo,*" Robo says to the bartender.

"Please to meet you," the bartender says in English. He has a wispy afro and long sideburns.

Boone nods without smiling, already in cop mode.

"*Dame dos tequilas,*" Robo says to the bartender. "*Tienes* Patrón?"

"*Simón.*"

"*Dos, por favor.*"

Boone says, "You're either drinking because you're nervous or because you're not. Which is it?"

Robo scratches the inside corner of his eye, digging deep. "I'm just trying to wake up," he says. "I went home and took a nap 'cause right after this I'm working security at a party downtown until four a.m."

The bartender drops two shot glasses in front of them and fills them with tequila.

"*Quieres sal? Limón?*" he asks. Freddy Fender. That's who he looks like. Boone's mom loved Freddy Fender.

"No, no. Everything's coolisimo," Robo replies. He picks up one of the glasses and motions with his forehead for Boone to take the other. "Here's to the truth," he says. "And those who seek it."

"Wow!" Boone says, clinking his glass against Robo's. "You really know how to make a girl weak in the knees."

"Drink, *gabacho;* don't talk."

The men toss back their shots and slam their empty glasses on the bar.

OSCAR ROSALES'S LAST address before he turned up dead on the bus is an apartment in a building on Westlake, around the corner from the Tango Room. Six stories, red brick, a rickety fire escape bolted to the facade. There are patches of tan paint on the bricks where someone who still cares has tried to cover the graffiti that crawls black and spidery over the other buildings on the block.

The neighborhood is a little dark because most of the streetlights have been shot out. Boone has heard that the local bad guys do this so the police can't keep track of what they're up to. It's noisy too. Sounds like a different radio station is blaring from each open window. A lot of people are out and about, lounging on stoops, congregating around certain cars. Robo and Boone get the stink eye from a pack of gangbangers gathered next to an ice-cream truck, and whistles follow them down the street, secret signals that tighten Boone's scalp.

The building's security gate is propped open with a cinder block, so Robo and Boone are able to enter without being buzzed in. Three toddlers play with a soccer ball in the dimly lit entryway, watched over by a sad-eyed girl sitting in a folding beach chair. She glances at the men as they step inside, then pretends to be absorbed in scolding one of the babies.

The apartment they're looking for is on the fourth floor, and the elevator is out of order. Robo is sweating and sucking wind by the time they finish climbing the last flight of creaky stairs. He waves at Boone to hold up so he can catch his breath.

Boone slips on the sport coat. The shadowy hallway is stifling, the air thick with the odors of food cooking. A TV plays loudly behind one door; a baby cries behind another. The linoleum covering the floor is worn through in places, revealing another, older layer of linoleum beneath it.

When Robo has recovered, they approach apartment 410. Boone stands to one side of the door, his back to the wall, so he can't be seen through the peephole. Robo tucks in his shirt, then raises his fist and knocks.

"*Quién es?*" a voice calls from inside.

"*Seguridad. Momentito, por favor,*" Robo says.

The deadbolt snaps, and the door opens about a foot. The little Latino guy standing in the gap has a lazy eye that makes it difficult to tell exactly what he's looking at.

"*Qué pasa?*" he says.

"*Conoces* Oscar Rosales?" Robo asks. Somewhere inside the apartment a dog is barking, which forces the men to raise their voices.

"*Quién?*"

"Oscar Rosales."

"*No, no. Lo siento.*"

The walleyed guy moves to shut the door, but Robo keeps it open using only the palm of his hand, no strain at all visible in his massive body.

Is anybody else here? he asks in Spanish.

The walleyed guy puts his back into it now, leaning against the door, determined to close it.

Relax, buddy, relax, Robo says while at the same time pushing the door open wider. *His family has a few questions, that's all. There will be no problems for you.*

Here we go, Boone thinks. He puffs himself up and steps out so that he's visible behind Robo. Maybe it'll make someone think twice about getting crazy. The first guy gives up and backs off, but a second rushes in, swinging a frying pan as Robo steps into the apartment. Robo grabs his wrist and gives it a little shake. The guy's eyes widen in pain, and the pan clatters to the floor.

"*Cálmate,*" Robo says, both hands raised in the air. "*Cálmate, hombre.*"

By now Boone has joined him in the tiny living room. The dog's barking grows more frantic, but there's still no sign of it. The walleyed guy dashes into the bathroom and slams the door. The other one crouches next to one of the three beds in the room. A third man, clad only in white briefs, cowers on another of the beds.

A dish breaks in the kitchen. Boone moves to the doorway and peers in. A fourth man is trying to squeeze through a small window over the sink, legs kicking wildly. Where the fuck is he going to go, four stories up? Boone grabs a foot and yanks him back inside, drags him off the counter, and slams him to the floor.

All the fight goes out of him, and Boone twists his arm up behind his back and marches him into the living room. Robo has rousted another man from the bedroom who now slouches red eyed and tousle haired on the junk-store couch, reeking of beer. Boone plops his guy next to him.

Boone's heart is pounding, but it feels good. He's always been at his best when things get rough. Nothing like a little close quarters combat to shake out the wrinkles.

You in the bathroom, please come out, Robo says. *We don't want trouble; we just want to talk. About Oscar.*

The bathroom door flies open. *Talk to him, asshole,* the walleyed guy shouts as a brindle pit bull charges into the room, a savage blur of thick muscle and bristling hair that leaps at Boone.

"Holy shit!" Robo shouts.

Boone manages to throw a forearm in the dog's way, and the animal's jaws clamp onto it. Boone grimaces, expecting pain, but none comes. The dog loses his grip and drops to the floor. He makes another leap and bites again, and again falls, unable to hang on.

Boone glances at his arm, confused. No damage to the sleeve of his coat, no blood. The dog is now gnawing on his shin. Boone reaches down and grabs the choke chain around the animal's neck and yanks it tight, forcing the dog to look up at him. The dog snarls and snaps, and Boone sees there's not a tooth in his head.

He releases the tension on the chain, and the dog sits beside him, suddenly calm and submissive, his fury spent.

"You okay, homes?" Robo asks, eyes wide.

"The fucking thing has no teeth," Boone replies as he checks his sleeve again.

"What do you mean?"

"I mean no teeth. The worst it could do is gum me to death."

The drunk on the couch laughs and points. *Did you see his face?* he says to his roommates. *That white boy shit his pants.*

Hey, you, quiet down, Robo says.

The drunk sneers defiantly but keeps his mouth shut.

Robo turns to the bathroom and shouts, *Come out now. Stop playing around.* After a few seconds the walleyed kid opens the door and sheepishly joins the others in the living room. He sits on one of the beds, and he and his four pals stare glumly at the floor. Boone checks the bedroom again to be sure. Three more beds, but no one else is hiding there.

It's Oscar's dog, the guy who wielded the frying pan blurts out, drawing disapproving glances from his roommates. *He brought it with him when he came back from the desert.*

What's your name? Robo asks him.

Carlos.

Good, Carlos, good. May I sit? Robo gestures to a white plastic chair. Carlos shrugs. Robo moves the chair to the middle of the room and sits facing the men. Boone stands behind him, arms crossed over his chest, and looks around the apartment.

A bunch of hardcore bachelors from what he can see. Clothes and blankets strewn everywhere, fast-food wrappers and empty beer cans, a small TV. The place stinks of work boots and sweat. A Guatemalan flag hanging on the wall, a couple of nude pinups, a baseball-card-sized painting of Jesus. It's clear that nobody's doing much more than crashing here between shifts, a couple of them probably sharing the same bed, one using it during the day, the other at night.

Robo leans forward in the chair, the legs bowing under his weight. *You heard about Oscar, right?* he asks Carlos.

That he's dead?

His grandfather has hired me to find out what happened. Perhaps you can help. How did you know Oscar?

Carlos scissors his legs open and closed and bobs his head. He's short and squat, with Indian features. A million years of history in that face, Boone thinks.

We grew up together in Guatemala and traveled to the U.S. together, Carlos says. *He lived here until he went to work in the desert, and we gave him a place when he returned.*

Tell me about the desert, Robo says. *Who was he working for out there?*

I don't know. A man he had been doing some painting for introduced him to the boss. It seemed like a good thing. More money, a chance to get out of the city. He was a country boy, you know. He had a son and a woman.

Yes, we talked to her.

He wanted to get married.

A helicopter clatters low over the building, rattling every loose item in the apartment—the change and keys on the coffee table, the dishes in the sink. Robo looks at the ceiling while he waits for it to pass, then asks, *What happened next?*

He was gone for six months, then returned suddenly, Carlos says. *He'd hitchhiked back. It had taken him three days. He'd been hurt, mauled by dogs, but wouldn't talk about it. He only said that the job had gone badly and that he was afraid there were men looking for him.*

The walleyed roommate, who's been lying back on one of the beds, suddenly sits up and hisses at Carlos. *You're going to get us killed too, you son of a bitch,* he says. *Shut your mouth.*

He was like my brother, Carlos replies. *Do you know what that means?*

The dog tenses at the sound of raised voices, stands and growls. Boone jerks the chain around his neck, and he sits again.

Nobody's going to get killed, Robo says. *Nobody will even know we were here. Who did Oscar think was looking for him?*

Men from the desert, Carlos says. *He said he had seen some bad things there, things he shouldn't have. His plan was to hide here until the bites healed, then return to Guatemala. But he wouldn't go to the clinic because he was afraid that the men who were after him would be watching it. We did the best we could to treat the wounds ourselves, but they got worse and worse.*

Tell the man the truth, the drunk slurs, waving his hand like he's swatting flies. *The boy was possessed. He was seeing devils and talking to angels. He made God angry. That's why he died.*

Shut up, Francisco, Carlos says. *That was only when his blood went bad.*

He turns back to Robo. *It's true that he was delirious at the end, but I know in my heart that he was truly frightened before then. He wouldn't leave the apartment for anything, not until the last days, when he was too far gone to care anymore.*

Was anyone actually after him? Robo asks.

I can't say for sure, but I know that he was scared enough that he chose to rot rather than get help.

Robo leans back in the chair and strokes his mustache. A shower goes on in another apartment, and the pipes rattle like someone is pounding on them with a hammer. The sound reminds Boone of prison. Suddenly, there's an icicle twisting in his gut.

Do you know the man who introduced Oscar to the man in the desert? Robo asks Carlos.

No, sir. I didn't meet him.

Did you have an address for Oscar when he was out there?

No.

Did he mention the boss's name? Anyone's name?

I've told you everything I know.

Francisco belches, then mumbles an apology.

How about his belongings? Robo asks. *Did he leave anything behind?*

The five men exchange embarrassed looks. Carlos bows his head. *We divided them up when we heard he was dead,* he says.

This was his, the kid who was going out the window says, tugging at his faded Rolling Stones T-shirt.

And these shoes. The walleyed guy points at his feet.

And then there's that fucking dog, Francisco says. He gestures at the pit bull. *His fish died, we gave the birds to a girl down the hall, but we can't even get a Chinese restaurant to take the dog.*

A few of the men stifle laughs. Robo smiles and nods, then stands with a grunt.

Well, I want to thank you very much for talking to us, he says as he tucks in his shirt. *It will mean a lot to Oscar's grandfather.* He reaches into his pocket and pulls out a roll of bills.

Peeling off a twenty, he hands it to Carlos, and says, *Keep this for yourself or share it, as you wish.*

Thank you, sir.

Boone reaches down to scratch the dog's head. The animal looks up at him with a silly toothless grin and licks his fingers. Boone notices for the first time how skinny the dog is, ribs and vertebrae protruding. A welter of gray scars crisscrosses his body, a map of past pain. Boone takes out his wallet with the intention of slipping Carlos a little money to buy the animal some food but instead says in Spanish, *I'll give you fifty dollars for the dog.*

"The dog?" Robo asks. "The one that just tried to fuck you up?"

Fifty, Boone repeats.

Fuck, man, Francisco says. *We won't take less than sixty for that champion.*

The other men laugh.

Sixty, okay, Boone says. He hands the money to Francisco, who fans his face with the bills and whistles loudly.

Does he have a name? Boone asks.

"His name is Joto," Francisco says in English. "Faggot."

The roommates laugh again. Boone tugs on the dog's chain, and the animal follows him to the door.

Once more, thank you for your time, Robo says before stepping out into the hall. *You gentlemen have a good night.*

Will you find out what happened to Oscar? Carlos asks from the doorway as Robo, Boone, and the dog walk to the stairwell.

I'm not the police, Robo says over his shoulder. *It's not my job. I only report to the grandfather.*

Carlos points at Boone. *What about him?*

It's not his job either.

Boone and Robo walk down the stairs and through the

entryway. Out on the street again, they head back toward the Tango Room. The dog is spooked by all the people milling about, all the noise. He cowers when an empty paper bag skids past, pushed along the sidewalk by a sudden gust of wind that slams windows shut up and down the block and ruins a hot hand in a car-hood poker game by flipping all the cards.

"You're pretty good at that questioning thing," Boone says to Robo. "You know, the LAPD is always looking for bilingual recruits."

Robo chuckles. "Shit, *ese,* you know what those guys make?" he says. "I can't support my family on that. And all the taxes?"

A disheveled woman in cutoff jeans and a flannel shirt stumbles out of an alley and almost bumps into them as she hurries to the curb. She sits hard and drops her head between her knees.

"So what now?" Boone asks Robo.

Robo shrugs and says, "That's it for me. I got no other addresses, no other leads. I'll tell the grandfather what I found out, and he can go to the cops if he wants, though he don't have much to go to them with."

One more mystery, Boone thinks. One more loose end in a world unraveling. "You gotta wonder what happened to that kid out there," he says.

"That's other people's problems," Robo replies. "I did my job, and I got paid."

"Case closed, huh?"

"For real, *ese*. It's all about the money, ain't a damn thing funny. I'm barely gonna turn a profit on this after paying you and that wetback."

"What about me?" Boone exclaims. "I got a fucking dog to feed out of the deal."

"*Orale,* Joto," Robo says, reaching down to pet the dog. The animal snaps at him, slinging slobber. Boone pulls the chain.

"Stupid motherfucker don't even know he can't bite no more," Robo says. "Still thinks he's some kind of killer. Good luck with that shit."

6

Boone returns to his car. Joto hops into the backseat without coercion and promptly flops down on his belly and goes to sleep. He doesn't stir when Boone stops at Vons for dog food, stuff that looks like it's soft enough for him to chew, and Boone has to shake him awake when they arrive at the bungalows.

As they are passing through the courtyard, the dog freezes, eyes locked on an overgrown bougainvillea bush, a low rumble thrumming deep in his chest. Boone tugs on his chain, but the dog refuses to move, so Boone crouches behind him and squints over his head in an attempt to figure out what's got him riled.

The bougainvillea is illuminated from below by the Malibu lights lining the walkway, and its leaves ripple in the breeze. Maybe that? That silvery shiver in the night? Joto's growl rises then, and Boone tenses up. A fat skunk waddles out of the flowerbed not ten feet in front of them, and Joto begins to bark. Boone recoils, startled, and almost falls on his ass.

"Easy, boy, easy," he croons, springing to his feet and tugging on the chain as the skunk disappears into the shadows.

The porch light at Amy's place comes on, and her door opens. She steps out wearing white shorts and a yellow T-shirt that says IT'S BETTER IN THE BAHAMAS and has a drawing of a sunset on it. Her dark hair is loose and spills over her shoulders. She's prettier every time Boone sees her.

"Jimmy?" she says, concern in her voice.

Boone raises a hand. "Sorry about the noise," he says. "You should have seen this skunk."

"I didn't know you had a dog."

"I don't. I didn't. It's a temporary thing until I can find him a home."

Amy steps off her porch and walks across the courtyard toward Boone and Joto. "What, is it a stray or something?" she asks.

"Kind of like that, yeah," Boone replies.

"Can I pet him?"

"Sure, but be careful. I haven't quite figured out his temperament yet."

Joto sniffs Amy's hand when she presents it to him, then licks it. She scratches his back.

"He doesn't have any teeth," Boone says.

"What?"

"I don't know why. He looks pretty unhealthy though."

Amy drops to her knees and runs a finger over Joto's gums. "That's so weird," she says.

"Best kind of pit bull to have, I guess," Boone says. "At least I don't have to worry about him mauling the mailman or anything."

"Does he have a name?"

"The people I got him from called him Joto."

Amy looks up at Boone and says, "That's Spanish, right?"

"It means *faggot*."

"Nice," Amy says with a chuckle. "Hey, wait a second, okay?"

She stands and walks back inside her bungalow, returning

a few seconds later with a bottle of wine, which she holds out to Boone. "I wanted to thank you for fixing my window," she says.

"Don't worry about it," Boone replies. "That's how I pay my way around here."

"Come on, come on, take it. Don't make me feel stupid."

Boone accepts the bottle and decides, what the hell, cop or no cop, might as well be neighborly. "Hey, if you're not doing anything right now, we could open this," he says. "Seeing as how it's Friday night and all."

Amy cocks her head for an instant, considering the offer, then says, "Sure. Okay. But my place is still a mess."

"Mine's not much better, but you're welcome to come over," Boone replies.

"Give me five minutes."

"No problem."

Boone leads Joto to his bungalow, unlocks the door, and ushers him inside. The dog sniffs his way around the place while Boone tidies up, tossing dirty socks into the closet and clearing junk mail off the coffee table. He scrubs the toilet, wipes out the bathroom sink, and, after a glance in the mirror, decides to change into a shirt he hasn't wrestled illegals in.

When Amy knocks, he's searching for a corkscrew, which he has, and wineglasses, which he doesn't. Joto goes nuts, leaping at the door and barking.

"No!" Boone yells. "Sit!" Remarkably, the dog obeys.

Boone lets Amy in, and he's suddenly aware of how impersonal his place is: no photos or houseplants or softball trophies. The bungalow is as stripped down as he used to keep his cell, like he's still worried the guards are going to bust in any minute and toss everything in a search for contraband. It's strange to him; he hopes it's not strange to Amy.

"All I've got are these," he says, and holds up two water glasses.

"That's cool," she replies. "The wine's just something that was on special at Trader Joe's."

Boone notices that she's applied fresh lipstick and run a brush through her hair. So she's trying too. Good.

He sets the glasses on the coffee table next to the wine, then remembers that he's forgotten to feed Joto. He mentions it to Amy, says, "It'll only take a minute."

She picks up the corkscrew and the bottle. "Go ahead," she says. "I'll handle this."

In the kitchen, Boone opens one of the cans of Alpo he bought on the way home and scoops it into a bowl. Joto sits at his feet, drawn into the kitchen by the smell. He stares up at Boone with his tongue hanging out, big drops of saliva splashing on the linoleum.

Boone puts the bowl down in front of the dog, and he's on it in an instant.

Amy comes in carrying two glasses of wine. "How's it going?" she asks.

"Poor guy's starving," Boone replies. He takes the glass she offers and sips from it as they watch Joto wolf down the slop. When the dog has emptied the bowl, Boone dumps in another can.

He and Amy return to the living room and sit on the couch, he leaning back on the cushions, she with one leg tucked under herself, facing him. She clinks her glass against his and says, "Here's to the handyman."

"So the window works okay?" Boone asks.

"Good as new. Was it a pain to repair?"

"The right tools, the right parts—piece of cake."

"Have you always been good at fixing things?"

"Not really," Boone says. "At one time I was better at breaking them—noses, arms." He stops suddenly and frowns. "I probably shouldn't be joking like that around you."

Amy draws back, confused. "What? Why?"

Boone can't believe he brought this up right off the bat, but now that he has, there's no graceful way to change the subject. "This is gonna sound bad," he says, "but while I was in your place this morning I saw some photos on your dresser."

"So."

Joto trots in from the kitchen, collapses in the corner, and begins to scratch behind his ears.

"So I didn't know you're a cop."

Amy narrows her eyes and smiles warily at Boone. "What's the problem?" she says. "Are you a criminal?"

"Ha!" Boone says, ignoring her question and hoping she'll let him slide.

"Actually, I'm an *ex*-cop, if that makes you feel any better," Amy continues. "I quit about five years ago and became an English teacher, middle school."

"That makes more sense," Boone says.

Amy gives him a dirty look. "Yeah? How so?"

"It's just that most cops... Well, you seem so cool."

"I *am* cool," Amy says, and they both laugh.

"Okay, so then let me ask you this," Boone says. "What made a cool girl like you want to be a police officer?"

Amy purses her lips, thinking. She looks down at her glass and swirls her wine. "Ah, jeez, man," she finally says. "Why does anybody want to do anything?"

"Well," Boone says, "I wanted to join the Cub Scouts so I could play with matches."

"Come on, you know what I mean," Amy says. She pulls a pack of American Spirits from her pocket. Something has made her nervous, Boone can tell. "Do you mind?" she says, opening the pack.

"No, no," he says. "It's fine."

He gets up and goes into the kitchen for a mug she can use as an ashtray.

"It's totally gross, I know," she calls after him. "But I only do it when I drink."

"Your dirty little secret," Boone says as he hands her the mug and sits on the couch again.

"One of them anyway," she says.

"So forget about being a cop," Boone says. "Tell me about teaching instead."

Amy smiles and takes a drag off her cigarette, blows the smoke out of the side of her mouth. "You're a nice guy," she says. "I'm only reluctant to talk about the cop thing because the whys of stuff are weird. They sound so stupid sometimes when you say them out loud."

"That's definitely true," Boone replies.

"Part of it was just that I wanted some excitement. I was working in a bookstore in Portland, and I was bored to death. But part of it was also that I believed—still believe—in right and wrong and good and evil. And that's silly, because I knew full well before I even put on the uniform that things don't break that cleanly, that that's just us trying to draw lines."

Boone sits back and raises his eyebrows. "Wow," he says.

Amy takes another hit of her cigarette. "Yeah, I'm full of shit," she says. "But you asked."

"You're not full of shit," Boone says.

"My parents sure thought I was. When I told them I was moving down to L.A. to go to the academy, they were like, 'Do you know what kind of people become police officers?

You have a college education. Just last month you were talking about going into the Peace Corps. You're a Democrat, for God's sake.' But that just made me want to do it even more. Now I had something to prove. I was going to be the one good cop in the whole wide world."

"Hoo-fucking-ray," Boone says.

"Exactly."

Amy exhales a cloud of smoke and sips her wine. Boone's a little dizzy watching her. You meet someone, you're not expecting anything, and *boom!*

"So what happened?" he says. "Why aren't you still protecting and serving?"

"Well, for one thing, I got shot."

Boone sits up straight, shocked. "Whoa! Really?"

Amy rolls up the sleeve of her T-shirt to show him a scar about the size of a quarter on her upper bicep and a long jagged one on the back of her arm.

"I chased down a thirteen-year-old psychopath high on paint thinner who'd cut up an old woman for her social security check, and he whirled on me and started shooting," she says. "My vest stopped two of the rounds, but the one that got through broke my humerus and nicked an artery. It's still a little numb sometimes, nerve damage, but nothing too bad."

"Jesus," Boone whispers.

Amy shrugs her shoulders as if to say, "There you have it."

"So then you were like, 'Forget this'?" Boone asks.

"It had been three years," Amy says, "and I was still reasonably happy, meaning I didn't dread going to work, but I was always glad to go home. I'd resigned myself to the fact that most cops are only out there for the money and the benefits, that it's just a job for them, one they don't particularly like.

And I'd accepted that most of the people you're dealing with on the street don't want your help. They want to be free to beat and be beaten, rob and be robbed, kill and be killed.

"I knew a lot of cops, though, who stayed cops because the years flew by and that got to be all they could do. I felt like I still had it in me to be something else. After I got shot, the way things panned out, I had a chance to leave the department without feeling like a quitter, so I took it and looked for another way to save the world."

"Did you find it?" Boone asks.

Amy smiles sadly as she tosses what's left of her cigarette into the mug on the coffee table and dribbles a little wine on it to put it out.

"Teaching?" she says. "Nah, that didn't turn out to be what I thought it would either. Most of the kids think they're smarter than me, even though they're reading at a third-grade level, and my job is to do what I can for the few who pay attention and try to keep the rest from killing each other on my watch. But it's one more step, you know. Hopefully, in the right direction."

"What's your master plan?" Boone asks.

Amy shrugs. "Move to Montana, open a used bookstore, marry a rich cowboy—something silly and selfish like that."

"Sounds like you've earned the right to be a little selfish," Boone says. "You've done your best to do good and paid your dues in full."

"I guess so," Amy says like she doesn't believe it. She thumbs the rim of her glass absentmindedly, suddenly somewhere else. Boone is about to say something to bring her back when she brightens and asks, "And what about you?"

"What about me what?" he replies.

"You ever done any good?"

Boone hesitates, unsure how to respond. He's never been much for tap dancing around the truth, but he also doesn't want to scare her off. "Let's just say that I did my best too," he finally replies.

"And let's just say that you're going to tell me all about it," Amy says. "I'm not going to be the only one to spill my guts tonight."

"How much wine is left?"

Amy picks up the bottle and holds it to the light. "Plenty," she says before topping off his glass, then hers.

"You're sure you want to hear this?" he says.

"Absolutely."

"It's not pretty."

"I was a cop, remember?"

Boone exhales loudly and settles back on the couch. This is going to hurt.

HE BEGINS WITH the rough period after his marriage to Lila ended. He was still installing stereos, still living in the apartment he'd shared with Lila, still wondering what had gone wrong with his life, when he got a call from his old Marine buddy and sparring partner Carl Perry. It had been a couple of years since they'd last talked, and Carl had some news: he'd started a bodyguard service in L.A. and wanted Boone to come up and work for him.

Boone turned him down, said it wouldn't be a good idea. He'd convinced himself he wasn't the man he'd been before the marriage, that the disappointment he'd experienced had diminished him somehow. Carl was persistent, though. "Come on, Jimmy. You're just the guy I need," he said. "You're tough, brave, smart. A little crazy, maybe, but honest about it. I'm looking for someone I can trust with my life, buddy, and that's you."

Carl's confidence in him shocked Boone out of feeling sorry for himself for half a second, long enough to realize that the man's offer was what he'd been waiting for all these months: a chance to get the hell out of San Diego and wipe the slate clean. He spoke quickly, before he could change his mind, told Carl that he'd drive up the very next day. If it was truly possible for someone to start over, he meant to.

Carl put him up in his apartment, and he became the newest operative at Ironman Executive Protection. He took all the shit work in the beginning. Things like accompanying a loudmouthed TV actor to clubs where Boone's job was to get between the punk and the girls he pissed off by grabbing their asses. Things like babysitting a famous model's pug while she spent hours snorting coke in the bathroom of a Beverly Hills restaurant. And then there was the senile movie producer who hired Boone to start his Mercedes and ride with him to the pharmacy because he was certain the Mob was still out to get him for some dirt he'd done back in 1972.

Boone was a hit. The clients liked him, requested him, and recommended him to others, and within a few months he was able to move into his own condo in Hollywood. Things continued to go well for the next six years. Boone became Carl's partner in the business, and they got bigger and better jobs. He accompanied a Saudi prince to Monaco and stood by his side while he gambled away a small fortune, and he and a team he assembled spent a whole month watching over a movie star and his family during their vacation in Hawaii. He moved into the Hills, leasing a house with a gym and a pool. He bought a Porsche 996 Turbo the first year they came out, dated a slew of very beautiful but very fucked-up actress/model/waitresses, and often lay awake at night marveling at where life had taken him. By the time he was thirty years old, he couldn't think of much more to ask for.

Then along came Tom and Jeannie Anderson.

The gig was cake. Tom Anderson, an oil-company executive from Houston, had a few weeks of business in L.A. and brought his wife, Jeannie, and eight-year-old daughter, Adelle, along with him, renting a villa in Malibu: a palatial main house, two guesthouses, a pool, and a tennis court, all on two acres overlooking a stunning sweep of California coastline. Ironman was hired to provide security.

Usually, Boone and Carl would have put a couple of new guys on such a routine assignment, but they were shorthanded, and Boone called heads when the quarter came up tails. He took days, and they gave nights to Rodney Parker, who'd played one season at tackle with the Oilers back in the seventies before blowing out his knee and was now the oldest guy on Ironman's payroll.

The two men set up camp in one of the guesthouses, which Rodney declared was bigger than any dump he'd ever lived in, and things settled quickly into a routine. During the week, Anderson left for work early in the morning and returned after dark. When Jeannie and Adelle went on shopping trips to Brentwood and Beverly Hills or jaunts down to the beach, Boone accompanied them, riding in the front seat of the limo. But mostly the girls hung around the house, where they ate lunch by the pool and watched lots of TV.

Jeannie was quite a bit younger than Anderson, one of those skinny, brittle blondes with perfect hair and makeup who seem born and bred to marry rich older men. She looked right through Boone when they had any occasion to interact, but this was nothing new. Many of his clients made it a point to ignore his presence, and they were doing him a favor, as far as he was concerned. Nobody yet had paid him enough to be their friend.

Little Adelle took after her dad physically: dark hair and big sad eyes. She hadn't learned the rules yet, so she often treated Boone and Rodney like babysitters, peppering them with silly questions and begging them to join in her games. She swam in the afternoons or sang along to her *Little Mermaid* DVD but still seemed a bit lonely stuck up there in that big house with Mommy and the help, once even asking Boone if he had any kids she could play with.

The vague air of unease that hung over the family was explained when Rodney heard Anderson and Jeannie arguing late one night as he was making his rounds of the property. "Going at it like a couple of back-alley knife fighters," he told Boone the next morning. "Screaming about divorce and custody, him saying if she ever leaves him, he'll fix it so she never gets any money or sees that little girl again." The tension between the couple was palpable after that, and Boone himself witnessed a couple of heated exchanges.

The second weekend the family was in town, Anderson threw a party for one hundred guests. Catered barbecue, a country band, cowboy hats—the full Texas hoedown. Boone and Rodney stuck to the perimeter, Rodney grumbling the whole time about having to turn around afterward and also work the night shift.

At one point Adelle and a couple other little girls approached Boone, and Adelle announced, "Here's our bodyguard. He has a gun."

"Really?" one of the girls asked.

"Show her," Adelle said.

"Come on, now, I don't need to carry a gun here," Boone

said. "Not with all these nice people." He was packing his Glock in a shoulder rig under his coat but certainly wasn't going to let the kids see it.

"Do you want me to get you some ice cream?" Adelle asked.

"No, I'm fine. Thanks," Boone said.

The little girl suddenly stepped forward and hugged him tightly around the waist. "Thank you for taking care of us," she said.

Something about that got Boone right in the chest. He reached down and tousled the girl's hair and had to swallow to get the quaver out of his voice before saying, "You guys better head back now. Sounds like the band is starting."

He turned to catch Jeannie staring at him so intently, it looked like she was trying to read his mind. Their eyes locked briefly, and then she walked off into the crowd of guests.

The last weekend of their stay, Anderson took Adelle to Disneyland, just the two of them, no Jeannie, no Boone or Rodney. This didn't sit well with Jeannie. She drank wine by the pool all day, threw a glass at the cook when he tried to serve lunch, and screamed to someone on the phone that she was going crazy.

That evening Rodney was on duty and Boone was watching TV in the guesthouse when there was a soft knock at the door. Boone answered and found a bedraggled Jeannie on the porch, eyes swollen from crying, hair hanging in her face. She needed to talk to someone, she said, and, in a hoarse whisper, asked if Boone would take a walk with her. Every alarm in Boone's head went off at once, but he couldn't come up with a reason to refuse her.

Jeannie was silent as they strolled side by side up the dimly lit path past the tennis courts to a bluff with a view of the moonlit ocean. She stood with her head bowed, her arms wrapped around her bare shoulders, and the same breeze that made her shiver in her thin sundress brought the faintest sound of crashing waves to Boone's ears.

"I think my husband is molesting my daughter," Jeannie blurted, as if the words burned her tongue.

Boone's stomach twisted, but he kept his voice calm as he asked, "What does that mean, you 'think'? Have you seen anything? Did Adelle say something?"

No, Adelle hadn't said anything, but there had definitely been some weird moments, Jeannie replied. She'd walked in on the two of them a few times, and Anderson had looked so...well...guilty. "I realize that's not any kind of proof, but I'm absolutely certain something's not right," she insisted. "A mother knows."

She turned to Boone then, tears shining on her cheeks, and said, "That's why I wanted to talk to you. What can I do about it?"

Without solid proof, Boone told her, not much. He suggested she keep an eye on her husband and talk to Adelle in a roundabout way, try to coax something out of her.

Jeannie cried harder. Boone laid a hand on her shoulder to comfort her, and she crumpled into him. "He's hurting my baby," she sobbed.

Boone walked her back to the main house after she'd calmed down. She thanked him for listening and apologized for being such a mess. When Boone told Rodney about it, Rodney said, "She's a client, Jimmy, and that's a personal problem. You see how much money this man has? He can fuck up your life in one hundred ways."

Boone didn't sleep at all that night. Sickening visions of Anderson abusing Adelle swirled in his head, and he twice ran into the bathroom, thinking he was going to vomit. He arose at dawn as jagged as a broken bottle.

Anderson and Adelle got back early Sunday, and the family began to pack for their return to Houston. Boone and Rodney packed too, so they'd be ready to roll as soon as the Andersons left for the airport the next morning.

Rodney was eager to get back to his wife and new grandson, and his happy chatter calmed Boone some. He started to think that Jeannie might have been overreacting the night before, that it might have been the wine talking. Truthfully, he just wanted the fucking job to end. He planned to fly to Vegas, hang out with a dancer he'd met on his last gig there, booze it up for a few days, and put the Andersons out of his mind.

About seven thirty, as the sun touched the ocean and set the sky on fire, he was making a final sweep of the grounds before turning things over to Rodney for the night. He was on his way back from checking the front gate when Jeannie appeared in the driveway in front of him. She approached at a run, her face clenched into a mask of agony.

"What's wrong?" he asked.

She thrust a pair of underwear at him, little girl's underwear—white cotton, flowers—and pointed out a spot of blood the size of a quarter.

"He's with her now," she rasped in his ear. "In the first upstairs bathroom. You have to stop him."

Her urgency propelled Boone into the house without further questions. The front door was wide open, and he raced through it, a human cannonball. He took the stairs two at a time, keeping to the edges to avoid squeaks.

Anderson's voice floated out of a room down the hall, something about "Love you, baby doll." Boone put his back to the wall and slid sideways toward the door, which was slightly ajar. He peeked through the crack.

Anderson was kneeling next to the bathtub with his back to Boone, wearing Bermuda shorts and no shirt. Boone could just see the top of Adelle's head. She appeared to be on all fours in the tub.

"I love you, baby doll," Anderson crooned again.

A bomb went off somewhere behind Boone's eyes. He drew his gun, moved away from the door. "Mr. Anderson?" he called out.

Anderson stepped into the hall, red-faced and scowling. "What are you doing up here?" he asked.

Boone stuck his gun in the man's ribs, hissed at him to shut the fuck up, then said, "Adelle, honey, I need you too."

"Now wait a goddamn minute," Anderson said.

Boone jabbed him with the gun again and said, "I *will* shoot you."

A few seconds later Adelle came out of the bathroom wrapped in a towel, wet hair plastered to her forehead.

"Go downstairs," Boone said, putting his hand on her shoulder and giving her a little shove. "Mommy's waiting." She was frightened and glanced up at Anderson as if asking if it was okay to leave.

"Go on, sweetie," Anderson said. "I'll be there in a minute."

The little girl ran off without looking back.

"What is this?" Anderson said to Boone. "A robbery?"

The outrage and disgust that had been building in Boone since the previous night got the best of him. He swung his gun, hitting Anderson on the side of the head. The man's eyes rolled, but he didn't go down, so Boone grabbed him by the throat, took him to the floor, and began punching him.

He kept it up until his hands hurt too much to go on and

Anderson's face was a bloody mess. When he finally came back to himself, he crawled over and sat against the wall, gasping for air. Footsteps pounded on the stairs, and Rodney appeared in the hallway.

"What the fuck did you do?" he yelled. "What the fuck did you do?"

The paramedics arrived, the police. They cuffed Boone and took him away. At the station he gave a brief statement about what Jeannie had told him, about what he'd seen in the bathroom, then decided he'd better keep his mouth shut until he talked to a lawyer.

It was touch and go for Anderson for a few days. Shattered cheekbones, a broken jaw, nose pulped, brain swelling. He pulled through, though, so murder wasn't added to the litany of charges against Boone, which included felony aggravated assault, felony battery, assault with a deadly weapon, assault with a firearm, attempted murder—it went on and on.

Ironman's attorney, Danny Berkson, showed up for the arraignment, where Boone pleaded not guilty. Carl posted his bond. A preliminary hearing was scheduled for a week later, and Boone kept close to home in that time, nursing two broken knuckles and replaying the scene in the Malibu house over and over. He'd fucked up for sure, gone way too far, but he figured he'd probably get off easy when what Anderson was doing to Adelle came out.

Berkson, a hulking, worn-out teddy bear of a man, paid him a visit the day before the hearing, his face grim, his shoulders more slumped than usual. "We're in a pickle," he said.

Turns out Jeannie had denied telling Boone that Anderson was molesting Adelle, denied showing him the bloody panties, denied there was ever any trouble at all. Furthermore, she claimed that Boone had been eyeballing her during the family's stay and, on a few occasions, had made comments that indicated he was attracted to her.

"You see how it looks, don't you?" Berkson said. "It looks like you busted into the house while Anderson was giving his darling daughter a bath and beat the guy half to death because you wanted to fuck his wife."

All the air went out of Boone, and he slumped on the couch, his chin resting on his chest. "Jesus Christ," he said.

"Do you know Him?" Berkson cracked. "Because we could sure use His help right about now."

"She played me," Boone said.

"How?" Berkson asked.

"I don't know for sure, but she played me hard."

Berkson leaned forward and clasped his hands between his knees. "Well, look," he said. "What it boils down to is that Anderson's attorneys have got the DA by the balls somehow, and he's saying that the only way he'll deal with us is if you retract your original statement about what Jeannie told you and what you saw in the bathroom."

Boone exhaled hard and shook his head. "This is so fucked up," he said.

"If you retract, they'll settle for eight years," Berkson continued. "With good time and work credits, you'll do four."

Four years. Boone stared out at his swimming pool sparkling in the sunlight. Four years. He felt like he'd been turned inside out.

"If you don't retract and this goes to trial, they're gonna come down on you with a sledgehammer," Berkson said. "That motherfucker was this close to dying, so we're talking fifteen, twenty years."

"Danny, man, what do I do?" Boone said.

"What do you do!" Berkson exclaimed. "Retract, retract, retract."

Boone could barely muster the energy to raise his head and look into Berkson's eyes. "At least you believe me, right?" he said.

Berkson smiled. "You gonna trust an old shark like me if I say I do?"

Boone briefly considered cutting and running. He could sell the Porsche and raise enough cash to make it to Panama or Colombia. But he wasn't the fugitive type. All that lying and hiding and scheming didn't sit right with him. So he took the deal, his hand shaking as he signed the papers. And when they cuffed him and led him out of the courtroom, he felt he might fall down dead of shame.

Not two months after he walked into the fish tank at Corcoran, he learned from Berkson that Anderson and Jeannie were divorcing. They'd share custody of Adelle, and Jeannie would receive a hefty settlement. *Ha!* he thought. *There it is.* He ran the whole thing through his head that night in his bunk.

It was clear that Jeannie was desperate to get out of the marriage and that Anderson didn't want to let her go. Hadn't Rodney heard him threatening to take the kid and give her nothing if she left? So she needed something to use against him. She revs Boone up with phony abuse stories, shows him a doctored pair of panties to push him over the edge, and lets his righteous anger do the rest.

The way it games out is, if he kills Anderson, she inherits everything. If he merely fucks him up, there's the abuse allegation, which she'll deny and make disappear in exchange for a divorce and enough cash. Either way, Boone is played for a fool and ends up behind bars. He chuckled bitterly as it all fell into place and thought, *Well, someday she'll get hers,* but that was bullshit, and he knew it, just something people comforted themselves with when they'd been had.

He kept his head down in prison, did his time. It was rough in the beginning. He had to go toe to toe with a couple of bone crushers to establish that he wasn't to be fucked with, and sustained a minor stab wound fending off a lunatic with a shiv who had some kind of beef with him. Word eventually got around that he was a righteous con, though, and the challenges stopped.

After that, his main problem was boredom, filling his days. He worked in the laundry, read paperbacks from the library, played cards, and exercised on the yard. In some ways it was a lot like the Marines. The easiest way to get by in Corcoran, just as it had been in the corps, was to stick to the program, follow orders, and not indulge in useless bitching and moaning. The few friends he made were older cons, go-with-the-flow characters who knew the secrets to living a quiet life in the midst of the chaos of prison.

Carl came up to see him a couple of times, Berkson too, but Boone was content to have little contact with the outside. His strategy was to ignore everything that didn't pertain to the day-to-day grind. Concrete, steel, shit, and sweat. He pulled back his horizons until they reached only as far as the razor-wire-topped perimeter fences and got very good at convincing himself that there was nothing he wanted, needed, or missed. But then a jet would pass overhead, bound for L.A. or San Francisco, or the yard would be swept by a breeze sweet with the smell of new-mown hay, and he'd crumble into dust.

Berkson picked him up when he was cut loose and drove him back to L.A. He'd come to believe that Boone had indeed been set up by Jeannie Anderson and felt awful about the way things had gone. Boone had sold everything he owned to pay his legal fees and fines and had only two grand left to his name. Carl had talked about him maybe returning to Ironman, but as a convicted felon—not even allowed to carry a gun—Boone wouldn't be much use, so Berkson set him up with the job at the Tick Tock and the gig managing the bungalows.

It's six months later now, and he hasn't yet figured out his next move. The only thing he's ever been good at is protecting other people, putting himself in harm's way for pay. Tending bar is nice and safe, but it sometimes feels like killing time. Lately he rouses from dreams of waiting and lies awake in the dark with the minutes flying past so swiftly, it takes his breath away. Then, suddenly, it's dawn, another day, and he's still a man becalmed, adrift a million miles from shore.

By the time Boone finishes up, his and Amy's glasses are empty, and so is the bottle. He's never laid the whole story out like this, told it from the beginning, and he's surprised at how drained he feels. He is also a bit embarrassed, thinking about Amy having to sit through all of it.

"Damn," he says. "Sorry about going on like that."

Amy sets her glass on the coffee table. "Don't be," she says. "You obviously needed to get it out."

"Yeah, okay, but that's what shrinks are for."

"Ahh, shrinks are expensive."

"Well, still, I'm sorry."

Amy pushes her hair back behind her ears. She reaches for her cigarettes, starts to pull one out, then pushes it back inside and closes the box.

"Look, I'm gonna go," she says. She stands suddenly, as if now that she's decided to leave, she can't wait to get away. "This is an awful lot to absorb, and I kind of feel like I need to be alone to do it."

"Sure," Boone says. "I understand."

Joto wakes up and lifts his head to watch as Boone walks Amy to the door.

"Do you have a blanket for him?" Amy asks. "Dogs like that, something of their own."

"I'll find one," Boone assures her.

She steps out onto the porch.

"The kids at school, what do they call you?" Boone asks.

"*Bitch* behind my back, I'm sure, but Miss Vitello to my face."

"Well, then, good night, Miss Vitello."

"Good night."

Boone watches her walk across the courtyard and actually feels pretty good, all things considered. He's done the right thing for once, putting everything out there. And Amy reacted just the way she should have. What woman wouldn't be turned around by a story like that? Maybe over time he'll learn a better way to tell it.

"Hey."

It's Amy, calling to him from her porch.

"What time are we going to breakfast tomorrow?" she says.

"Excuse me?" Boone replies, wondering if he missed something.

"I'll have all this sorted out by morning and be dying to talk about it."

"Is nine okay?" Boone asks.

"Nine's fine," Amy says. She walks into her bungalow and closes the door. A few minutes later the light in her living room goes off.

Boone stands on his porch for a long time, listening to the freeway traffic in the distance and watching the spotlights slide across the purple sky above Hollywood. It might be the wine, but he's moved—by the night, by the city, by the gently swaying silhouettes of the palm trees overhead. By Amy's kindness and by Berkson's faith in him. Beautiful, he thinks. All of it. Tomorrow, things will go to hell again, but tonight he's not going to question his contentment; he's going to accept it for the fleeting gift that it is.

7

William Taggert slips out of bed at dawn as he does every morning. Part of it is that he can't stand to waste daylight, but the other part is that his dreams have turned weird lately. Lots of running, lots of hiding. Half the time he wakes up more tired than when he sacked out.

Olivia mumbles something angry in her sleep and curls into a tighter ball, and Taggert takes a moment to admire her long legs, her smooth skin, thanking his lucky stars for the thousandth time before covering her with the sheet. A quick piss, and he steps out into the front yard in his boxers and a T-shirt, raises his arms over his head, and groans as he stretches.

The surrounding desert blooms pink and purple, the sun just now climbing above the horizon. Taggert watches a baby cottontail nibble at a clump of weeds until a barking dog over at the barn spooks it, sending it bounding for cover. A couple of little brown birds perched on the old horse trough in Olivia's cactus garden dip their beaks and fluff their feathers. These truly are the finest five minutes of every day.

Miguel, the kid who looks after the animals, steps out of his trailer over by the barn and waves. T.K.'s Explorer is parked next to the bunkhouse, a battered seventies singlewide set up on a flat a hundred yards down the hill. Taggert heard him and Spiller get in around eleven last night but didn't feel like dealing with it. He and Olivia had already killed a pitcher of margaritas and were in the middle of *The Godfather.* She'd never seen it before, but that didn't surprise him. She's twenty-five; he's fifty-five. He's seen a lot of things she hasn't.

He puts on khaki shorts with lots of pockets and a pair of flip-flops, then pours himself a cup of coffee and sips it on his way down to the bunkhouse. The mobile home shakes when he pounds on the door. Something falls off a shelf and clatters to the floor.

"Rise and shine, bitches," he yells.

Spiller opens up, that stringy red hair of his, what's left of it, hanging in his face, a bandage on his neck.

"Morning, boss," he mumbles.

"Another job well done, huh?" Taggert says.

"What were we supposed to do, the fucker pulls a gun?"

"Reason with him? Talk him down?"

"No time. The guy was half a second from opening up on us."

T.K. appears in the hallway behind Spiller, nods, and says, "Hey, boss," before shutting himself up in the bathroom.

"What'd you do with the garbage?" Taggert asks Spiller. "I didn't see anything in your vehicle."

"We dropped everything off at the shack on the way in. T.K. was worried about it leaking on his upholstery."

"And the kid?"

Spiller jerks his head toward the couch, and Taggert leans in to see a pair of scared eyes peering at him over the armrest. The punk does look a little like Olivia.

"Hey there," Taggert says. "Welcome to the ranch."

"Thank you, sir."

"It's Virgil, isn't it?"

"Yes, sir."

"Well, Virgil, I bet your sister's gonna get a big kick out of seeing you. Spiller and I have some chores to do, but what say we meet at the house at ten for breakfast?"

"Cool," Virgil says.

Cool, huh? Taggert kicks himself in the ass. He should have had Spiller and T.K. put the kid down with that other piece of shit. Olivia would never have been the wiser; bad boys like Virgil drop off the face of the earth every day of the week. But he blinked because of her. Because she calls him Big Poppa and Sweet Tea. Because sometimes she smiles right when he needs her to. Because she gets him hard just by walking into a room.

"Put some fucking pants on," he says to Spiller, the guy standing there in his Jockeys like it ain't no thing.

TAGGERT WALKS BACK up to the house, which started as a simple vacation cabin in the fifties but has since mutated into a sprawling three-bedroom jumble of dubious structural soundness thanks to various owners' additions and improvements. Taggert bought the place a couple of years ago for the land—two hundred acres of sand, chaparral, and rocks—and when the new house he's building on the butte is finished, this rattrap will be torn down and hauled away.

He climbs into his old Dodge truck and drives down to pick up Spiller at the bunkhouse. They bump along a washboard road until they reach the abandoned homesteader's shack where T.K. and Spiller stashed Eton's body and the bags containing the pieces of chair and the bloody linen. There's a funky smell in the air when they step inside the shack. Flies are already gathering, their frenzied buzzing enough to make your head spin, and a long line of fat black ants marches across the shower curtain to squeeze through a hole in the plastic and get at the corpse.

"They sure don't waste any time," Spiller says as he bends over to grab Eton's feet.

"When'd you last turn down a free meal?" Taggert replies, lifting his end.

They carry the body out to the truck, lay it in the bed, then load the bags. Taggert slides behind the wheel again and turns onto a side road that climbs into a narrow box canyon. The canyon dead-ends at the entrance to an old mine, a five-foot-square vertical shaft that extends down who knows how far, but enough that the beam of a powerful flashlight doesn't reach the bottom.

Spiller hops out of the truck and walks over to the mine. He cranes his neck to peer into the hole and says, "I bet there's a way to figure out how deep this goes by counting, like you do with thunder."

Taggert has dropped the tailgate of the truck and is dragging out the body. He says, "Maybe one day you'll wind up down there yourself, and all your questions will be answered."

"I'm not that curious," Spiller replies as he walks to the truck to help.

They carry the body to the shaft and toss it in. Spiller stands at the edge with his hand cupped over his ear, listening for it to hit.

"I got to four," he says. "What's that mean in feet?"

"Hey," Taggert growls, already back at the truck. "How about getting over here and grabbing some of these bags."

When everything has been disposed of, Taggert drives Spiller up to the site of the new house, the highest point on the property. From here they can see the little town of Twentynine

Palms, the Marine base that keeps the town from drying up and blowing away, and part of Joshua Tree National Park. He and Spiller stand on the concrete foundation, which was poured six months ago. It's taken two years to get this far on the place, with Taggert putting every bit of extra cash he can into it. All the sacrifices will be worth it when the house is done though. Taggert takes a deep breath, filling his lungs with the cleanest air he's ever tasted.

The sun is fully up now, and the only thing marring the pale blue sky is a pair of jet contrails arching over their heads and already beginning to feather and fade. Taggert walks to the truck and retrieves the blueprint for the house from behind the seat. He unrolls it on the slab, weighting the corners with rocks. He dreamed last night that the south wall was off by six feet and wants to put his mind at ease.

He bends to examine the plan. Thirty-one feet, it should be. Taking a tape measure from the pocket of his shorts, he hands the end of it to Spiller.

"Hook this over there," he says. "I need to check something."

Spiller moves to the end of the slab while Taggert walks backward, extending the tape. Thirty-one feet exactly. So everything's copacetic. Taggert scratches his goatee and shakes his head. Fucking dreams, man. And the fucking fools who dream them. He rolls up the blueprint and sits on the foundation to admire again the view he'll have from the front window of the house. Spiller plops down beside him, lights a cigarette.

"If I was smart, I'd have moved here years ago," Taggert says.

"It's nice," Spiller says. "Quiet. Makes you feel close to God."

"God?" Taggert says, then spits in the dirt. "There's no God out here, man. No God, no devil, just the wind. And shit lasts forever in this dry air. Leave a junk car sitting outside, it'll take years to rust. People too. They've proven that you actually live longer in a climate like this."

"I believe that," Spiller says. "You seen those mummies cruising around Palm Springs, so shrunk up they can barely see over the dashboard? All you can make out from behind is big-ass knuckles clutching the steering wheel."

The guy thinks he's cute, making fun of old folks. He doesn't realize yet that someday he's going to be old too and have young assholes cracking wise about him. Taggert doesn't say what he was about to say next, that he's thinking about throttling back soon, taking it easy. He doesn't want to hear any more jokes.

But it's true. He's working on a retirement plan for himself. If this thing that Benjy is setting up comes through, he'll have enough cash to last him for as long as he keeps ticking. He'll finish the house, pay off his debts, and then he and Olivia will sit back and watch sunsets and drink margaritas until they're bored to death with each other.

A buzzard circles in the distance, its ragged black wings outstretched, its shadow sliding over the rocks below. Spiller takes a deep drag of his cigarette, tilts his head back, and fires off a few smoke rings.

"Boss," he says, "I want to come right out with you about something."

"No, you can't suck my cock," Taggert says.

"Seriously, bro," Spiller says. "You know I've been in a custody fight with that whore I was married to for half a second and that part of the deal is I got to have some of my ink removed."

Taggert looks down at his own forearms, which are covered with ancient tattoos that have faded into mush.

"Well, that shit's expensive, the treatments," Spiller continues. "And what I was wondering is, I think I've been doing good work for you these past few years, and it seems to me that it's time I get a bigger cut, if you see what I'm saying."

Taggert puts his palms behind him on the slab and leans back. The concrete is already warming up. He wouldn't trust Spiller in a dark room with a sharp knife, but the weasel does what he's told and isn't afraid to mix it up if it comes to that. Has it really been three years he's been part of the crew? Must be. He was around for the Russian thing and the AK-47s.

"I'll never hold it against you, you asking for what you want," Taggert says. "I mean, how else are you gonna get it, right?"

"So I'm gonna get it?" Spiller says.

"What if you don't?"

Spiller frowns. Taggert can tell that he feels like he's being fucked with and that he doesn't like it.

"I might have to take on some side work," Spiller says. "Stony's been after me to ride with him on some shit."

"Petrovich? Good luck. Word is ATF is all the way up his ass, and he's going down any day now."

"I'm just saying. That's one thing."

Taggert cups his hands over his eyes to cut the glare and squints down the hill toward where he thinks he saw a flash a moment ago—the sun on an old beer can maybe—but it's gone now. He turns to face Spiller.

"You're a good soldier," he says. "I won't play about that. Hold off on freelancing for a while, because between you and me—and I said between you and me—there's something in the wind that could put us all in the black for a long time."

"For real, man?"

"On my skin. Give me like a week."

"That's good to hear," Spiller says. " 'Cause I really don't want to work for anybody but you."

Taggert doesn't tell Spiller that there's no way he'd have let him work for anybody else, least of all Stony Petrovich, and that, in fact, he's a little pissed that he's even been talking to the guy. He swallows the bubble of anger in his throat and returns to thinking about tile, what color he's going to use in the master bath, while Spiller removes one of his sneakers and shakes out a pebble that's been bothering him.

A few minutes more, and they head back to the truck. They're almost there when a rattle sounds, stopping them in their tracks. Taggert spots a huge Mojave green coiled in the sand a couple yards from where Spiller is standing. A real monster. Five feet long and as big around as an ax handle.

Spiller sees the snake, too, and all the color drains out of his face. "Hey," he whines. "Help me, boss."

"Keep still," Taggert says.

As far as he's concerned, rattlers have more right to be out here than he does, but if they make the mistake of challenging him, they're going to get the short end of the stick. He walks over to the truck and leans in the open window to retrieve his vintage Colt, a big old cowboy-movie six-shooter that he carries in the glove box.

"Hurry," Spiller says. "I think I'm gonna puke."

Taggert finds a good spot, raises the revolver, and blows the snake's head off, the shot echoing from rocky hill to rocky hill. Spiller's legs give way, and he sits hard on the ground.

Taggert shoves the Colt into his waistband and takes out his lockblade. He walks over to the snake and cuts off its rattle, then whips what's left of the beast into the scrub. When he goes to put the knife back into his pocket, it slips out of his hand and falls to the ground. Panic constricts him for an instant, a cold finger pinging his spine. It's nothing, he thinks. Clumsiness. Still, he flexes the hand, opens and closes it, testing the muscles for weakness.

"PHOENIX EYE," T.K. says, forming a fist from which the second knuckle of his index finger protrudes. "Very nasty if you catch someone in the throat with it, or the eye, or—" Before Virgil can react, T.K punches him in the hand, finger bone striking wrist bone. Virgil yelps and recoils as pain like an electric shock shoots up his arm.

"Yo, man, that ain't cool," Virgil says.

"You asked me to show you some stuff," T.K. replies.

"That don't mean you can whale on me though."

Virgil walked out of the mobile home earlier to find T.K. practicing kung fu, kicking and punching imaginary opponents in what looked like some kind of lethal dance, his massive chest and arms gleaming with sweat. The big man said he'd teach him how to put the hurt on someone, but all he's done for the past ten minutes is use him for target practice.

Virgil was tripped out to wake up here in the middle of nowhere this morning. It was so dark on the way in last night, there was no way to tell just how much nothing there was around. It's freaky, all this dirt, all this sky, the sun sitting right on top of you, no place to hide. It makes him dizzy.

He's pretty sure he's not going to end up like Eton—at least it doesn't feel like they're about to shoot him every other second anymore—but when Taggert banged on the door this morning, man, Virgil almost swallowed his tongue. The guy is all the way o.g.: silver hair slicked straight back, thick goatee, prison muscles straining the sleeves of his T-shirt, a gnarly scar on his throat. An older dude, sure, but one who could break you in half if you crossed him. And that voice of his, a rusty whisper that you're forced to listen closely to because you don't dare ask the man to repeat himself.

"Okay, throw a couple jabs at me, then a right," T.K. says.

Virgil's ready to go back inside and see what channels the mobile home's TV pulls in, but he puts up his dukes and tosses a few halfhearted punches.

"Stick some dick into it, boy," T.K. says. "Let's see some of that white power you woods are always going on about."

Jab, jab, stopping inches from T.K.'s jaw, then a hard right.

"Better," T.K. says. "Again."

Jab, jab, right, and all of a sudden Virgil is bent backward over T.K.'s thigh, a sweaty forearm pressed to his throat. If T.K. hadn't stopped him midfall, he'd have ended up in the dirt.

"That was a sweeper kick, a great way to take someone to the mat," T.K. says. He returns Virgil to his feet and releases him, and Virgil moves away, rubbing a twinge in his lower back.

"Forget this shit," he says. "I ain't nobody's punching bag."

T.K. wipes the sweat off his forehead with his palm and says, "You got to have patience. Guys come in and want to be Jet Li right off the bat, but it doesn't work like that."

"How long till Taggert and Spiller get back?" Virgil asks. "I'm fucking starving."

"Couldn't say, man," T.K. replies. "Nobody tells me nothing."

Virgil walks over and sits on the steps of the mobile home. A couple of dogs are barking somewhere nearby. They've been at it all morning. Virgil picks up a stick and drags it through the sand, drawing naked women, while T.K. goes back to practicing punches and kicks.

"So what are you, man? Chinese, black, what?" Virgil asks.

"When they ask, I check 'other,' " T.K. replies.

"You been with Taggert long?"

"Couple three years or so. Me and Spiller joined up about the same time, after his old crew fell apart."

"What happened?"

"Ah, you know, something about somebody fucking somebody else's. Taggert's a legend, so I jumped at the chance to get in with him. He stood up to the Mexicans, the Colombians, the Angels. He's a fearless motherfucker."

T.K. keeps going. He tells Virgil how Taggert was born in Kentucky into a family of coal miners and moonshiners, how he was drafted right out of high school and did a tour in Nam but was finally booted out of the service for being part of a ring that was hawking weapons stolen from the base armory.

He tried mining after that, concluded that it was a job for men who sold themselves cheap, and eventually ended up in Louisville, where he fell in with a local mover who taught him to run whores, put money on the street, and set odds. The mover disappeared a few years later, and Taggert took over his operation, adding dope dealing to the menu. This didn't sit well with certain old-timers. A shooting war broke out, and lots of people from both sides fell into shallow graves. Taggert came out on top but a year later went down for a truck hijacking and did a bit in the Kentucky state pen.

It was 1979 when he got clear of that, and he decided to kiss the Bluegrass State good-bye and try his luck in California. Washing up flat busted in San Diego, he quickly found work smuggling Mexicans and marijuana across the border and in time put together his own crew and started pulling off jobs—bank robberies, credit card scams, shakedowns—all over the Southwest. He took another fall in the early nineties—assault—and did a couple years behind that, which is when he got his throat cut and fucked up his voice. It's been up, up, and away since then though. People want a car, they come to Taggert. Dope, guns, explosives, chemicals—the man has connections.

And he's still as tough as he ever was. There's the story about him walking into a bar in Tijuana, blowing away three crooked *federales* who fucked him over on a coke deal, then spending the afternoon drinking mescal with his boots propped up on the corpses. Or how about when he drove five miles north on the southbound side of the freeway to shake the CHP?

"See, what it is, he doesn't give a shit about dying because he should be dead already," T.K. says. Having finished his workout, he crouches in the shade next to the mobile home. "His granddad, his dad, his brother, they all died from strokes before they hit forty. His uncle lived through his but wound up paralyzed, being fed through a tube. The poor bastard couldn't see, couldn't swallow. Taggert finally snuck in one night and pulled the plug on him.

"All them dying like that? From the same thing? Taggert is cursed, and he knows it. Any minute now some fucked-up little vein in his head will pop, and he'll either be dead or drooling all over himself and shitting in a diaper. He stares at death in the mirror every morning and carries it around inside him every day, and that gives him all the power in the world. Look into his eyes next time you get close. The end of everything is in there. You can't reason with a man like that. You can only kill him or follow him."

Virgil shivers, a little spooked. "Damn, man," he says. "You ain't hungry yet?" He should have brought some weed, that's for sure. Definitely should have raided Eton's stash before leaving the house. He stands and stretches, and a cloud of dust catches his eye, a truck speeding up the dirt road toward the ranch. Taggert and Spiller. Virgil's legs shake and his heart races. Goddamn T.K., talking all that shit.

8

Boone wakes before dawn and can't get back to sleep. He tosses and turns for an hour or so, his mind swirling with thoughts of Oscar Rosales. The kid was no saint, but by all accounts he was trying to do the right thing by Maribel and the baby, trying to get his life on track. So how, then, did he wind up being mauled, and who frightened him so badly that he refused to seek treatment for the wounds? Exactly what kind of craziness did he run into out there in the desert?

Boone's brain feels like it's going to explode, so he gets up and takes a cold shower, trying and failing to wash Oscar out of his thoughts. He walks into the living room afterward and notices a puddle of vomit on the floor.

"Did you do that?" he says to Joto.

The dog, curled up on the ragged comforter Boone laid out for him to sleep on, opens his eyes briefly, then closes them again. Boone kneels beside him and puts his fingers to the animal's nose. It's warm to the touch. Not a good thing, Boone remembers hearing somewhere.

He and Amy are supposed to go to breakfast at nine. At eight thirty he walks across the courtyard to her bungalow.

"You're a little early," Amy says when she opens her door. She's wearing jeans and a red tank top, and her hair is pulled back into a ponytail.

"There's kind of a problem," Boone says. "The dog's sick. He's been throwing up and seems really lethargic. I hate to flake on you, but I should probably get him to a vet."

"The poor thing," Amy says. "Do you mind if I take a look?"

"Please," Boone says. "I know squat about animals, so maybe I'm freaking out over nothing."

Joto barely reacts when they walk into Boone's place. Amy sits on the floor beside the dog and lifts his head to peer into his eyes.

"I'm not an expert or anything, but I think you're right to be worried," she says. "Do you have a vet?"

"I didn't even have a dog until last night," Boone replies.

"My friend is a total animal nut. If you want, I can check with her and see if she has any recommendations."

"That'd be awesome."

While Amy is at her place, making the call, Boone lifts the bowl of water sitting next to the comforter to Joto's mouth to encourage him to drink. His tongue flaps once or twice, but then he turns away and drops his head onto the blanket. Boone fingers a scar on the dog's flank, traces its path down his leg. "Don't worry, buddy," he says. "You'll be all right."

"Everything's cool," Amy says when she returns. "My friend told me about a vet in West Hollywood who specializes in pit bulls. I called, and she's in the office this morning and can see you."

"Can we move breakfast to tomorrow then?" Boone says.

"Or how about this," Amy says. "I'll help you transport Joto, and we can grab something while we're out."

Transport. A cop word. It makes Boone smile. "Kind of a lame way to spend Saturday morning," he says.

"You don't know lame. For a while I was going to a knitting club. *That* was lame."

When it's time to leave, Joto yelps and snaps at Boone as he picks him up.

"Easy, boy, easy," Amy says, stroking the dog's head.

Boone carries him to the Olds while Amy runs ahead to spread the comforter over the backseat. She sits with Joto during the ride. The weekend morning traffic is so light, it only takes them five minutes to reach the animal hospital on Santa Monica.

There are two other people in the reception area, older gay men with an empty cat carrier. Boone is embarrassed to tell the receptionist Joto's name in front of them, so he says he doesn't know, the dog's basically a stray.

"Does he bite?" the receptionist asks.

"He tries," Boone replies, "but he doesn't have any teeth."

She says Joto will have to wear a muzzle anyway and retrieves one from a cupboard. Boone can't figure the goddamn thing out. Amy has to help him put it on the dog.

After completing the paperwork, Boone sits with Joto in his lap. The dog is weaker than ever, can barely keep his eyes open. Boone stares at a poster hanging on the wall: photos of all kinds of animals and the words REAL DOCTORS TREAT MORE THAN ONE SPECIES. One of the gay men begins to cry, and the other reaches over and takes his hand. Amy gives Boone a pout in sympathy with them.

The vet, Dr. Sanchez, is a short, stocky woman with bleached blond hair moussed up into a faux hawk. She has multiple piercings in her ears and is wearing camouflage pants under her white smock.

She notices Joto's missing teeth as soon as she removes the

muzzle and questions Boone about it, rank suspicion in her tone. He explains that he bought the dog last night because he thought he was being mistreated but has no idea how he got so messed up. Sanchez continues the examination but seems a little edgy. She asks Boone to leave Joto with her and come back in an hour.

"Was it just me, or was she ready to kick my ass?" Boone says to Amy as they're walking out.

"I imagine she sees some pretty sick shit," Amy replies.

There's a café across the street from the animal hospital. Boone and Amy sit outside at one of the tables on the sidewalk. The other diners are all men, muscular guys in tight T-shirts with expensive haircuts and fake tans. Boone and Amy order coffee from the waiter and look over their menus.

"Ever been down here on Halloween?" Boone asks. "They block off the street, have a big party. Guys dress like Marilyn Monroe, Pam Anderson, pink flamingos."

"My friend Victor lives close by, and I came over last year," Amy says. "He went as J. Lo, and I swear he looked exactly like her. Hotter even."

"And you've got the Russians now too," Boone says. "That must be a trip, coming from Moscow to Boys Town."

"Hey, it's a crash course in America. Might as well throw them into the deep end."

Boone orders oatmeal. He's been putting on weight lately, living on hamburgers and french fries from the Tick Tock. Amy asks for eggs over easy, bacon, tomatoes instead of potatoes, and sourdough toast. She's wearing sandals, and Boone notices that her toenails are painted the same color as her shirt. Cute. The conversation stays surfacy, which is a relief after last night. She hates shopping; he has an unnatural love for Kevin

Costner movies; neither has been to a nude beach, but neither has completely ruled out the possibility. They laugh a lot, something Boone hasn't done in a long time.

The food arrives, and they can't believe how hungry they are, how good everything tastes.

"You know how sometimes you find yourself shoveling it in without enjoying it?" Amy says. "Like you might as well be eating hay?"

"Mmmm," Boone replies, his mouth full of toast. He tells a story about a Filipino kid he knew in the Marines, Mike Dagdag, who hit his head in a motorcycle accident and lost his sense of taste and smell. He and Boone became friendly, and Boone figured out a way to turn Dag's misfortune into easy money for both of them: they'd show up at the bars in Oceanside and convince their fellow jarheads to pay to see Dag do crazy shit like drink entire bottles of hot sauce or eat ten jalapeños, one after another.

Boone acted as Dag's manager, lining up the action and taking twenty-five percent for his efforts, and they had a good run for a while. Cash poured in, a couple hundred bucks a night, more on paydays. Guys would challenge Dag and wind up passing out or puking, trying to do what he did.

But then Dag got born-again, thanks to some girl he was dating, and started questioning the morality of their scam. Boone told him he could deliver a little sermon afterward, say it was the power of the Lord that enabled him to guzzle cod-liver oil, or he could give his share of the take to missionaries in China or Ethiopia or wherever. Dag wouldn't have any of it, though. God had spoken to his heart.

"It was tough watching my dreams die," Boone says with a smile. "Especially knowing God was behind it."

When they finish eating, Boone tells Amy he owes her for finding the vet and coming along with him and picks up the check. Amy protests just enough before giving in, and they walk across the street to the animal hospital. The two men and their cat carrier are gone. Boone hopes everything worked out okay for them.

Sanchez takes Boone and Amy back to the examination room, and a girl brings Joto in. The dog is livelier already. He barks at the sight of Boone and tries to lick his face through the muzzle when the girl sets him on the table.

"What do you know about this animal's history?" Sanchez asks, hands on her hips.

"Nothing," Boone replies. "Like I told you before, I bought him from some guys in MacArthur Park. He woke up sick this morning, so I brought him in."

"Well, he's a real mess," Sanchez says, consulting a clipboard. "He's malnourished and dehydrated. He has worms, a broken leg that wasn't set properly, mange, and fleas. And then someone took it upon themselves to remove his teeth."

"Remove?" Boone says.

"Someone pulled them for no reason that I can see. And not a professional."

"Jesus," Amy hisses.

"He was a fighting dog," Sanchez continues. "Thus, all the scars. And this—" she points inside his right ear. Boone bends to look and sees a small red star and the number 102 tattooed there.

"That's the mark of a breeder and trainer we've seen before," Sanchez says. "His name is Bob Morrison, and we've been trying to stop him for years with no luck. He's got a kennel out in Vernon. Sickos pay fifteen hundred dollars for his dogs, then throw them in a ring and let them tear each other apart while other sickos bet on the outcome. This dog's actually pretty lucky. He survived somehow."

Boone drifts off for a second, losing track of what Sanchez is saying. He's thinking that Robo should talk to this Morrison. If Joto really is one of his dogs, Morrison might know something about what happened to Oscar.

"Do you plan to keep him?" Sanchez asks.

"Huh?" Boone says. "No, I mean, I can't where I live. I thought I'd take him to the pound or get him adopted, whatever people do."

Sanchez taps her pen on her clipboard and says, "I know someone who rescues pit bulls. She's found homes for dogs a lot more screwed up than this one. I'll give you her number."

"Sounds good."

Sanchez then lists all the things it'll take to get Joto in shape—antibiotics, worm medicine, shampoo for the mange—and the whole time Boone is thinking there goes the little bit of money he has stashed under his mattress. She even recommends special food, saying that the vomiting and listlessness were likely caused by what Boone fed him being too rich for his system after he'd gone without eating for so long.

"Basically, he's got a tummy ache," she says. "It should clear up in a few days."

She writes down the number of the rescue woman on one of her business cards, and Boone says, "When you say you've been trying to stop this Morrison, what do you mean?"

"It wasn't me, exactly," Sanchez says. She tugs at one of the thin gold hoops in her ear. "It was some friends of mine, pretty serious animal activists. They were all over the bastard a couple years ago, picketing his place, videoing his every move and posting it on the Web, but they could never get the officials interested. Morrison ended up taking them to court, and the judge made them back off."

Boone rests a hand on Joto's head and says, "You know, it's kind of personal for me now, what they did to this dog. Is there any way for me to get in touch with your friends to make a donation or something?"

"Sure," Sanchez says. "Just go to Stop the Slaughter dot org."

Boone writes the address next to the rescue lady's number on the card. After removing the muzzle from Joto, he carries the dog out to the Olds while Amy follows with the food and medicine. She again rides in the backseat with Joto, who has enough energy now to sit up and snap at a fly that buzzes too close.

They're headed up Highland when a cop steps into the street and holds up his hand for them to stop. Boone hits the brake hard and feels his scalp tighten, the con in him expecting the worst. But then he notices the trailers, the equipment trucks. It's a location shoot, and the cop is stopping traffic while the crew films on the sidewalk. Looks like a man and a woman having an argument. The guy is carrying a bunch of yellow smiley-face balloons.

"Hooray for Hollywood," Boone says.

"Recognize anybody?" Amy asks, leaning forward to look out the windshield.

"I'm no good at that," Boone says. "Although I should be, considering all the time I spent on sets when I was working security."

"That must have been exciting, being around the actors and stuff," Amy says.

Boone wrinkles his nose. "I don't know. I was always thinking, 'What's this guy got that I don't? He can't even throw a punch that looks real.' And they're a strange bunch, that Hollywood crowd. They've got so many people saying yes to them all the time, they forget how to take no like everybody else has to."

"Yeah, okay," Amy says. "But you'd still trade places with them in a second."

"Absolutely," Boone replies.

They both laugh as the crew gets the shot and the cop waves them on.

WHEN THEY GET back to the bungalows, Joto is strong enough to walk from the car to Boone's place on his own. Amy helps Boone open a can of the new food and dope it with Joto's meds. The dog gobbles the mess, then trots into the living room and curls up on his blanket.

Boone is at the sink washing dishes. Amy leans against the counter, watching him. The silence between them stretches into something noticeable, and things are awkward for the first time this morning.

"So last night," Amy says, finally getting around to it.

Boone doesn't look up from the plate he's rinsing. He's suddenly a little nervous, worried what's on her mind. "That was weird, huh?" he says. "Superweird, in fact."

"It was definitely up there," Amy says. "But I also think it was pretty brave of you to be so honest about your arrest and prison and everything."

"I want you to know that's not my usual technique for getting women to like me," Boone says. "That was special, just for you."

Amy reaches out and lays her hand on his arm. "Seriously, Jimmy, look at me for a second," she says. "Every instinct

I have tells me that you're a decent guy, so I'm not going to second-guess you on what happened in Malibu. It was you in that moment, only you, and I was a cop long enough to know that things happen so fast sometimes, there's no thinking involved. It's pure aggression and adrenaline, and you sort it out later."

"Yeah, but I should have seen it coming," Boone says. "And that wasn't the first time I'd been stupid."

"But that's it: You weren't stupid. You met an evil genius."

Boone dries his hands on a towel and says, "What?"

"They're out there," Amy continues. "People who are so bad, it's like a talent."

"Evil geniuses."

"Sure, and think about it: How's a decent person supposed to anticipate what an evil genius is going to do? They can't. That's like trying to outthink Einstein. Our brains don't even work the same way."

Boone looks down at Amy's smiling face. He wants to kiss her right now, right on the mouth. "You're crazy," he says.

"No, I'm not. I'm right."

"Okay, then, so tell me straight up: is this your way of saying that we can be friends?"

Amy fishes the sponge out of the sink and wipes the counter. "We can give it a shot, right?" she says.

"Right," Boone replies. He pulls himself away from her to toss the empty dog food can in the trash. Take it slow, he thinks. Try for something real this time.

VIRGIL IS LYING on the couch in the mobile home watching cartoons with half a hard-on when T.K. comes out of the bathroom, freshly showered and smelling like aftershave, and says,

"Breakfast time." Fucking finally. Virgil feels paper-thin as he jumps up and puts on his Rays jersey and cap. Can't they see he's a growing boy?

He and T.K. walk up the dirt road to Taggert's house, which looks like an overgrown shack that might crash to the ground if you leaned on it the wrong way. Must be painted five different colors, every one of them fading to gray. There's all kinds of junk scattered around it too—pieces of cars and motorcycles, an old washing machine, a couple of shot-up stereo speakers. Virgil whips a rock at a lizard sunning itself on a discarded toilet bowl. A trickle of sweat runs down the crack of his ass. What kind of place is this hot at ten in the morning?

Taggert waves a spatula from a patio shaded by a tin awning. He's cooking steaks on a gas grill. Spiller is there too, comfortable in a folding lawn chair, the beer in his hand tucked into a green coozie from Joshua Tree Liquor, and there's a Mexican kid about Virgil's age kicked back on the bench seat from an old car.

"You two sure make a cute couple," Taggert rasps as Virgil and T.K. approach.

"Steak again," T.K. says. "Man, I sure miss my Cheerios."

Taggert motions to a cooler. "Grab yourselves a couple Buds," he says.

T.K. waves him off. "Little early for me."

"Not me," Virgil says. He reaches in and takes a cold, wet can from the ice.

Spiller holds out a fat joint and says, "You probably want some of this too."

Virgil hits it hard, then croaks around the mouthful of smoke, "You guys are my new best friends." Taggert gives him a look he can't figure out, half like a smile, half like he'd like to strangle him, and Virgil decides to keep his mouth shut for a while. He passes the joint to the Mexican and just grins and nods when Taggert says, "I hope you like your meat rare and your eggs scrambled, 'cause that's the only way I do them."

"Check this out," Taggert says. He pulls something from his pocket that makes a sizzling sound when he shakes it and tosses it to T.K. "Got those off a snake we saw up at the new house this morning. Thing was huge, a man-eater. Spiller nearly dookied when he tripped over it."

"Nice place you got here," T.K. says. "Fucking snakes and scorpions and tarantulas and buzzards." He passes the rattle to Virgil, who pinches it gingerly between his thumb and index finger.

"It's what you call harsh beauty," Taggert says. "Everything out here has to be tough or smart to survive, has to be ruthless."

"I'll take my chances in the hood," T.K. replies. "Least motherfuckers there ain't sneaking around trying to bite you."

Taggert laughs and turns the steaks. Virgil holds out the rattle to him, but Taggert says, "Go on, keep it for a souvenir."

Virgil would like to know when he can get out of here, back to L.A., but is too scared to ask. His sister, Olivia, might dig all this sand and sky, but it just makes him feel lost. He's got enough cash left for a bus ticket to Tampa, and that'll be that. He's had his fill of California. Everything is so goddamn serious out here, and the cost of living way too high. A yellow jacket lands on the rim of his beer can, and he flicks it off.

Taggert closes the lid of the grill. "Watch the beef," he says to Spiller, then turns to Virgil. "Come on. I've got something to show you."

Virgil is fine where he is, thanks very much, but there's no way he's telling Taggert this. He drags his feet when they step from the shade into the sun and has to squint to see as they walk across the yard.

"Are there a lot of snakes out here?" he asks.

"Man, this is snake heaven," Taggert replies.

He leads Virgil down a dirt road toward the barn, a big corrugated steel structure set off a couple hundred feet from the house. They pass a rooster on the way, scratching in the sand, and a twitchy black cat Taggert calls Satan. A dog barks as they get closer, then another, then another, until Taggert practically has to shout to be heard when he says, "It's like a goddamn zoo out here."

Next to the barn is a coop full of muttering hens and a pen containing a small herd of goats. The goats rush the fence, climbing all over one another to poke their noses through. Virgil reaches down to scratch a few chins. They're kind of cute, except for their devil eyes: yellow, with strange, slitlike pupils.

Taggert opens a gate and steps inside the pen, and the goats gather around him, some standing on their hind legs to rest their front hooves on his thighs. He bends over to take hold of a little brown one with a white muzzle, picks it up, and cradles it against his chest. "Hey there, kiddo," he growls as he backs out of the pen and closes the gate.

The barn's sliding door is halfway open. Virgil follows Taggert inside. The barking of the dogs is louder than ever, bouncing around the cavernous space. Thin shafts of light squeeze through pinholes in the walls and ceiling and spark the dust that swirls in the air. Virgil, really feeling the weed now, can't ever remember seeing anything so beautiful. It looks like stars, like rivers of stars.

Taggert flips a switch, and the lights—big, bowl-shaped fixtures that hang from a beam overhead—go on. A tractor sits in one corner, partially covered by an oily canvas tarp. There's also an assortment of hand tools, a table saw, and the chassis of a VW bug. In the center of the barn is a pen with three-foot plywood walls. It's maybe twelve by twelve and floored with a piece of badly stained green carpet.

Taggert walks to the pen and sets the goat down inside it. The animal bleats forlornly and butts the wall with its tiny horns. Beyond the pen are five cages. Three are occupied by pit bulls, the source of the barking. The cages extend through holes cut in the rear wall of the barn to allow the dogs access to sun and fresh air. The concrete floors are clean, and there are troughs of fresh water.

"Miguel takes good care of my boys, doesn't he?" Taggert says as he and Virgil walk over to the cages. He stops in front of the first one, which holds a big red dog with one eye, and sticks his fingers through the chain-link fencing to let the animal lick them.

"This is Butcher Boy, a dead game fighter," he says. "I traded a nice shotgun for him. He's won five matches for me so far and once, no shit, took down a Rottweiler that outweighed him by forty pounds. They should make men as brave as this dog."

The barking starts to get to Virgil, makes his guts jump around. And it's hot in here too, stuffy. He feels like he can't get enough air. He nods when he's supposed to, but he's not actually listening to Taggert go on and on about his fucking dog. He just wants to go outside.

Taggert grabs a leash off a hook on the wall and tells Virgil to stand back. "They'll tolerate Miguel and me, but anybody else, we train 'em to go right for the balls," he says.

Virgil moves toward a workbench and considers climbing on top of it as Taggert opens the cage and attaches the leash to a chain around Butcher Boy's neck. As soon as the dog is outside the enclosure, he lunges at Virgil, barking wildly and foaming at the mouth, his single eye practically popping out of his head. Virgil backpedals into the bench and grabs a hammer.

"That's real smart," Taggert says, pulling the dog up short. "Now he thinks you're threatening me. Put that fucking thing down." Virgil lays the hammer on the bench, and Butcher Boy settles a bit. Taggert leads the dog to the pen containing the goat and motions for Virgil to follow.

"This is the pit where we fight them," Taggert says. "We've had some epic bouts here, dogs in from Arizona, Mexico, New Orleans. This old boy from Memphis walked away with ten grand one night when his dog came back from the dead to beat a bruiser named Capone."

Taggert opens a gate in one wall of the pit, and he and the dog enter. Butcher Boy goes nuts again when he sees the goat, which cowers against the far wall, clearly terrified. Taggert bends over the dog as the goat mewls plaintively.

"Gonna get him, aren't you," he whispers into Butcher Boy's ear. "Gonna sic, sic, sic." He unhooks the leash, and before he can stand upright, the dog is halfway across the pit. He leaps on the goat, clamps his powerful jaws onto its throat, and shakes his head. The bleating stops, and blood spurts. Virgil looks away. He killed a cat once with a twenty-two when he was a kid, but nothing like this. When he turns back, the dog is flinging the dead goat around the pit like a stuffed toy.

"Get me a breaking stick off that bench," Taggert says. "Looks like a cutoff broom handle."

Virgil locates the splintered length of wood and hurries to the pit to hand it to Taggert. Taggert stands over Butcher Boy and grabs his collar, then jams the stick into the back of the dog's mouth, behind his teeth, and twists it to force his jaws open. The goat drops to the carpet, and Taggert leashes the dog and drags him out of the pit.

"You got to let them kill something every so often," Taggert says. "That's how you keep them good and crazy."

He leads Butcher Boy to his cage and locks him up again. Virgil glances down at the goat. Its head is almost separated from its body, and there's blood everywhere. Virgil flashes back on Eton and the whole scene at the house and gets a weird taste in his mouth, something sour. How fucking unfair can you get? The poor thing didn't have a chance.

All of a sudden Taggert is standing right beside him, too close, crowding him. "We need to talk," he says. His voice is little more than a whisper now that the dogs have quieted down.

Every muscle in Virgil's body draws taut, and he has to stop himself from running away. "Yeah?" he says.

"That fucker who drew down on T.K. and Spiller and got shot to pieces, was he a friend of yours? Ethan?"

"Eton," Virgil says.

"Eton. Right. Eton Dogfood." Taggert smirks and spits on the floor. Virgil can smell the beer on his breath. "So he was your buddy?"

"I actually barely knew him," Virgil says. "Olivia set it up, me staying at his house."

"Still, it must have been pretty fucked up seeing him get killed like that, right in front of you."

Virgil shrugs, trying not to give anything away.

"Yes? No? You ever see anybody shot before?" Taggert asks.

Virgil feels a sob building in his chest. He fights to keep it down, shakes his head.

"Answer me out loud," Taggert snaps.

"No, sir."

"Call me Bill."

"Okay."

Taggert reaches up and massages his forehead with the fingertips of his right hand. He licks his lips and says, "I'll tell you this one time that I'm real sorry about what happened, but you're a man, and you'll get over it. If that kind of stuff bothers you, you should pick nicer playmates and take a job at Walmart, right?"

"Right," Virgil says.

"In fact, it's not you I'm worried about; it's your sister," Taggert continues. "I know Olivia was tight with Eton, and it would tear her up if she found out what happened to him. I don't want her to go through that; know what I mean?"

Taggert is still all up in Virgil's personal space. Virgil tries to put some distance between them, a few inches even, while looking around for something to swing in case it goes like that.

"I ain't gonna say nothing," he mumbles.

"Nothing, right?"

"Nothing."

"Good," Taggert says. "And what about when she asks how you ended up out here? What are you going to say then?"

"What do you want me to say?"

Taggert places his hand on Virgil's shoulder and squeezes once, hard. "Tell her that my guys showed up to make a delivery, and you all got to talking," he says. "Eton mentioned that Spiller and T.K. worked for Olivia's boyfriend, and you decided that you wanted to visit her and asked if they could give you a ride. They called me, I said sure, and here you are."

"Okay."

"You got that?"

"I got it."

Virgil remembers what T.K. said about Taggert's eyes—look in them, and you'll see the end of everything. He forces himself to raise his gaze to meet Taggert's, but all he sees in the scary bottomless blackness is his own reflection.

Taggert moves away then, going to the wall to take down a saw hanging there. He holds the handle in one hand, the end of the blade in the other, and shakes it so that it makes a sound, a metallic wobble.

"I used to know a man who could play a saw like a fiddle," he says. "You ever heard that? It's a real sad sound."

Virgil wishes he wasn't sweating so much, wishes he'd been born with better luck, wishes lots of things. "No," he says.

Taggert puts the saw back on its nail and says, "That idiot'll charcoalize those steaks if we don't stop him."

Virgil lags behind on the walk to the house, his legs a little unsteady. He blames it on hunger, but it's something more. He feels ashamed, like he's backed down from a fight. He knows what Taggert was doing with the goat and everything: he was trying to put the fear of God in him.

Someone else is sitting under the awning now, on the car seat next to the Mexican. Olivia. She's wearing a hippie skirt, a black bikini top, and a trucker cap that says CSI on it. Her hair is blond this time, short and shaggy.

Taggert leans down and kisses her on the cheek; says, "Mornin', sunshine."

She looks past him at Virgil and frowns. "What the fuck are you doing here?" she asks.

Virgil raises his hand in a weak wave and says, "Surprise, Olly."

9

NOTHING SPECIAL FOR MR. KING TONIGHT, THE USUAL martini on the dry side, one olive. Boone pours him Sapphire, instead of the well rotgut, a little treat. And why not? Delia, the other bartender, actually showed up for her shift, and it's been nice and slow for a Saturday.

Besides Mr. King and Gina, the only other customers left on his end of the stick are four Germans—big, blond, sunburned beer-drinkers who've been tipping a lousy buck a round. He's not about to let that dampen his mood though. He turns it into a private joke, ignoring them until they're practically banging their glasses on the bar to get his attention.

Mr. King looks like he started early tonight. His tie is crooked, his hair mussed. He attended the funeral of an old friend earlier in the day, and it's made him nostalgic.

"To Ben Crosson," he says, raising his glass.

Boone raises his too, the martini Mr. King bought him. Might as well let the man get it out of his system.

"Ben and I met on a Western in forty-five, right after the war," Mr. King continues. "We were production assistants, so low on the totem pole we had to provide our own meals. He was missing the little finger on one hand. A Jap—Japanese—sniper shot it off on Guadalcanal. Someone'd be half in the bag, and Ben would hold his hands up in front of the guy's face and ask, 'How many fingers do you see?' Guy'd always say 'Ten.' Funny, you know. Ben was funny."

Mr. King removes his glasses and swipes at his bloodshot eyes with the napkin from under his drink. Gina pats his arm and says, "Talk about something else, Papa. No be sad."

They're singing "Happy Birthday" at a table in the restaurant, the waitresses joining in. Boone sips his drink and glances at the Germans. This might be a good time to check on them, let the old man pull himself together.

"I'm not sad," Mr. King says. "I'm telling stories that need to be told. Every day a little more of my past disappears, and, by God, I'm going to do something about it. Jimmy, my boy"—he reaches across the bar and grabs Boone's forearm—"I want you to remember what I'm saying tonight. Remember it for me and for Ben."

"You got it," Boone replies.

"He used to do this other trick too," Mr. King says. "You'd leave the room to answer the phone or step out of the editing bay for a cigarette, and when you came back, he'd be sitting right where you left him, doing exactly what he was doing before, only buck naked, starkers, not a stitch on him. I'd laugh till I thought I was going to pass out."

"A real wild man, huh?" Boone says.

"Oh, he was, he was," Mr. King says. "He was *wild*. Best editor I ever worked with. We wouldn't see each other for years at a stretch, but I'd think of him now and then, and all of a sudden I'd be happy just knowing he was somewhere out there in the world."

He finishes his drink in a gulp, then slides off his stool and steadies himself against the bar. "Is the music always so goddamn loud in here?" he asks before heading off to the men's room.

Delia announces last call, and the Germans order a round. One of them asks Boone where he and his buddies can meet women. Boone suggests they talk to Robo out front but doubts their stonewashed denim shorts and "Venice Beach Lifeguard" muscle shirts will pass muster at any of the clubs in Hollywood.

He's helping Gonzalo unclog the ice machine when his phone rings.

"Jimmy Boone?"

"This is he."

"My name is Loretta Marshall. I do pit bull rescues."

Boone had called the number the vet gave him and left a message before coming to work.

"Sorry to get back to you so late, but I couldn't sleep thinking about that dog you found," Loretta continues. "I want to start trying to find it a permanent home as soon as possible."

Boone glances at his watch. Almost midnight. So she's a little kooky. Lots of that going around.

"When can I come over and see—what's the dog's name?" Loretta asks. "Is it a boy or a girl?"

"Male," Boone says. "The people I got him from called him Joto."

"Joto. That's kinda sweet."

"It's Spanish for *fag*."

"Oh," she says. There's a long pause. "Well, when can I come see him?"

Simon crosses from the restaurant to the bar and frowns when he notices Boone on the phone, motions for him to hang up. Boone raises a finger. One second.

"How about tomorrow afternoon, around noon?" he says to Loretta.

"Lovely. I can meet you and the dog and fill you in on what I do."

Boone gives Loretta his address and hustles the good-byes. Simon is leaning on the stick, waiting for him to finish. "You know the rules," he says, holding out his hand, palm up. If he catches an employee making a personal call while on the clock, that employee has to pay him a five-dollar fine.

Boone reaches into his pocket, throws a crumpled bill onto the bar.

"Don't be mad at me," Simon says as he picks up the money. "It's your own fault."

Yes, it is. This and every goddamn thing that's brought him to this point. No arguing with that. Simon stands there grinning his mean little grin, and before he puts his fist in the middle of it, Boone calls to Delia, "I missed my last break, so I'm taking it now."

He ducks under the bar and walks out the front door.

Robo is standing on the sidewalk, talking to the valets. He's wearing a suit tonight, per Simon's order. It's black, looks almost like wool, and fits pretty well, considering the acreage it has to cover. He's also got on a white shirt, which has come untucked, and a red tie.

"Check you out," Boone says.

Robo opens the jacket and slides his thumbs under the suspenders that hold his pants up. "*El rey de los reyes,*" he says.

"Where'd you score it?"

"Over in Santee Alley. Homeboy's friends with my dad and hooked me up on short notice. Now fucking Simon can kiss my big brown ass."

Hollywood Boulevard is bumper to bumper with kids in from the Valley, East L.A., the Westside, all looking to get crazy on Saturday night, get wasted, get laid. Music thumps out of open windows, and neon reflections whirl over hoods and windshields like out-of-control carnival rides. Boone watches the traffic stream past and wonders what Amy's up to, if she's having fun.

"How's that dog?" Robo asks.

"Had to take him to the vet this morning," Boone replies. "Cost me two hundred dollars to find out he had a stomachache."

"If you need extra cash, come with me tomorrow. I'm gonna repo a forty-two-inch plasma from some *pendejo* who quit making payments to the dude who sold it to him. I'll toss thirty bucks your way."

"I don't think so, bro," Boone says. "No more rough stuff for me."

Robo makes a pair of pistols with his fingers and points them at Boone. "Come on," he says. "We're a good team. Fatman and Robin."

A stretch Hummer rolls past with bellowing frat boys hanging out of every window. They disappear like frightened chipmunks into their holes when an LAPD cruiser chirps its siren and a cop using the car's loudspeaker orders the driver to pull over. One of the valets says something in Spanish that Boone doesn't catch. Robo clucks his tongue and shakes his head.

"Did you talk to Rosales, tell him what you found out about Oscar from Maribel and the roommates?" Boone asks Robo.

"All that nothin'?" Robo says. "Yeah, I told him. I also refunded him sixty bucks, meaning I made shit on that job."

"Well, check this out," Boone says. "The vet I took the dog to said he was used for fighting and that he has a tattoo in his ear that identifies his breeder. I was thinking if you found this breeder, he might know something about what happened to the kid."

"Yeah? So?"

"So, maybe you can get more money out of the old man to look into it."

Robo waves his hand dismissively. "Shit, *ese,* that *borracho* don't have no more money, and I sure as hell ain't working for free."

Boone pushes a bottle cap into the gutter with the toe of his shoe. "It's your thing," he says. "Just letting you know." He's disappointed. He's been thinking about Oscar all day and had hoped to ease his mind by getting Robo to follow up on the lead.

"You want to do something for me," Robo says, "find me some jobs that pay."

Mr. King and Gina walk out of the Tick Tock, Mr. King leaning heavily on Gina. He looks old and frail, almost trips over a buckle in the sidewalk.

Robo turns to the couple and spreads his arms wide. "Hey, hey, hey, the beautiful people," he says with a big smile. "Where you off to now? One of them Beverly Hills parties? Some dancing maybe?"

Mr. King hands the valet his ticket. "Straight to bed, Robert," he says. "The sooner this one ends, the better."

"It do go like that sometimes, don't it?"

Boone heads into the restaurant. "Ben Crosson," Mr. King calls after him. "Remember, Jimmy."

"I will," Boone says.

The Smashing Pumpkins' "1979" is playing on the sound system when he gets back inside, a song he's always liked. One of the waitresses is into oldies, she told him earlier, and this is her CD. So the Smashing Pumpkins are oldies now. What a kick in the ass.

BOONE IS WIRED after closing, so he walks down Hollywood to Skooby's for a chili dog, stepping on the sidewalk stars of all kinds of people he's never heard of, probably more of Mr. King's friends. A flock of homeless punks are hanging out at the stand, along with a couple of girls dressed for the clubs in short skirts and high heels. The girls pick at their fries with long, painted fingernails and crane their necks awkwardly as they bite into their dogs to avoid dripping mustard on their outfits.

Boone eats at the outdoor counter, spinning around on his stool to watch the late show on the boulevard. Two bums come to blows over a Starbucks cup filled with vodka, and a skeev dressed like Superman limps past, yelling into a phone.

A guy who looks like Charlie Brown, if Charlie Brown were black and homeless, approaches Boone and holds out a battered video copy of *Grease*.

"You want to buy this?" he asks.

"Nope," Boone replies.

"One dollar."

"Nope."

Charlie looks like he's about to cry as he waddles away.

Boone finishes his food and ducks into the Internet café across the street, Cyberplace, a long, narrow room lined with computers and lit by the kind of fluorescent tubes that always put him back in prison. He hasn't sprung for a computer of his own yet—other things keep coming up, like two-hundred-dollar vet bills—so this is where he checks his e-mail.

There's only one new message, from his old partner at Ironman, Carl Perry. He wants Boone to come to his place Friday to watch a pay-per-view boxing match. "The wife will be there, so bring a date, if you got one," he adds. Boone has turned down a number of invitations from Carl since being released from Corcoran. They've talked on the phone a couple times, exchanged e-mails, but Boone's been putting off a face-to-face. He's told himself it's because he's been busy getting back on his feet in the outside world, but that's only part of it.

The truth is, Ironman took a hit when Boone attacked Anderson. As word of the incident spread—crazed bodyguard beats client—business suffered, and the company is still struggling almost five years later. Boone feels guilty about this, and that's why he's been avoiding his old friend. But he also knows that it's high time he look Carl in the eye and apologize for ruining the good thing he had going, so he e-mails back that he'll be there for sure on Friday.

Then, just for kicks, he pulls out the card the vet gave him and types in the address of her animal activist buddies' Web site, the ones who went after Morrison, Joto's breeder. The group is called TMW, which stands for This Means War. A headline on the page reads "Stop the Slaughter Now!" and there are lots of gory pictures of fighting dogs with their ears torn off, their eyes gouged out, their intestines exposed.

These animals are tortured for the sick pleasure of those who wager on them, an essay on the site explains. *They live short, horrible, brutal lives and are expected to kill other dogs in order to earn their keep. Win or lose, however, they die slow, cruel deaths and are often kept in appalling conditions. We at TMW are committed to stamping out this sickening "sport" BY ANY MEANS NECESSARY.*

At the bottom of the page is a link to contact the site's owners. Boone clicks it and types, *I'm a filmmaker putting together an antidogfight documentary, and I've been trying to track down Bob Morrison, a notorious breeder and trainer of fighting dogs. My plan is to interview him with a hidden camera to gather footage that can be used to put him behind bars once and for all.*

My vet, Dr. Sanchez, mentioned that you were trying to take Morrison down but were unable to do so due to legal complications. We have the funds, we have the lawyers, and, if you'll provide us with contact information for Morrison (an address?), we'd be honored to finish what you started. Sincerely, Ben Crosson.

Boone chuckles to himself as he hits SEND. He doesn't really expect his ruse to work. The people at TMW will surely want proof that he is who he says he is, or they'll demand to be involved in the film in some way or will ask for payment for any information they give him. It's L.A., after all. Everyone has his hand out, even the do-gooders. Everyone wants a screen credit.

BOONE DIDN'T SET the alarm when he went to bed, planning to sleep in for once, but Joto barks him awake at seven thirty, excited about taking a piss and licking the dew off the grass. He's already looking less sickly and certainly has more energy. Boone clips the leash to his collar, and the dog practically drags him into the courtyard.

Amy's place was dark when Boone got home last night, and there's no sign of her now. Mrs. Hu is up, though, on her knees in front of her bungalow, planting bright red flowers.

"Morning," Boone says.

"Pets are against the rules," she replies, without looking up.

"I know. I'm trying to find him a home."

"I'll shoot him if he comes near me," Mrs. Hu says, patting the bulge, that .38, in the pocket of her housecoat.

Boone pulls tight on the leash and says, "I'll keep a good eye on him, don't worry."

"And you better clean up after him too, the shit."

"I will, Mrs. Hu. Anything else?"

The old woman doesn't reply, just stabs at the dirt with her trowel.

Boone and Joto walk over to Bronson and head up into the hills, where multimillion-dollar homes line the streets. Boone used to live not far from here when he worked for Ironman. He had a view of Catalina on clear days, a pool, a maid, and a gardener. He'd always felt that it was too good to last, though, always known he'd blow it somehow. An ex-jarhead from Oildale living next to movie stars? It didn't compute.

A pretty woman walking a pair of whippets gives Boone a friendly smile, but all hell breaks loose when Joto lunges for her dogs, growling and snapping his toothless jaws. Boone has to yank him onto his hind legs to make him break off the attack, and the woman lectures him over her shoulder as she hurries away, something about how vicious dogs shouldn't be out in public.

After dropping Joto at the bungalow, Boone goes for a run, then hits the gym for an hour, banging the heavy bag until he can't hold his arms up. By the time the dog-rescue woman arrives at noon, he's showered, eaten lunch, and picked up the place a bit.

Loretta Marshall is a very big girl in very tight clothes—jeans and a pink T-shirt with the slogan LOVE ALL LIVING THINGS. Her blond hair has been teased and sprayed into a nest of stiff curls, and diamond rings glitter on every finger.

"Let me see this sweet boy of yours," she says, and Boone

invites her inside. Joto licks her face when she drops to one knee and baby talks him.

"Where did you get him?" she asks Boone.

"I found him," he replies. No need to get into it.

"He's so beat up."

"The vet said he was used for dogfighting."

"And his teeth?"

"Someone pulled them."

Loretta gasps. Her hand goes to her mouth, and her eyes fill with tears.

"He also has mange and worms," Boone continues. "But he's pretty good-natured despite all that."

Loretta's whole body is shaking, and she looks like she's about to keel over. Boone helps her up and sits her on the couch, asks if she wants some water.

"Please," she gasps. "And a tissue."

She regains her composure a few minutes later, after blowing her nose and dabbing at the tears on her cheeks. She takes a sip of water and says, "Okay, so I'm a crier. But it just wrecks me the way people treat the most innocent, trusting, loyal things God put on this planet."

"I understand," Boone says.

Loretta reaches into her cavernous purse for a pink compact, opens it, and checks her hair and makeup in a little mirror. "So now you're thinking: 'How can this crazy lady get so worked up about dogs when there are babies dying every day in Africa?' " she says.

"It's a rough old world," Boone replies, keeping it noncommittal.

"You know what I think?" she says as she snaps shut the compact. "I think there's a battle between good and evil being fought right this minute, and I think that every wrong you right, every bit of kindness you show, no matter how small, is a blow against that evil."

"That's a nice way to look at things," Boone says.

"It is, right?" Loretta says. "Because that means that with every rescue, I'm helping to chip away at the darkness. It might not be much, but at least it's something, and every little bit helps."

She's one of the lucky ones, someone with a worldview. Boone keeps waiting for the pieces to come together for him like that but doubts they ever will.

Loretta dives into her purse again and comes up with a digital camera. "I need to take some photos for my Web site," she says. "Also, do you mind if I change his name to something nicer? How about Toto? That shouldn't confuse him too much."

"Whatever you need to do," Boone says.

Loretta slips off the couch and crouches in front of Joto to snap a few shots. "That's a cutie," she coos to the dog. "That's a cutie." When she's finished, she asks Boone, "Why don't you want to keep him?"

"I guess I'm not a dog person," Boone replies.

Loretta smiles and says, "That's what my husband used to think before we got married, but he came around. You seem to be doing a wonderful job."

"My life's kind of up in the air right now."

"Nothing like a dog to ground you."

"It wouldn't work," Boone says. "Trust me."

Loretta lifts her penciled-in eyebrows like she doesn't believe him, like that's a cop-out, then drops the camera into her purse. She puts one hand on the couch and one on the coffee table and groans as she rises from the floor. Boone reaches out to steady her.

"Thanks," she says. "These old knees of mine."

After bending once more to pet Joto, she moves to the front door and says, "So what I'll do is put Toto up on our Web site this evening and make a few calls."

"How long does it usually take to place a dog?" Boone asks.

"Depends. Puppies go first, of course. And Toto's kind of a special case, with his teeth and all. That sort of thing either melts someone's heart or totally turns them off."

Boone follows her onto the porch and thanks her for coming by.

"Please," she says. "This is how I nourish my soul." She hands him a card with her phone number and e-mail address on it and says, "And if you know anyone who needs a Realtor, I'm also really good at that."

The flowery smell of her perfume lingers in the bungalow for hours after she departs.

THAT NIGHT, WHEN he gets off work, Boone stops at Cyberplace again. First, he checks out Loretta's adoption site. Joto's, or Toto's, information is on the main page under the heading REAL HEARTBREAKER: *This lovable fellow could use a friend who understands his special needs. He's a brindle male, approximately two years old, with a few minor medical problems. In addition, his teeth have been removed. He's likely been used for fighting and should be kept away from other animals but is still a sweet, friendly boy who would make a great companion for someone who can provide him with the TLC he deserves after all he's been through.*

In the photo, Joto's head is cocked to the side and his tongue is hanging out. Cute as can be. You can barely even see the scars.

There's also a message from TMW: *Dear Ben: After we were forced by the court to end our campaign against Morrison, we moved on to other projects, but we'd be happy to do whatever we can to help you expose the bastard. As far as we know, he still operates his kennel and training facility at 25620 Leonis Boulevard, in Vernon, CA.*

Warning: Be extremely careful when you approach him. He's an alcoholic with a violent temper and has been known to carry a firearm. If we can be of any further assistance, don't hesitate to contact us, and good luck on your film. Stop the slaughter now!

Boone writes Morrison's address on the back of Loretta's card and slips the card into his wallet. It's time to stop kidding himself. The mystery of Oscar's death has been haunting him for days, and the only way he's going to get any peace is by looking into it further. He realizes that this is what he's been waiting for when he wakes in the night, his body tense, his mind racing: a mission. A rocky path to some untamed form of redemption. Something terrible happened to the kid, and it's up to him to find out what it was. And the first step is to track down Morrison.

What was big, beautiful Loretta talking about? Chipping away at the darkness? Christ, Boone thinks, I'm crazier than she is.

10

OLIVIA SEARCHES THE SKY FOR SHOOTING STARS, HER HEAD full of wishes. A coyote yips somewhere in the hills, and the dogs in the barn answer back. Olivia shudders and draws her jacket tighter around herself. What if they're plotting to band together and take down the humans? That's what she'd do.

"Man, I'm superstoned," she says.

Virgil grunts in reply. He's nothing but a boy-shaped stain blotting out a chunk of the night sky until he lights a cigarette and his face glows for an instant like a Halloween pumpkin.

Olivia brought him up here to show him her hideout, a natural rock bench overlooking the ranch where she comes to get away from Taggert when he's mad at her or when she can't stand his touch anymore. She trips out on the stars up here, watches sunsets. She even came up during a thunderstorm once, and lightning struck so close, she could taste the sizzle in the air afterward.

Virgil isn't interested in any of this though. He's still upset about what happened yesterday. He was hinting about going back to L.A. with T.K. and Spiller, but then Taggert said he'd like him to hang out a while longer and asked Olivia didn't she want him to stay too. She said yes, thinking it would be fun to have some company. Taggert offered to pay Virgil for helping

Miguel with the dogs, and today he let him ride one of his dirt bikes, but still, ever since T.K. and Spiller drove off without him, the kid's been moping around and whining to her that he feels like some kind of prisoner. She thought bringing him up here to smoke a joint would brighten his mood, but it doesn't seem to have worked.

She leans back against the rock, which is still warm from the day just passed, and stares into the dark desert stretched out in front of her. She can see the lights of the house and the barn and, in the distance, Twentynine Palms and the Marine base. She has to admit that she feels like a prisoner too, sometimes. Though Taggert says she's free to come and go as she pleases, he always finds a reason to tag along with her to the supermarket or the drugstore, and on the rare occasions when he lets her go into Palm Springs alone to shop for clothes or have her hair cut, he's calling on the phone every ten minutes.

"So you had fun with Eton?" she asks Virgil. The boy is drawing circles in the air with the cherry of his cigarette, making tracers. He gazes at them intently, like a man trying to hypnotize himself.

"It was cool," he says.

"He still going out with that Korean girl, that porn star?"

"Nah, but he talked about her a lot when he got drunk, which was pretty much all the time."

"He sure saved my ass when I first got to L.A.," she says. "I was such a poo butt, didn't know nothing. He took me in, let me work for him, kept me off the street."

"That's what he said, you were like a sister to him."

Olivia nibbles at a hangnail on her thumb. All that seems like a million years ago. She barely remembers who she was back then, so much shit has happened since.

"You gonna stay with him when you go back?" she asks.

Virgil doesn't answer. A gritty wind has come up, and Olivia thinks maybe it snatched her words away.

"I said, Are you gonna stay with him when you go back?" she asks again.

"Nah," Virgil replies. "I met some guys, and we're gonna get a house over in Hollywood, a party crib."

Party, party, party. She was the same way at his age, couldn't get enough of anything. Must be in their blood, she thinks.

"Have you talked to Daddy lately?" she asks.

"Nope. You?"

"Nope."

Their parents were hard-core dope fiends when they met, Momma hooking to feed her habit, Daddy stealing cars and slinging meth. Momma was doing a six-month bit when she found out she was pregnant with Olivia, and she and Daddy decided it was time to clean up, settle down, and try to do the right thing by their baby girl.

Daddy got a job at a frozen-food plant in South Carolina, and Momma kept house and sold Avon. They lived in a nice mobile home on Daddy's Daddy's land, joined a nice church, and played penny-ante poker every Friday night with their nice neighbors.

Everything was fine until Momma got depressed after Virgil was born and began to look backward instead of forward, regretting things she'd done, dwelling on things that had been done to her, and mining her own pain. It started with her not wanting to get out of bed to care for her newborn son and ended a month later when she died from an overdose of something the doctor had prescribed.

Olivia was seven, Virgil barely three months old, and Daddy

left them with Grandma and Grandpa while he ran off and tried to kill himself too.

Olivia has heard what happened next a hundred times because Daddy loves to tell anybody who'll listen to the story of how he was saved. He recites it at church, at family gatherings, at AA meetings. After two years of pure evil, he was all fucked up in a Houston flophouse when a black angel, the angel of death, appeared at the end of his bed and said, "Buddy Ray, if you really want to die, I'll send you to hell right this minute. But if you want to live, then hit your knees and ask Jesus to forgive you, and he'll see that you get back to your children and become the father you should be to them."

Daddy dropped to the floor and prayed until morning, when he bummed enough cash to catch a bus to Blacksburg. Everybody welcomed him with open arms except Olivia, who'd been having doubts about things like angels ever since she wasn't struck dead the first time she kissed old Deacon Cullum's thingy for Barbie money.

She sat silently in a corner and smirked at everyone praising God and gobbling about miracles until Daddy finally knelt in front of her, sobbing and snuffling into a wad of pink toilet paper like an old woman, and said he understood if she was mad at him right that minute, but from then on his whole life would be devoted to making her and Virgil happy.

Of course, the first thing the son of a bitch did was go out and marry a woman who hated both of them. Julie, or Mama Juju, as Virgil called her, was a tall, skinny Jesus freak with a wispy black mustache and two kids from a previous marriage. Daddy said it would be like that old show *The Brady Bunch,* but it sure wasn't.

Virgil was still a baby, so Olivia got the worst of it. Mama

Juju would dump the garbage on Olivia's bed if Olivia forgot to empty it, make her scrub the kitchen floor on her hands and knees, and smack her with a wooden spoon if she complained. Her own kids, Brian and Stacy, she treated like a little prince and princess, even when they called Olivia "trash" and "orphan" and kicked her in church so she'd scream and get in trouble.

Olivia ran away for the first time when she was eleven, right after they'd moved to Tampa, where Daddy had a job cutting the grass at a golf course. She was already drinking by then, smoking weed, and she officially lost her virginity at age twelve to a PCP freak named Starman. Daddy threw her out for good at fifteen, after she broke Princess Stacy's nose and stole her car, and she's been on her own ever since.

This isn't the story she tells people when they ask, though, because then they'd make all kinds of nasty assumptions about her. She usually says her dad works for the phone company and her mom runs a jewelry store. Taggert thinks she was a cheerleader in high school and got a volleyball scholarship to the University of Florida. Whatever works, is how she feels about it. People are always talking up the truth, but the truth—and everybody knows it—is that little white lies make the world go round.

"Last I heard, Stacy was pregnant again, and Brian was going to Afghanistan," Virgil says. "They took off Mama Juju's tits too, you know. Cancer."

"Boo hoo," Olivia replies. She reaches over and steals Virgil's cigarette and watches an airplane pass overhead, tracks the blinking lights weaving among the stars as she takes a drag.

"I wish you hadn't left me there when you split," Virgil says.

"You were eight years old," Olivia replies. "What was I

gonna do, bring you with me? Besides, you were the baby. That bitch treated you a lot better than she treated me."

"Is that right?" Virgil says. He grabs her hand and runs her fingers over a lump on the top of his head. "Feel that? That's where she hit me with a bean pot when I was ten and knocked me out. And I got more if you want to see them."

"Why didn't you tell Daddy?" Olivia asks.

"Why didn't you?"

" 'Cause he's a total idiot when it comes to her."

"I know," Virgil says. "That old witch must give a hell of a blow job."

Olivia laughs so hard she coughs. Virgil laughs too, until he notices the glowing red dot trembling in the center of his chest. He swipes at it like it's something that might rub off, then says, "What the fuck?"

"What is that?" Olivia asks.

"I don't..." Virgil's expression slides from confused to terrified. He jumps to his feet and scrambles for cover behind the rock.

Olivia, ducking instinctively herself, shouts "What?"

"Someone's lighting me up with a laser sight," Virgil yelps.

"That you guys?" Taggert calls from the house.

Olivia stands and looks down the hill and sees him slouched in the doorway, a rifle cradled across his chest.

"Who else would it be?" she yells.

"Just checking," he says. He waves the rifle over his head and walks inside.

Olivia turns to Virgil and says, "It's okay; he's gone now." It's a struggle to keep the anger out of her voice.

Virgil steps out warily from behind the rock, his eyes locked on the house. "I told you he wants to kill me," he says. He sounds like he's about to cry.

"He didn't mean anything by it," Olivia replies, not sure if that's true.

"Come on, Olly. That was fucking crazy."

"He probably thinks he was being funny."

Virgil brushes dirt off his pants and shakes his head. "You gotta ask him when I can go back," he says.

"I will."

"I got shit going on, deals and stuff. I'm losing money out here."

Olivia hands him his cigarette and zips up her coat. "I said I'd ask," she says. "But don't do anything to piss him off in the meantime."

TAGGERT IS IN the kitchen fixing himself a rum and Coke when Olivia returns to the house. He's wearing his reading glasses on a chain around his neck, something he only does in front of her. Anyone else, he says, would jump on it as a sign that he's getting old, getting weaker. Even a little thing like that could give a shithead ideas.

"What the fuck were you doing, pointing a rifle at my brother?" Olivia asks after slamming the door.

Taggert continues to stir his drink. He doesn't even bother to look up. "Just fucking around," he says.

Olivia stands with her hands on her hips. "Why'd you want him to stay out here if you're going to treat him like that?" she says.

Taggert shuffles past her to the refrigerator, his flip-flops slapping the floor. He opens the freezer. "I'm gonna make some Pizza Rolls," he says. "Want some?" He turns to shake the box at her, raises his eyebrows.

Like she's a dumb bitch. Like he doesn't have to take what she says seriously. Olivia lashes out, slapping the box from

Taggert's hand, and frozen Pizza Rolls skitter across the worn linoleum.

"Don't ever do me like that again," she yells. She's right in his face now, her finger inches from his nose. "I'm not your fucking cum rag. All I asked was a question, and all you had to do was answer me. That's how normal fucking people do it."

Taggert exhales heavily and says, "Are you going to pick that shit up off the floor on your own, or do I have to make you?"

Olivia's hand clenches into a fist, and she draws it back to punch him. She stops herself at the last instant though. Last time she hit him, he hit back and almost busted her nose. Got to be smarter than that now.

"I'll pick them up," she says, "and then later I'll cut your throat while you sleep."

He shoots her a mean smile and points to the Pizza Rolls again, giving her a silent order.

Tears spring into Olivia's eyes. This always happens when she's angry, and she hates it. She can't let Taggert see her cry because he'll take it as a win. "You think I'm afraid of you?" she screams. "I'm not fucking afraid of you!"

Taggert doesn't follow when she bolts for the bedroom.

THEY MET AT a club in Upland. Olivia was dancing there after she'd sworn she'd never dance again, and, worse yet, dancing nude instead of topless, which she'd also sworn she'd never do again, because it made her sick to her stomach to have guys staring at her cookie.

She'd quit a good gig cocktailing in Hollywood to move with some girl she was crushing on out to the Inland Empire, a pretty name for what was actually a hot, smoggy shitpit rotting at the rim of the desert. Things went great for a couple of months, until her girlfriend came home one afternoon and told her that she was going back to doing guys and that Olivia would have to get out of the apartment they'd been sharing.

So now Olivia needed money and needed it quick, and it turned out that dancing was the only job that close to the edge of the world that paid a decent wage. Taggert came in to the club about a week after she started. She noticed that he moved from the bar to the rail for her set and laid down a twenty after each of her songs, so she snuggled up to him afterward and asked if he'd like a couch dance in the VIP lounge. He leaned in close enough that his breath tickled her ear and said, "That kind of thing might make these other hillbillies jizz in their Fruit of the Looms, but I've got five hundred dollars set aside for some straight up fucking and sucking."

Any other night she would have had him thrown out, because she'd also sworn to herself that she wasn't going to trick again, but the security deposit on the condo she wanted was fifteen hundred dollars and she was pretty twisted on some Percocet one of the bouncers had given her, so she drove over to Taggert's motel when her shift ended.

He wasn't exactly her type—he was a guy, number one, and old, and kind of crusty and scarred up—but for some reason they hit it off. He was gentle in bed, funny and appreciative, and she wound up staying the whole night. Over pancakes at IHOP the next morning she told him about having to move—her boyfriend had dumped her, she said—and Taggert offered to help her get a place if he could have visitation rights. He claimed to be a salesman who passed through town two or three times a week and liked to have a girl on call, but Olivia knew that was bullshit. She recognized an outlaw when she saw one.

A month later she was kind of in love with him. They had

a blast whenever he showed up, and he never once tripped on her. Wrapped in his big arms, Olivia felt as safe as she ever had with a man. Then one day he drove her out to the ranch and told her if she wanted, she could quit dancing and move in with him, and he'd take care of her. It seemed like a chance to leave a lot of bad stuff behind all at once and make a stab at some sort of normal life, so she hugged him and cried her best fake tears of happiness and said she'd stand by him forever.

Now, though, eight months into it, she's feeling restless. Besides occasional shopping days in Palm Springs and at the outlet malls, they've only been away from the ranch twice, for a week in Vegas and a week in San Diego. Both trips were related to jobs Taggert's crew was pulling, so he was paranoid the whole time, always worrying that they were being tailed and barking at her whenever she strayed from his sight. He got so pissed at a blackjack dealer at the Mirage who was flirting with her that she thought he was going to kill the kid or drop dead from a stroke, like his dad.

He treats her like one of his dogs now, doesn't give her a say in anything. Yes, he pays the bills, but that doesn't mean she's just a fuck toy. In fact, she's been after him lately to let her be more involved in his business. What crew couldn't use a hot chick who knows her way around a hustle?

He always has excuses, though: things are going to get physical this time, a new face might queer the deal. The guy doesn't even have the balls to tell her no outright. And now this shit with Virgil? Terrorizing him like that? Could be it's getting time to hit the road.

THERE'S A KNOCK at the bedroom door.

"Baby," Taggert says. "Can I come in?"

Olivia sits up in bed and scrubs the smeared mascara off her face with the sheet. It's been over an hour since she stormed out of the kitchen.

"It's your house," she says.

Taggert opens the door and sticks his head inside.

"You're not gonna shoot me?" he says.

Olivia ignores him, keeps staring at the TV playing in the corner. He shuffles in and sits on the edge of the mattress.

"Baby," he says, "what happened out there earlier, I don't want us to be like that."

Let him do the talking, Olivia thinks.

"Why did I want your brother to stay?" he continues. "Because I thought it'd be good for the two of you to hang out for a while. I know you get bored out here, and I thought it'd be a treat for you. But if he wants to go, and you want him to go, Spiller and T.K.'ll be up on Saturday, and he can catch a ride with them when they leave."

Olivia turns to look him in the eye. It's one of her tricks. Most people don't meet his gaze, she's noticed, so when someone does, he pays attention. "You scared him tonight," she says. "He's not as tough as he acts."

"I know, I know, and I'm going to apologize to him," Taggert says. He rests a hand on Olivia's knee, a hand that's broken bones, a hand that's killed. He could crush her, tear her to pieces. She's frightened by that and turned on at the same time. It's like being close to a wild animal. She gets hot sometimes, thinking of all the ways he could hurt her.

"I want to apologize to you too," he continues. "I'm sorry I treated you like I did. I was just being cruel. You...you're precious to me."

Olivia pulls away from him. She knows she's won this time but wants him to suffer a little more. "I wish I could believe that," she says.

"You wait," he replies.

"For what?"

"I'm going to make you believe it; you'll see."

"Yeah, okay," she says, smiling a little. "But I'm still going to kill you in your sleep."

Taggert takes her face in his palms. "I love you, baby," he says, then kisses her forehead.

"I love you too."

"You sure?" he asks.

Olivia nods.

"Good," he says. " 'Cause I got something to show you."

He stands and motions for her to move over, give him some room on the bed. Reaching into his pocket for his wallet, he removes a hundred-dollar bill, lays it on the sheet, and asks, "What's this?"

"Mine," Olivia says, snatching up the money.

"Come on," Taggert says. "I'm schooling you here."

Olivia pouts as she puts the bill back on the sheet.

"So, what is it?" Taggert asks again.

"Money. A hundred dollars."

Taggert drops another bill next to it.

"And what's this?" he asks.

"Another hundred."

"All right, so which is the fake?"

Olivia picks up both bills and rubs them between her fingers. She holds them to the light, snaps them, even smells them. The paper of one seems to be a bit thinner than the paper of the other, so she waves that one as the phony.

"Wrong," Taggert says.

"Man," Olivia says, examining the counterfeit hundred. "This is amazing."

"It's a fucking masterpiece is what it is," Taggert says. He grabs the bill from her and gazes at it with wonder himself, like he still can't believe it's that perfect.

"Where'd you get it?" Olivia asks.

"They print them in Mexico using the same process the U.S. Treasury does. They're undetectable by sight and feel, as good as the supernotes the North Koreans and Colombians make."

"So what's the deal?" Olivia asks.

Taggert sits next to her on the bed and hands her the phony bill. She's never seen him this excited. He's practically bouncing up and down as he says, "The deal is, it's a totally new operation, barely starting out, and they're looking for a partner. They've got old women bringing bundles of this stuff in their underwear across the border, and they need someone over here to take it from there. Benjy has family in the crew running it. He says he can get me as much as I want for fifteen percent of face, and I've got a guy, this Iranian cat, I can lay it off on for forty-five percent."

"That's big money," Olivia says.

"*Big* money," Taggert replies. He stretches out on the bed, hands behind his head. " 'Fuck you' money."

"What do you mean?"

"I'm thinking this: I make three or four big deals with these guys, the Mexicans and the Iranian, and then I get out. Out of everything. I buy another Harley, play golf, build birdhouses—whatever retired guys do. And we'll travel—Hawaii, Mexico, cruises. We could even get married, if you want."

He reaches out and runs a finger up the inside of her thigh toward her crotch. She slaps it away playfully, but her stomach sours as she imagines being pushed around by him for the rest of her life. He says he's trying to change, but that's never going to happen. Fucker's been the boss for, what, thirty years now? Has guys asking "How high?" when he says "Jump." Then, all of a sudden, he's just another citizen, no crew to lead, no jobs to plan. First thing he's going to do is try to control her even more than he does now so he feels like he still has some power, and the first thing she's going to do is fight back. And when he gets tired of her bucking, she's going to wind up out on her ass with nothing. Again.

"You *know* what I want," she says, climbing on top of him and peering into his face.

"I do?" he says.

"I want my own money. I want a piece of this."

"And you're going to do what to earn this piece?" he asks.

"Whatever you need me to. Whatever those retards Spiller and T.K. do. You're the captain; put me to work."

Taggert hisses disgustedly, then pushes her off him and swings his legs over so that he's sitting on the edge of the mattress. "I guess you didn't hear me propose to you a minute ago," he says.

Olivia rolls onto her stomach and raises herself up on her elbows. "Wouldn't it be better to marry a girl who has her own money?" she asks.

"I like taking care of you."

"I like taking care of myself."

Taggert scratches his goatee and says, "If I promise I'll look to see if there's somewhere I can bring you in on this, will that be good enough for tonight?"

"If that's all you *can* do, it'll have to be," Olivia replies.

"It's all I *can* do because I haven't even met with Benjy's man yet. We're hooking up later this week. I won't know what's going on until then."

The same old runaround. Olivia feels like screaming but decides to keep playing it cool, give that a try for once. "Okay, so meet with them, and we'll talk afterward," she says.

"Sure," Taggert says. He stands and walks to the door. "I'm getting a drink."

Olivia falls back onto the pillow and gives him a sexy smile. "Bring me one too," she says in her fuck-me baby voice.

"Two large rum and Cokes," Taggert says. "And why don't you put on *Law and Order.*"

Olivia waits until he leaves the room, then lets her face go blank. Pulling the sheet up over her head, she lies as still as she can, like a corpse in the morgue on one of those cop shows Taggert's always watching. She holds her breath and rolls her eyes. I'm going to get what I want this time, even if it kills me, she thinks. Even if it kills me.

11

ON WEDNESDAY AFTERNOON BOONE SITS IN HIS CAR, HELD up by a big rig that's blocking both lanes of a narrow street in Vernon as it attempts to back into the parking lot of a clothing factory. It's a tricky maneuver, the driver moving up three feet, back four, up five, back six, aided by a spotter who stands in the road and directs him with frantic hand signals and shouts of "Left, left—now crank it right!" that can barely be heard over the tooth-rattling rumble of the truck's engine. A knot of workers gathered around a catering wagon parked at the curb in front of the factory sip coffee and eat tacos as they watch the truck finally squeeze through the gate in the chain-link fence that surrounds the building and inch up to the loading dock.

Boone is lost, took a wrong turn somewhere. As traffic starts to move again, he glances down at the map he printed out yesterday at Cyberplace. Bob Morrison's last known address is somewhere nearby.

Grinding away on the edge of downtown L.A., Vernon is the dirty, noisy, gas-guzzling, smoke-spewing engine of the city. Twenty-four hours a day it clanks and roars and hisses as its factories turn out toy cars, baseball hats, salsa, concrete, chrome exhaust pipes, cardboard boxes, miniblinds—products of every description—and trucks come and go, picking up merchandise and delivering raw materials.

Boone passes a local landmark, the Farmer John slaughterhouse, where each day thousands of pigs are killed and processed into bacon and Dodger Dogs. The immense compound is surrounded by high walls decorated with block-long murals depicting man and swine living together in blissful harmony in a bucolic green world of forests and pastures. They chase one another playfully, roll in the mud, and cuddle in the shade of leafy trees, and Boone can't decide if the message is that pigs are like people or that people are like pigs.

When he finally finds Leonis Boulevard, he drives slowly down the street, checking addresses; 25620 is a large windowless factory with a faded sign, USA FASTENERS. The building appears to be deserted—no cars in the parking lot, all the rollup doors shut tight. It's separated from the street by an eight-foot fence constructed of spearlike steel rods painted black.

Boone pulls into the driveway and steps out of the Olds. The sliding gate is secured with a thick chain and heavy-duty padlock, and there's no way to climb over the fence without being gutted. Boone walks up and down the sidewalk, looking for another way in. "Hey!" he shouts. "Anybody home?" Dogs bark somewhere behind the factory. That means Morrison's here; must be.

Frustrated, Boone grabs the gate and gives it a good shake. The padlock falls to the ground, and the chain swings free. Whoever entered last neglected to snap the lock shut.

Before good sense can stop him, Boone slides the gate open and drives onto the lot, then swings the Olds around and parks so that it's facing the exit. As he's walking toward the factory he contemplates turning back and grabbing the tire iron stored in his trunk, but what kind of message would that send?

The main entrance to the building is a thick steel door with a small wire-reinforced window set into it. Hands cupping his eyes, Boone peers through the glass but can't make out anything inside. There's a sign on the wall next to the door—PLEASE RING FOR SERVICE—and below that a little white button, like a doorbell. Boone doesn't hear anything when he pushes it, and nobody responds.

He moves toward the rear of the structure, sticking close to the wall, his system awash in adrenaline. The person from TMW said Morrison carries a gun, so Boone shouts "Hello" a few times to let him know he's coming. This gets the dogs going again.

When Boone reaches the rear of the factory, he discovers the source of the barks: on the other side of a fifty-foot expanse of asphalt is a row of kennels lined up against the ten-foot-high cinderblock wall that marks the end of the property, each kennel containing a dog. There's also a small dilapidated trailer, an aluminum storage shed, and a corrugated fiberglass awning sheltering a treadmill, a weight bench, and other workout equipment.

Boone steps out from the shadow of the building into the sunlight and shouts, "Mr. Morrison?" as he approaches the compound. He's in the open now, a clear target, and his heartbeat is loud inside his head as he scans for movement. Nothing but the dogs pacing in their cages and the flapping of a plastic grocery bag caught on the concertina wire topping the wall behind the kennels.

Boone walks to the trailer and raps on the door.

"Mr. Morrison?" he calls again.

The distinctive *shlock shlock* of a shotgun shell being chambered cuts through the dogs' racket and stops him cold.

"Put your hands behind your head and lace your fingers," someone with a heavy English accent says.

Boone does as ordered.

"Now, down on your knees."

Again, Boone complies. Out of the corner of his eye he sees a man emerge from between two of the kennels and advance toward him, leading with a pistol-gripped twelve gauge.

"Is Morrison around?" Boone asks.

"How'd you get in here?" the Brit says. He's standing directly behind Boone now, out of his range of vision.

"The gate was unlocked. I came to see Morrison about buying a dog. Sorry if I startled you."

The Brit chuckles and says, "You didn't fucking startle me, mate. It was the other way around. I'm going to pat you down now, if you don't mind."

He rests the muzzle of the gun against the back of Boone's neck as he runs his hand over Boone's torso. Boone wrinkles his nose at the whiskey funk oozing from the guy. Satisfied that Boone's not carrying, the Brit reaches into the back pocket of Boone's jeans and removes his wallet. Boone imagines him flipping it open to check the driver's license.

"James Boone," the Brit says, then tosses the wallet on the ground. "You can pick that up and get to your feet now."

Boone stands after retrieving his wallet and turns to see the Brit backing away but still holding the gun on him.

"I'm Morrison," the Brit says. He's fifty or so, built like a beer keg, short and squat with thin, spindly legs. His black hair is slicked into an elaborate pompadour, but it looks like he hasn't shaved in a week. A white scar cuts across his forehead right above his piggy blue eyes.

"Still breeding winners?" Boone says.

"What would you know about that?" Morrison replies.

Boone launches into the story he concocted on the way over. "I'm looking to buy a dog," he says. "You were recommended to me by Oscar Rosales." He watches Morrison's face for a flicker of recognition or panic or fear but sees nothing.

"Never heard of the cunt," Morrison says.

"We met at a match in Tijuana," Boone continues. "He had this dog that was incredible—strong as hell, but smart too. He said he got it from you. Told me your dogs are the best there are."

Morrison shrugs. "Still never heard of the cunt."

"When I got back to L.A. I looked you up on the Internet and found your address."

"The Internet?" Morrison says. He blows his nose on his fingers and wipes them on his grimy Led Zeppelin T-shirt. "How am I on the fucking Internet? I don't even have a computer."

"Everybody's on the Internet," Boone replies.

Morrison rubs his forehead scar with a fat knuckle, contemplating this, then says, "Christ, these really are the last days, aren't they?"

He lowers the shotgun, and Boone relaxes a bit. Seems like the guy's buying what he's selling.

"So are all your dogs as good as the one I saw?" Boone says.

"I've got a few nice prospects," Morrison replies. "Come have a look, if you like." He turns and starts for the kennels. Boone follows.

"I wasn't sure I had the right place," Boone says. "Almost drove right past."

"It's my brother-in-law's factory. My sister married a Taiwanese Chinese something or other, some kind of rich ching-chong. All the company's crap is made in Mexico now, but he hasn't sold the building yet. It's my job to make sure the Zulus don't overrun the fort."

Leaning the shotgun against the wall of the shed, Morrison

grabs a leash off a rack and approaches one of the cages. He opens the door and clips the leash to the collar of the dog inside, a black pit bull.

"This is Charles the Second," he says as he leads the dog to the treadmill under the awning. "He's from a long line of absolutely fearless fighters."

The dog steps onto the machine like he's done it many times before, and Morrison punches a few buttons on the keypad. The treadmill begins to turn, and the dog has no problem keeping pace. Morrison increases the speed, forcing Charles to trot.

"Look at that," Morrison says. "That's the result of a hundred years of good breeding. The grain in the wood."

Boone is mesmerized. The dog's thick muscles ripple beneath his hide with every step, and his jaws look as if they could splinter bone. The animal exudes the same primal power as the guillotine, the AK-47, the cruise missile—devices engineered solely for killing; devices whose lethal potential repulses some to the point of nausea but compels others to reach out a trembling hand to touch.

"He's beautiful," Boone says.

"A beautiful, bloodthirsty bastard," Morrison replies. "He's been in the pit three times now, massacres all. Nearly tore the last cur's head off before I could separate them. It's been hard to make a match for him after that. Have to travel down south, maybe, where nobody knows him."

"What's a dog like that go for?"

Morrison pushes a button to slow the treadmill and says, "Oh, he's not for sale, mate. I'll fight him a couple more times, then make my money off stud fees. I've got others nearly as good, though, if you're interested."

Charles hops off the machine, and Morrison leads him to

his cage. He removes the leash from the dog's collar and says, "There you go, your majesty," before locking him up.

"I really liked the dog I saw in TJ," Boone says. "Rosales was the owner's name, I'm sure. A brindle male. Had a tattoo in his ear."

"A tattoo?" Morrison picks up the shotgun and turns to look at Boone over his shoulder.

"A red star and the number one oh two."

Morrison knuckles his scar again as he processes this information. After a long pause, he says, "Care for a drink?"

Boone is a little worried about where this is going, but he nonetheless follows Morrison to the trailer, a corroded relic with flat tires and a decided list, like a boat well on its way to the bottom. Morrison opens the door and ducks inside, only to poke his head out an instant later.

"Mind you scrape your shoes," he says, then laughs uproariously, revealing a mouthful of twisted yellow teeth.

Boone gets the joke as soon as he steps inside. The trailer is filthy. The windows have been covered with tinfoil to block out the sun, but Boone can still make out the dirty dishes piled in the sink of the tiny galley kitchen and the empty cans of baked beans and boxes of macaroni and cheese that litter the stovetop, the counter, the floor.

He steps over the garbage to get to where Morrison is sitting, at a table in a kind of booth lit by a bare fluorescent bulb. Above the Brit is the bunk where he sleeps, a rat's nest consisting of a sleeping bag, a tangle of greasy blankets, and what looks like his entire wardrobe. The whole space is not much bigger than Boone's cell was in Corcoran.

"Cozy, innit?" Morrison says as Boone swats at a fly buzzing his nose and joins him in the booth.

The guy is trying too hard to be funny. Boone figures that he read the disgust on his face when he saw the state of the trailer and suddenly realized how bad things had gotten. Now he's embarrassed and overcompensating. He offers Boone a Marlboro, which he declines. A clattery fan pushes around stale air that reeks of rotting food, sweat, and sewage, and it's a relief when Morrison lights up and blows out a stream of smoke.

The shotgun sits on the table between them, along with a half-empty bottle of Jameson's and an abalone shell overflowing with cigarette butts. Reaching behind his head, Morrison opens a cabinet and, without looking, locates a shot glass amid the junk stored there.

"What's a fancy fucker like you doing getting into dogs?" he asks as he unscrews the cap on the whiskey, pours a shot, and motions for Boone to take it. "Tennis lost its luster?"

Boone downs the drink and improvises: "It's something my dad loved when I was a kid in Texas. Maybe it's genetic."

Morrison nods thoughtfully and refills the glass. "Myself, I got the sickness from my grandfather," he says. "He was the finest trainer in East London. Had me exercising dogs as soon as I could walk."

He tosses back the shot, then digs through the stack of porn videos and paperback spy novels piled on the shelf beside him, coming up with a red spiral notebook. On the cover, in vaguely Gothic script, someone has written MORRISON KENNELS and drawn a logo of sorts, the silhouette of a dog inside a five-pointed star.

Morrison parks his cigarette in the corner of his mouth and, squinting one eye against the smoke, leafs through the notebook. When he finds the page he's looking for, he runs his finger over the words written there.

"See, I knew I wasn't crazy," he says. "One oh two, right? I tattoo all my dogs to prove they've come from me. One oh two is Henry the Fifth, and I sold him to a nigger called Big Unc a year ago March. When was the match in Tijuana?"

"Three, four months ago."

"Big Unc must have sold Henry to this Rosales. Or maybe the bastard stole him. Sounds Mexican, after all."

Boone glances at the page Morrison referred to and sees a phone number next to Big Unc's name. Before he can commit it to memory, however, Morrison slides the book aside in order to pour another drink.

"As for your needs," Morrison says, pointing at the glass, then at Boone. "I've got a pup here by Henry's dam and another sire that's showing a lot of promise. I'll need to work with him for a few more months to get him into fighting shape, but he's already quite game."

Boone swallows the whiskey and sets down the glass. "That's cool," he says. "I won't be ready to take him for a while anyway."

Morrison fills the glass again. Trying to find a way to stall him in hopes of getting another look at the notebook, Boone points to a photograph hanging on the wall. It's of Morrison in some kind of uniform Boone can't identify.

"That you?" he asks.

Morrison glances up at the photo and says, "I was a handsome lad, wasn't I? Downright fuckable."

"So, what, you were a cop in England?"

"A cop?" Morrison says, mimicking Boone's American accent. "Fuck off, mate. I was a legionnaire in the bloody French foreign legion. Second Regiment Etranger de Parachutistes, based in Corsica."

Standing to reach another shelf, he pulls down a white,

billed cap and places it on his head. "The képi blanc?" he says. " 'March or die,' *Beau Geste,* all that? Don't they teach you anything in school over here?"

He snaps to attention, salutes, and bawls, "Sergeant Morrison, *cinq ans de service. La mission est sacrée, tu l'exécutes jusqu'au bout, à tout prix.*"

"I don't know what the fuck you're saying," Boone says, "but it sure sounds impressive."

Morrison is pumped now. His cheeks are flushed, and his eyes have come to life. He's eager to show Boone that he's not just some geezer who lives in more filth than his dogs do.

"Were you ever in the military?" he asks Boone.

"The Marines, four years."

"Ever bloody your hands?"

"It was peacetime."

Morrison snorts and says, "No such fucking thing, mate."

He takes off the hat and sets it on the table, then reaches up to the shelf again, for a hinged case covered in black leather, like something a fancy watch might come in. He opens the case and passes it to Boone. Inside, nestled in red velvet, is a medal, an iron cross with a snarling leopard head in the center and a pair of crossed rifles behind.

"That's the Croix de la Bravoure Militaire from the Republic of Zaire," Morrison says. "It was presented to us by that bastard Mobutu himself, for Operation Léopard."

"I haven't heard of that one."

Morrison chuckles as he lowers himself back into the booth. "That don't surprise me," he says. He picks up the glass of whiskey from the table and downs it, his face suddenly serious. "Pour yourself another," he says, "and I'll teach you something."

Boone fills the glass but doesn't drink it. Morrison taps his fingers absentmindedly on the top of the hat, then leans back, closes his eyes, and begins: "On the thirteenth of May, 1978, two thousand rebels from the Congolese National Liberation Front swept into Zaire from Angola. They overran the town of Kolwezi and proceeded to do what fucking savages are wont to do, which is lay waste to everything, raping the women and children, killing and mutilating the men, and emptying out the shops.

"Business as usual on the dark continent. Except this time there were a couple thousand Europeans living in the town, most connected to the mining industry there, gold and copper. The rebels rounded them up and announced that they were all to be executed. Now, niggers killing niggers, nobody gives a damn, but niggers killing whites, that's unacceptable. So France decided to send us in."

He lights another cigarette off the butt of the last one as he continues talking.

"At four p.m. on the nineteenth, four hundred of us legionnaires parachuted into a field on the outskirts of Kolwezi and immediately began taking fire. We were pinned down in elephant grass three meters high that made it impossible to see anything, rounds zipping every which way like bloody mosquitoes.

"It was my first time in combat, and I had no idea what the fuck I was doing. My first official act of the battle was to press my face into the dirt and recite every prayer my mum had ever taught me. Eventually, thank Christ, better soldiers than myself took care of the gunmen, and we regrouped and advanced into town.

"Town"— he snorts in contempt—"that's being polite. It was a mud-brick and concrete slum, a filthy maze of dirt streets and alleys. Open sewers, communal wells—fucking medieval, man, a fucking idiot's dream of civilization. First thing I saw was two skinny dogs tearing into something in the road. From far off it looked like a bag of dirty laundry, but as we got closer I saw that it was a human torso. Someone shot the dogs, and we kept going."

Morrison pauses, and his hand plays over the shotgun. Boone tenses up.

"It was house-to-house for the rest of that day," Morrison continues. "Small bands of rebels had holed up in schools, in hotels, in private homes, and it was our job to flush them out and release any hostages. Usually they'd bugger off after we sent a few rounds their way, but every once in a while they'd put up a fight, and if they did, we were merciless.

"Some criticized us later, saying we killed every nig-nog we saw without trying to sort the good from the bad. They might have been right, but they also weren't there. You kick open the door of a house you've been taking fire from for ten or twenty minutes, and five black bastards rush you, yelling booga this and booga that—well, you're not a fucking diplomat. You toss a grenade, slam the door, and *blammo*. One problem solved, on to the next.

"But there was something else that drove us to be so thorough. That first body, the torso, was nothing compared to what we came across later. The streets were filled with the corpses of townspeople who'd been mutilated by the rebels. I'm talking cocks in mouths, intestines unspooled, pink meat peeking through charred flesh.

"The smell was so overwhelming, hard-as-nails twenty-year vets were puking their guts out. You could see it in everyone's eyes: This will not happen to me. I will not end up with a pry bar shoved up my ass and a niggertown stray eating my balls.

We killed every black thing that moved, killed them twice. And you would have too."

He rests his cigarette in the abalone shell and picks up the hat and turns it over in his hands. "By the end of the second day it was done," he says. "Two hundred and fifty rebels killed, two thousand hostages rescued, five legionnaires killed, twenty wounded.

"Those two days were like ten years of university for me, like reading the Bible and Freud and Darwin and bloody fucking Plato all in forty-eight hours. I knew everything I needed to know about the world after that."

The Brit's hand trembles as he picks up the glass and gulps down the whiskey in it. Boone runs his finger over the medal, picturing an army of damaged soldiers marching, halt and haunted, across a blighted field. He's met men like Morrison before, warriors undone by war, made strange by the savagery revealed in themselves and others.

"Oh, God," Morrison groans suddenly, clutching his stomach. "Excuse me a moment." He slides out of the booth and hurries to the bathroom. Sickening spattering sounds fill the trailer as soon as the door closes behind him.

Boone reaches for the notebook. A pencil is stored in the wire binding, and he uses it to write Big Unc's phone number on a gas station receipt he fishes from his pocket.

By the time Morrison returns, everything is arranged as it was when he left. Boone tells him that he has other appointments.

"Come along then," Morrison says. He picks up the shotgun and sets the képi blanc on his head. "On your way I'll show you the dog I was telling you about."

Boone stumbles stepping out of the trailer. The whiskey and the heat and the smell have done a number on him. He follows

Morrison to the kennels, where the Brit takes down a leash and enters one of the pens, emerging a few seconds later with a sleek brindle puppy.

"This is Richard the Second," he says, "my best student these days."

"You mind if I touch him?" Boone asks.

"Go on. He's quite friendly."

Boone crouches next to the dog and hopes he looks like he knows what he's doing as he runs his hands over the animal's neck and legs. The dog licks his face, and Boone hates to think of him being torn to pieces in a fight someday.

"Come back in three months, and he'll be a devil," Morrison says. "You can match him with the best, make some real money."

"Sounds good," Boone says, rising to his feet. "Three months then. You want me to lock up on my way out?"

"I'll walk you," Morrison replies. He grabs the shotgun from where he left it leaning against the shed, and he and Boone and the dog set off across the lot toward the Olds.

"Next time just pull up to the gate and honk SOS in Morse," Morrison says. "They teach you Morse code in the Marines, don't they?"

"It's been a while."

"Dot dot dot dash dash dash dot dot dot. I'll come out and let you in."

"Got it," Boone says as he slips behind the wheel of the Olds and starts it up.

"We've got to stick together, us dog men," Morrison says.

"We sure do."

The Brit raises his hand to the bill of his hat in a salute and begins singing in French—"*Tiens, voilá du boudin, voilá du boudin...*" Driving out of the gate, Boone watches him in the rearview mirror and marvels again at all the many ways a man can be fucked.

He checks his messages after he gets on the freeway. There's one new one, from Amy, responding to a call he made earlier, asking if she'd like to go with him to Carl's on Friday. "Yeah, sure, that'll be fun," she says, and the sound of her voice makes him wish for another, better world.

12

THE CASINO RISES OUT OF THE DESERT LIKE A GLEAMING spaceship set down on Mars. Taggert, driving west on the 10 Freeway, spots it from miles away, the mirrored windows of the twenty-seven-story tower brighter than the afternoon sun.

The place is run by the Morongo Band of Mission Indians. Twenty-five years ago they were nearly extinct, the reservation consisting of a few old-timers living in mobile homes and relying on the take from a small bingo operation to keep from starving. That all changed when a group of businessmen and attorneys concocted a scheme to expand the state gaming laws to allow slot machines and blackjack on Indian land, using sovereignty guarantees and years of poverty and official neglect as levers.

A few contributions to the right politicians, a couple of well-funded ballot initiatives, and now the businessmen and attorneys are raking in a fortune, and each and every tribe member receives a check for twenty grand a month, thanks to the busloads of retirees from Palm Springs and L.A. who show up to dump their Social Security money into the nickel slots.

Elaborate scams like this make Taggert feel small-time and stupid. He's always gone for the short con, the easy score, never thinking big enough. He blames it on the way he was raised. His parents were a couple of by-the-book worker bees, folks so averse to risk that they never even bought a new car on credit, instead paying cash for used heaps with God knows how many miles on them because how would they make payments if Daddy were to lose his job? The only chance they ever took was splurging on a few Christmas raffle tickets from the church once a year.

As a young man, Taggert was disdainful of their caution, saw it as weakness, a contemptible lack of faith in themselves, yet how many times has he bowed out of opportunities that would have netted him millions because he couldn't bring himself to lay it all on the line? How many jobs has he walked away from because the stakes were a bit too high? The guys who had the guts to tempt fate are living in castles in Mexico now, living on the beach in Hawaii, watching surfers catch big waves, and here he is, still in the shit, still duking it out every day. It's embarrassing, really, a guy his age. But that all ends now. This time he's going for broke.

He exits the freeway at Cabazon, where two sagging concrete dinosaurs sit baking in the heat, and drives down a frontage road to reach the casino. Benjy should be waiting for him at the bar. A quick drink to get the juices flowing, and they'll be off to a suite in the hotel to meet the point man for the Mexicans who produced the C-note that impressed Olivia so much. A little "How you doing?" a little back-and-forth, a handshake, and Taggert will leave here having made the deal of his life.

He's driving his good truck today, the new F-150, so he decides to valet it. A skinny black kid in a red vest opens the door for him, and Taggert steps out into the porte cochere. It's hot even in the shade. The kid's face is shiny with sweat.

"Welcome to Morongo Casino Resort and Spa," he says, handing Taggert a ticket.

"Where you gonna put it?" Taggert asks.

"We got a special lot over there." The kid gestures vaguely toward an expanse of shimmering asphalt where hundreds of vehicles sit unprotected from the relentless sun.

"I want to be in the shade," Taggert says. "My dash'll crack out there."

"But that's the valet lot, sir."

Taggert opens his wallet and pinches out a twenty. "Put it right here," he says, pointing to an empty spot at the curb with one hand and passing the money to the kid with the other. "I'll only be a half hour or so."

The kid bobs his head in acknowledgment of the payment as he shoves the bill in his pocket. "I'll see what I can do, sir," he says.

Two sets of heavy glass doors keep the heat outside. Taggert pushes through them and enters the air-conditioned bubble of the casino. The electronic whoops and giggles of the slot machines swirl in his head as he makes his way to the bar, and he wonders how the dealers and cocktail waitresses stand the noise all day long. It would drive him nuts.

He's passing the penny slots when a fat old gal slides off her stool and lands flat on her back on the carpet in front of him. He looks down at her bulging eyes and flushed face and knows right then and there that it's all over. Nonetheless, he crouches beside her and says, "Hey, can you hear me? Are you okay?"

No response, not a flicker.

"Carol?" another old broad calls, hobbling toward them down the narrow aisle separating the rows of machines, a long cigarette scissored between her fingers. "Carol, honey?"

Carol is tethered to the slot by a pink plastic spiral cord, one end of which is clipped to a belt loop on her pants, the other to her casino rewards card, which is still inserted in the machine she was playing when she collapsed. Taggert reaches up, slides the card out, and sets it on the floor beside her. His mind flashes to Daddy and Paw Paw and his brother, James, to Uncle Ralph, how they all dropped in their tracks just like this, and the thought hollows him out so that everything echoes longer and louder than it should.

Someone is calling for security. Foam bubbles between Carol's lips, which have turned blue. Her friend kneels and takes her hand. "Hold on, honey," she says.

A security guard, a big Indian in a dark suit, sidesteps through the gathering crowd and squats next to Taggert.

"What happened?" he asks.

"No idea," Taggert replies. "I was coming in and saw her fall."

"She has heart trouble," the friend says.

The guard pulls the mic of his headset closer to his mouth. "I need medical at the penny corral."

"Come on, sweetie," the friend says, lifting Carol's lifeless hand to her cheek. "Come on, now."

Taggert stands as the guard sticks his fingers into Carol's mouth to clear it in preparation for CPR. The Indian begins chest compressions, then places his mouth over Carol's and fills her lungs. The air rushes back out between her slack lips with a sound like a Bronx cheer.

Taggert turns away and comes face to face with the onlookers. Their eyes are bright as they watch the guard attempt to pump life back into the woman, their expressions full of hope. A pack of rubes waiting for a miracle—angel fire and heavenly harps. One guy even has his head bowed and is mumbling a prayer. He must be seventy years old. You'd think someone who'd lived that long would have learned something. Taggert pushes past him and bumps his way out of the crowd. Anybody says a prayer for him when he drops, he'll come roaring back just to punch them in the mouth.

The bar where he's meeting Benjy is located in the middle of the casino. He passes two EMTs humping plastic cases and rolling a gurney on his way there. Benjy is standing at the railing that separates the bar from the casino floor, watching the commotion. Taggert sidles up to him and says, "You fucking turkey vulture."

"What happened?" Benjy asks.

"Some old lady died," Taggert replies. "Let's have a drink."

They move to the bar, snag a couple of stools. Benjy calls for a beer; Taggert goes for bourbon. He's tense about the meeting. Things can go to hell in an instant, and here he is, no gun, no knife, Benjy's contact having insisted they show up unarmed. That should have been out of the question.

Taggert sips his Maker's, then sets the glass on the bar and rotates it slowly, his fingertips barely touching the rim. "You speak to your man?" he asks Benjy, who is intently pushing buttons on his phone.

"He's got a couple bitches with him right now," Benjy says without taking his eyes off the screen. "Said he'll call when he's ready."

"Glad to see he's taking this so seriously."

Benjy shrugs. "What do you want me to do?"

"Nothing," Taggert says. "Just keep right on diddling that thing."

Benjy looks up, irritated. "I'm texting my mom, okay?" he says, then goes back to the keypad. Taggert has known Benjy since the guy was a little *vato* hustling eight balls of stepped-on coke to college kids. Now he's losing his hair and has wrinkles around his eyes.

The bartender, a cute young blonde, drops a glass, and

some asshole sitting across the bar from Taggert applauds. The girl ducks her head and massages her temples, then crouches to pick up the pieces. Taggert thinks about walking over and popping the loudmouth but instead adjusts his stool and has another sip of bourbon.

He decided to wear a suit today as a sign of respect—no tie, but a nice jacket and slacks—and here's Benjy in jeans and a T-shirt. Now Taggert wonders if he's overdressed. Used to be he could give a shit, went everywhere in motorcycle boots and greasy Levi's. These days, though, he's trying to be more professional, trying to elevate his game. Looks like he's the only one.

Benjy's phone blares a tinny tune. He jabs a button, puts it to his ear. "*Sí,*" he says, then, "*Bueno.*" He snaps the phone shut and says, "Time to go."

They finish their drinks and leave the bar. The EMTs are loading Carol onto the gurney. She's still dead. Taggert follows Benjy across the casino to the hotel lobby. They find the elevators and step into an empty car. As the doors are closing, a woman carrying two suitcases rushes over.

"Hold that, please," she says.

"Sorry, full up," Benjy replies. He and Taggert exchange smirks as the doors slide shut in the woman's face.

Taggert straightens his jacket when they step out onto the Mexican's floor. He follows Benjy down the hall to the suite and waits with his hands clasped behind his back while Benjy knocks. A bodybuilder with a woman's eyes opens the door.

"We're here to see Mando," Benjy says.

The bodybuilder looks both ways, checking the hall, then quickly pats Benjy down and motions him inside. Taggert is next. The muscle takes his time with him, makes him open his jacket, and runs his hand up and down his torso, his legs. The guy smells like a woman too. Must be the crap he uses in his hair. He squeezes Taggert's nuts as a final flourish, then steps aside to let him pass.

Mando, standing behind a table, is silhouetted against a big window that frames a view of rocky desert and, beyond that, the snow-covered crest of Mount San Gorgonio. Benjy strides across the room to shake his hand, and Taggert follows. The way the light is, Taggert can't see Mando's face until he's right up on him. Curly black hair, a nose that looks like it's been busted a few times, a gold tooth. His hand is hard and rough, like a seashell. A working man.

"Sit, sit," he says, sinking into a chair.

Taggert and Benjy take seats across from him. On the table are the remains of a room-service platter of chicken wings, a mound of tiny bones surrounded by half-eaten celery sticks and small plastic cups of dressing. Mando slides the platter out of the way and motions for the bodybuilder to do something with it.

"You speak Spanish?" he asks Taggert.

"*Dos tacos, por favor.* That's about it," Taggert replies. He rests his forearms on the table and turns his hands into fists.

"So we speak English then," Mando says with a smile.

"I've shown him your paper," Benjy says.

"Good stuff," Taggert interjects. "Best I've seen in a long time."

"And you seen a lot, huh?" Mando asks. He leans back in his chair and fades into shadow against the window again, playing hide-and-seek.

"Can we close the drapes?" Taggert says. "I like to look in a man's eyes when I'm doing business."

Mando says something in Spanish to the bodybuilder, who moves to the window and yanks the cord that draws the curtains shut. They sit silently in the dark until the muscle turns on an overhead light.

"Okay now?" Mando says. "You are comfortable?"

Taggert nods. He can tell the guy is irritated with him, so he tries to keep things moving. "How many of the hundreds can you get?" he asks.

"How many you want?"

"What about half a mil to start with?"

Mando purses his lips and rocks his head from side to side, thinking. "This will cost you seventy-five thousand," he says.

"I can handle it."

"You sure?"

"And if everything works out, I'll take more next time."

Mando smiles and says, "You got a lot to prove before then, hombre." He hooks his thumbs into the belt loops of his jeans and tilts his chair onto its rear legs.

Everything he says and does seems like a challenge to Taggert, an invitation to fight. Even his shirt—blood red with a scorpion embroidered on it, two rhinestones for eyes, another sparkling at the tip of its tail—pisses Taggert off. There's a chance, though, that the guy is just testing him to see if he's some kind of hothead whose anger could blow everything, so Taggert swallows the insults boiling up into his throat and asks, "How will it work, the exchange?"

Mando puts one snakeskin boot on the table and leans way back. "Is it true you burned a man a little by a little because he stole from you?" he says.

Breezy Petty, about five years ago. Nasty. Very nasty. "Yeah, it's true," Taggert replies.

"How you do this?"

Taggert scratches the scar on his throat and squints, pretending he has to dig up the details from his memory. "I started with his right hand," he says. "Dipped it in gas, set it on fire, and let it burn a while, then put it out. Then his left hand, left foot, right foot, and so on. He hung in there for a long time. I think I eventually had to put a bullet in him."

Mando licks his index finger and idly rubs at a scuff on the toe of his boot, like he's bored by the story, like he's all kinds of rough and tough. "I'll talk to my boss in Mexico," he says. "If he says okay, we come up with a way to get the paper to you. I'll contact him"—he motions to Benjy.

There's a knock at the door. Worry ripples across Mando's face. He slides his boot off the table and sets the chair down. Taggert tightens up, like there's a big screw in his stomach that's attached to everything. Again he thinks how dumb it was not to bring a piece.

He turns to look over his shoulder as Mando waves the muscle to the door. The guy puts his eye to the peephole, then curses under his breath. When he opens up, another bodybuilder, not as pretty as the first, steps into the room and rattles off something in Spanish.

"An old woman is died while playing a machine," Mando says. "Enrique is afraid. He thinks it could be a bad sign."

"We saw it," Benjy says. He points at Taggert. "He tried to help her."

"Really?" Mando says to Taggert. "So now maybe you have a ghost following you."

"I don't believe in ghosts," Taggert replies.

"No?"

"No."

Mando shakes his head ruefully. "We got a lot of ghosts in Mexico," he says. "A lot. I have seen some myself."

"Oh, yeah?" Taggert says.

"Seriously, hombre. In my town, the children, we play by the water, the stream, you know? One time after the rain the stream flooded, and the water took away a little girl, Rosa. The men search and search but never find her. Her family buried an empty coffin.

"A month later, another girl, Isabel, woke up crying. Her mother says, 'What's wrong, Isabel?' and the girl says, 'I'm not Isabel; I'm Rosa.' The mother tells the girl it's wrong to talk that way, but Isabel is still crying and still saying she is Rosa."

Music blasts on the other side of the closed door separating the bedroom from the rest of the suite. A woman laughs.

"Hey!" Mando yells. "Hey!"

The door opens, and a dark-haired girl in a tiny bathing suit pokes her head out. Taggert can see another girl, a blonde, sprawled on the bed behind her.

"We are talking," Mando says.

The dark-haired girl rolls her eyes and closes the door. The music cuts off.

"So, anyway," Mando says, picking up his story, "Isabel's father brought the priest to talk to Isabel. The priest ask her questions about Rosa's family, about her house, and Isabel answered them all. She tell the priest she wants to see her mother, and then she will show him where her bones are.

"The priest took Isabel to Rosa's house. I remember I seen them walking. The girl looked strange to me, and I was scared, you know, very scared. Rosa's mother speaked to the girl and couldn't believe it. It was really Rosa's ghost in Isabel's body.

"They talked for a while, then the ghost said she must go. Rosa's mother begged her to stay, but the ghost said God was waiting for her.

"The priest put Isabel on a burro and took her into the desert. They came to a place where all the garbage from the flood was piled up, and Isabel told the priest where to dig.

"Right there he found Rosa's body. Isabel, she was asleeping then, and he couldn't wake her. He wrapped Rosa's body in a blanket and tied it to the burro and carried Isabel all the way back to the pueblo.

"Isabel waked up like normal two days later, only talking about a dream of heaven. I remember the whole pueblo came when they dug up the empty coffin and put Rosa inside."

One of the bodybuilders crosses himself, and Mando raises his hands and tilts his head as if to say to Taggert, "Ghosts. What more proof do you need?" Taggert can't suppress a snicker.

"You don' believe me?" Mando says, his heavy eyebrows crashing into each other above his nose.

"Oh, I believe you," Taggert says quickly. "It's just it sounds a little crazy, you know?"

"It's not crazy," Mando says.

Taggert leans back in his chair, trying to ease the tension. "Look," he says. "I just wanted to come here and let you see my face, let you see the kind of man I am."

"A man who don' believe in ghosts," Mando says.

"A man who's all about putting money in his pocket," Taggert says. "The same kind of man as you."

Mando flashes his gold tooth in a quick smile, but Taggert doesn't trust it.

"Okay," Mando says. "I talk to my boss and contact you soon."

The music starts in the bedroom again. Mando tenses as if he's about to shout once more, but then something sly comes into his expression, and he turns back to Taggert.

"Party girls," he says with a shrug.

"Best kind," Taggert replies.

"You like to party? With girls?"

"Who doesn't?"

Mando stands and walks to the bedroom door. He opens it and says, "Come, come, ladies, to meet someone."

The girls step into the doorway on either side of him, and he wraps his arms around them. Nice stuff. The best money can buy.

"This is Tanya," he says, kissing the blonde on the cheek. "And this is her friend..." The name escapes him.

"Vallee," the dark one says.

"Vallee, Vallee." Mando kisses her on the cheek too, then says to Taggert, "You want to party with them?"

"Some other time," Taggert says. "I've got places to be, people to see."

"Come on," Mando says. "Pick one. Or both."

"Really, bro, thanks and all, but..."

"You are a faggot?" Mando says. "No, you are not a faggot."

Taggert colors as he tries to hide the anger rising inside him. This is no test. Mando is fucking with him, pure and simple. Got to let it go, though, to make this deal.

"Maybe you are a cop," Mando continues, his face tight behind his fake smile. "Maybe that's why you won't fuck my girls."

"You know I'm not a cop, man," Taggert growls. He plants his hands flat on the table and pushes himself up out of his chair. Mando flinches a little as he approaches him and the girls.

"You want to watch?" Taggert asks him.

The smile disappears from Mando's face. He steps away

from the girls, and Taggert takes his place between them, ushering them into the bedroom. The door closes behind them, and over the music Taggert hears Mando say something in Spanish that makes the bodybuilders and Benjy laugh. A joke about him, no doubt.

13

FRIDAY AT NOON BOONE DIALS THE NUMBER HE GOT FOR BIG Unc from Morrison's notebook.

"Playpen," barks the man who answers.

Boone is taken aback but recovers quickly. "Is Big Unc there?" he asks.

"He comes in around two. Who's this?"

"Who's this?"

"This is Tim."

"Tim, right," Boone says. "Thanks, Tim."

"Hold on, now," Tim sputters. "Who the fuck is *this?*"

Boone hangs up. He can pull the address for the Playpen off the Internet and drive over to talk to this Unc about Joto this afternoon and still be back in plenty of time to pick up Amy and go to Carl's to watch the boxing match.

He walks into the kitchen and opens a can of food for Joto. The dog dives right in when he sets the bowl on the floor. Boone hasn't heard anything from Loretta about someone wanting to adopt him. She should shoot some new photos once he's healthier.

"Henry," Boone says, trying out the name Morrison mentioned. "Hey, Henry." The dog doesn't look up.

Boone makes himself a ham and cheese sandwich, pulls a beer out of the refrigerator, and returns to the living room to eat in front of the TV. The news is on. Car bombs and Internet sex stings, miracle babies and tainted meat. Payday's tomorrow, and he's got thirty bucks to last him until then. Shouldn't be any big thing though. The Olds has half a tank of gas in it, and there's a decent bottle of wine in the cupboard to take over to Carl's.

He tosses Joto a corner of his sandwich and changes the channel. "Today we're talking to teenage tramps," some white-haired joker says.

A new crack has appeared in the ceiling of the bungalow, like a black bolt of lightning in a white sky. Boone wonders if there was an earthquake yesterday. Sometimes, when you're on the move, you don't even feel the little ones.

THE PLAYPEN TURNS out to be a bar on the weedy fringes of Compton, a windowless pink stucco box right there between the Louisiana Fish Market and Kisha's Hair Affair. Boone is parked in front, working out what he's going to say to Big Unc, when a couple of kids walk past and give him hard looks. He doesn't blame them—white faces down here usually mean nothing but trouble—but before they can set off any alarms, he steps out of the Olds, takes three quick breaths as he crosses the sidewalk, and ducks into the bar.

He pauses just inside the door to let his eyes adjust. Everybody can see him, but he can't see anyone. As soon as he's able to make out an empty stool, he slides onto it. The bartender, a short old guy in a Laker T-shirt and thick glasses, is on him immediately.

"Can I help you?" he asks. Boone recognizes the gravelly voice from the phone. Tim.

"How about a Bud."

"You got ID?"

Boone unfolds his wallet and lays it on the bar.

"I need for you to take it out," Tim says.

The old man's sweating him, but Boone keeps his mouth shut and slips his driver's license from its clear plastic sleeve and hands it to him. Tim examines it up close, then at arm's length. He stares at Boone, then the license, then back at Boone before saying, "What you want again?"

"A Budweiser."

Boone scopes the place out while Tim shuffles to the cooler with deliberate slowness. It's a narrow room, bar on the left wall, red vinyl booths patched with duct tape on the right, a couple video games blinking in back. The jukebox is playing Marvin Gaye, and both of the other customers, shadowy figures slouched a few barstools apart, are smoking, even though it's against the law.

Boone nurses his beer after Tim delivers it and tries to come up with a way to ask about Big Unc without spooking him. He watches a spiderweb up near the ceiling that's situated directly in front of an air-conditioning vent. The cold wind blasting from the vent has stretched the web to its limits, puffing it like a parachute. It's torn from its mooring when the front door opens with a whoosh and a blade of sunlight stabs the darkness, then withdraws.

"Unc here?" the newcomer asks.

Tim hooks a thumb over his shoulder. "He in back, fucking with that machine."

Boone smiles at his good luck.

The newcomer steps up to the bar not five feet from Boone and says, "Let me get a couple drinks here." He's tall and skinny, wearing a black nylon do-rag, a clean white T-shirt, and baggy jeans. With him is a girl, maybe eighteen, tight skirt and blouse straining to contain her big ass and titties, a braided blond wig hanging to the middle of her back.

"Vodka and cranberry," the guy says. "What you want, baby?"

"Ya'll got wine coolers?" the girl asks Tim.

"We got wine coolers," Tim says. "We got whatever you want."

He moves off to fetch the drinks, and the new guy looks down at Boone and says, "How you doin', my brother?"

"Better by the beer," Boone replies.

The guy smiles, showing the whitest teeth Boone has ever seen. "Let me ask you," he says. "They a KKK meeting around here somewhere?"

"Oh, shit," the girl hoots.

Boone looks down at his beer and shakes his head. "Ahh, man, why's it got to be like that?" he says.

"Nah, I'm just fucking with you," the guy says. "You cool, you cool." He turns to the girl. "You know who he look like? Like that dude in that movie."

"Brad Pitt?" the girl says.

"Brad Pitt? He don't look like motherfucking Brad Pitt. You need to get over to Laser Eye Center, get you some LASIK."

Tim delivers the vodka cranberry and the wine cooler. The guy passes the cooler to the girl and picks up his drink.

"Cheers," he says to Boone.

Boone raises his bottle and tilts it toward the guy's glass, then watches him and the girl walk to the back of the bar. The guy knocks on a red door, and he and the girl disappear through it after someone on the other side opens up.

Boone finishes his beer while listening to "Me and Mrs. Jones" on the jukebox. He's all revved up. The next few minutes could go a million different ways. He almost knocks over his stool when he stands and walks down the bar to where

Tim is working a word-search puzzle and asks, "Where's the bathroom?"

Tim points toward the back and says, "You need paper? We keep it behind here."

"Nah, I'm good," Boone says. Just past the video games he spots the men's room on his left. On his right is the door the young couple went through, with a peephole and a PRIVATE sign. The door is slightly ajar, and Boone hears music playing on the other side and someone rapping, "I like big butts, and I cannot lie." He doesn't like the idea of barging in unannounced, especially when Unc has company, but this might be his only chance to get to the man. Changing course abruptly, he shoulders open the door and steps over the threshold.

The room is bigger than he expected it would be. Five video poker machines are lined up along one wall, and there's a blackjack table and a craps table. The couple, sitting on a worn leather couch in a lounge area with a small bar, stare up at him, startled. An older man stands in front of a karaoke machine, microphone in hand. He's wearing some kind of loose-fitting canary-yellow pajamas, and his hair is braided into cornrows.

"The fuck you doin'?" he shouts over the music.

"Everything's cool," Boone says. "I just want to ask you some questions."

Unc's eyes narrow, his free hand darts toward his pocket. Before it gets there, Boone is on him. Boone had hoped it wouldn't zig this way, but now that it has, he's got to take control immediately. He drives an elbow into Unc's chest and grabs his wrist, which stops him from drawing whatever he was after. Unc swings the mic, but Boone blocks the shot with his forearm and throws another elbow, this time to the man's

Adam's apple. Unc sinks to his knees, retching and clutching his throat.

Boone turns to check on the couple and steps right into a smack on the forehead from the guy, who moves in closer and hits him again with the butt of a Beretta. Boone is blinded by pain for an instant but manages to knee the guy twice in the nuts and drive him backward into the wall. Grabbing the guy's arm, Boone slams his gun hand into a black velvet poster of Tupac until he drops the weapon, then muscles him to the couch, where he tumbles onto his cowering girlfriend.

Boone stoops to pick up the Beretta. Unc is on his knees now, one hand digging in his pocket. Boone kicks him there, in the pocket, and Unc howls and withdraws the hand while Boone stands over him and presses the Beretta to the back of his head.

"Get what you were getting, but slowly," Boone says.

Unc reaches into his pocket with bloody fingers and comes out with a little chrome pistol.

"Toss it away," Boone says, prodding the man's skull with the gun.

Unc slides the pistol across the floor. It caroms off the wall and ends up under the craps table.

The karaoke machine is still blasting Sir Mix-a-Lot. Boone yanks the plug out of the socket. He glances at the Beretta in his hand and realizes that he's way into felony territory now. Too late to back down though.

"Go on over there with your friends," he says to Unc. "I get my answers, and I'm gone."

Unc rises slowly from the floor and limps to the couch, cradling his injured hand in his good one. He sits next to the girl and glares at Boone, beads of sweat glistening like tiny jewels on his forehead.

Boone closes the door and flips the deadbolt, all the while keeping the Beretta on Unc and the couple. He's feeling sharp again after a few dizzy seconds following the blows to the head, but something warm and sticky is dripping into his left eye, distorting his vision, blood from a cut above his eyebrow.

"You got any towels in here? Any napkins?" he asks.

Unc points to the bar and says, "What you want to ask me about?"

Boone moves to the bar and finds a stack of drink napkins with the name of another establishment, the Home Stretch, printed on them. He wipes his eye clear with a few, then presses more to the cut to try to stop the bleeding.

"About a dog," he says.

"A dog?" Unc says. "All this fucking drama for a dog?"

Boone shrugs. "You're the one who went for his gun."

"And you're damn lucky I didn't shoot you," Unc says. The girl next to him on the couch adjusts her skirt, jostling him. "Be still," he snaps.

She gives him a dirty look and crosses her arms over her chest.

Boone leans against the bar and says, "You bought a dog from a guy named Morrison. Henry the Fifth, a brindle pit bull."

"Man, I sold that motherfucker more 'n six months ago."

"To who?"

"To none of your goddamn business," Unc says. "Unless you're the IRS, I don't have to open my books to you." The girl beside him fidgets again. He elbows her and says, "Bitch, I told you to quit knocking into me."

The guy on the couch with them leans forward to look around the girl at Unc and says, "Listen up, nigger, don't be calling my girl a bitch."

"What are you saying to me, boy?" Unc replies.

Boone grabs a bottle of Courvoisier off the bar and hurls it across the room. It explodes on the wall with a crash. Unc and the couple duck and turn their attention back to him.

"What, was that you getting all badass?" Unc says.

There's pounding on the door. "Unc? Unc?" Tim calls.

"Everything's cool," Unc says. "Get your ass back behind the bar."

Boone gives everybody a second to calm down, then says, "So, who'd you sell the dog to?"

Unc exhales loudly through flared nostrils. "Some cracker name of Taggert," he says.

"That his first name, last name?"

"I don't know, man. Taggert, motherfucking Taggert. Lives out in the desert, Twentynine Palms or some shit, out by the Marine base. Puts on a dog fight now and then. Me and the crew been out there a couple times. He liked one of my dogs, made me an offer, and I sold it to him right out the pit."

Twentynine Palms. Boone's sure he's on the right track now. Both Maribel and Oscar's roommate said Oscar's last job was somewhere in the desert, working with dogs.

"You got an address for Taggert? A phone number?" Boone asks.

Unc draws back his head and smirks. "Oh, yeah, sure," he says. "Let me get right on that for you, boss."

Boone swings the Beretta over and squeezes the trigger, putting a round into the karaoke machine. The girl on the couch claps her hands over her ears and closes her eyes.

"*That* was me getting all badass," Boone says. "And next I fuck up one of your pretty poker machines."

"All right, all right," Unc says. "Get me my phone. It's over there where you are, with my keys."

Boone picks up the phone from the bar and walks it over to

Unc, then moves out of reach. Time to get a move on. Someone's bound to call the cops after the gunshot.

Unc pushes a few buttons, stares down at the screen. "You know you're putting my life in danger," he says. "Taggert finds out who gave you this information."

"Your name won't come up, I promise," Boone replies.

"He a stone killer. You fuck with him, and there ain't gon' be none of this nicey-nice we got going on here."

"Thanks for the warning."

Unc snorts derisively and says, "Warning? Boy, I *hope* that crazy motherfucker rips you in half."

Boone pulls the wad of napkins away from his forehead. They're soaked through with blood. The cut's a real gusher, the kind of thing that might need stitches. Doesn't hurt though. Not too much. Not yet.

"Here," Unc says, holding out the phone. There's an address and number for Taggert on the screen. Boone copies these onto a napkin, using a stub of pencil he finds on the bar, then picks up Unc's gun from under the craps table and slips it into the pocket of his hoodie.

"All righty then," Boone says. "If you'll escort me out, this meeting is adjourned."

Unc rises grudgingly from the couch and walks to the door. Boone stands behind him as he unlocks it, lets him feel the Beretta against his spine.

The main room is empty now, except for Tim behind the bar, pointing a shotgun.

"Tell him to put that thing down," Boone says to Unc.

"You heard the motherfucker," Unc says to Tim.

Tim sets the gun on the bar and slides it out of his reach. He thrusts his arms into the air, bent at the elbows, a look of pure hatred twisting his face.

It's a long twenty feet to the door. Boone shifts the Berreta between Unc and Tim all the way. Unc pushes the door open, and the sunlight claws at Boone's eyes. He squints and steps around Unc so that he's facing him.

"Let the door close behind you, and stay in front of it," he says.

Unc stands in the doorway as Boone backs across the sidewalk to the Olds. A woman steps out of Kisha's Hair Affair and lights a cigarette but hurries inside when she sees the gun in Boone's hand.

Boone moves around to the driver's side and tosses the bloody napkins into the street. He takes Unc's pistol from his pocket, drops it and kicks it under the car, then grabs his keys. Still covering Unc with the Beretta, he unlocks the door and swings it open. In one motion, he ducks inside, shoves the keys in the ignition and starts the car. Just as he's pulling away, he throws the Beretta out the window.

In the rearview mirror he watches Unc charge out of the doorway and pick up his pistol. He goes into a crouch and points it two-handed at the Olds but doesn't fire. Boone cuts loose with a victory whoop and slaps his palm against the steering wheel. That was a close one. The best kind.

THE CUT ON Boone's head is still oozing blood, but the flow has slowed considerably. He reaches into the backseat for the towel he uses at the gym and presses it to the wound during the drive home. The towel is still damp with sweat from his morning workout, and the salt stings.

He stops at a pay phone in the parking lot of a gas station and punches in the number he got for Taggert, just to see what happens. After one ring a message comes on saying that the number is no longer in service. Of course it isn't. Which means there's nothing to do but drive out to Twentynine Palms and talk to Taggert, the stone killer, in person.

He knows he's nuts to put himself in that kind of dangerous situation, but at the same time there's a fire burning inside him that he hasn't felt in years. "You're so goddamn stubborn," Carl used to say when Boone kept coming at him in the ring even though Boone was so exhausted he could barely keep his gloves up, and Boone always took that as a compliment. Finding out what happened to Oscar Rosales has turned into a bigger-than-life quest for truth for him, and even though everything about it stinks of trouble, he's going to keep moving forward until he runs headfirst into a wall.

Back at the bungalow, he uses a butterfly bandage to close the gash on his forehead and covers it with gauze. He'll need to come up with a story to explain the wound to Amy when he picks her up. The cut is throbbing some, so he pops a beer and downs a couple Advil. Joto pokes his head into the kitchen, ever hopeful.

"It's not time to eat yet, you greedy bastard," Boone says.

The dog follows him into the bathroom and watches as he turns on the shower. Boone bends down to pet him, feels the scars marring his hide. He's surprised at the anger that wells up so suddenly in him.

"We'll get them," he tells the dog. "Every last one."

14

What happened to you?" Amy asks as soon as she opens the door of her bungalow and gets a look at Boone.

He reaches up to touch the bandage on his forehead and says, "Sparring accident at the gym. Dude went high; I went low."

"You boys should be more careful," she says, stepping out onto the porch. She's wearing a yellow sundress, and her hair is loose around her shoulders.

"It's no fun if nobody gets hurt," Boone says.

He begins to feel anxious on the drive over to Carl's place. He tries as best he can to keep up the small talk with Amy, but his mind is elsewhere.

When Anderson hired Ironman to guard his family, Carl and his wife and two boys were settling into their dream house in Pasadena. Great neighborhood, great schools, great life. A year later, after the beating, after Boone went to prison, after business at Ironman tanked, they had to move to a two-bedroom condo on the bad side of Culver City, where they're still living today.

Boone doesn't know how to apologize for this or if he should even try. He's put together a dozen different speeches expressing his remorse, but that was never how he and Carl were with each other. At this point he wishes he'd never said he'd show up for the fight tonight, the way his stomach is twitching.

"Are you okay?" Amy asks.

"Me? Sure. Why?" Boone replies.

"I just asked who was going to be at this shindig and you said, 'Sure.' "

The Robertson exit is coming up. Boone tightens his grip on the wheel and moves out of the fast lane. "I guess I'm nervous," he says. "I haven't seen Carl since I was released, and I don't think his wife ever liked me much as it is."

"What's her problem?"

"I was the single friend, the one who was going to lead her man astray, push hookers and blow on him."

Amy reaches over and squeezes his arm. "Jimmy, this guy was your partner for years," she says. "Everything's going to be fine."

THE CONDO IS in a gray stucco building with rounded corners that was built around the time of the '84 Olympics. It looks like all the minimalls that sprang up back then, with pale green balcony railings and pale pink trim. Someone has tagged the wall next to the front door in big black letters, some ragged nonsense. Boone bets that kind of stuff doesn't happen in Pasadena. He pushes the button next to Carl's name on the intercom. A few seconds later a child's voice blasts out of the speaker.

"Hello?"

"It's Jimmy Boone."

A buzzer goes off, and the lock on the door clicks.

Carl lives on the third floor. Boone and Amy take the elevator and get out in a hallway that smells faintly of bug spray. Boone's knock triggers a stampede inside the condo. Carl's sons, Dennis and Warren, are still squabbling over who gets to answer as the door opens. Dennis was five when Boone went away. He's nine now, trim but sturdy like his dad. Warren, who wasn't even a year old back then, is five. He's wearing a bright red football helmet and carrying a cheese grater.

"Remember me?" Boone says.

Dennis shakes his head no and steps aside to let them in.

"I'm Jimmy, an old friend of your dad's, and this is Amy."

"Nice helmet," Amy says to Warren. "What position do you play?"

He makes a fart sound with his mouth and runs off.

Carl pokes his head into the entryway. "Hey, Jimmy," he says and rushes over to give Boone a hug. "Long time, man. Too long."

He looks the same: a running back's body, skin the color of coffee with two creams, hair cut close to the scalp, a thin mustache. "It's great to see you too," Jimmy says, a little choked up, all the good years coming back to him at once, then the bad ones.

Carl extends his hand to Amy.

"Carl Wright," he says. "Welcome to our home."

"Amy Vitello."

"My man treating you right?" Carl asks.

"Can't complain yet," Amy replies.

"Well, you let me know," Carl says. "I'll whip his ass into shape if need be." He points to the bandage on Boone's forehead. "You been scrapping?" he asks.

"Only in the gym," Boone replies.

Carl takes them into the kitchen to see Diana, his wife. She's darker than Carl, has her hair braided. She kisses Boone on the cheek and greets Amy warmly. If she's upset about all the trouble Boone has caused her family, she's too classy to show it.

Warren is standing on a step stool at the counter, grating cheese, more of which is ending up on the floor than in the bowl.

"Jimmy Neutron," he says to Boone.

"Gotta blast," Boone replies. He ends up on Nickelodeon now and then while channel surfing.

Diana takes Amy up on her offer of help and gets her started making a salad. Carl hands Boone a beer and walks him into the living room, where a couple of the current employees of Ironman are watching a baseball game on TV.

They look like straight-up thugs: shaved heads, warm-up suits, lots of gold. A black guy and an Armenian. Carl has to prompt them to stand and shake hands. Times must be hard if he's hiring humps like these. In the past, anyone working for the company had to have at least enough manners to get by in polite society. These two would scare the shit out of Ironman's old clientele.

"Come on with me while I check these ribs," Carl says to Boone.

Boone follows him out to the condo's small balcony, most of which is taken up by an enormous gas grill.

"I hauled this over from Pasadena," Carl says. "Had a hell of a time getting it up here." He opens the lid and bastes the meat with sauce from a bowl on the grill's counter. "Di parboiled these, so it shouldn't take too long," he continues. "Why don't you close that door so we don't smoke everyone out."

Boone slides the glass door shut and leans against the wall.

"Things coming together?" Carl asks him.

"Yeah, man, they are," Boone says. "You probably heard that Danny found me a bartending gig and hooked me up with a place in Hollywood."

"He's a cool old dude, Danny is."

"I'm just trying to keep my nose clean, you know, get back in the groove."

Carl lowers the lid of the grill and drops the basting brush into the bowl of sauce. "Got yourself a nice girl," he says. "That's a good start."

"You believe she used to be a cop?" Boone says.

Carl grins and raises his eyebrows.

"I know, man," Boone says. "It's some crazy shit."

He sips his beer and watches Carl's back as he fiddles with the grill, adjusting the temperature and checking the propane connection. Busy work, like he knows what the next question is going to be.

"How about you?" Boone asks, not because he wants to but because he's got to.

"Oh, we're doing fine," Carl says, his back still to him. "Not as good as before, but pretty damn good. Business is picking up. I'm branching out."

"Yeah?"

"Yeah. You know, someone needs talking to, dude hires me to do the talking, that kind of thing."

Rough stuff. They were offered those kinds of gigs all the time back in the day, but Carl always turned them down. He wanted Ironman to be a legit operation, no arm twisting, no leg breaking, nothing shady. Things must be worse than he's letting on if he's stooping to muscle jobs.

"Just be careful," Boone says.

Carl whips around to face him, and Boone can feel the heat coming off him from six feet away.

"I thank you for that advice," Carl says, "but things ain't like they used to be. You heard that saying 'Beggars can't be choosers'? It's no more Bahamas and Maui and Aspen, Jimmy.

Those folks don't call no more. There ain't no more office, neither. I run shit out of my bedroom now, dealing with all these so-called rappers and so-called self-made millionaires. Half the time they flat-out refuse to pay their bills, and the other half they try and nickel and dime me to death.

"I had to make some hard choices in order to keep my family fed, and I ain't so high and mighty anymore. I ain't so philosophical. These days I'll bust a head if I have to; I'll deliver a package."

He opens the lid of the grill and slops more sauce on the ribs. Boone keeps his mouth shut. He deserved every bit of that. A car alarm goes off somewhere, turning the silence toxic. Boone recalls a time when Ironman was just getting going and he and Carl were working security at a party in Newport Beach. A crazy drunk pulled a gun on Boone, and Carl took the guy out with one punch before he could squeeze the trigger. And that was only the first time he saved Boone's ass.

After a few tense seconds, Carl's shoulders slump, and he bows his head. "Sorry about that," he says.

"Shut the fuck up," Boone replies. "I'm the one who's sorry. I screwed everything up by beating that man down, and that's all there is to it."

Carl turns to him again, softer now. "Maybe so and maybe not, but I never doubted you," he says. "I believed you saw what you thought you saw in that house, and later I believed that bitch set you up. Shit, you tell me today that the sky is pink instead of blue, I'm still going to believe you, because you're an honest motherfucker, Jimmy."

Boone shuffles his feet and shoves his hands in his pockets. "Not really," he says. "But thanks for saying it."

"I ain't letting the past tear me up, and you shouldn't either."

"I'm trying not to."

Carl chuckles and shakes his head. "We are a couple of sorry pieces of shit, ain't we?"

"Hey," Boone replies, "at least we're still pretty."

"There you go."

A muffled shout rises on the other side of the glass door, one of the thugs reacting to the game. "We best take these ribs in there before those cavemen eat my babies," Carl says.

Everybody squeezes in around the dining-room table and fills plates with ribs, beans, salad, coleslaw, and macaroni and cheese. The thugs wolf down their food and head back into the living room for the undercard, the kids pick at their macaroni then ask to be excused, but Boone and Amy and Carl and Diana take their time, eating and talking.

Carl and Boone tell Amy war stories about Ironman, crazy stuff that clients said and did. Like the Japanese businessman with a thing for ghetto poon who would fly into town every few months and hire two guys to accompany him to the nastiest South Central strip joints. He was like an alien popped in from outer space, sitting there in his business suit, drinking watered-down Hennessy and dropping thousands of dollars on the very appreciative dancers. And then there was the guy who hired a man to stand next to him while he told his wife that he'd wrecked her car, he was so afraid she was going to kick his ass.

When the main event begins, they grab fresh beers and move into the living room. It's two Mexican fighters, quick little men, one with a particularly sweet right hook. Boone gets into it, the first fight he's watched in a while, and pretty soon he's yelling at the screen right along with Carl and the thugs.

The kids come out of their bedroom to see what the commotion is all about and stand silently for a while, a bit uneasy, watching the men get loud and jab imaginary opponents as they re-create the action. At one point the Armenian yells something about one of the fighters being a motherfucking pussy, and Carl shouts, "Hey!" and jerks his head toward the boys. The Armenian grits his teeth and clamps a hand over his mouth.

The bout goes all twelve and gets gory in the later rounds. Boone turns to check on Amy now and then—she's sitting beside him on the couch—but she seems to be fine, rooting quietly for the underdog and rolling her eyes at the men's boisterousness. He decides it's silly to worry about her. She probably saw more blood in her years as a cop than he's seen in his entire life.

As soon as the fight is over—José Right Hook in a controversial decision—the thugs make a quick exit. Off to the clubs, they announce. Boone offers to do the dishes, but Diana insists that's Carl's job. "He's gotta pay somehow for putting me through this tonight," she says with a laugh.

A few minutes later Boone finds her packing up the leftovers in the kitchen when he goes in to get another beer. She checks to make sure Amy and Carl are talking in the living room, then leans in close and says, "You know it broke his heart that you didn't come see him when you got out."

Boone stares down at the beer in his hand. "I felt so bad about what happened with the business and everything," he says. "I still do."

"Come on, Jimmy," Diana says. "You guys were friends. Partners. I don't care how bad you felt; you owed him a visit. And if it turned out he wanted to cuss you up and down for what happened, you owed him that too."

"You're right, Di."

"I got to tell you," she says as she scoops coleslaw from a bright green bowl into a plastic storage container, "I thought you were a better man than that."

"So did I," Boone says.

"But you're here now, so I guess it's all good."

"You know, I want to apologize to you too," Boone says.

Diana waves him off. "Shit," she says. "Don't waste your time. I got a good husband, great kids. I got everything I need to be happy forever. Go do your penance elsewhere, Jimmy Boone."

Carl pokes his head into the kitchen and asks, "What's going on in here?"

"Jimmy's telling me dirty jokes," Diana says. "You better get him out of my face before I wash his mouth out with soap."

At about ten Carl lets a yawn escape, and Boone decides it's time to go. He and Amy say good-bye to Diana and the boys, and Carl walks them to the elevator.

"You hear of any jobs for me, you let me know," Carl says to Boone as they wait for the car to arrive.

"Absolutely, man. No problem."

"I'm not picky; know what I'm saying?"

The elevator doors open, and Boone reaches out to shake hands with Carl, looks him right in the eye. "I know what you're saying," he replies. "Thanks for everything."

"And be sweet to this girl," Carl says, hugging Amy.

"I will."

When the doors close and the elevator starts to move, Amy says, "So? How'd it go?"

"It went," Boone replies.

"Are you glad you came?"

Boone reaches up to touch the bandage on his head. The cut is throbbing again. "Yeah," he says. "Yeah, I am."

IT'S A QUIET ride home. Both Boone and Amy try to start conversations, but they peter out before they get going. Which is silly, Boone thinks, because they definitely have a connection. In fact, he feels it now more than ever. Maybe she does too. Maybe that's why things are suddenly a little sticky.

Back at the bungalows, they linger in the courtyard in front of Amy's place. She finishes up a story about something funny that happened at school, something silly one of her students said. He laughs when she gets to the punch line, but then there's another long silence. Their eyes meet briefly, and Boone looks away first.

"Thanks for coming with me tonight," he says.

"It was fun," Amy replies. "They're nice people. Good friends to have."

"And sorry if we got a little loud during the fight."

Amy shrugs. "Bloodlust. What can you do?"

Boone smiles, but he's shaking inside.

"Up for a nightcap?" he says. "All I have is beer and bourbon, but..."

"Sounds lovely," Amy says. "But I've got to be up early tomorrow for a carnival at my school, a benefit."

Then, somehow, they're in each other's arms; they're kissing. It's a good one, a long one, and kind of a relief, like they've both been waiting a while for it.

They separate and try to figure out where to look and what to do with their hands.

"Well," Boone says.

"Well, well," Amy replies. She moves onto her porch, turns to glance at him over her shoulder.

"Sleep tight," she says.

"Fat chance," Boone replies.

Amy smiles and goes inside.

Boone feels good as he walks to his place. It's like they've pulled something off and managed to make a clean getaway.

15

SATURDAY MORNING BENJY IS SITTING AT TAGGERT'S kitchen table, trying to drink his way out of a hangover. He showed up at the ranch half an hour ago looking like he'd fold up on himself if you bumped him, and three beers later there's still sweat shining on his upper lip. His hand shakes as he lifts a cigarette to his mouth. Taggert smiles and slaps the table hard just to see him jump.

"What the fuck, Bill?" Benjy whines.

"There was a fly. Sorry," Taggert replies.

Benjy buries his face in his hands and presses his temples with his fingertips. "You got any aspirin?" he asks.

Taggert is frustrated. Here Benjy's supposed to be giving him the word on whether Mando's bosses okayed the deal, and the guy can barely sit upright. Normally, Taggert would lay into him for being such a pussy and tell him to come out with it already, but this is still the big one, and a wrong move could send it spinning out of reach, so he's willing to be patient, even if it comes down to hand-holding a grown man who whines like a bitch after a night of drinking.

"How about some Tylenol three?" Taggert says, standing up from his chair. "The codeine should put you right."

As he's retrieving the pills from the medicine cabinet in the bathroom, he glances out the window and sees Olivia and

Virgil walking up the hill from the bunkhouse. They're passing a joint back and forth and giggling at something stupid. The kid is supposed to be helping Miguel set up for tonight's dogfights over at the barn. Thirty or forty guys will be arriving at six, and things need to be squared away. Taggert raises his hand to open the window and yell at the punk to get his ass in gear but then stops himself. He can never tell what's going to piss Olivia off these days.

Benjy is sitting with his mouth open and eyes closed when Taggert returns to the kitchen. Taggert sets three pills on the table in front of him. Benjy swallows them with gulps of beer.

"You want some food?" Taggert says. "I'll scramble you some eggs."

Benjy belches long and loud and shakes his head. "I'm good," he says. "Them beers are finally working."

Enough of this shit. Taggert leans forward in his chair and scratches his neck. "So back to Mando," he says.

"Our man Mando."

"What's the deal?"

"Well, they want to work with you."

"That's good."

"The problem is, they want you to take a million instead of five hundred thousand, meaning you've got to come up with a hundred fifty grand instead of seventy-five."

Taggert winces. "The fuck's that about?"

"Truthfully?" Benjy replies. He flicks the tab on his beer can with his thumb. "Mando told them they should make you prove you got what it takes. They don't want to play with low rollers."

If Mando was here, Taggert swears he'd cut his heart out. It's clear that the guy has a hard-on for him. Goading him into balling those chicks, telling ghost stories in the middle of a negotiation, and now this. Taggert keeps his face blank, though, says nothing. This Mando could be Benjy's cousin or his uncle. Benjy could be feeding him all kinds of information. Never trust a middleman. He's got no loyalty to anybody but himself.

One hundred fifty thousand dollars means that every bit of Taggert's ready cash will be tied up in this one deal. If something goes wrong, he'll be wiped out. Flat busted at fifty-five years old. That's the kind of hole you don't climb out of. On the other hand, if he doesn't go for it, no matter what excuses he makes, what it really comes down to is that Kentucky won out in the end. That at heart he's as chickenshit as any of them back there who kept digging coal even though they knew it was killing them, because they didn't have the balls to take a chance on anything else.

He looks past Benjy at the cracked walls and sagging, stained ceiling of the kitchen, at the ancient stove, the faucet dripping rusty water. It's going to take money to finish the new place, and big scores like this one don't come together every day. If he really wants what he thinks he wants, he'll have to swallow his pride, put up the money, and show everybody that he's ready to sit at the grown-ups' table.

Olivia's voice grows louder as she approaches the kitchen door. No time to think. "Make the call," Taggert says right before she steps inside. "Tell them I'm in."

Olivia enters and walks over to the table. "Benjy," she says. "When'd you get here?"

"I don't know. An hour ago?"

She's wearing her cowboy hat and a pair of short shorts. Taggert grabs her arm and pulls her onto his lap. He's feeling better already, full of the relief that comes after a hard decision has been made.

"Where you been?" he asks her.

She struggles playfully to get away from him. "Down at the bunkhouse," she says. "Watching TV with Virgil."

"Watching what?"

She breaks free and backs out of his reach. "Nothing," she says. "What are you guys talking about?"

"Nothing," Taggert replies, imitating her voice.

"Yeah, right," she snaps. Before he can say anything else, she storms out of the kitchen. Goddamn, Taggert thinks. The bitch gets an idea in her head and will not let it go. She won't be satisfied until she's his right hand on this thing.

He waits until he hears the bedroom door slam, then says to Benjy, "What about the transfer? How's that go down?"

VIRGIL WALKS TO the barn after dropping Olivia off at the house. Taggert wanted him there an hour ago to help Miguel, but fuck that noise. For the past week the guy's been ordering him around like he signs his check. This is Virgil's last day at the ranch though—tomorrow morning he's riding back to L.A. with T.K. and Spiller—so the old man can kiss his ass.

He passes the goat pen and chicken coop and enters the barn. Miguel has cleared a space around the pit to accommodate spectators, and now he's dragging the blood-stained square of green carpet out of the enclosure. Virgil gives him a hand tossing it. Miguel points out a new piece of rug, beige this time, and they position it in the pit. Virgil tacks it down with a few nails. It feels good to swing a hammer. Maybe he'll do construction when he gets back to Tampa. Decent money in that.

One of the dogs begins to bark until Miguel yells something in Spanish that shuts it up. Miguel is setting up a bar on the workbench. Vodka, tequila, bourbon, plastic cups. A big tin washtub holds beer.

Virgil sweeps the floor around the pit and arranges a few folding chairs. The dust in the air tickles his nose and makes him sneeze. He goes to the tub and pulls out a beer. There's no ice yet, so it's warm, but he pops it open and takes a swig anyway.

Moving to the cages, he walks up and down in front of them. He's been helping Miguel feed and water the dogs for the past few days, and it feels like they're getting to know him. They don't bark at him as much as they used to and sometimes even seem happy to see him.

He stops in front of Butcher Boy's pen. The dog is hunched in the shadows, his single yellow eye a baleful beacon. Virgil kisses at him but gets no reaction. He crouches and calls, "Come here, boy," and still the dog doesn't stir. It makes no sense. Just yesterday he let him pet him and everything.

Virgil pokes his fingers through the mesh and wiggles them. Suddenly, silently, the big red dog launches himself. All Virgil sees are teeth flying toward him out of the darkness. He yanks his fingers free and tumbles backward as Butcher Boy slams into the gate with a snarl.

Virgil scrambles to his feet and examines his hand, ignoring Miguel's laughter. A single puncture wound, where the dog nipped the tip of his middle finger, oozes blood. Virgil pops the finger into his mouth and sucks on it.

"You see that shit?" he asks Miguel. "Motherfucker charged me."

"He's fighting tonight," Miguel says. "He's nervous."

The kid's nutty, thinks dogs are almost human. He told Virgil the other day that they talk to each other like people do.

Virgil returns to the tub to replace the beer he dropped when he fell.

"They ever bite you?" he asks Miguel.

"I don't make them mad," Miguel replies. He picks up the beer can Virgil left in front of the cage and, after turning it over to make sure it's empty, drops it into the trash bag he's carrying.

"One bited the boss once though," he says.

"Who, Bill?" Virgil says. "That must have been great."

Miguel glances at the open door of the barn to make sure nobody is in earshot, then leans in close to Virgil and says, "No, man, no. It was very bad."

He motions Virgil to the workbench. "I was only helping then," he continues. "This other guy, Oscar, was taking care of the animals. The dog, Henry, he bited the boss's hand. The boss says it was because he came from a black man.

"He make me and Oscar and Spiller hold the dog, then"—he picks up a pair of pliers off the bench and waves them around—"he pull all that dog's teeth."

"That's fucking sick," Virgil says.

"It was, man. So bloody, and the dog escreaming so loud."

"My sister didn't see it, did she?" Virgil asks. He can't imagine Olivia standing by and letting that happen.

"No, she was in the house," Miguel says. "Then the boss, he give Oscar a gun and tol him to take Henry away and kill him. But Oscar can't do it because he love that dog, you know?"

"Miguel!" Taggert calls from outside. Miguel freezes like he's been caught stealing, then rushes to the door. Virgil follows.

T.K. and Spiller have arrived in T.K.'s Explorer. Taggert and his guy, Benjy, are standing with them next to the truck.

"Yes, boss?" Miguel says.

"Unload this before it melts, throw it on those beers."

T.K. opens the rear door of the Explorer. The cargo area is filled with bags of ice. Miguel trots down the road to the truck without another word, his feet kicking up little dust blooms.

Virgil ducks inside the barn before Taggert calls on him to help. He feels like hiding somewhere until tomorrow morning, when he plans to be out by the Explorer as soon as the sun rises, all packed up and ready to go.

OLIVIA LEANS BACK in the car seat on the patio of the house, exhales loudly, and tries again to thread her needle. She snagged the sleeve of her favorite blouse on a barbed-wire fence the other day and has decided to mend it so she can wear it tonight.

The problem is, she can't sew. Mama Juju tried to teach her, but Olivia didn't want to learn anything from that bitch. She knows how you start though—slide the thread through the tiny hole at the top of the needle—and the rest of it can't be that difficult if every old lady in the world can do it.

Slowly, slowly. She doesn't understand why her hands are shaking so much. It's been hours since her morning coffee. Maybe she should smoke another joint. A drop of sweat rolls down her nose and hangs off the tip. The thread approaches the hole, bumps the edge once, twice, then slips through. She ties the ends of the length of thread together—she remembers that much—and picks up the blouse to examine the tear more closely.

The screen door opens, and Taggert steps out onto the patio. Ever since Benjy left a few hours ago, he's been busy getting ready for tonight's dogfight, ordering Virgil and Miguel around, sprinkling the parking area with water to keep the dust down, and changing the propane tank on the grill. He pops open a Dr Pepper and sits down beside Olivia on the car seat.

"I'm thinking I ought to yank another case of burgers out of the freezer," he says. "Don't want to run out like last time."

Olivia shrugs, not looking up from her sewing. She can tell he's excited about having his friends come to the ranch, and he loves fighting those dogs, but she'll be damned if she's going to buy into it. Not when he hasn't said word one about the counterfeit bills since that night in the bedroom, even though he promised to fill her in on what happened at the meeting with the Mexicans. And what were he and Benjy talking about earlier, in the kitchen? The fucker probably thinks that if he puts her off long enough, she'll say, "Oh, well," and give up her demand for a cut, but he's dead wrong.

"You gonna chop the onions and lettuce and stuff?" he asks.

"Soon as I finish this," she snaps, letting him know she's irritated with him. She jabs the needle through the blouse, draws her first stitch tight. It looks like crap, the fabric all puckered, and the second is even worse. She has to stop herself from ripping the blouse to pieces.

The sun drops below the patio's awning, and a wave of warm red light washes over her and Taggert. Pretty soon the surrounding hills will take on that color as the day slowly dies. Taggert leans back in his chair and fiddles with his glasses, which are hanging around his neck.

The goats are crying down at the barn. T.K. and Spiller toss a football in front of the bunkhouse, and their occasional exclamations drift lazily up the hill a second or so after they leave their mouths, a disconcerting trick of distance.

"Okay, so listen," Taggert finally says. "Tell me what you think of this." He leans forward and motions for her to do the same, then uses his index finger to draw two parallel lines about a foot apart, one above the other, in the dust that covers the patio. “That’s Interstate 15,” he says, pointing at the top line, “and that’s the 40.”

He scratches another line, this one joining the midpoint of the top line to the midpoint of the bottom line. “This here’s a little dirt road that runs between the two freeways through a patch of desert called the Mojave Preserve,” he says. “Nothing on it but an old ghost town.” He makes a dot on the new line, right in the middle. “Ghost town. Got it?”

Olivia nods.

“Now, come Tuesday, there’s two cars, ours and theirs,” Taggert continues. “Two cars, two people in each, no guns. That’s the setup. They’ve got one million in funny money, we’ve got $150,000 of the real stuff. They come down from the 15 on the dirt road, we come up from the 40, and we meet in the town.” He taps the dot. “An old post office, a couple of abandoned houses. No people, not for years. Just snakes and shit. So we meet there, make the exchange, then they drive out the way we came in, and we go out the way they came in. Done deal.”

Olivia examines the map. She can’t believe that Taggert is giving her so many details and wants to come up with something that’ll show him she’s on the ball. “What’s to stop them from coming in with twenty guys and a whole bunch of guns?” she says.

Taggert smiles. “Aha!” he says, then leans over and makes two new dots at both ends of the dirt road, where it intersects the freeways. “We’ll have a guy here, where the road meets the 15, to check their car, and they’ll have someone down at the 40 to inspect ours. If everything’s cool, our guy calls to let us know. Same with their guy and them.”

He sits up and rubs the dirt off his finger with his thumb, then sips his Dr Pepper.

Olivia continues to stare down at the map. The plan seems awfully complicated. "What's wrong with meeting in a parking lot somewhere?" she says.

Taggert shrugs. "Benjy said they're paranoid as shit about surveillance cameras and that this is the way they do things in Mexico. He said if I want in, it's how it's got to be."

"Well, I don't like it," Olivia says.

"The way I look at it, they're taking as big a chance as I am," Taggert says. "They don't know me from Adam either. We're all going into this with our dicks hanging out."

"Is it worth the risk?" Olivia asks.

Taggert nods. "Yeah. Yeah, it is. I've tucked my tail too many times, missed out on big scores because I was too goddamn cautious. This one's mine. I want it, and I'm going to get it. Now that doesn't mean I've got my eyes closed. At the first sign of anything fishy, I'm out. These guys seem like the real deal, though, and you know what, fuck it, I'm the real deal too."

Olivia picks up the blouse from her lap and begins sewing again. Her mind's not on the task though; it's just something to get her hands moving. Her heart is pounding as she says, "So what's my part in it?"

"Not this one," Taggert says.

"But you promised."

"I did not."

"You said—"

"I said I'd see if there was somewhere we could use you, and I'm sorry, but there isn't." He reaches over and squeezes her knee. "Something'll come along soon, though, I promise."

Olivia's disappointment instantly, uncontrollably swells into rage. She digs her nails into her palms and swallows hard.

Taggert sits there drinking his soda and staring out at a dust devil whipping across the yard. All kinds of junk is caught up in it—a Doritos bag, newspaper, part of a NO TRESPASSING sign. Olivia watches him watch the swirling column.

When the dust devil passes, Taggert turns to her and says, "What's that you're doing there?"

"Fixing a rip," she replies.

Holding out his hand, he says, "Let me see."

She passes him the blouse. He squints at her handiwork, then remembers his glasses on the chain around his neck and puts them on.

"This is all fucked up," he says. "Didn't your mom teach you anything?"

Olivia doesn't reply. She's got to hold back, not come at him with her claws out. Taggert reaches into his pocket for his knife and uses it to tear away her awkward stitches.

"Gimme the thread," he says. She hands it to him, and he unspools a length, runs the end of it through his lips and rethreads the needle in nothing flat. "Amazing, the shit you pick up in the joint," he says as he sets to work on the blouse.

When she can't control herself any longer, Olivia says, "I could go with you to the ghost town. All that's gonna happen is a few bags changing hands."

Taggert looks at her over the top of his glasses and says, "It's not gonna happen, babe. These Mexicans are macho motherfuckers, and they don't let their women get involved in their business. They're just waiting for me to fuck up, and I can't be throwing curveballs our first time out. Maybe later, when they trust me more, you can ride along, but not this time. No way. Put it out of your head."

He resumes sewing.

Olivia is so angry, she has to work hard to draw a breath.

The man's such a fucking liar. Tears sting her eyes, and she barely manages to get out, "It's always going to be something, isn't it?" without sobbing.

"Look, if this is about you having your own money, I'll start paying you for all the stuff you do around here," Taggert says. "Cooking and cleaning and everything."

Olivia springs to her feet and says, "I don't cook, Bill. I don't clean. All I do is fuck you. Is that what you're going to pay me for?"

Taggert looks up at her pleadingly. "Please, babe, not tonight," he says. "I got all these people coming and everything."

Olivia can't stand looking at his ugly face any longer, can't talk to him. She runs into the house, slamming the door so hard, the window in it cracks. Across the kitchen she goes, down the hall and into the bathroom, where she presses a towel to her mouth to muffle her screams of frustration.

16

Boone works the day shift at the bar, then gets on the road about six, headed east on the 10, after throwing an extra shirt and a toothbrush into a backpack and leaving the key to his bungalow with Amy so she can feed Joto. Off to visit an old Marine buddy, he tells her. The real deal is, he's going to find Taggert's place this evening, sleep somewhere in the Olds, then approach the guy tomorrow morning, have a little chat about dogs and such, see if he can shake anything out of him.

Traffic is heavy all the way to Pomona. Boone watches the sun sink lower and lower in the rearview mirror and listens to what passes for country music these days on the radio. He's nervous about what lies ahead, can't stop tapping his fingers on the steering wheel.

L.A.'s sprawl dries up somewhere past Banning, giving way to ugly scrubland and wind-scoured hardpan. Boone pushes the Olds to eighty-five as he zips past the outlet malls, the Indian casino, then drops into the Gorgonio Pass. The two tallest mountains in Southern California rise straight up from the desert to scrape the purpling sky on either side of the freeway, San Gorgonio to the north, San Jacinto to the south.

The hundreds of towering high-tech windmills arrayed in martial ranks on the surrounding hillsides and plains whirl silently, transforming the energy of the ceaseless wind into electricity. They're ominous in the half-light of dusk, a new species freshly risen from the sand pausing to gather strength before marching to the sea.

A mile or so past the turnoff for Palm Springs, Boone leaves the 10 and drives north on the 62, which passes through Yucca Valley and Joshua Tree before becoming the main street of Twentynine Palms. The little town is sandwiched between Joshua Tree National Park and the Twentynine Palms Marine Corps Air Ground Combat Center, the largest Marine base in the world, home to ten thousand jarheads and their families. It doesn't look to Boone that it's changed much since he and his unit came out here for war games when he was a grunt: the same barbershops offering cheap high and tights, the same tattoo parlors, the same fast-food restaurants, the same joyless cinderblock bars.

He pulls into a gas station to buy provisions for his car campout. A chime ding-dongs when he walks through the door, and the clerk, a ravaged old speed freak with a homeless tan and no front teeth, waves and calls out, "Hi, howdy, how you doing?"

The only other customer is a heavyset Indian woman pushing an empty baby stroller and wearing a T-shirt with the American flag and an eagle on it. She and the clerk talk about someone named Dodo, who just went to jail, while Boone picks up a bottle of water, two cans of Red Bull, a couple of Snickers bars, and two tuna sandwiches sealed in triangular plastic containers. That should get him through the night.

"And I'm gonna fill up on pump eight," he says to the clerk after the man rings up his purchases with trembling hands.

"Going rock climbing?" the clerk asks. A red USMC baseball cap is perched atop his greasy gray hair.

"Not this time," Boone replies.

"They got great rock climbing in the park," the clerk says. "Folks come from Germany, Japan, San Francisco."

"Fucking idiots," the Indian woman says. "You got a dollar for me, man? Something?"

"Goddamn it, Martha!" the clerk shouts. "Do not beg from the customers!"

Nope, things haven't changed much. Boone picks up the bag containing his supplies and says, "You two have a good evening."

The chime sounds again when he walks outside. The first stars are blinking in the sky. He flinches as something flits past his face. A bat, on its way to feed on the insects swarming around the station's lights. Martha comes out of the store while he's pumping his gas. She walks to the side of the building, hikes up her dress, and squats to pee.

THE MEN BEGIN arriving for the dogfights, their trucks and SUVs throwing up rooster tails of dust as they haul ass on the dirt road leading to Taggert's spread. Taggert sits on the patio with T.K. and Spiller and greets his visitors with handshakes and backslaps. A bunch of rednecks mostly, a few Mexicans, one black dude.

Before they showed up, Taggert pulled Virgil aside, pressed a couple of hundreds into his hand, and said, "You're working tonight. Miguel's going to be busy with the dogs, so you'll be making drinks and anything else I need you to do."

Virgil felt like telling him he was nobody's nigger but held his tongue. He doesn't want any trouble on his last night here.

"Virgil," Taggert calls now from the yard, where he's admiring a dog in a portable kennel in the back of a pickup. "Bring old Stank a beer." Stank, a fat, red-faced man in a cowboy hat, is the dog's owner.

Virgil gets up from his chair on the patio and walks to the cooler. Spiller is flipping burgers on the grill. "When you're done with that, I need more buns," he says.

"Yeah, yeah," Virgil replies.

T.K., sprawled on the car seat, says, "And then you can come over here and scratch my balls." He and Spiller laugh uproariously.

Virgil ignores them. He wonders what's wrong with Olivia. He hasn't seen her since this afternoon. When he asked Taggert about her, he said she was asleep, not feeling too good. They must be fighting again, because she was fine earlier.

Virgil claws a can of beer out of the ice and carries it to Stank.

"Thanks, son," the cowboy drawls around a mouthful of Red Man.

"Look at this dog, Virgil," Taggert says, motioning him to the truck bed. "What's his name again?" he asks Stank.

"Super Trooper."

Virgil bends to look into the cage. Inside, a tan pit bull with a black muzzle chews contentedly on a dried pig's ear.

"He's in the first bout tonight," Taggert says. "You should lay some of that cash I gave you on him. He's pretty much a sure thing."

"Maybe I will," Virgil says. It makes him uneasy, Taggert being so nice to him now after ignoring him completely since lighting him up with the laser sight.

Stank spits a big brown gob and scrapes dirt over it with his boot. Another man in a cowboy hat walks up and says, "Bill, where you keeping the whores tonight?"

"You're shit out of luck," Taggert says with a laugh. "Your sister never answered the phone."

Someone turns up a car stereo, blasting Guns N' Roses.

"Put some real fucking music on," Stank yells.

Virgil walks to the patio and is about to sit down when Spiller says, "Hey, man, I told you I need buns."

"Sorry," Virgil replies. He lets the screen door slam behind him on his way into the kitchen.

EVERYONE MOVES DOWN to the barn a little before eight. It's hot inside, steamy, even with a pair of big industrial fans going full tilt. Sounds are amplified in the cavernous space—the raucous banter of the men, the barking of the dogs—and Virgil has to strain to catch the orders shouted at him at the makeshift bar. He hands two beers to a couple of heavily tattooed bikers. The drinks are free and nobody's tipping, so he's not working too hard.

There are four bouts tonight. The first is between two forty-pound dogs, Stank's Super Trooper and Buck, a grizzle mix breed. The spectators gather around the plywood pit, and an old man in sunglasses and a Cubs cap works the crowd, taking bets.

"Who's next?" he shouts.

"Fifty on Buck," someone shouts back.

"You got it, baby. At three to two."

Virgil waves to attract the tout's attention and bets one of Taggert's hundreds on Super Trooper at two to one. Easy come, easy go. He stands on the workbench to get a better view as Stank carries the dog into the pit and sets him in his corner, facing the wall. Buck is brought in next, and men in the crowd shout for their favorites.

The referee, a Mexican with a long white goatee, stands next to the pit and yells, "Face your dogs."

Stank and the other handler turn the dogs so that they can see each other, gripping the animals tightly with their knees.

The dogs struggle to break free, eager to get to it. A high-pitched scream rises from deep in Buck's throat, and Super Trooper barks once.

Virgil leans in as the referee shouts, "Let go!"

The handlers release the dogs, and both animals charge hard to meet in the center of the pit in a tangle of teeth and fur. Buck clamps onto Trooper's ear and shakes hard, but Trooper ducks and manages to get a hold on Buck's front leg and flip him onto his back.

The dogs remain in this position for a minute or more—Trooper on Buck's leg, Buck on Trooper's ear—not making a sound, not moving except to tighten their grips. The crowd yells at them to fight, fight, for fuck's sake fight.

Buck makes a sudden grab for Trooper's nose and bites down on it. Trooper releases Buck's leg, which allows Buck to spring to his feet. He moves from Trooper's nose to his throat, gets a mouthful of loose skin, and Trooper takes hold of his ear. The dogs roll over and over joined this way, like some broken beast sprung from a nightmare.

Buck winds up pinned on his back against the wall of the pit. Thrashing wildly, he's able to grab Trooper's hind leg and take him to the carpet. Trooper, on *his* back now, clamps down on Buck's hind leg, up in the thigh area.

Again the dogs are locked in a stalemate. Buck gnaws on Trooper's leg, and Trooper gnaws on Buck's. Both dogs are breathing hard. Their eyes roll, and thick strands of bloody saliva dangle from their quivering jaws.

"Come on, Trooper," Stank yells, clapping his hands to encourage his dog. "Come on, boy."

A minute passes, three, five. The crowd grows more boisterous. Supporters of both dogs trade insults, and two men come to blows at the edge of the pit and are quickly separated. Dust kicked up by the spectators rises into the air, which has the primal tang of blood and whiskey. It's both thrilling and terrifying to watch the dogs act on savage instinct, a heady brush with an earlier time, a rawer state. Virgil feels like he's buzzed on some new drug. He stomps the workbench and whistles as someone yells, "Fight, you fucking curs."

Men drift to the bar for drinks during the lull, and Virgil hops down from his perch to serve them. Then a shout goes up, and all eyes swing to the pit. Virgil climbs onto the workbench again to see that the dogs have finally separated. Buck charges in and bites Trooper's chest, but Trooper wriggles out of it and takes Buck's hind leg again, shaking him hard, punishing him. Buck quails and tries to pull away.

In his attempt to flee, Buck turns his head and shoulders away from Trooper, and the ref shouts, "Turn! Handle your dogs." Stank and the other handler rush to the combatants. The men scoop up their animals, carry them to their respective corners and face them to the wall. Stank pours bottled water into Trooper's mouth, and the dog's tongue flaps greedily.

After a twenty-five-second rest, the ref calls for the handlers to bring the dogs around so that they're once again facing each other. The animals aren't as fiery as they were at the start of the bout. Both look tired, and Buck is bleeding from a wound on his hind leg and another on his snout.

Because he turned, Buck must now prove that he's still willing to fight, or the match will be stopped. A strip of duct tape on the carpet—the scratch line—divides the pit diagonally in two. In order for the bout to continue, Buck must cross this line within ten seconds on his way to engage Trooper.

"Let go!" the ref shouts, and Buck is released. The dog

races across the pit without hesitation, favoring his injured leg only slightly. As soon as he passes over the line, Stank releases Trooper.

The dogs slam into each other and swap holds, Trooper grabbing Buck and Buck shaking him off, Buck grabbing Trooper and Trooper shaking him off. The exchange continues for some time, triggering a new round of betting, the favorite being whichever dog is on top at that particular moment.

Suddenly, Buck is down with Trooper clamped to his throat. Trooper shakes his head, tearing through flesh and muscle. A jet of bright red blood shoots into his eye as he hits an artery, but he doesn't let go.

Buck's handler hurries over and kicks Trooper in the ribs in an attempt to back him off.

"Foul!" Stank bawls.

"Foul!" the referee echoes.

Stank charges Buck's handler head down, like an angry bull, and knocks him on his ass. A spectator leaps over the plywood wall into the pit to swing at Stank. The two men square off and exchange awkward, flailing punches to the delight of the crowd. Virgil adds his shouts to the chorus and flings his half-empty beer into the pit.

Buck's handler scrambles to his feet and approaches the dogs again. Taking hold of Trooper's hind legs, he pulls him off Buck and tosses him aside. Buck tries to stand, a gash in his neck spurting rhythmically. His handler gathers him up and rushes him out of the pit. Stank, meanwhile, has beaten his opponent to the ground and now grabs the exhausted Trooper and hoists him into the air as the ref declares the dog the winner of the bout.

The spectators stream out of the barn for fresh air and cigarettes. Virgil opens another beer and gulps down half of it to wash the dust from his throat. His ears are ringing from all the shouting, but he's stoked at having doubled the hundred he bet on the match. He drifts over to the kennels where Taggert's dogs are kept and stops in front of Butcher Boy's cage.

"What up, motherfucker?" he says.

The dog paces back and forth, unsettled by the noise and unfamiliar scents. Virgil kneels in front of the pen and pours beer onto his fingers. He presses his hand to the gate, and the dog glares at him with his one good eye before slinking over to lick his thumb.

"You like that, huh?" Virgil says. "Not gonna bite me now, are you?"

He dribbles more beer onto his fingers, and again the dog laps it up.

"Good boy," Virgil coos.

"What the fuck do you think you're doing?"

Virgil spins to find Taggert standing over him, his blank black eyes flashing with rage, like distant bombs exploding in the night.

"Nothing," Virgil replies quickly.

Bam. He's on his back on the ground, and for a few weird seconds he thinks he's been shot. Then the pain coalesces on the left side of his face, where Taggert's fist caught him, and his eyes gush tears.

"I should fucking kill you," Taggert rages. "What are you thinking, giving that dog beer when he'll be fighting in an hour?"

"I'm sorry," Virgil blubbers, more humiliated than hurt. Taggert draws back a leg to kick him, and Virgil curls into a ball, arms whipping up to protect his head.

The kick never comes. Instead, Taggert growls, "Get out of my barn, you worthless piece of shit."

Virgil crawls on all fours until he's beyond Taggert's range, then rises to his feet and sprints for the door.

The cooler air outside is like a reviving slap. He weaves through the loudmouthed drunks haw-hawing in front of the barn on his way to the house. His anger toward Taggert fills him with false courage. He'll burn the place down. He'll blow it to shit. He'll get a gun and shoot Taggert dead. Put bullets in both kneecaps to make him suffer, then another right between those evil-ass eyes of his.

BOONE PULLS OVER at the intersection of Amboy Road and Cholla, a dirt track leading to several properties set back in the hills to the east. The last trace of daylight is fading fast, and more stars pop into the sky every second. When he rolls down the window of the Olds, the smell of sage fills the car. He checks the address he got from Unc against the reflective numbers on the sides of the mailboxes lined up at the intersection and finds one that matches.

The original plan was to park somewhere nearby for the night, then visit Taggert's place bright and early tomorrow. Now that he's here, though, he's thinking why not take a walk up the road a ways, do a little recon? It can't hurt to get the lay of the land before putting himself into a potentially volatile situation. Makes good sense to have as much information as possible. And what else is he going to do to kill time tonight?

He decides he's got more reasons for doing something stupid than any man needs to have, so he continues along Amboy for a hundred yards or so before pulling onto the shoulder. After eating one of the sandwiches and drinking a Red Bull in the gathering dark, he stuffs his backpack with the water, a Snickers bar, a penlight, and a pair of binoculars.

He steps out of the car and slips his arms through the backpack's straps. Lifting the top strand of a sagging barbed-wire fence, he steps over the middle strand onto private property. The sandwich sits like a stone in his stomach as he trots along at double time, following the fence.

A half moon hanging just above the horizon provides enough light to navigate by, an eerie glow that permeates the sand and throws the chaparral into spiky relief. He stumbles once, crossing a rocky dry wash, and once he stops and spins around, certain he's being stalked by some kind of predator. Nothing shows itself, though, and he decides that the sound he heard must have been his own blood whooshing past his ears.

Upon reaching Cholla Road, he crouches in the moon shadow of an enormous Joshua tree to rest a minute and drink some water. He has no idea how far up the dirt track the turnoff to Taggert's place is. Could be a quarter mile, could be five. He glances at his watch. A little before nine. He'll walk for half an hour. If he hasn't reached the ranch by then, he'll turn back and fly blind tomorrow.

The whine and clatter of a vehicle approaching from the direction of the ranch breaks the silence. A pair of headlights rise like twin suns, and Boone hides behind the Joshua tree and closes his eyes to protect his night vision. A pickup races past in a swirl of dust. Its taillights flash as the driver stops briefly at the intersection before swinging out onto Amboy Road, headed toward town.

Boone resumes his trek, paralleling Cholla now, but keeping a safe distance from the road, in case of more traffic. Five minutes of walking brings him to the crest of a low rise and a narrower road that branches off Cholla and snakes up another hill toward a cluster of structures awash in white light, a bright oasis wrested from the surrounding darkness. The numbers nailed to a post at the turnoff match those on the mailbox below. It's Taggert's place.

Boone moves out into the desert away from the road and drops to his knees to scan the compound with his binoculars. Some sort of gathering is in progress. Dusty pickups and SUVs are parked helter-skelter all over the property, and groups of men mill about in front of what looks to be a barn. There's another permanent structure, a house, and also a mobile home, a small trailer, and a corrugated steel water tower.

The breeze shifts toward Boone, and borne upon it are scraps of sound: the rhythmic rise and fall of boisterous conversations; barking dogs; a man's jagged laughter, the kind that cuts through everything else. Unc said that Taggert hosted dogfights, and that must be what's going on tonight.

Boone knows he should turn back, steer clear of the commotion, but he's come this far already, and it shouldn't be too difficult to sneak up to the perimeter of the compound for a closer look. If he breaks off now, he's going to regret it as soon as he gets back to the Olds, see it as a failure of nerve. Cursing his bullheadedness, he tightens the backpack's straps, ducks low to the ground, and sets off at a jog toward the ranch.

17

The second match of the evening is about to begin. Two twenty-five-pound dogs, Tombstone and Scarface. Spiller throws a hundred on Tombstone at two to one, even though it's the dog's first fight. He wants to make back the fifty he lost on Buck.

The kid, Virgil, isn't at the bar like he's supposed to be, so Spiller helps himself to two cans of beer and pushes his way to the wall of the pit as the ref calls for the handlers to face their dogs.

Scarface is a nervous black wriggler who bounces up and down between his handler's knees. Tombstone, on the other hand, stands stock-still, no barking, no whining, eyes locked on his opponent. A real killer, Spiller's sure. This one is definitely in the bag.

"Let go!" the ref shouts.

"Tear him up, Tombstone!" Spiller yells.

The dogs meet in the center of the pit. After a few minutes of exchanging holds, Scarface grabs Tombstone's chest and flips him onto his back. Tombstone wriggles free but turns while doing so.

Spiller claps his hands and says, "That's okay. That's just fine," as the handlers return the dogs to their corners.

Twenty-five seconds later they face the dogs again. Tombstone is released first and races for the scratch line. Before crossing it, though, he veers suddenly to the left, leaps over the pit wall, and sprints for the barn door, dodging the kicks and stomps of angry spectators.

Spiller howls along with the rest of the crowd as Scarface is named the winner. Fucking Tombstone turned out to be nothing but a two-balled bitch. Spiller slams his fist into the wall of the pit and snorts at his luck. T.K. pops up beside him and waves a fan of twenties in his face.

"Always bet on the black," he taunts.

"Go fuck yourself," Spiller replies.

He pops open his second beer and makes his way through the crowd to the door. Time for a piss. On his way out he passes Taggert and Miguel. Taggert's all worked up. One of his dogs is fighting in the next bout, and he'll be handling him.

"What about the first-aid kit?" Taggert asks the kid.

Miguel grimaces and fidgets.

"What?" Taggert says.

"I left it in the trailer," Miguel replies.

"Well, get the fuck over there," Taggert says. "But first, grab me a bottle of water from the box by the bench."

Spiller decides then and there to bet against Taggert's dog. It's only a hunch, but a strong one, the kind he's always reminding himself to listen to.

In front of the barn men drink and smoke and bullshit as they wait for the next fight to start. At the edge of the ragged circle of light cast by the bulb over the barn door, Spiller comes upon a small group set apart from the rest: two men standing and one sitting in the dirt, cradling a bloody dog. The dog is Buck, the man holding his lifeless body, his handler.

"You did everything you could," one of the standing men says.

"I know," the handler replies. A few tears have blazed muddy trails down his cheeks.

"He was a toughie," the other standing man says. "Game right to the end."

"He sure was," the handler says.

Pathetic, Spiller thinks. Crying over a fucking dog, an animal that eats its own shit.

He moves past them into the moonlit scrub in search of a private spot to take a leak. His heart shudders as he thinks about all the critters out there hunting under cover of darkness. Coyotes, mountain lions, snakes. Better to stay close to the light than be attacked by a rabid possum. Who cares if anybody sees?

He tilts his head back as he pisses. There are so many stars in the sky, it makes him woozy, and he almost topples over. He surveys Taggert's spread, and something catches his eye over near the little trailer where Miguel stays, movement in the chaparral.

He shakes off and buttons his jeans, squinting for a better look. Yup, yup, there it is. A figure dressed in dark clothing creeps out of the shadows to try the door of the trailer. Finding it unlocked, he opens it and slips inside.

Spiller jumps at the sound of approaching footsteps and turns to see Miguel running up the path to the trailer to fetch the first-aid kit. He almost shouts a warning, but why spook the prowler and scare him off? It'd be much better to catch the guy and bring him to Taggert. That'd for sure be worth a few extra points on the next job.

He slips his Hawg from his ankle holster and moves deeper into the brush, keeping low and to the darkness, any fear of marauding animals shunted aside as greed takes over.

* * *

BOONE MAKES A final dash to a small trailer at the edge of Taggert's compound and squats beside it. He's fifty yards from the barn now and can clearly hear the conversations of the men gathered there. It's a dogfight, as he suspected. The talk is of bets won and lost, grand champions, and spectacularly violent past matches.

Boone lifts his binoculars to his eyes and glasses the rest of the property. The house is quiet, as is the mobile home. Maribel said that Oscar lived in a trailer on the ranch where he worked. Could be the one he's leaning against right now. Might as well take a look inside, see what there is to see.

He pushes himself to his feet and runs for the door, exposed for a long second to any roving eyes in the crowd. Nobody calls him out, so he ducks in the shadow cast by the water tower and reaches up to knock lightly on the door. No answer. He tries the knob, which turns easily, then opens the door and slithers inside.

Pulling the door shut behind him, he crouches in the darkness, sweat dripping off his face, and flashes back to the cabinet-shop burglary in Oildale. All the years since have taught him nothing. Here he is again, sneaking around somewhere he shouldn't be, fear drying his mouth and straining the muscles in his neck.

He thumbs the penlight and cups the beam to contain it. The trailer is tiny, even smaller than Morrison's. Just enough room for a two-burner propane stove, a sink, and a narrow bunk. It's clean, though, immaculate even. Bed made, clothes hanging in the small closet and folded neatly in the drawers of a built-in dresser, cans of beans and Styrofoam cups of ramen noodles stacked in the cupboard. A picture of the Virgin of Guadalupe shares a wall with a magazine shot of a Ferrari.

Boone picks up a Spanish Bible off the counter. A photo slips from between the pages and falls to the floor. He snatches it up, shines his light on it. A Polaroid of Oscar, Maribel, and little Alex. Looks like it was taken at a barbecue. Boone rides a momentary rush. He's done it, definitely established that the kid was here.

The door rattles. Someone is coming in. Boone switches off the flashlight, but there's nowhere to hide. As soon as the door opens, he reaches out and grabs the shirt of the figure standing on the threshold, yanks him inside. Driving the intruder backward until he flops onto the bunk, Boone pins him to the mattress with a knee to the groin and a hand pressed to his mouth.

In the dim light filtering in from outside he sees that he's jumped a kid, Mexican or something. The boy doesn't struggle, just lies there looking up at him with big, scared eyes.

"I'm not going to hurt you," Boone says. "Okay?"

The kid nods once.

"I'll take my hand away now, let you up," Boone says.

The kid nods again, and Boone lifts his palm from his mouth. When the boy doesn't raise holy hell, Boone backs off and allows him to sit on the edge of the bunk. The kid rubs his lips, his eyes locked on Boone. Boone picks up the photo of Oscar and Maribel and shows it to him.

"You know who this is?"

The kid shakes his head no.

"It was in your Bible."

"Thas not my Bible," the kid replies.

"Whose is it?"

The kid wrinkles his nose, a nervous tic. "Some guy use to work here," he says.

"Oscar? Oscar Rosales?"

The kid looks down at the floor and nods. Boone moves in on him to intimidate him some.

"What happened to Oscar?" he asks.

"He quit. Went away."

"Why? Why'd he quit?"

The kid begins to fidget, his knee bouncing uncontrollably. "I got to get back," he says. "The boss is waiting."

"Taggert?" Boone says.

The kid nods again.

Boone realizes that any chance of stealth has been blown. As soon as he lets the kid go, there'll be nothing stopping him from running to Taggert and reporting what happened here. When Boone returns tomorrow, Taggert will be ready for him, loaded for bear. Either that or he'll make himself scarce. Better to confront him now. With all these people around, things can only get so wild.

"Take me to Taggert," Boone says to the kid.

"I got to get the first-aid kit," the kid replies, gesturing toward his bed.

"Go on," Boone says.

He watches as the boy slides a plastic storage tub from under the bunk. The kid then moves to the door, opens it, and steps outside. Boone is right on his heels.

Boone has barely cleared the trailer when a donkey kicks him in the head, almost sending him to his knees. He sees a little redheaded turd with tattoos and a ponytail draw back a length of pipe for another swing and throws up an arm to deflect it, but his reflexes have been scrambled by the first whack, and the pipe slams into his skull above his ear.

The stars overhead grow painfully bright, then abruptly die, like someone blowing out a candle. Boone crumples onto the sand, and the last thing he hears before he slips away is a dog's angry bark.

Olivia is holed up in the bedroom, guzzling rum and fuming over being duped again. It's time to face the fact that Taggert is never going to let her join the crew. She has the TV up so loud, to drown out the noise from the dogfight, that she almost doesn't hear the knock at the bedroom door. Lowering the volume with the remote, she calls out, "What?"

Her brother slips into the room. His eyes are red and swollen, like he's been crying, and there's a walnut-size lump on his left cheek that's on its way to purple.

"What happened?" Olivia asks as Virgil sits on the edge of the bed.

"Your boyfriend worked me over."

"What do you mean? What for?"

Virgil shrugs. "He caught me messing with one of his dogs."

He tries to shake Olivia off when she grabs his chin, but she bats his hand away and turns his face toward her to get a better look at his injury.

"That motherfucker," she says. "I'll get some ice."

Virgil reaches out to stop her. "Fuck that," he says. "I'm here to tell you something. You're gonna be mad I didn't tell you earlier, but I couldn't."

A numbness spreads through Olivia, moving up from her toes to her legs to her stomach. It's something that happens whenever she knows she's about to hear bad news.

"Go on," she says.

Virgil launches himself off the bed and walks toward the TV but spins around to look at her with frightened eyes before he gets there.

"Eton's dead," he says in a loud whisper.

Olivia half smiles, not wanting to believe what she heard. "What?"

"Spiller and T.K. killed him."

"Why?"

"Something about some money he owed Bill," Virgil says. "T.K. and Spiller came to collect and told Eton he had to get out of the house. He freaked and pulled a gun, and they blew him away."

Olivia gasps and feels the first sting of tears. She squeezes them back, though, because she's done crying. She doesn't think she'll ever cry again.

"They were going to kill me too, but I remembered that Bill was your boyfriend," Virgil continues. "They called Bill, and he told them to bring me here. He warned me not to say anything to you about what happened; said he'd kill me if I did."

Olivia starts to stand, then crumples back onto the bed. The son of a bitch goes on and on about how much he loves her and how close they are and then kills one of the only people who's ever been decent to her. Everything inside her is twisting and turning into new configurations. She's made of stone now; she's made of steel.

"That's it," she says, straightening up.

"What?" Virgil replies.

"I'm not letting him get away with this."

Virgil's eyes widen, and he talks very fast. "Okay, fine, yeah. But whatever you're doing, wait till I'm gone. I've got a clean shot out of here tomorrow. Don't fuck it up for me."

"We're both leaving," Olivia says. "Tonight."

"No, Olly, come on."

"Stop being such a little bitch."

Olivia grabs Virgil's arm and pulls him with her as she hurries out of the bedroom and down the hall to a walk-in closet. She uses a stepladder inside the closet to climb to a panel in the ceiling. Sliding the panel aside, she reaches into a crawl space and brings out a sawed-off shotgun, which she passes down to Virgil, and a Glock. She replaces the panel and turns to a shelf for a box of nine-millimeter rounds and some shotgun shells.

Then it's back to the bedroom. She picks up Taggert's cargo shorts off the floor and sticks her hand in the pocket, coming out with his keys.

"We'll take the F-150," she says. "As soon as everyone leaves, we'll get the fuck out of here."

"Let's go now, while he's busy," Virgil says.

"I'm gonna talk to him first," Olivia says. "I want him to know why I'm splitting."

Virgil holds the shotgun gingerly, as if he'd like to pass it off to someone else. "Don't be stupid because you're mad at him," he says. "The guy's a psycho."

Olivia snatches the shotgun away from him. "Go on then," she says. "I don't need you."

"That's not what I'm saying," Virgil whines.

"So you're with me?"

"We're not gonna kill him, are we?"

"I don't think so," Olivia says.

"Swear."

Olivia smirks and says, "I swear."

Virgil holds out his hand for the shotgun, and she passes it back to him.

"Get your clothes and shit together so we'll be ready," she says. "But be cool. Don't let anybody see you."

Virgil hesitates in the hallway outside the bedroom. He opens his mouth to say something, then decides against it and heads for the front door.

Olivia sits on the bed, drops the magazine out of the Glock and begins filling it. She had a cop boyfriend once who taught her all about guns—another dirtbag, another liar. Ended up using her as bait when he ripped off dope dealers. Motherfuckers are all the same, cops or criminals.

Her heart feels like it's beating way too fast. She lifts a hand to her chest and presses down hard, as if she could calm it that way. Doesn't help, though, so she goes back to what she was doing, picking up another round off the bedspread and shoving it into the magazine.

18

Taggert sees Miguel enter the barn carrying the first-aid kit and signals the referee to start the match.

"Boss," Miguel says when he reaches the pit. "Spiller—"

Taggert cuts him off. "Where the fuck you been?" The referee is waving him over, so, without giving the kid time to answer, Taggert leads Butcher Boy into the pit and turns him into his corner.

Butcher Boy's opponent, Cisco, is a buckskin dog with a blaze on his forehead and a butterfly nose. His owner is some loudmouth from Porterville, some used-car dealer. Both dogs weighed in at forty-five pounds.

Taggert looks up, takes in the crowd, and feels nothing but disdain. A pack of jokers sloshing beer on each other, screaming nonsense, playing grab-ass. They don't deserve to watch a warrior like Butcher Boy fight.

"What's he gonna do, that one-eyed cur?" one of them shouts. "I'll take Cisco at any price."

They win a hundred bucks, lose a hundred, go home and sleep it off. Not one of them understands what they're witnessing. This is a contest where gameness—the mysterious quality that drives some dogs to get to their feet even after being hurt, that sends them charging again into the fray—often triumphs over brute strength. Taggert identifies with this. He's never been the smartest or the richest or the toughest, but he's also never backed down from a fight, and he always gives as good as he gets.

The ref calls for him and the car salesman to face their dogs. Taggert swings Butcher Boy around and feels him tense at the sight of his opponent across the pit. He squeezes the dog tighter with his knees and whispers at him to calm down, but Butcher Boy lunges anyway, and Taggert has to grab the scruff of his neck to stop him, pulling him back so that just the dog's head protrudes from between his legs.

When the order to release the dogs comes, Butcher Boy streaks across the carpet and pounces on Cisco before the other dog can build much momentum. He grabs Cisco's throat in his jaws but gets only flesh, and Cisco is able to shake him off.

The dogs trade holds for a bit—noses, ears, legs—tiring each other out. Butcher Boy eventually clamps onto the back of Cisco's neck while Cisco takes hold of Butcher Boy's front leg. They remain locked together like this for almost ten minutes, both dogs occasionally jockeying for better leverage but neither able to gain an advantage.

Taggert shouts encouragement. "Sic, sic, sic," he hisses. He wipes the sweat from his forehead with the palm of his hand and backs into the dog's corner.

"Give me some water," he says to Miguel, who is stationed on the other side of the plywood wall. Miguel passes him a plastic bottle, and he takes a swig.

"Boss," Miguel says.

"Not now," Taggert snaps, eyes on the fight.

Cisco suddenly releases Butcher Boy's leg and rolls over in an attempt to dislodge the dog from his neck. He's successful but turns his head in the process. The ref calls it, and Taggert darts in to grab Butcher Boy and carry him to his corner.

The dog is panting, tongue hanging out, sides heaving, but it's still all Taggert can do to keep him from running across the pit to engage Cisco again. He dribbles water into the dog's mouth and aims a portable fan at his muzzle.

He and the car salesman face the dogs again, and the salesman releases Cisco, who crosses the scratch line without hesitation. Taggert looses Butcher Boy, and the dogs battle for position, biting each other but not hanging on. Cisco eventually grabs Butcher Boy high on a hind leg, and this time it's Butcher Boy who's called for a turn.

Per the rules, Taggert stands by until Butcher Boy manages to twist himself out of Cisco's leg hold, then scoops him up and returns him to his corner. There's blood on the leg, and when Taggert squeezes it, the dog yelps and snaps at him. It's not broken, but the bite is deep.

"Don't worry," Taggert whispers. "You'll have another chance at him."

Now it's Butcher Boy who must cross the scratch line within ten seconds. He springs from between Taggert's legs as fresh as the first time and rockets toward Cisco, who balks slightly upon his release but then moves forward to meet Butcher Boy's charge. Butcher Boy barrels into him head-on and sweeps him off his feet. The momentum carries both dogs into the wall of the pit with a loud bang.

Butcher Boy chomps down on Cisco's right front leg at the joint, and a sickening *crack* elicits a groan from the crowd. Cisco turns with a yelp and struggles to escape, but Butcher Boy holds on and shakes his head, doing even more damage.

Taggert crouches on the carpet, ready to rush in and pull

Butcher Boy off Cisco when the salesman throws in the towel, but the concession doesn't come. Butcher Boy eventually releases the leg, and Taggert and the salesman retrieve their dogs and return them once again to their corners.

Now, Taggert thinks, the salesman will surely call for the fight to be stopped, his dog being in no shape to continue. When it's time to face the animals, however, the salesman brings Cisco around. A few spectators protest, but the rules state that the fight will continue until one of the handlers concedes or until one of the dogs is unwilling or unable to cross the scratch line.

The ref, his face impassive, directs the salesman to release Cisco, who limps over the line on three legs, still game. Taggert releases Butcher Boy and feels like closing his eyes as the dog charges.

Butcher Boy hits Cisco hard, knocks him onto his side, and takes hold of an ear. Cisco doesn't make a sound as Butcher Boy drags him around the pit, just flails with his paws in an attempt to dislodge the other dog. The ear finally tears away from Cisco's skull, and he limps away. The ref calls the turn. Butcher Boy drops the bloody ear and moves toward Cisco, but Taggert grabs him before he can bite again.

"What the fuck is this?" he yells at the salesman.

"You handle your dog; I'll handle mine," the salesman replies.

More men demand that the fight be ended, but just as many call for it to continue. Cisco is released again, and again crosses the line on three legs, blinking away the blood in his eyes. Taggert knows now that the salesman is going to let the dog die in the pit. This sickens him, but the rules are what make the sport, so he opens his legs and looses Butcher Boy once more.

Butcher Boy tears into Cisco, and the buckskin barely puts

up a fight. Taggert's dog attacks at will, tearing flesh and drawing blood. Cisco rallies once to shake Butcher Boy off a thigh hold, but when Butcher Boy grabs his muzzle, he cries out and flees to his corner. The ref calls another turn.

Taggert glowers at the salesman as they face each other across the pit, dogs between their legs. Cisco is released first and stands dazed for a long second, looking about as if realizing for the first time where he is and what's about to happen to him.

The dog takes one faltering step toward the scratch line, two, then falls onto his side on the blood-stained carpet, his body spasming uncontrollably. The crowd shouts for him to get up, but it isn't to be. After ten seconds the ref declares Butcher Boy the winner of the match.

Taggert hands Butcher Boy off to Miguel and strides quickly across the pit, hands tightly fisted. He bumps the salesman with his chest and growls, "I ought to beat your fucking head in."

The salesman stands his ground. "If you ain't got the stomach for the game, don't play," he says.

"Oh, I got the stomach, you son of a bitch," Taggert says.

Two men come up behind Taggert and pull him away with shouts of "Whoa, now" and "Take it easy, boys." Taggert shrugs himself free of the peacekeepers and leaves the pit. He walks over to the kennels, where Miguel is using a garden hose and a plastic tub to wash Butcher Boy.

"How's the leg?" Taggert asks.

"A small cut."

Taggert reaches down to scratch the panting dog's head. "Make sure you put plenty of antibiotic on it," he says. "Hit him with a shot of penicillin too."

Spiller walks up and says, "I need to talk to you, boss."

"Here I am."

Spiller leans in close. "Some dude named James Boone broke into Miguel's trailer while he was fetching the first-aid kit. He grilled him about Oscar, then said he wanted to see you. I clocked him on his way out and tied him up."

"Oscar?" Taggert says. He turns to Miguel. "Why didn't..."

"I try, boss, remember," Miguel says.

"What'd he want to know?"

"He ask what happen to Oscar, and I tol him he quit a long time ago, thas all," Miguel says.

"Why the fuck did you tell him anything?" Taggert says.

"He surprise me, boss."

Taggert turns back to Spiller and asks, "A cop?"

"I don't think so," Spiller replies.

Taggert pats the dog once more. What the fuck is this about? Right when he's got this big deal coming down, there's an ambush around every corner. Suddenly, he's bone tired. He has the feeling that something big is barreling down on him and hopes to God he'll be able to get out of its way.

He watches the salesman carry the dead dog out of the barn, one hand clutching the scruff of its neck, the other between its hind legs. "We got one more bout," Taggert says. "We'll handle this after all these fuckers clear out."

BOONE SITS ON the edge of the bunk in the trailer. His wrists are bound behind his back with duct tape, his legs at the ankles. Another strip of tape covers his mouth. This is where he came to after being knocked unconscious by the redheaded turd. His skull hurts, and one eye is swollen shut. He has no idea how long he was out. The noise from the dogfight has quieted down, but it's still night.

The turd pokes his head through the door and tells the

Asian-looking black dude who's been silently watching Boone for the last hour or so to step outside.

" 'Bout time," the black dude grumbles. "It's hotter than a motherfucker up in here."

As soon as the door closes behind them, Boone twists his sweat-slicked wrists, working to stretch the tape and foul the adhesive. He's been at it every chance he's had since regaining consciousness and is close to being able to free himself. Then what, he doesn't know.

The door opens, and the turd enters the trailer, followed by the black dude, who points a gun while the turd flips open a knife and approaches Boone.

"Twitch, and I'll take your nose off," the turd says. He kneels in front of Boone and slices through the tape around his ankles.

"Get up," he says, backing away and pulling his own gun.

The black dude leaves the trailer, then Boone, then the turd, his pistol pressed hard into Boone's back. The cooler air outside clears Boone's head, sharpens him up. The goons put him in front, and they walk down a narrow path that runs between the trailer and the barn. If he tried to flee now, they'd drop him before he could take two steps, so he goes nice and easy.

The vehicles that were parked around the property earlier are gone, and the night is profoundly quiet, just the crunch of their footsteps on the hardpan. The turd shoves Boone toward the barn's tall sliding door.

Boone steels himself, ignoring the pain in his head, his throbbing eye. He feels like he used to when stepping into the ring for a bout, the same cold flutter in his stomach, the same single-mindedness. It's too late to put on the brakes now. All he can do is keep his guard up and use every opening to his advantage.

He steps into the barn, passes from the darkness into bright light. A tractor and other farm machinery, tools, a few folding chairs. Empty beer cans litter the floor. Looks like it was a hell of a party.

In the center of the space is a plywood enclosure. The pit. The man standing next to it in the Harley T and jeans is tall and muscular, with a silver goatee and thick silver hair. An ugly scar stretches across his throat like a permanent smile. He crosses his arms over his chest and motions with his chin to one of the chairs. The redheaded turd steers Boone toward it and orders him to sit.

The guy with the goatee grabs another chair and walks toward him. In one smooth motion he swings the chair up over his head with both hands and brings it down on Boone, catching him where his neck meets his collarbone. Boone grits his teeth behind the tape over his mouth as a red-hot bolt of pain zips down his right arm.

Unfolding the chair, the guy with the goatee sits backward on it, facing Boone. He reaches out and rips the tape from Boone's mouth.

"Mr. Boone," he rasps, something wrong with his voice. "You were trespassing."

"I'm here to see Taggert," Boone says.

"Did you think he lived in that trailer you broke into?"

Boone sits up straight, wriggles the fingers of his right hand. Everything seems to be working okay. "Taggert's got a reputation," he says, still pretending he hasn't figured out that this is the man. "I thought I'd check things out before showing up on his doorstep."

"Well, at least I know you're not a cop," Taggert says. "No cop's that stupid."

A dog begins to bark. The Mexican kid Boone jumped in the trailer hurries over to a row of cages set into the rear wall of the barn and whispers something in Spanish that quiets the animal.

"I'm Taggert," Taggert says. "What do you want to talk about?"

"Oscar Rosales," Boone says.

"Who?"

"Guatemalan kid. About eighteen. He turned up dead in L.A. last month, and his grandfather hired me to find out what happened."

"And what the fuck would I know about that?" Taggert says.

"People said he worked for you for a while. I was hoping you could fill in some blanks."

"People are wrong," Taggert says. "I never heard of him."

"Okay, then," Boone says. "So I'll get out of your hair, let you all go to bed."

The redheaded turd steps forward and says, "He's fucking with you, boss." He hands Taggert the photo of Oscar, Maribel, and the baby. "Miguel says he got this out of a Bible in the trailer. Had it in his pocket when I took him down."

Taggert strokes his goatee and stares at the photo, expressionless. He holds it out to Boone and says, "What were you going to do with this?"

"Give it to the kid's grandfather," Boone says. "Maybe get a little more money out of him."

"Or give it to the cops," the turd says.

"Come on, man," Boone says. "I'm a fucking felon, still on paper. You think I want anything to do with the cops?"

Taggert reaches into his pocket for a cigarette lighter.

Holding the Polaroid by one corner, he sets fire to it and watches it blacken and curl before dropping the charred remnants to the floor.

So much for talking my way out, Boone thinks. On to plan B. Two guns, twenty-five feet to the door, half a mile or so to the car in the dark, no flashlight. It isn't going to be easy.

Taggert stands, raises a booted foot, and slams it into Boone's chest, knocks him over backward.

Boone's head bounces off the floor, and his vision blurs. Three Taggerts stand over him, three boots move toward his throat. Taggert presses on his windpipe just hard enough to make breathing difficult and trigger a panic reaction in Boone when it seems like he won't be able to draw enough air into his lungs.

"I don't have time for this shit," Taggert growls.

He lifts his boot from Boone's throat and motions to his two goons, who each grab an elbow and yank Boone to his feet. Boone takes a deep breath and winds himself up. The next opportunity for escape that presents itself, no matter how crazy, he's got to go for. It's either that or die here tonight. He sees that now.

Taggert jerks his head in the direction of the pit, and the goons drag Boone toward it.

"Miguel, bring the dogs," Taggert says.

When the goons and Boone reach the pit, Taggert opens the gate so the goons can walk Boone into it. They all stand inside, on a square of bloodstained carpet.

"Give Miguel a hand," Taggert says to the goons. The black dude passes Taggert his Glock on his way out, and Taggert holds it at his side, ready to swing it up should Boone make a move.

"Really, man," Boone says. "I meant you no harm. Don't make this uglier than it has to be."

Over at the cages, Miguel leashes a fawn pit bull and hands him off to the redheaded turd. The animal strains at the tether as the turd walks him to the pit. The black dude is close behind with a second dog.

"Oscar died?" Taggert asks Boone.

Boone nods. "Infection, dog bites."

"He should have put that cur down when I told him to," Boone says. "Biggest mistake of his life, I guess."

"I guess," Boone says, sounding more angry than he meant to.

Taggert glares at him.

The dogs enter the pit, and Taggert takes the leash of the third one from Miguel. He's a big red one-eyed monster with fresh cuts on his muzzle that are still oozing blood. Taggert kneels beside the animal and strokes his flank.

"The difference is, I liked Oscar," he says to Boone. "I called the dogs off him after a while. I even let him take the dog he saved with him when he left. You, on the other hand, I don't give a flying fuck about."

Boone twists his wrists, desperately trying to free himself from the tape as Taggert unclips the leash from the red dog's collar and hisses, "Sic, sic, sic."

The dog charges, and Boone backs away until he's stopped by the plywood wall. The dog grabs his thigh, and the animal's teeth tear through the denim of his jeans to sink into his flesh. Boone grunts as he kicks once, twice, and manages to dislodge the animal, which immediately makes another run at him, this time latching onto his ankle. The sensation of teeth grinding against bone almost makes Boone puke, but he kicks again until he breaks the dog's hold.

The goons release the other dogs, and they bound across the pit to join in the attack. Boone deflects one by jamming his knee into the animal's head, but the other slips past and leaps up to bite him in the stomach, ripping away a chunk as it drops to the carpet.

The red dog suddenly collapses, his head a stew of blood and brains and bone. A gunshot rings in Boone's ears, and the other two dogs, spooked by the sound, flee the pit and scamper to their cages. Boone again works his wrists against the tape binding them, and it gives way at last.

Taggert and the goons are transfixed, their gazes locked on two figures standing in the doorway. Boone is on the redheaded turd in a flash. He punches him in the face, then slips behind him and throws an arm lock around his neck in order to use him as a shield. With his free hand he snatches the man's pistol from his belt and points it at Taggert.

"Everybody stop where you are!" a woman's voice shouts.

Boone turns to see a blond girl with a Glock and a kid with a sawed-off walking toward the pit. His injured ankle is about to give way, so he shifts all his weight to his other foot. He's doing his best to keep a clear head, but the pain from his injuries is making it difficult. Blood seeps from the bite in his stomach, soaking his T-shirt.

"Throw your guns over here," the girl says.

Boone waits for Taggert to toss the Glock before he underhands the turd's Hawg toward the girl. He keeps his arm tight around the turd's throat.

"You too," the girl says to the black guy.

"I got nothing," he replies. He lifts his shirt and turns around to show her.

"Make Miguel lock up the dogs," the kid with the shotgun says, sounding scared.

"Do it," the girl says.

The Mexican boy scurries to obey as Taggert opens his arms wide and says, "What the fuck are you doing, Olivia?"

"What the fuck I'm doing is leaving, Bill," Olivia says. She and the kid stop ten feet away, guns trained on Boone, Taggert, and the goons.

"Great," Taggert says. "But you didn't need to make this kind of mess—kill my dog, put a gun on me."

Olivia points her pistol at Taggert's face. "Oh, yeah?" she says. "What happened to Eton?"

Taggert shoots the kid a murderous glance, then drops his arms and shakes his head. "I'm sorry about that."

"You never would've told me, would you?"

"There was gonna be a right way, a right time."

"How much did he owe you?" Olivia says.

Taggert smirks. "None of your business."

"Come on, I want to know how much you killed my friend over."

Taggert raises a warning finger. "Whoa, baby, back it up. I didn't kill anybody. Your boy brought it on himself. He pulled a gun on Spiller and T.K., and they were just covering their asses."

"You could have sent me," Olivia says. "I'd have got you your money."

"For fuck's sake, Olivia," Taggert growls. He tenses up like he's thinking of rushing her.

Olivia turns to Boone. "How much do you owe him?" she asks.

"Nothing," Boone replies. It hits him that he's seen the kid before. At the Tick Tock. The dope dealer they rousted last week. "Someone hired me to look into the death of Oscar Rosales, a boy who used to work here," he continues. "I came to talk to Taggert about him."

"Jesus, Bill," Olivia exclaims. "You killed Oscar too?"

Taggert jerks his thumb at Boone and says, "This scumbag is full of shit. We caught him—"

Boone interrupts. "He put the dogs on Oscar just like he did me, and they tore him up. Oscar made it back to L.A., but the bites got infected. He didn't go to the hospital because he thought these guys were after him."

"We weren't after him," the turd says, wriggling in Boone's hold. "We let him go." Boone punches him in the ear and squeezes his neck tighter.

"That's enough," Olivia says. She points at the turd. "Let Spiller loose."

Boone pushes the turd away from him hard enough that he falls to the carpet. The guy gets to his feet and moves over to stand with Taggert and the black dude. Olivia calls the Mexican back from the kennels.

Boone recalculates the odds of a successful escape. Olivia and the kid are between him and the door. They're both armed, but there's a chance he could outrun their aim. It's risky, though, dizzy as he is, and on a bad ankle.

"What are you gonna do now?" Taggert says. He steps out of the pit and creeps toward Olivia and the kid. The kid tenses up, unable to conceal his fear of the man. "Kill me?" Taggert says. "Kill all of us?"

Olivia fires the Glock. The round throws up dust as it hits the floor a few inches in front of Taggert's boot, stops him in his tracks.

"I can't even tell you how bad you're fucking up," he says.

"On your bellies," Olivia says. "Everyone except you." She points her gun at Boone.

Taggert, Spiller, and the black dude obey reluctantly, stretching out facedown on the floor. The Mexican too.

"Think fast," the kid from the bar says as he tosses a roll of duct tape to Boone.

"Tie them up, hands and feet," Olivia says.

Boone approaches Taggert and kneels beside him. He unrolls a length of tape and wraps the man's wrists behind his back, then binds his legs together, from ankles to midshin. Next is Spiller, then the black dude, then the Mexican boy.

The kid from the bar picks up Spiller's Hawg and the Glock, shoves them into the pockets of his hoodie. Virgil. Virgil Cherry. Boone can still picture his ID. The dickhead doesn't seem to recall him though.

When Boone is finished with the tape, he stands and raises his hands.

Olivia lowers her Glock, more relaxed now. She walks to Taggert and flips him over so that he's on his back. Straddling him, one foot on either side of his chest, she squats until they're face to face and says, "Take a long last look at the best thing you ever had."

"Listen, baby," Taggert says.

"Nope, baby, nope, nope, nope." Olivia holds out her hand to Boone for the tape, tears off a piece and slaps it over Taggert's mouth. "No more bullshit." She dangles a set of keys. "We're taking the Ford," she says. "You owe me that much."

Taggert glares at her as she turns and struts toward the door.

"I guess you want to get out of here," she says to Boone.

"That'd be nice."

"Well, hurry your ass up. The last bus is leaving."

"Spiller has my wallet and keys."

"Get 'em," Olivia says.

Boone bends over Spiller, digs his stuff out of the guy's pocket.

"Be seeing you, dog," Spiller says, giving him a crazy smile.

"Can't wait," Boone replies. He limps over to join Olivia and Virgil. They walk out of the barn, and Virgil slides the door shut and secures it with a padlock. The three of them set off down the dirt road leading to the main house, Boone doing his best to keep up.

"What's your name?" Olivia asks him.

"Jimmy Boone," he replies.

"This is your lucky day, huh, Jimmy Boone?"

"Proof everybody gets one now and then."

A black F-150 is parked next to the ramshackle house. They put Boone in the backseat, Olivia slides behind the wheel, and Virgil rides shotgun. The truck starts with a roar, and Olivia backs up at high speed, barely missing the propane tank. A cloud of dust billows as she wheels around and steers for the main road.

She's driving too fast. The headlights bounce crazily over the scrub, the world beyond their reach as good as gone. A sudden dip lifts them all out of their seats and slams them down again. Boone feels like he's full of broken glass.

"I'm free!" Olivia yells with mock exuberance. "I'm free!"

A few minutes later, when they reach Amboy Road, Boone calls out to her to stop.

"What?" she says as she hits the brakes.

"My car's over there."

"Oh," she replies, a bit confused. "Okay."

Boone steps out and thanks them for the ride. The truck squeals onto the asphalt and speeds away.

Boone walks as fast as he can along the shoulder to his car. It won't take Taggert and his crew long to free themselves, and then there's always the chance the local cops might happen by and demand an explanation for his bloody clothes and bruises.

He lifts his T-shirt to check the bite on his stomach, but it's too dark to see much.

The pavement in front of him sparkles, and a roadside reflector flares to life. Not the moon. Too bright. He turns to look behind him and spies headlights. He's only twenty yards from the Olds, can see it there, on the side of the road, but he'll never reach it in time. With the sound of the approaching vehicle's engine growing louder, he veers into the chaparral and dives to the ground.

Taggert's truck races past and screeches to a stop next to the Olds.

"Jimmy," Olivia yells out the window. "Hey, Jimmy Boone."

Virgil hops down and runs around the truck to try the door of the car.

"Locked," he calls to Olivia.

"Where the fuck'd he go?"

Boone decides to show himself, find out what's going on. He stands and steps into the road.

Virgil points and says something to Olivia. She puts the truck in reverse and backs up to meet Boone, sticks her head out the window. "Were you hiding from us?" she says.

"I thought it was Taggert," Boone replies.

Olivia pushes her wispy blond hair out of her eyes and says, "This truck is going to be a lot more hassle than it's worth. We need a ride to L.A."

Boone hesitates. These two are clearly trouble, and this is nothing he needs to be mixed up in.

"Come on, dude," Olivia says. "We saved your ass."

"A ride," Boone says. "That's all. No fucking around."

"A ride," Olivia repeats, a little offended. "Meet me at the turnoff."

While Boone walks the rest of the way to his car, Olivia

executes a three-point turn and heads back to the intersection with Cholla. Virgil is waiting for Boone, leaning on the hood of the Olds when he reaches it.

"You're taking me and my sister?" Virgil says.

"Looks like it," Boone replies.

"So everything's cool."

"And let's keep it that way," Boone says.

The car starts right up, and he and Virgil drive to the turn-off. Olivia has wedged the F-150 sideways across the dirt road, blocking it. She's waiting beside the truck with a couple of suitcases and a gym bag at her feet, the shotgun and Glock in her hands.

She calls Virgil out of the Olds and passes him the sawed-off. Boone can't hear what they're saying to each other, but all of a sudden they raise their weapons and begin firing at the truck. Muzzle flashes light up the night as shotgun blasts shatter the windshield, the rear window, the headlights. Olivia puts a few rounds through the grill into the engine, then walks around and shoots all the tires.

Before the echoes of the shots bounce away, Olivia and Virgil have scooped up their belongings and piled into the Olds, Olivia in back high-fiving her brother in the passenger seat. They're sweaty and breathless as Boone pulls away.

"We fucked his shit *up!*" Virgil crows.

"Between his truck and his dog, that motherfucker's ruined for life," Olivia says.

Boone flicks on his brights. He should have stayed hidden by the side of the road. There's too much pent-up anger in these two, and not enough sense.

Virgil notices the supplies Boone purchased earlier. He reaches into a bag, comes up with a Snickers bar and says, "Can I have this? I'm fucking starving."

"Sure," Boone says. "Eat whatever you guys want."

He checks the rearview mirror every few seconds until they get through Twentynine Palms. By the time they hit the 10, Olivia and Virgil are sound asleep, her lying across the backseat, him crumpled openmouthed against the window, the Glock nestled in his lap.

19

TAGGERT IS SLUMPED IN A RECLINER IN HIS LIVING ROOM, NO television, no music, just silence and darkness, the drapes keeping out the morning. He can't sleep. Every time he starts to doze off, something twitches inside him and jolts him back to wakefulness.

He and Spiller and T.K. drove down to Amboy Road after they freed themselves last night and found the Ford shot full of holes but no sign of Olivia, Virgil, or Boone. Took them almost until dawn to tow the truck back to the ranch.

It hurts like hell, Olivia leaving. He can't believe it, but it does. His whole life he's laughed at guys who talked like this, but here he is with tears in his eyes over a woman. He chews his thumbnail and stares at a stain on the carpet. He should have told her about Eton right when it happened. If he'd played it that he was as broken up about it as she was, she might have gone for it. Instead, she busts in while he's dealing with Boone, and he looks like a lunatic.

She's probably halfway back to Florida by now, putting as many miles between him and her as she can. After the deal with the Mexicans is done, maybe he'll fly out and track her down. Fuck the truck, he'll say, fuck the dog. That'll surprise her. She knows how he usually handles those who cross him, so she'll realize how much she means to him. And then he'll surprise her even more. He'll say, "Let me make things up to you." God knows she's the kind of girl who'll let him try.

As for Boone, the guy can't prove anything about anything. If some heat does come down, the story is that he got bit while trespassing, while breaking and entering. He'll have Miguel take down the pit today just in case, then send him on a long trip to visit his family in Michoacán to get him off the property for a while. He can't trust the kid to keep his mouth shut if they put the screws to him.

He stands and stomps the feeling back into his feet. Time to pull his head out of his ass, take the wheel again. Drawing a glass of water in the kitchen, he walks out onto the patio. The sun is already high in the sky. Heat shimmers off the hard-packed earth of the yard, and insects sizzle in the chaparral. He strolls out to the gut-shot F-150 and runs his fingers over a bullet hole in the fender. The metal is warm to the touch.

Down the hill at the bunkhouse, T.K. and Spiller are preparing to drive back to L.A. They're supposed to stay at their places in town tonight, then drive back tomorrow evening, but Taggert's having second thoughts about that now.

As he's walking over to talk to them, the muffled *boom boom boom* of distant artillery drifts up from the Marine base. Live-fire exercises. They're almost constant these days, the corps busy turning out grunts for Iraq and Afghanistan. Poor bastards. The sound disturbs a raven perched on a nearby boulder. The big black bird croaks twice, then lumbers into flight with long, lazy flaps of its wings.

Spiller steps out of the mobile home when Taggert approaches. "Hey, boss," he says, raising a hand to cover the bruise on his cheek where Boone punched him last night. "We're about ready to roll. You want us to bring you anything back?"

"I've changed my mind," Taggert says. "You two are gonna hang out until we finish this thing."

T.K. appears in the doorway. "What's up?" he says.

"There's a lot less chance of something going wrong if we stick together."

"Ain't nothing gonna go wrong."

"Yeah, well, you'd have said that yesterday too, and look what happened."

T.K. isn't happy. "I got things going on," he grumbles.

"More important than this?" Taggert replies.

The guy doesn't answer, just stands there looking pissed until Spiller pipes up with, "Whatever you think's best, boss."

T.K. grunts and fades back into the bunkhouse. Taggert cuts him some slack this time, but the guy better adjust his attitude before he finds himself in a world of hurt.

"Come to the house in a bit," he says to Spiller. "I'll put on some steaks."

His knees feel a little creaky going up the hill. A cloud slides in front of the sun, and the light changes in an instant, the shadows losing their hard edges, all the shiny spots their piercing glare.

BOONE LIES ON the couch in his bungalow and listens to the purr of a nearby lawnmower. It's 9:00 a.m., a new day. He and Olivia and Virgil arrived back in L.A. about two. Olivia made a few calls but couldn't find anybody willing to take in her and her brother, so Boone let them crash at his place. He made it clear, though, that they'd be on their own in the morning.

They squawked some when he ordered them to hand over the weapons they were carrying, but he locked the pistols and the shotgun in the toolshed after wiping his prints off the Hawg he took from Spiller. Virgil then proceeded to try to drink all the beer in the fridge, and it was another hour before Boone got them settled in the bedroom.

Joto walks over and licks his face. He pushes the dog away and sits up. So many parts of him scream out in pain that he pauses for a minute to catch his breath: the cut he got during the tussle at Big Unc's, the knot on his head from Spiller's pipe. His collarbone is sore where Taggert hit him with the chair, and he can't lift his right arm without wincing.

Then there are the dog bites. The one on his thigh consists of two deep punctures accompanied by bruising. The one on his stomach is nastier, a raw, red hole a couple inches in diameter. He covered it with gauze when they got back, and that seems to have stopped the bleeding. The bite on his ankle doesn't look too bad, but the joint buckles when he stands, so he assumes the dog's teeth did some damage beneath the skin.

He limps into the bathroom to take a shower, then applies Neosporin to his wounds and covers them with fresh dressings.

Someone bangs on the door as he's finishing up.

"You almost done?" Virgil calls. "I got to take a wicked piss."

Boone opens the door and squeezes past the kid. Glancing into the bedroom, he sees Olivia sitting on the bed, hair tousled, a blank look on her face.

"Is there any coffee?" she asks around a yawn.

"I usually go out," he says.

"Shit."

He leashes Joto for his morning walk. It feels strange leaving Olivia and Virgil alone in his place, but, hell, there's nothing for them to steal.

Joto takes his time dumping out, passes up all his favorite spots to finally squat on a patch of dead grass three blocks away.

He's in no hurry to get back either. Every tree trunk, every garbage can, every telephone pole, merits special attention.

A few bees hover over an orange peel lying in the gutter, and ranchero music plays nearby. Boone takes a deep breath, smells jasmine and frying bacon. He's disappointed at how his little investigation turned out. Even if he could get the police interested in what happened to Oscar, there's nothing tying the kid to the ranch, so all Taggert has to do is deny ever knowing him. And to get the cops interested, Boone would have to admit to violating his parole in so many ways, they'd throw away the key.

It's a fucked-up situation: he uncovers the truth, but the truth isn't enough. Joto smiles at him and lifts his leg on one of the Olds's tires.

Olivia and Virgil are smoking on the couch when he returns. A water glass serves as an ashtray.

"This okay?" Olivia asks, holding up her cigarette.

"Yeah, yeah, fine," Boone replies.

She's a pretty girl, but there's a hardness in her face, in her eyes, all out of proportion to her years. Too many late nights, too much dope, too many bad men—something is grinding her down.

She's wearing cutoff denim shorts, a purple cropped T-shirt, and flip-flops, and Virgil is in his baby blue warm-up suit, the one he was sporting the night they busted him at the Tick Tock. Both of them have the same dangerous vibe that a lot of guys in the pen had: like they could joke with you at ten, gut you at eleven, and have trouble remembering any of it by noon. The sooner they're out of here, the better.

Boone walks into the kitchen and opens the fridge. A carton of eggs and a twelve-pack of Pepsi.

"You guys want a soda?" he calls into the living room. It's not coffee, but it might help them get their asses in gear.

"What kind?" Virgil replies.

Boone carries the cans to them and walks over and opens a window to let out some of the smoke. Joto is standing in the middle of the room, his eyes locked on the newcomers. At the same time, Boone feels Olivia watching him, sizing him up, trying to figure out how big a mark he is, how much she can take him for.

Virgil pats the couch and calls to Joto. "Here, boy."

The dog considers the request for a moment before walking over and sniffing the kid's outstretched hand.

"Looks like he's done some fighting," Virgil says as he scratches Joto between the ears.

"So they tell me," Boone replies.

Olivia lifts her Pepsi can from her bare stomach, wipes away the condensation left behind with her index finger, then slides the finger between her lips, all the while staring at Boone with a sly smile. Flat-out stripper stuff, supremely strange this early in the morning.

"What are you going to do now?" she asks him.

"Now?" he replies.

"Now that you know what happened to Oscar."

Boone shrugs. "Not much I can do, considering my circumstances."

"What's that mean?"

"It's none of your business, but I just got out of the joint, and I'm still on parole."

Olivia sips her Pepsi and peeks at him over the top of her can. "For what?"

"Like I said, none of your business," Boone replies.

"Come on. You think you're gonna freak *me* out?"

"I beat the shit out of someone I shouldn't have," Boone says. He feels like he's bragging now, like some kind of asshole.

Olivia smiles. "See, I knew you were a badass," she says. "The way you took Spiller out, that was, like, totally professional."

Boone points to his bruised and bandaged face. "Totally."

Virgil is watching him with a strange expression. When Boone catches his eye, the kid looks away. Boone wonders if he finally remembers their previous encounter. All the more reason to get them moving.

The kid tugs on Joto's ears and says, "What's up with dude's teeth?"

"Taggert," Boone replies.

"Is this that dog?" Virgil says. He turns to Olivia. "I told you about that shit."

"I thought he looked familiar," Olivia says.

"Oscar brought him home from the ranch and took care of him until he died," Boone says. "I bought him from Oscar's friends."

"Fucking Taggert," Virgil says.

"How do you get by?" Olivia asks Boone. "Like for money?"

"Again, none of your business," Boone replies. The girl already knows where he lives, what kind of car he drives, that he's still on paper. He's not going to give her anything else she can use. She reaches down to scratch her ankle, then runs her hand all the way up her leg to her thigh while Boone tries not to stare.

"They make it hard for a con, don't they?" she says.

There's a knock at the door, and Joto barks. Boone presses his eye to the peephole. Amy.

She looks puzzled when he opens the door.

"I thought I heard voices in here," she says. She notices the new damage to his face and raises a hand to her mouth. "My God. What happened?"

Boone smiles sheepishly. "In case anybody ever asks you, don't spar with eighteen-year-old jarheads after a few beers." Another lie. They're coming easier and easier.

Darkness flits across Amy's face. She doesn't believe him but isn't going to pursue it. "Looks painful," she says.

"It's not too bad."

"I was coming over to check on Joto." She holds up the key Boone gave her so she could feed the dog while he was in the desert. "I didn't think you'd be home until later."

"I decided to cut out early, beat the traffic," Boone says as he takes the key.

"Probably smart," Amy replies. She looks past him at the two on the couch.

"My buddy's kids, Olivia and Virgil," Boone says. "He asked me to give them a ride back to the city. Guys, this is Amy."

Olivia and Virgil wave. Amy doesn't wave back.

"Well, stay out of trouble," Amy says coldly, all done pretending that everything's fine. She walks off the porch, and Boone knows she's insulted by his lame attempt to put something over on her. The woman's an ex-cop. She can smell hinky a mile off.

"Hey, wait," he calls and limps into the courtyard after her. She turns to face him, looking dubious. He puts his hands on her shoulders and draws her close to whisper in her ear.

"Some wild stuff's obviously gone down," he says. "As soon as I'm clear of it, I'll explain everything."

"What makes you think I want to know?"

"Let's talk later, when I get home from the restaurant tonight."

"I have to work tomorrow," Amy says. "I can't be up that late."

"In the morning then, before you leave."

She pulls away. "Jesus, Jimmy, you're bleeding."

He looks down at a fresh spot of blood on his T-shirt, seepage from the bite on his stomach.

"Please?" he says, covering the stain with his hand.

Amy shakes her head disgustedly and walks off. Boone turns back to the bungalow to see Olivia watching from the porch. She takes a deep drag on her cigarette, blows out a cloud of smoke, and tosses the butt in the flower bed.

"Girlfriend's pissed, huh?" she says with a mocking tone as Boone approaches.

"Get in there," he replies.

Olivia steps inside the bungalow. Boone follows and pulls the door shut. Virgil has the TV on and is surfing the channels.

"You got B-E-T?" he asks Boone.

Boone snatches the remote out of his hand and says, "Time for you two to go."

"Girlfriend's *really* pissed," Olivia says.

"Get your shit together and call whoever you need to call."

Olivia cringes and affects a hurt expression. "Wow," she says. "Some thank-you this is."

"What do you want?" Boone says. "Breakfast? I'll make you some eggs."

Olivia sits on the arm of the couch. She sips her Pepsi and says, "Let me ask you something: do you want to get back at Bill for what he did to you?"

"What are you talking about?" Boone says.

"I've got a way to fuck him over."

Boone raises his hand palm out, like a traffic cop. He wants her to stop right now, doesn't want to hear anything that could pull him in any deeper.

"As far as I'm concerned, I got what I deserve for being stupid," he says.

"What about Oscar?" Olivia replies. "He get what he deserved?"

Boone walks toward the kitchen. "You like toast?" he says. "I have some bread."

"I'm not talking about killing him," Olivia says. "I'm talking about ripping his ass off."

Boone's injured ankle gives way when he turns to face Olivia. He grabs the door frame to keep from falling.

"What'd this guy do to you to piss you off so bad?" he asks.

"Let's see," Olivia replies. "He killed my friend. He treated me like a whore. He beat up my brother."

"Which was a total shock, right?" Boone says. "Because you thought he was a perfectly nice guy going into whatever arrangement you had with him, a different kind of asshole from all the other assholes you'd hooked up with before."

Olivia loses it then. She leaps up from the couch to stand chest to chest with Boone and screams, "Don't act like you know my life, motherfucker!" Saliva spatters Boone's face. He reacts instinctively, shoving Olivia backward. She almost falls over the arm of the couch but manages to stay upright. When it looks like she's going to charge again, Boone points a finger and says, "Don't."

She holds back, seething. Virgil pops up like he's going to get into it, and Boone shifts the finger to him.

"Get your stuff and get out," he says.

"Big man," Olivia says with a sneer. "You're cool pushing

girls around but scared shitless to go up against a dude who beat you down and humiliated you."

"Spare me the lowlife logic," Boone says.

"Ooooooh, logic. A smart man too," Olivia says. "Big and smart. Wow."

Boone refuses to be drawn in by her taunts. "Hit the road," he says. "Now."

Olivia and Virgil walk into the bedroom and reappear a moment later carrying their bags. Boone herds them to the front door.

"Get our guns," Olivia says.

"Why? So you can shoot me?" Boone replies.

"Shit, dude, you are so not worth the trouble."

Boone is uneasy about handing over the weapons but doesn't want to give the duo any reason to hold a grudge. He leads them out to the shed and unlocks the door. After pulling on a pair of work gloves, he opens the cabinet where he stowed the pistols and the shotgun and hands them over one by one.

"Be careful with these," he says.

"Oh, we will, Daddy," Olivia says.

She and Virgil bury the firearms in their bags, then head off down the concrete path to the street.

"Sorry you're such a loser," Olivia calls over her shoulder.

"You have a nice life too," Boone replies.

"Don't worry about that, bitch."

Mrs. Hu is standing on her porch when Boone limps back to his bungalow. She glares at him with her hands on her hips, and Boone tosses off a quick wave and sorry.

As soon as the door closes behind him, he lies down on the couch, lost in a whirl of anger and pain. It's half an hour before he can muster the strength to walk into the kitchen for a bottle of Jack Daniel's and a handful of Advil. Time to put in a call to Doc Ock.

"I KNOW THAT guy, Jimmy," Virgil says after he and Olivia manage to flag down a cab.

"Yeah?" Olivia replies.

"I just now figured it out: he was the bartender at this place where they busted me for dealing. Him and this other guy took me into an alley and stole my stuff."

"Seriously?" Olivia says. "He doesn't seem like that kind."

"Seriously," Virgil replies. "Man, I wish I'd have remembered earlier. I'd have fucked his shit up good."

Olivia doesn't know whether to believe him. Virgil is so stoned half the time, he doesn't know if he's coming or going.

The cab driver is a raghead who barely speaks English. That kind of thing makes Olivia angry. Like the Russian girls she's danced with at clubs, the Thai girls fresh off the boat. If you want to live in this country, you should learn the language. She looks out the window at the stores along Sunset with signs in all kinds of Spanish and Chinese, all kinds of other *alphabets,* some like a retarded kid's scribbles. It's not right.

She tried calling some old friends to see if anyone would pick them up, but their numbers weren't in service or they didn't answer, so now she and Virgil are stuck paying this fucking terrorist for a ride. All because Mr. Jimmy Boone all of a sudden freaked on them, the ungrateful prick. He's gonna get his though. She has big plans for that boy.

Virgil is listening to his iPod. His head bobs up and down like he's nodding yes over and over. The driver's phone rings. He answers it and starts talking that camel talk, starts shouting, really. Olivia slips her hand inside the bag on her lap and wraps her fingers around the Glock hidden there. Armed and dangerous, the only way to be.

They stop at a red light, and she watches a homeless woman wrapped in black plastic garbage bags push a shopping cart overflowing with junk into the shade of a bus kiosk and sit heavily on the bench. The woman's bare feet are swollen and caked with dirt. That's you, if you don't change shit up, Olivia tells herself. But then another voice says, No way, girl. You got brains, and you got beauty. Good things are coming your way. The woman on the bench lifts the bags covering her pendulous breasts in an attempt to cool off. Olivia grimaces and looks away.

Eton's house is exactly like she remembers it, the front yard a little more overgrown, the roof a little saggier. She and Virgil get out of the cab, and the driver hops out to unload their bags from the trunk, where he insisted on stowing them. He must think they'll tip bigger if they see him actually working.

"Okay," he says as he sets the bags on the sidewalk. He's a little man, round, with heavy five o'clock shadow. He's wearing some kind of slippers on his feet.

"Okay," Olivia says, mocking him.

"Is twelve seventy-five."

"In dollars?" Olivia says.

"Pardon me?"

Olivia gives him a twenty. He reaches into his pocket for a wad of bills, peels off a five right away and hands it to her. He's expecting her to let him keep the rest, but she doesn't like him. And not just because he's a foreigner. He hasn't smiled once since he picked them up, and what was that about, talking on the phone when he had customers? People don't want to hear that kind of crap. Finally, reluctantly, he hands her two ones and a quarter.

"Tank you," he says sharply as she and Virgil walk away.

"No, thank *you,*" Olivia says, carefully enunciating each word.

Virgil leads the way up the path to the house. They climb the steps, and Virgil tilts a shriveled potted cactus on the porch to retrieve the spare key hidden under it.

He holds out his hand and says, "I'm shaking."

"What, do you need me to open the door?" Olivia snaps, sick to death of gutless men.

"I'm just saying it's weird," Virgil replies. "Coming back after what happened here."

He inserts the key, twists the deadbolt. The door opens, and a gust of Lysol-scented air trapped inside since Spiller, T.K., and Virgil scrubbed the place clean whooshes out.

Olivia enters first, steps into the living room. You can't even tell someone was murdered here. An ornate cobweb cuts the room in two. It glistens in the sunlight streaming through the open door. Virgil walks to the couch.

"I was sitting right here," he says. "Eton was over there. They took the chair he was in because it was all bloody."

The place looks the same to Olivia as it did last time she stopped by, a couple of years ago. Same creepy knickknacks and paintings, same old-lady furniture. The flat screen is new, the Xbox. She raises her bag and uses it to break through the spiderweb on her way to the kitchen, which is as filthy as ever. A pot on the stove is caked with dried refried beans, and the trash is overflowing.

A bunch of photos are stuck to the refrigerator door with skull-and-crossbones magnets. One of them is of her and Eton way back when. She has blue hair and a nose ring; he's sticking his finger in her ear and making a funny face. The one time they tried to fuck, he couldn't get it up. Sad. Her anger at

Taggert flares again, hot and bright, and the plan she's been putting together begins to solidify.

She and Virgil walk through the rest of the house, the three bedrooms upstairs. Eton's looks like a teenager's hideout. Mattress on the floor, computer, two guitars on stands, amps, and posters of old punk bands tacked to the walls.

Virgil grabs a key ring off the nightstand. "Sweet," he says. "Now we can use his van." He moves to a three-drawer file cabinet, tries the top drawer and finds it locked. It takes him a few tries before he hits on the right key. Inside the drawer is a stash of marijuana divided into eighths, quarters, and ounces—a pound or so—a small quantity of black tar heroin and orange prescription bottles containing various pills.

"We're rich," Virgil says. "We move this shit, we could make, like, thousands."

Olivia rolls her eyes. The kid's so small town. He doesn't even know how close he is to real money.

The second bedroom contains a bed, a dresser, and a bookcase full of dusty old books. Hanging above the bed is a painting of a glowing angel watching over two kids as they cross a rickety bridge. Someone has drawn a Hitler mustache on the angel and scratched 666 across her forehead. Virgil drops his gym bag on the floor and says, "I call this one."

"Whatever," Olivia says.

The last room is Eton's grandma's, the one left untouched as a kind of shrine to her memory. Her clothes are still in the closet, her gray hair tangled in the hairbrush, and there's half a pack of Marlboro Lights on the nightstand and an ashtray full of lipstick-smeared butts.

It used to creep Olivia out back in the day. She'd get high and sit in the hall, put her ear to the door and listen for ghosts on the other side. What a dipshit she was. There's nothing in here but a bunch of junk that smells of mothballs and mildew. She picks up an old-fashioned perfume dispenser from the dresser, leaving behind a perfect circle in the dust, and squeezes the bulb a few times. Roses. She carries the dispenser with her when she and Virgil step back into the hall and close the door behind them.

They go back downstairs to the living room. Virgil dumps a bag of Eton's weed on the coffee table and sets about rolling a joint. He's got one of the Glocks sitting there, thinking it gives him that gangster lean.

Olivia runs through her scheme to get back at Taggert once more in her mind, and excitement rises like a piston from her belly to her throat, crowding out everything else. It could work. It could definitely work. But they have to move fast.

"Yo, hold up," she says to Virgil as he's about to light the spliff.

"What?" he snaps, irritated.

"We've got stuff to do yet. I need you to be on the ball."

"What stuff?"

She reaches out and snatches the joint from his fingers and says, "Is that any way to talk to the girl who's about to change your life?"

20

BOONE SITS IN A FLIMSY PLASTIC CHAIR IN THE WATCH-repair shop that serves as Doc Ock's waiting room. The shop, barely the size of a walk-in closet, is wedged between an Armenian bakery and a Thai restaurant on Hollywood Boulevard, near Western. The old man behind the counter peers down at an antique pocket watch through a pair of magnifying lenses clamped to his regular glasses and uses what look like dental tools to poke at the timepiece's works. Russian folk music plays softly somewhere.

Boone reaches down and squeezes his ankle. It hurts most at the top of the joint, right below the shin. That's where the dog's teeth dug in, tearing through everything. He hopes it's something Ock can fix.

Ock—née Aleksei Sokolov—came over from Russia ten years ago. He was a doctor in Moscow but hasn't yet gotten around to taking the courses and doing the paperwork that would allow him to practice legally in the U.S. Instead, he works out of the back room of his uncle's shop, cash only.

In addition to poor families from the neighborhood, his patients include gangbangers, mobsters, and other shady types who sneak in to have bullets removed, knife wounds stitched up, and broken bones set without the scrutiny they'd face at a hospital or clinic.

Boone first visited Ock in the Ironman days. Carl recommended him when Boone dislocated his shoulder fending off a photographer for a client, and Ock patched him up for fifty bucks. The price was right, and Boone liked the guy, so he kept coming back even after he could afford a legit doctor.

Ock's uncle's cell phone beeps. He glances down at it, then whistles and jerks his thumb over his shoulder, the signal that the doctor is ready. Boone steps through a gap in the counter and opens the door to the examination room, which is tricked out with the usual paper-covered table, scale, blood pressure apparatus, and cabinets full of supplies.

"Hello, Jimmy," Ock says with a thick Russian accent. He's about fifty, as tanned and handsome as a movie star, with gleaming teeth and suspiciously black hair. His white coat is spotless, and a stethoscope hangs around his neck. "How are you?"

"Not so good," Boone replies.

Ock pats the table to indicate that Boone should sit and says, "Tell me the problem."

"I got hit a couple times, bit by some dogs," Boone says.

"Such excitement. When did this happen?"

"Last night."

"Show me."

First, Ock looks at the lumps on Boone's head, and then, after Boone takes off his T-shirt, pokes at his bruised collarbone and has him raise his right arm two or three times.

"Does that hurt?" Ock asks.

"Like a mother," Boone replies.

Boone pulls the gauze away from the bite on his stomach, and Ock probes the wound with his fingertips.

"What else?" he asks.

"I'll have to take my pants off," Boone says.

Ock raises his eyebrows and motions for Boone to stand. Boone slides off the table, removes his shoes, and drops his jeans.

"Here," he says, pointing to the teeth marks in his thigh, "and here," at his ankle.

"Ahhh," Ock says. "When you say take off pants, I am thinking..." He cups his crotch and grimaces.

"Nope. Got lucky there," Boone replies.

"You have been drinking?" Ock asks. "Your breath."

"Couple shots," Boone says. "Makes the Advil work better."

Ock examines the ankle, twisting it this way and that and asking, "This hurts? This?" Finally, he stands and says, "Okay, not too bad. I can x-ray ankle and shoulder if you like. New machine. Digital. But it will cost you more."

"What do you think?" Boone asks.

"I think is fine. If I wrap, should be okay."

"How much?"

"Fifty dollars for treatment, twenty for antibiotics. You want pain pills?"

"Bourbon's cheaper."

"Also, we should to think about rabies. I have no vaccine here. I can get, but is very expensive."

"The dogs weren't rabid," Boone says.

"They should be tested."

"They weren't rabid."

"Okay, then," Ock says with a sigh. "Seventy dollars."

"Deal."

Ock shakes Boone's hand, then sets to work on the bites. The stomach wound first. Boone grits his teeth as Ock rinses it, slathers it with antibiotic ointment, and covers it with fresh gauze. The puncture on his thigh gets the same treatment, and then Ock cleans the bite on his ankle and wraps it tightly in an elastic bandage. A tetanus shot, a dose of penicillin, a sling for Boone's arm, and he's finished.

Boone looks at the photos hanging on the wall while he's dressing. Ock's wife and kids; his house in Glendale; his cars, a Mercedes and a Land Rover; and a big sailboat.

"That is new," Ock says, pointing at the boat. "Svetlana, same name as my wife. Someday we will sail to Hawaii together, the whole family."

Boone ties his shoes. The American dream. He's glad somebody's living it.

Ock hands him a bottle of pills. "Two of these every eight hours, and change the bandages often."

"Thanks, Doc," Boone says.

"And stay out of the doghouse."

"What?"

"A joke," Ock says.

"Oh, the doghouse," Boone replies. "Good one."

A Latina cradling a crying baby is waiting in the watch-repair shop when Boone passes through on his way to the street. Ock's uncle waves her into the back of the store.

Outside, Boone tests his ankle, stands on one foot. It feels better already. A bus pulls up to the curb and discharges its sweating passengers in a cloud of exhaust fumes. The sky is a worrisome shade of brown, and a dead bird festers on the sidewalk. Hawaii. Boone wonders if he'll ever get back there. Seems a million miles away today, that's for sure. He limps to the Olds. Another drink would set him right, but he's due at work in three hours. Better to grab a nap. He takes the sling off his arm. Can't tend bar one-handed.

AT 11:00 A.M. Amy drives to the Short Stop in Echo Park. She's meeting Tom and Karen Takeshi, friends of hers, teachers at her school. They have an extra ticket for today's Dodgers game and have invited Amy along.

The Short Stop was a watering hole for Rampart cops before turning into a divey hangout for neighborhood hipsters. The bar opens early when there's a game because the stadium is just up Sunset. It's pitch dark inside and packed with fans in Dodgers drag who are excited to be sucking down two-dollar PBRs before noon. The din of all their voices raised at once is topped off by the Stones' "Midnight Rambler" blasting out of the jukebox.

Amy squeezes her way to the bar and orders a Coke. She's pacing herself so she can do a yoga class after the game. She spots Tom and Karen back by the wooden gun lockers, where, in the old days, patrons were required to stow their sidearms before getting shit faced. There's someone with them, a tall, skinny guy in a Dodgers cap and black-framed glasses. He smiles at Amy as she approaches.

"Hey, girly, how you doin'?" Karen shouts over the music, already a little buzzed.

"Great," Amy replies.

"This is Dean," Tom says. "Dean, this is Amy."

"Hey, Amy," Dean says.

Dean. Right. Karen has mentioned him a couple of times. Friend of Tom's, does something in computers at one of the studios. They shake hands. He's got that glint in his eye that says that he thinks he knows more about her than she knows about him. Karen must have been talking her up. Too bad, because Amy can already tell he's not her type, just by his slouch. Looks like his bones are too soft to hold him up.

Coming here wasn't a great idea. She's still off balance after what happened with Boone this morning, wondering how something that seemed to be going so well went south so quickly. She liked Boone from the moment she met him. He was handsome and funny, sweet with Joto, and there was something kind of noble about his determination to get beyond the mistakes of his past. All good stuff.

But then he goes and lies to her face about those people at his place, about what he's been up to. Does he think she's some kind of idiot? She's looking to the future now, not just playing around, so if he doesn't get back to being real next time they talk, if he tries to snow her in any way, that's that.

"Did you come here when you were on the force?" Dean leans in to ask. Yep, Karen's been running her mouth.

"That was a little before my time," Amy says. "I heard lots of stories though."

"I like cops," Dean says with a smile, and Amy wonders how she's supposed to respond to that.

Pretty soon they leave the bar to join the parade of fans walking to the stadium. It's a hot day. Too bright, even with sunglasses. Tom and Dean take the lead while Amy and Karen hang back.

"You guys hitting it off?" Karen asks.

"I'm kind of out of it today," Amy replies.

"He's cute though, right?" Karen says.

"Sure."

"Makes good money too. Drives a Benz."

"Woo hoo!" Amy hoots with false enthusiasm.

"Hold on," Karen says as she drops to one knee to tie her black Converse. There's a red tint in her hair that lights up when the sun hits it. She looks at Amy and says, "You're not in the market for a handsome rich guy?"

"That's creepy, 'in the market,' " Amy replies.

"Nothing wrong with setting parameters."

"You sound like one of those people on TV."

Karen stands and brushes the dust off her jeans. "So you're an 'It's gonna happen when it happens with whoever it happens with' kinda girl?" she says.

They turn onto Stadium Way and start up the hill. Tom and Dean are waiting for them.

"No, I'm an 'I'm gonna kick your ass if you don't change the subject' kind of girl," Amy says before they reach the guys.

"I used to believe in magic too," Karen says. "I really did."

At the top of the hill they cross the chaotic parking lot, which reflects the heat like the bottom of a skillet. The shade of the stadium is a welcome relief, and Amy is happy to find that their seats are in a kind of cave, well back under the upper deck.

She drinks a beer, eats a hot dog, and feels better. The players loping across the green, green grass, the excitement of the crowd, the palm trees in the distance—there are worse ways she could be spending today. And Dean isn't a bad guy, just a little dopey.

Unfortunately, he gets dopier by the beer. During the third inning he tells her all about his last few girlfriends, tossing around the word *bitch* a little too freely. In the fifth inning he slips while trying to bat a beach ball that's making its way across the section and spills his beer on the woman sitting in front of him. He's slurring by the seventh, when he moves in close and asks Amy if she'd like to frisk him.

She says her good-byes then, fibs about suddenly remembering that she has to be somewhere by four. Dean offers to walk her down the hill to her car, but she insists he stay for the rest of the game. She looks at her watch as she crosses the parking lot, a roar rising from the stadium behind her. If she hurries, she can still make that yoga class.

* * *

VIRGIL IS ASLEEP in the driver's seat of Eton's van, reclined all the way back, mouth agape. Olivia is in the passenger seat, watching the bungalows across the street where Boone and Amy live. They've been here since noon and seen Boone leave twice, once for about an hour, and then again twenty minutes ago, dressed for work in a white shirt and black slacks. Both times they ducked and kept quiet until he got into his car and drove away.

Still no sign of Amy though.

Olivia decides to stretch her legs. She grabs a cigarette from Virgil's pack, his lighter, and steps out of the van. While she's pacing up and down the sidewalk, smoking, she remembers coming to a party around here once, some rock star's place. The guy was shooting coke and screaming about Ozzy Osbourne.

A car turns onto the street from Franklin. Olivia ducks behind a truck and watches it pass. A silver Honda Civic. It pulls over to the curb in front of the bungalows, and Amy gets out and runs up the stairs.

Olivia hurries back to the van. Virgil moans and rolls over when she climbs in. He's been no help at all since they left the house, dragging his feet every step of the way. When this is done, she doesn't care if she ever sees the little shit again.

"She's here," she says, slapping his arm.

Virgil sits upright, the seat springing up behind him. He yawns and rubs his eyes. "Finally," he says.

Olivia reaches for her bag, opens it to make sure the Glock is there. She'll knock on Amy's door and pretend to be looking for Boone, say she left something behind at his place. As soon as Amy opens up, she'll show her the gun and lead her out to the van.

"Oh, great," Virgil groans.

Olivia looks up to see Amy come down the stairs and return to her car. She starts it and flips a U, heading back to Franklin.

"Follow her," Olivia says.

Virgil cranks the van to life and chases the Honda down the hill. He reaches the intersection just as Amy makes a right onto Franklin.

"Stay with her," Olivia says.

"You got to hang back when you're tailing someone," Virgil replies. "That's how the real dudes do it."

He turns onto Franklin too but allows one car to squeeze in between the van and the Civic, then another. Olivia leans forward in the passenger seat and struggles to keep the Honda in sight.

"Turn signal, turn signal," she yells.

"I see it," Virgil replies. "Relax."

They follow the Civic down Gower, under the 101 and across Hollywood Boulevard, where the car turns abruptly into a parking structure adjacent to a large health club. Virgil stops at the entrance.

"Should I go in?" he asks.

Olivia tries to think. She didn't plan for this. A car behind the van honks, wanting to get by. Okay, fuck it. She grabs her bag and hops out.

"Wait at the exit," she says to Virgil before slamming the door.

She dashes into the parking structure in time to see the Civic heading up the ramp in search of an open space. There's a stairway in the corner, and she climbs to the second floor, pushing past two old Korean women who are taking forever.

The second floor is full too, and the Civic moves on to the

third. Olivia crouches in the stairwell until the car passes, then runs up another flight.

When she reaches the third floor, a Prius is backing out, and the Civic is waiting to take its spot. She reaches into her bag for the Glock. The Civic pulls into the Prius's space, and she emerges from the stairwell.

Amy is halfway out of the car when Olivia swoops down on her. She keeps the gun low, out of sight of passersby.

"Freeze, bitch," she hisses.

Amy looks up at her, eyes wide with surprise, before dropping back into the seat, her legs still outside the Honda.

"Move to the other side," Olivia says. "Kneel on the floor and put your face on the seat."

"Olivia, right?" Amy says. "What are you doing?"

Olivia hesitates upon hearing Amy use her name. Maybe she should have worn a mask or something. But then she gets angry. The bitch thinks she's slick, stalling like this. Olivia grabs a handful of her hair, yanks her head sideways, and presses the gun to her temple.

"I'm not here for girl talk," she says.

Amy climbs over the center console, slides down into the space between the passenger seat and the dash, and presses her face into the cushion.

"Hands behind your head," Olivia says as she sits in the driver's seat and closes the door. She reaches for the ignition and feels like kicking something. Stupid, stupid, stupid.

"Give me the keys," she says to Amy.

Amy raises a finger. Her key ring dangles from it mockingly. Olivia grabs it and says, "If you don't want to die, do everything I tell you."

Olivia holds the gun on Amy as she starts the car and spirals down through the parking structure to the exit, where Virgil is waiting in a loading zone. Pulling up beside the van, Olivia lowers the passenger-side window.

"I'll follow you," she says.

Virgil's face blanches when he sees Amy curled up on the floor of the Civic.

"You really did it?" he says.

"D'you think I was joking?" Olivia replies.

"Nah, nah," Virgil stammers. "It's just..."

Olivia rolls up the window to end the conversation. If he doesn't blow this, it'll be a miracle.

Virgil moves out into traffic, and Olivia slips in behind him. They head south on Gower to Sunset and make a left. Amy shifts her position a little, rearranges her legs.

"Keep still," Olivia snaps.

"You don't have to do this," Amy says. "I'll give you money. You can have the car."

Olivia presses the gun to the back of Amy's head, pushing her face into the seat.

"I'm not going to tell you to shut up again," she says.

Amy is silent then. Olivia glances out the window at the Hollywood sign propped up on a hill in the distance and remembers the first time she saw it, the morning she arrived from Florida, and knew, just *knew,* that her whole life was going to change. What a joke. Not one goddamned thing turned out like it was supposed to.

21

THE CAR COMES TO A STOP, AND AMY SNEAKS A GLANCE AT her watch. They've been driving for ten minutes in stop-and-go traffic, surface streets. That puts them anywhere from West Hollywood to Koreatown to the East Side. She tries to remember what they learned at the academy about hostage situations.

Rule number one was, if they've got you outgunned, don't fight with your captors during the abduction. They'll be so hopped up on adrenaline and who knows what else that you could very easily get your head blown off. Rule number two was be observant. Take in all the information you can about where you're being held and who's holding you. And rule number three was wait for your moment. Don't try to escape until it looks like you have a reasonable chance of getting away.

Olivia hands her a black sweatshirt. "Put this over your head," she says. "Cover your eyes."

Amy looks down the barrel of the Glock and does as she's told.

"All clear?" Olivia calls out.

"If you fucking hurry," a voice responds.

Amy's door opens and someone grabs her arm and lifts her out of the car. She's hustled blind into some sort of structure and up a flight of stairs. When the kid, Virgil, yanks off the sweatshirt, she finds herself sitting on a bed in a room furnished with antiques. An old bed in an old house with cracked plaster walls, scarred wainscoting, and a creaky wooden floor.

"Come on, guys," Amy says, friendly as can be. "What's going on here?"

"Shut it," Olivia says. She hands Virgil the gun and begins to rifle through Amy's purse. "Where's your phone?" she asks.

"In the zipper pocket."

Olivia pulls it out and says, "You're going to call your job and tell them you won't be in for a couple of days."

"They're going to ask for a reason," Amy says.

"Tell them you're sick. Tell them someone died."

Amy reaches for the phone, thinking she might be able to—

"I'll dial," Olivia says. "What's the number?"

Amy hides her disappointment. "It's in there, under 'school,' " she says.

Olivia scrolls through the phonebook, finds the entry, and hits the call button. She waits until the recording starts, then passes the phone to Amy as she signals Virgil to raise the gun. He points it at Amy's head.

Amy leaves a message saying she has some kind of bug and will be out tomorrow and probably Tuesday as well and promises to call back with an update.

Olivia snatches the phone away from her as soon as she ends the call. "I didn't tell you to say anything about an update," she says.

"That's how it works," Amy replies with a shrug. "How do I know today that I'll still be sick on Tuesday? It's official procedure."

"Don't get smart, or I'll beat your ass."

And fuck you too, bitch, Amy thinks.

"Is there anyone else who's going to be worried if they don't hear from you?" Olivia continues.

"Jimmy Boone," Amy says. "I'm supposed to see him tomorrow morning."

Virgil and Olivia grin at each other, and Olivia says, "Your boyfriend's gonna be way too busy to worry about you, sweetie."

"Jimmy has something to do with this?" Amy asks. Of course he does, goddamn it.

Olivia takes the gun back from Virgil and tells him to tie Amy up.

The kid opens the top drawer of the dresser and rummages around a bit, coming up with a pair of hose.

"These'll work," he says.

He moves to the bed and sets about binding Amy's hands behind her back. Try to evoke sympathy from your captors, she remembers. "Please let me go," she whispers, forcing tears into her eyes and a tremor into her voice.

"Everything's cool," Virgil says. "We're gonna take good care of you."

"But I don't even know what's happening."

"You're lucky," Virgil says. "Knowing stuff is highly overrated in this case."

"Don't talk to her," Olivia snaps.

Virgil moves down and ties her ankles together. When he's finished, Olivia sets the gun down and picks up Amy's phone again. Pointing it at Amy, she snaps a photo of her sitting on the bed, her back resting against the ornately carved headboard. Virgil leans over to look at the screen with her.

"That's awesome," he says.

Olivia grabs the Glock and bends to press the muzzle to Amy's forehead. Amy closes her eyes but is more angry than scared.

"Be good," Olivia says, then she and Virgil walk out the door.

Downstairs, Olivia finds Boone's number on Amy's phone and calls him. The call goes straight to voicemail. She leaves a message: "Check out the photo and call back, bitch. And don't even think about going to the cops. I got eyes on you." She then sends him the picture she took of Amy on the bed.

So now the fuse has been lit. Nothing to do but wait for the explosion.

Virgil passes Olivia one of the joints he rolled with Eton's weed, and she pours more 151 into her glass of Diet Pepsi. They've been sitting on the couch all afternoon, watching TV and checking Amy's phone every five minutes. First *People's Court* and now *Maury*. This black chick screams and falls to the ground when a DNA test reveals that her boyfriend is not the father of her child, and Virgil imitates her, moaning, "No, no, no." Olivia laughs so hard, she has to run into the bathroom to catch her breath.

The pizza guy rings the bell. Another motherfucker who can't speak English. Virgil pulls out one of the hundred-dollar bills Taggert gave him for helping at the dogfight, but the kid can't break it, so Olivia grabs a twenty from her wallet. Then Virgil tries to tip the dude with a joint. The kid's eyes grow wide, and he shakes his head before backing quickly off the porch.

"No, no, no," Virgil says again, and Olivia cracks up.

They dig in to the pizza, and Olivia smiles to herself, as happy as she's been in forever. She thinks of Taggert and can't believe how much time she wasted on that bastard. That control freak. That user. That liar. He deserves everything she's about to bring down on him.

"Awww, fuck," Virgil moans. "This isn't what I ordered."

Olivia looks down at her slice. "What?"

"It's got peppers on it. I'm allergic to peppers."

"So pick them off."

"But they're touching everything else." The kid looks like he's about to cry.

AMY SCOOTS TO the edge of the bed. It's been hours since Olivia and Virgil left her here, and she can't lie still doing nothing any longer. She swings her legs over so they're hanging off the side of the bed and slides forward until her feet touch the floor.

The only window in the room is covered with thick drapes. She stands and makes her way toward it, the pantyhose around her ankles giving enough to allow her to build to a slow shuffle. If she can get a look outside, she might recognize the neighborhood. That'll come in handy if she gets hold of a phone.

She pauses when she reaches the window, listens intently. The TV is still blaring, music and voices seeping up through the floorboards. She nudges the drapes aside with her nose and comes face to face with her reflection in a pane of cracked glass. A sheet of plywood has been nailed to the frame from the outside and blocks the view.

Okay, so much for that. She's about to return to the bed

when she notices the sharp end of a nail protruding about an inch from the wall. Turning around and backing up, she scrapes the pantyhose binding her wrists across the point. With each stroke the nylon frays a bit.

After a few minutes she pauses to test her bonds. Definitely looser. A few minutes more, another test. This time the nylon gives way when she flexes her wrists. Her hands are free. She sits quickly on the floor and goes to work on the hose wrapped around her ankles.

She has them almost untied when she hears footsteps on the stairs. Her heart pounding, she tears at the last few knots. Just as she looses herself and scrambles to her feet, Virgil opens the door. He's carrying a couple slices of pizza on a plate in one hand, a gun in the other.

"Whoa!" he yells. "Whoa!" He drops the pizza and almost drops the Glock.

Amy launches herself at him and grabs his gun arm. Her momentum throws him off balance, and they both go down hard. She twists his wrist and tears the pistol out of his hand. He rises to his knees, but she kicks him in the chest and knocks him over.

Olivia appears in the doorway. Amy swings the pistol back and forth, covering both of them.

"Stay where you are!" she shouts. She's breathing hard, sweating.

Olivia smirks and shakes her head. "You got us, huh?" she says. "Do we give up now?"

"On your bellies!" Amy shouts. "Arms straight out from your sides."

Olivia laughs and says. "Virgil, get up and take that fucking thing away from her."

Amy points the Glock at him, says again, "On your belly!"

"Take it," Olivia says.

Virgil gives Olivia a worried look. "What do you mean?" he asks.

Olivia snarls with disgust and steps over him to approach Amy.

"Final warning," Amy says, aiming the gun at Olivia's chest. Something's not right, she thinks. Olivia's not this crazy. She pulls the trigger as the girl reaches for the pistol. Nothing happens.

Olivia wrests the Glock away from Amy, then slaps her across the face. She racks the slide on the gun, points it at Virgil, and pulls the trigger. Again nothing.

"I put in an empty clip while you were taking a shit," she says to her brother. "You think I'm going to let you hold a loaded gun, stoned as you are?"

"That's fucked up," Virgil says.

"Next time I tell you to do something, you do it," Olivia says.

It's do or die now. Amy makes a run for the door, but Olivia grabs her hair as she passes by, stopping her short, and Virgil throws his arms around her knees. Her head strikes the dresser on the way down. She's seeing stars when she hits the floor.

"Tie her up," she hears Olivia say. "And make sure she can't get loose again."

She doesn't struggle when Virgil takes hold of her T-shirt, jerks her to her feet, and drags her to the bed, where he begins lashing her to the frame with more pantyhose. She's dizzy, nauseated. Better to conserve her strength than to continue to fight now, in case she gets another chance later.

"When's he going to call?" Virgil whines as he pulls a knot tight. "It's been hours."

"How the fuck should I know," Olivia says. "Hey! Hey, bitch!" she says, addressing Amy.

Amy looks over to see her drop the empty magazine out of the gun and slide in a full one.

"Next time, it's for real," Olivia says.

BOONE CARRIES SIX shot glasses to the sink, throws away the peels from a dish of lime wedges, and wipes down the bar. A bachelorette party has just tossed back their last belts of Patron and stumbled out to a waiting limo, ready to move on to the next stop on their Hollywood pub crawl. They were a shrill bunch, drunk and demanding, and Boone's headache is glad to see them go.

He checks on his other customers: three party boys in fancy jeans and dress shirts silk-screened with skulls and AK-47s who spend more time texting than talking to one another. They've been to a screening at the Arclight and are desperately trying to wrangle an invitation to the afterparty at a club down the boulevard. When Boone asks if they need anything else, one of them frowns and waves him away like smoke.

He pulls out his phone. Fucking hell. The thing's completely dead. He forgot to charge it before coming in. Robo sidles up to him and whispers, "The first rule of fight club is, you do not talk about fight club."

"What are you mumbling about?" Boone says.

"Your face, homes. Yesterday you showed up with that cut on your head, and tonight you look even worse."

Boone touches his forehead, then picks up a folded bar towel, unfolds it and folds it again to hide his nervousness.

"What's the big deal?" he says. "Some kid with cheap gloves gave me the cut at the gym, and this morning I walked into a cabinet door."

"And you're limping," Robo says.

Boone unfolds the towel again. "You must love my ass, all this attention you're giving me," he says.

Robo moves in closer. "It ain't me, dog, it's Simon," he says. "Dude's freaked out. Says you look like a bum and that your face scares the customers."

Boone saw Simon walk past a few times earlier this evening but ignored him because he doesn't have the stomach for any hassles tonight. He wonders if he should stop him next chance he gets and give him the phony explanations for his injuries but then decides why the hell should he? If the guy has a beef, let him step up and say something about it.

"*My* face upsets the customers," Boone says to Robo. "What about yours?"

Robo frowns and hitches up his pants. "That's cold," he says. "I'm just trying to warn you."

"I know, bro, and thanks," Boone replies. "My shit's been crazy lately, that's all."

It's a relief when Simon leaves for the night a short time later. He doesn't even acknowledge Boone as he walks out the front door with a couple of cute young things in tow. The guy's so sketchy, he probably forgot what he said to Robo as soon as it came out of his mouth.

Doesn't matter, though, because Boone isn't going to give him anything else to get bent out of shape about. From now on, it's all about slinging beers, scooping tips, and saving pennies. No more looking for trouble.

The last few hours of his shift crawl by. He can't even muster an enthusiastic greeting for Mr. King and Gina when they show up. And, of course, Mr. King wants to be creative tonight, ordering something called a Bronx and calling out the ingredients for Boone: gin, sweet vermouth, dry vermouth, and orange juice. Tastes like crap, and Boone dumps his in the sink when the old man is looking the other way.

22

Boone's alarm goes off at six. He showers and gets dressed, then crosses the courtyard to Amy's bungalow to catch her before she leaves for work. He knocks, waits, and knocks again. No response.

Her car isn't parked out front either. He walks Joto all the way down to Franklin to be sure. So she must have left for school already. He wonders if she's avoiding him. If she gives him a chance to explain what's been going on, he's sure he can make her understand why he lied to her. He's off tonight. Maybe she'll let him take her to dinner.

He tests his sore arm as he watches Joto sniff something in the gutter. It feels pretty good this morning. He can lift it over his head without wincing. The day is warming up quickly, and the palm trees shy away from a hot, dry wind that makes it difficult for the birds to get where they're trying to go. A frond torn loose by a powerful gust sails through the air and lands in the middle of the street.

Back at the bungalow, Boone lies down on the couch with the newspaper and falls back asleep until nine. He gets up and feeds Joto, then pulls his phone off the charger, thinking he'll try to call Amy. As soon as the phone powers up, though, it chirps to signal that he has a message from her.

Boone pushes the button and can't believe what he hears.

It's Olivia, saying something about a photo, the cops, people watching him. He brings up the picture: Amy, bound hand and foot, a stunned expression on her face.

Jesus. Fuck. This is insane. Boone closes his eyes and waits for his initial panic to subside before calling Amy's phone.

Olivia answers. "About fucking time."

"Where is she?" Boone says.

"Staring at the business end of a shotgun," Olivia replies. "If you want to see her again, be at Hollywood and Highland in half an hour, at the entrance to the subway station."

"Wait. Hold on."

"That's all for now, except that my people better not see anybody who even smells like a cop within a hundred yards of you. But you're smart enough to know that, right?"

"Listen," Boone says. "Bring Amy along. You can take me instead."

Olivia chuckles. "Not gonna happen," she says.

"At least put her on for a second; let me talk to her."

"Fuck you, man. Half an hour," Olivia snaps, then ends the call.

BOONE MAKES IT to the meeting place in fifteen minutes, the mall at the corner of Hollywood Boulevard and Highland Avenue. A Gap, a Coach store, Hot Topic, and restaurants catering to the tourists who come to see the stars' hand- and footprints at Grauman's Chinese Theater next door.

The subway station is located a couple of stories beneath the mall. Boone plants himself at the top of the escalators and scrutinizes every passing face. Throngs of tourists wander around like they're lost. They've seen the footprints and the sidewalk stars, posed with the hustlers dressed as Batman and SpongeBob, and now they're wondering what else there is to do. Boone feels like the world has taken a sickening tilt. He wants to shout a warning at them.

An ambulance races past, siren going full-bore. Boone checks his watch and finds that two minutes have gone by since he last looked. He crosses his arms and uncrosses them, about to come out of his skin. A bum asks for a dollar and scoffs at his curt refusal.

Olivia materializes out of the crowd. She's wearing big black sunglasses and a little green dress.

"Hey, sailor," she coos.

"What the fuck's going on?" Boone says.

"All kinds of fun stuff. Let's take a walk."

She was smart to meet in public. If they were anywhere else, Boone would take her down right now and start breaking things until she told him where Amy was. They head west, toward the theater.

"First off," Olivia says, "your girlfriend's fine."

"Let her go," Boone says. "Whatever this is, it's stupid to involve her. I barely know her."

"Really?" Olivia says sarcastically. "Okay, let me make a quick call."

One slap, Boone thinks. Just to wipe the smirk off her face.

"If you hurt her..." he begins.

"Let's get past this part," Olivia says. "If I hurt her, you'll fuck me up or hunt me down or whatever. I know you're the king of the badasses. That's why you're here. I need a badass."

Boone grabs her arm, yanks her to a stop. "I mean it," he says. His reflection glowers back at him from her sunglasses.

Olivia's smugness disappears, replaced by sudden rage. She pulls away from Boone and holds up a phone. "In about three minutes this is going to ring," she says. "Touch me again, and I'm going to tell my friend on the other end to kill your girl."

He could call her bluff, but it's too risky. The bitch is crazy—her and her brother. A couple of mean dogs who've jumped the fence and can't figure out who to bite first. He raises his hands in surrender, and they start walking again, detouring around a woman taking a picture of a teddy bear sitting on Jackie Chan's star.

"How do I get her back?" Boone asks.

"You're going to help me on something, a job I planned," Olivia replies. "If you do your part right, hooray for our team. If you blow it, think about going back to prison. Or worse. Think about you dying, or your girl, or both of you."

They've reached the theater. The forecourt is packed with tourists who occasionally drop to their knees to place their hands in the impressions left in the concrete by the hands of Marilyn Monroe or Tom Cruise. Olivia watches the ritual with a superior smile twisting her lips.

"What kind of job?" Boone asks.

"Tomorrow Bill is meeting some Mexicans in a ghost town out in the desert," Olivia says. "He'll have one hundred and fifty thousand dollars in cash, and the Mexicans will have a million in counterfeit hundreds. Both groups will have been searched beforehand to make sure nobody's carrying weapons. You're going to be there too, you and your crew, hiding somewhere nearby with lots of guns.

"Right when Bill and the Mexicans are about to make the exchange, you'll pop out and jack them for the real money and the fake shit, fucking over everybody all at once. Then you'll get the hell out of there, and me and you will hook up later. You'll hand me the take, and I'll hand you your girlfriend and twenty thousand dollars."

Boone goes cold. He's got to think fast, talk Olivia out of this madness.

"That's great and all," he says, "but can I point out a few problems?"

"No," Olivia snaps.

"First, the crew you mentioned? I don't have one."

"Put one together."

"And I don't have any guns either."

"You're in L.A., dude. Guns grow on trees."

"Okay, this ghost town. Where exactly is it? What's it called? I need to know these things."

"How much longer are we gonna go on like this?" Olivia says with a sigh. "It's in the Mojave Reserve or Preserve or something like that. I'm going back to Bill's today to get all the details, and I'll call you with them later."

"Last I saw, you and Bill were pretty much on the outs," Boone says. "Something changed since then?"

"I'm done with you," Olivia says.

Boone winces with frustration, pauses for a moment to regain control of his voice, then says, "Olivia, listen to what I'm telling you. This is way over your head, and way over mine. I was a bodyguard, not a robber. You picked the wrong guy."

Olivia glares at him, anger flushing her cheeks. "Okay, you know what?" she says. "You might as well shut up now, because nothing you say is going to change this. You've got two choices: Do as you're told, and Miss Amy lives. Don't do as you're told, and she dies. Real simple."

"Tomorrow is too soon," Boone says.

"I've got no control over that. Better get to stepping."

"Olivia, please."

The girl turns and walks away. Boone thinks about following her, but that would be a mistake if she's actually smart enough to have someone watching him. A fresh load of tourists streams off a bus, and Boone loses her in the mess. His heart is banging a mile a minute, but his mind is strangely calm as he jogs across Hollywood Boulevard against the light to reach his car, ignoring the honks and shouted curses. It's blood-and-guts time now, and there'll be no stopping until Amy is safe.

BOONE CALLS ROBO when he gets back to the Olds.

Robo answers with a sharp "*Dígame*."

"It's Jimmy," Boone says. "I need to talk to you."

"Yeah?"

"Not on the phone, in person. Can we meet somewhere?"

"What do you mean? I'll be at work tomorrow."

Boone touches the bandage on his forehead. "This can't wait that long," he says.

"I don't know what to tell you. I'm watching the kids right now. My old lady's out shopping with her sister."

"I'll come there then."

Boone hears children in the background on Robo's end. Robo lowers his voice and says, "It's barely ten in the morning, bro. What the fuck's going on?"

"I want to talk to you about a job."

"One of them kind that can't wait?"

"One of them kind that pays real well. Come on and give me your address."

HALF AN HOUR later Boone pulls up in front of a two-story duplex deep in Van Nuys. Robo's family occupies the bottom unit. The building's yellow stucco is cracked and flaking, and the windows are covered with iron security bars. Boone steps over a tricycle on his way to the front door. Other toys are scattered across the dead grass in the yard.

The door of Robo's unit is open, so Boone sticks his head inside. Robo, dressed in a T-shirt and sweatpants, is passing out bananas to a pack of rambunctious kids and shouting to be heard over the cartoon on the TV.

"Hey, *mijo!* Don't be so grabby," he says to one of the boys.

"Junior took my baby," a little girl wails.

"What you want with a doll?" Robo asks Junior, a chubby five-year-old. "You're a boy. Give it back."

"Hey," Boone calls out.

"Hey, *ese,*" Robo says, raising a hand. "Hold on a minute. I'll be right there."

The kids all turn to look at Boone with big brown eyes and quizzical expressions. He takes in the wall of family photos, the well-worn furniture, the fresh roses in a vase on the dining-room table and knows he shouldn't be coming to Robo with a thing like this. It's a lot hairier than the guy's usual snooping and strong-arming.

But then he flashes back on the picture of Amy that Olivia sent, the fear and confusion in her face. If Robo says no, he says no, but Boone has to ask. He moves outside to wait on the porch while the fat man settles the children in front of the TV.

Robo joins him a few seconds later, shouting over his shoulder, "Stop banging that candle! Now!" Sweat shines on his face and neck.

"Damn, man, how many kids you got?" Boone says.

Robo passes him a can of Budweiser. "That's my sister-in-law's too. A whole fucking circus."

He pops open his beer and leads Boone to a wrought-iron table and chairs set up in a shady spot in the yard. Boone takes a seat and watches a couple of *vatos* pedal past on lowrider bicycles.

"So what you got for me?" Robo asks.

Boone starts talking without a solid pitch. A mistake, probably, but time's short. He leaves out Amy and Olivia—too much to go into right now—and plays it instead that he heard about the meeting between Taggert and the Mexicans from a prison buddy looking to hire anonymous gunmen to ride out to the desert and rob the businessmen on both sides of the deal.

Robo shakes his head when Boone tells him his cut will be ten thousand dollars. "Damn, *ese!*" he says. "What happened to you? A week ago I could barely get you to come with me to push a couple wetbacks around, and now you're talking about robbing motherfuckers."

"Shit changes," Boone says with a shrug. "You interested?"

Robo sips his beer and scratches his belly. "That's some straight-up thugging," he says. "Been a long time since I got into something like that."

"You asked me to find you jobs that pay," Boone says, then jerks his head toward the duplex. "I understand if you're not into it, though, the family and all."

"Fuck, man," Robo exclaims. He slouches in his chair and holds his head in both hands.

A panel truck sidles up to the curb, and the driver sounds a horn that plays "La Cucaracha." He jumps out, hurries to the back, and slides open the door to reveal crates of battered vegetables and a small selection of packaged goods: cooking oil, tortillas, sacks of rice and beans. A few housewives drift over from the complex across the street, the one that looks more like a prison than apartments, and gather around the rolling grocery store.

"Remember how I told you George needs an operation on his eyes?" Robo says.

"At Denny's the other day, sure," Boone replies.

"Yeah, well, now they're saying it has to be done soon, before he gets much bigger."

"That's rough," Boone says.

"I work my ass off, you know. Fuck."

Boone reaches down and picks up a Matchbox car off the grass to avoid looking Robo in the eye. If he does, he's going to tell him to forget it, he'll find someone else.

"My share's ten grand?" Robo says.

Boone turns the car over in his hands, a Mustang. "That's what the man's promising."

"Tomorrow?"

"We'll leave this afternoon to make sure we're set up."

Robo goes silent and squints off into space like he's in pain. Boone watches a ratty-looking squirrel scamper down an avocado tree in short, startlingly quick bursts. When it reaches the ground, it paws at the dirt, searching for something it buried earlier.

"Dad!" a little girl calls from the porch.

"What?" Robo responds, without turning around.

"George spilled some water."

"So clean it up."

The girl gives a frustrated moan and steps back inside. A second later every kid in the apartment is screaming.

Robo drains his beer, belches, and hurls the can at the squirrel, which races back up the tree.

"Okay, I'm in," he says, holding out his fist.

Boone pounds it and says, "You sure?"

"No, but don't worry," Robo replies.

"We're gonna need guns," Boone says.

"What kind?"

"Big as you can borrow. We want to look like the baddest motherfuckers walking. AKs, AR-15s—like that."

Robo grimaces. "That's short notice, dog."

"I know, man, I know," Boone replies.

"You're lucky I got the friends I got."

The girl reappears in the doorway and yells, "Dad!"

Robo stands with a grunt. "I'm gonna go whip some little asses," he says. "And you better split before my wife gets home. I don't need to be answering all kinds of questions about what that white boy wanted."

"Thanks, Robo," Boone says.

"I should be thanking you, right?" Robo says as he waddles toward the duplex. "You're the dude who hired me."

The women shopping at the vegetable truck steal leery glances at Boone as he walks out to his car. Once behind the wheel he shuts his eyes and takes a second to process everything. A little bit of doubt tickles his brain, a little bit of "This is happening too fast," but he pushes it aside and slips the Olds into drive.

OLIVIA SWEEPS THROUGH the front door all amped because her plan is in motion, but Virgil doesn't acknowledge her, doesn't even turn away from the TV. This whole thing has him so stressed, he took what he thought was a Xanax from Eton's stash, and now everything's kinda off, kinda wavy, and he's wondering if it might have been something stronger.

"How's our girl?" Olivia says as she plops down beside him on the couch.

"Fine, I guess," he says. "I took her some cereal a while ago."

"You got to keep a good eye on her, like every fifteen minutes."

Virgil ignores her, stares at the TV.

"I mean it," she says.

Definitely stronger than Xanax. Judge Judy has green dots all over her face. "How'd it go with what's-his-nuts?" he asks, hoping to switch Olivia to another subject.

She sits back and puts her feet on the coffee table. "He threatened me and shit when I told him we had his chick, but I let him know we weren't fucking around," she says.

"That's cool."

"The next thing I've got to do is call Bill and get back in good with him."

"How you gonna do that?" Virgil says.

Olivia leans forward to scratch her knee. "The guy's crazy about me. Like, really crazy," she says. "If everything's cool after I talk to him, I'll leave in an hour for the ranch, find out what I need to know, then come back here as soon as they take off for the meet. Tomorrow afternoon we'll swap the bitch for the money, and it's 'See ya, motherfuckers.' "

"Be careful," Virgil says.

"What do you mean?"

"He could get you out there just to shoot you."

Olivia is quiet for a second, staring at the TV. "You don't suppose I know that?" she finally says.

Virgil closes his eyes and thinks, Where you gonna go?

"What?" Olivia says, and Virgil realizes he must have spoken out loud.

"Where you gonna go?" he repeats, louder.

"What do you mean?" Olivia snaps. "The ranch, you idiot."

"No, after, with your share."

"I don't know. Maybe Costa Rica. A girl I know said it was superchill down there, supernice."

"Need a passport," Virgil says. His head is suddenly too heavy for his neck.

Olivia leans forward to look into his face. "What the fuck are you on?" she says.

Virgil shakes himself out of his nod, swallows hard. "I'm just tired."

"Well, straighten your ass up and come with me to check on Amy."

This is Olivia's thing and all, but her bossy tone makes Virgil's balls ache. He heaves himself off the couch and lurches into the kitchen, where he stands at the sink and scrubs his face with cold water. "Huh," he grunts. "Huh, huh, huh." He dries off with a sour-smelling dish towel and does a set of jumping jacks to get his heart going. By the time he heads up the stairs, he's feeling steadier on his feet.

Olivia is waiting in the hall, her ear pressed to the door of Eton's grandma's room. She's carrying both of the Glocks, hands him one. Amy is looking right at them when they push into the room. She's tied hand and foot to the bed.

"How are we?" Olivia says.

"I have to go to the bathroom," Amy replies.

"You just went a couple hours ago."

Amy shrugs, like, What do you want me to do?

"Cut her loose," Olivia says to Virgil.

Virgil sets the Glock on the dresser and takes out his pocketknife. This is the third time the chick's had to go today. He steps to the bed and slices through the pantyhose securing her to the frame, then moves down to free her ankles. He notices her tits again. Nice ones. Big ones.

"Everything's going good," Olivia says as Virgil helps Amy sit on the edge of the bed. "You'll be home by tomorrow afternoon."

Amy doesn't reply, just reaches her bound hands down to rub the red welts on her ankles. Being ignored like that infuriates Olivia. She walks over and jerks the woman up off the bed, shoves her toward the door.

"Cop an attitude with me, and you'll be pissing in that bed," Olivia says.

Amy walks out into the hall with Olivia and the Glock right behind her, and Virgil sits on the bed to await their return. The room spins in slow circles. It'd be great to lie down for a few minutes, but Olivia would shit if she caught him. He pops to his feet and slaps himself in the face a couple times. They're going to need more pantyhose to replace the ones he cut. He steps to the dresser and grabs another pair. After this he's going to hit Eton's stash again, this time for something that will wake his ass up.

WHEN BOONE TELLS him it's something serious, Carl has him meet him at the Burger King on Venice instead of at the condo, because Diana is home sick from work today. Boone arrives at the restaurant before Carl does, buys a Coke, and sits in one of the booths. He watches a fly stagger across a poster advertising something called the Bacon Double Homestyle Melt. Two goth teenagers at the next table feed each other french fries. The girl has a zit on her chin that weeps through her thick makeup.

Carl strides in slow and easy, radiating calm. He points to acknowledge Boone before stopping at the counter for coffee. He's wearing a pink Polo, khakis, and some kind of loafers. Boone almost smiles. The guy has always dressed like a frat boy. Boone used to tease him about it, tell him he was the lamest brother he'd ever met.

Boone stands when Carl approaches the booth, a weirdly formal gesture that he chalks up to nervousness.

"What, you want to change tables?" Carl asks.

"No, we're cool, we're cool," Boone says as he sits again.

Carl slides in across from him.

"What's on your mind?" he says.

"I need your help," Boone replies.

"You got it."

"I wouldn't sign up so quickly."

Carl leans back and looks Boone over for the first time since his arrival. "Somebody been beating on you again?" he asks.

"Amy's been kidnapped," Boon replies.

"Come on, man."

"Some fucking psychos I got mixed up with snatched her."

"Jesus," Carl exclaims. "What kind of shit have you got yourself in now?"

Boone explains the situation in a rush, going all the way back to his and Robo's meeting with Oscar's grandfather. He tells Carl how he tracked Taggert to the ranch, what happened there and afterward, and how that led to this, him being forced to rob Taggert in order to free Amy.

Carl whistles at the conclusion of the tale and shakes his head. "This is deep, Jimmy."

"I know, man, I know," Boone says. "That's why I'm coming to you. I need you to ride out there with me and help me do this. It'll be me, you, and Robo. They're promising me twenty grand, which you and Robo can split for your trouble."

"This Robo cat, he solid?" Carl asks.

"I think so. I hope so. How can you know?"

"And we're talking about leaving today?"

"Soon as we can."

"But we don't know where we're going or when this thing is going off?"

"Fucking ridiculous," Boone says.

"There's no ice," a guy in a hard hat and an orange vest standing in front of the drink dispenser yells at the people behind the counter. "Hey, no ice!"

Carl lays his hand over the top of his cup so that the steam from his coffee is trapped beneath it, then turns the hand sideways, releasing the steam all at once, in a puff, like he's sending smoke signals.

"Know what I did last night?" he says.

Boone wonders why the hell he wants to talk about this now. "Took Di to Red Lobster?" he jokes.

"This dude Chemo—'cause he had cancer when he was a kid—hired me and those two you met at my place to round up some poor motherfucker who burned him in a Mickey Mouse dope deal," Carl says. "We swarmed the guy at a titty bar downtown, bounced him around in the bathroom, and told him that Chemo was waiting for him, and we'd be happy to give him a ride over to straighten things out.

"This brother was afraid of Chemo, but he was even more afraid of the linoleum knife that Armenian kid, Aram, was waving around. We drove him to an old rail yard down by the river, where Chemo was waiting. The deal was, we'd hold the guy but wouldn't hit him. Any heavy shit was on Chemo.

"Now, Chemo, man, he's an ugly bastard, looks like he's still got cancer, like a skeleton. He stepped out of the dark, and homeboy from the strip club was crying even before he hit him the first time. He kept yelling he didn't have any money, but five minutes and a few busted teeth later, he pulls a roll of bills out of his sock. Didn't make any sense to me to take a beating like that, but, you know, man, I've given up trying to figure people out.

"Chemo skimmed five hundred off the roll and handed it to me, then told us our work was done. We left him stomping on that poor bastard's head. Didn't look like he was gonna make it through the night."

Carl frowns and sips his coffee.

"That's fucked up," Boone says.

"What I'm saying," Carl continues, "is that if you squint,

we're the good guys in this thing of yours, and it's been a long time since I felt like a good guy."

"Seems like I've been doing a lot of squinting lately," Boone says.

"There's no other way to get Amy back?" Carl says.

"Not that I can see," Boone replies.

Carl extends his hand across the table for Boone to shake. "Well, then, what can we do but what we got to do?" he says.

23

OLIVIA PULLS OUT FROM BEHIND A SEMI IN THE SLOW LANE and presses the accelerator to the floor. The battered Econoline has no guts though. Olivia creeps up beside the big rig, bouncing in her seat as if that'll make the van go faster, but then the engine starts whining, so she takes her foot off the gas. No sense risking a breakdown in the middle of the desert.

The first thing she did when Taggert answered the phone earlier was apologize for shooting up his truck and running off, but he wasn't having any of it. He cussed her every which way and said he couldn't believe she'd pull that kind of stunt with this deal coming up, that she'd humiliated him in front of Spiller and T.K., and that he'd tried his best with her even though he knew damn well that you can't turn a whore into a housewife.

The whore part made her bite the inside of her cheek, but she waited until his rage had burned itself out, then laid on the sob story she'd worked up: she and Virgil had returned to Eton's house and grabbed his stash with the intention of selling it, but then, while she slept in their motel room, Virgil had skipped out with the dope and all her money.

"Oh, baby," she said. "What the fuck have I gone and done?" She never should have left the ranch, never should have let her anger get the best of her. As soon as she'd driven away, she'd known it was a mistake. It was awful being apart and scary how much she missed him. Didn't he feel it too, that this thing between them was so much stronger than anything either of them had ever had before?

Of course he did. He was all alone in the middle of nowhere, all alone in the world, and his secret weakness, Olivia knew, was that he needed someone to care about and someone who cared about him in order to feel human. Without that, every time he looked in the mirror he saw an animal staring back at him, a low and vicious beast, and despised himself for his savagery.

"Let me come home," she said. "You can deal with me however you see fit, but let me come home to you."

Taggert was silent for a long time, then finally growled, "Do whatever the hell you want," and ended the call.

He's not going to kill me, Olivia assures herself. Anybody else, maybe, but not me. If she's misread him, though, she's dead. Simple as that. He'll cut off her head and hands and scatter her bones. But that's the risk you run when you try to steal the monster's treasure.

She reaches up to pull down the visor. The sun's right in her eyes. The van's air conditioner makes lots of noise, but no cold air. When she rolls down the window, seeking a little relief, the blast of gritty wind just makes her hotter. The sand outside glows white. The top floors of the Indian casino look like they're about to burst into flame.

For a second Olivia wishes she was headed there instead of the ranch. She imagines checking into a room, eating a nice dinner, and playing blackjack, like in the commercials. Thing is, she only has forty dollars to her name.

She could go ahead and stop, but dinner will be McDonald's, and she'll lose all her cash in the first hour and spend the rest of the night hustling drinks and video poker money from the truck drivers and retirees there for the seafood buffet. One of them will ask if she's working, and if she's drunk and desperate enough, she'll turn a trick, then pass out in the van until she wakes up sweaty and hungover to a sun so bright it shows every secret.

Not again, she thinks as she rattles past the casino. Never again. This time tomorrow, she'll be a whole new person, someone with money and choices, someone who has and keeps things. A bug hits the windshield and explodes red and yellow like a skyrocket. She drifts into the next lane trying to turn on the wipers, and a car behind her honks. She sure wishes the radio worked.

BOONE DRIVES BACK to Hollywood. The wind is picking up. Jumpy as hell, he slams on his brakes to avoid a cardboard box skittering across Franklin like a wounded animal; almost gets rear-ended. The giant inflatable tooth perched on the roof of the dental clinic strains at its tethers. He parks in front of Cyberplace. Three different gutter punks ask for change while he's feeding the meter.

A computer search for the Mojave Preserve turns up a map. It's out past Baker, nestled between the 15 and 40 freeways, a million and a half acres of desert, hundreds of miles of road, a dozen ghost towns. He and Robo and Carl will head out toward the preserve and hope that Olivia's call comes somewhere along the way. If not, they'll gas up in Baker and wait there to hear from her.

After printing out the information Boone walks down the boulevard to the army surplus store to pick up ski masks.

"Knocking over a bank?" the burly guy behind the counter jokes.

"Liquor store," Boone replies.

"Careful of those security cameras."

His next stop is Food For Less. He pulls into the parking lot and chases down a cart. The little plastic flags strung between the light poles snap like firecrackers in the wind.

The music is too loud in the store, some kind of happy-dappy smooth jazz, and the air conditioner is cranked all the way up. Boone hurries down the aisles, grabbing jugs of water and Gatorade, a loaf of bread, packets of ham and bologna, a jar of mustard, and a couple bags of ice.

Back at the bungalow, he pulls his sleeping bag off his bed and brings in a cooler from the shed. He dumps some ice in the cooler, along with the food that needs to be kept cold, sets the cooler by the door. He adds a hoodie to the pile, and the flashlight he keeps under the kitchen sink. And a machete. Always good to have a machete. Joto follows him around like he knows Boone's leaving soon.

Carl insisted they take his Xterra to the desert because he doesn't trust the Olds to make the trip. "I don't want to be making a call to the Auto Club with a load of guns and counterfeit money," he said, and Boone couldn't argue with that. Carl arrives at two. His knock startles Boone, makes him bite his tongue.

"You're not fucking around, are you?" Boone says when he opens the door and sees Carl's desert cammies.

"Are *you?*" Carl replies, clearly displeased by the grin on Boone's face.

"Absolutely not," Boone says, gesturing at the gear and supplies he's collected. "I'm ready to do this thing."

"What's all that?" Carl asks.

"Food," Boone says. "Water."

"Come on, man," Carl scoffs. "You're a Marine, not a Boy

Scout. Grab the water and your sleeping bag. I've got enough MREs for all of us."

Boone opens a couple of cans of food for Joto, then he and Carl toss his stuff into the Xterra and drive out to the valley. Boone calls to let Robo know they're on their way.

When they arrive, Robo is sweating on the curb, a cooler, a propane stove, and firewood heaped on the sidewalk behind him.

"It's only one night," Boone says.

"One long-ass night," Robo replies.

Boone introduces Robo to Carl while they sort through Robo's piles, picking out the essentials. The two men shake hands.

"Good to meet you," Carl says.

"You too," Robo replies.

When they've loaded the truck, Robo lifts a last duffel bag and unzips it just enough that Boone catches a glimpse of black steel and plastic and smells gun oil.

"The *cuetes,*" Robo says. "Two M-16s, a 12-gauge, and a couple nines for backup."

"I'm covered there," Carl says and pats his favorite Smith & Wesson .45, which is nestled in a shoulder rig under his cammies.

"Daddy!"

The men turn to watch Robo's son Junior stagger toward them, struggling to carry a shovel twice his size.

"Do you need this for your hunting?" he asks.

Robo takes the shovel and kneels in front of the boy.

"I don't think we're going to be digging any holes, *mijo*," he says.

"Uh-huh, to hide in," Junior says.

"They got bushes and stuff for that," Robo replies.

Boone watches as he scoops up the kid and carries him to the duplex. If anything happens to him tomorrow, or to Carl—Boone doesn't want to, can't let himself, think about that.

It's purely for show that he asked them to come along anyway, a couple of big guys with big guns. During the actual robbery, he'll be the one to step out while they remain under cover. Before Taggert and the others even figure out what's going on, he, Robo, and Carl will be safely on their way.

Robo stands in the doorway, kissing his wife and babies, then breaks free and lumbers out to the Xterra.

"*Vámonos*," he says. "They act like I'm leaving for a year."

Boone takes the passenger seat, and Robo squeezes his bulk in back, with the weapons and some of the gear. Carl drives to the 101, gets on heading south. There's a rattle in the cargo bay, and Robo reaches back and rearranges the load until it stops.

"You guys like tamales?" he says when he's finished. " 'Cause my old lady made me bring a shitload of them."

THE SUN IS still high when Olivia reaches the turnoff to the ranch, and the surrounding hills are being scoured by the wind. Fear catches up to Olivia, the sudden taste of it sour on her tongue, as she drives the dirt road through the scrub. She tops the last rise, and the ranch comes into view. The heat bears down on it like a boot heel. She hates this place, always has.

The compound looks deserted. No movement at all except for what the wind's got hold of. Taggert's old truck sits in the yard, and the bullet-riddled corpse of his new one. T.K.'s Explorer is up at the bunkhouse. Olivia's heart judders behind her ribs when the road spits her onto the property. She kills the engine and steps out with her arms crossed protectively over her chest.

The dogs are raising hell over at the barn. Olivia approaches the house slowly. "Bill?" she calls out, hating the quaver in her voice but knowing it's something Taggert will be listening for. The man doesn't miss much.

"I'm here," he says.

She can barely make him out, slumped there on the car seat under the awning, a beer in his hand. She moves toward him, unsure what to do now, what to say. Before she can come up with something, her legs give way, and she sinks to the ground in front of him. He doesn't stir when she rests her cheek on his thigh and begins to cry. The tears are mostly from fear, but he doesn't know that. Olivia lets them come. They're a good addition to her act.

"I'm sorry," she sobs.

Something brushes the back of her head, and she tenses up. She doesn't want to die. Not here. Not now. Not on her knees in front of this man, any man. It's only Taggert's fingers, though, lightly stroking her hair.

"I never told you I had a son," he says.

"No," Olivia replies. "You didn't."

"Bill Junior. Billy. By my first wife, Clara, the girl I married right after graduation, back in Kentucky."

Olivia sniffs and reaches up to wipe her nose. She can see the sky from here, full of dust, no color she can name.

"We didn't last long," Taggert continues. "Things were rotten between us before I went into the army and got worse when I mustered out. I'd blown a man's head off from five feet away, and Clara was worried about what to make for Sunday supper. She had this idea of the way things ought to be, and it was a joke. Shit jobs, a little house, church—that stuff just made me laugh. The rules didn't apply to me anymore, and she thought the rules were all there was."

Taggert falls silent, and Olivia hears him sip his beer. He's been at it a while, she can tell. His voice has that lazy drawl it gets.

"Billy was born while I was in the jungle," he says. "He was about six months old when I first saw him and screamed bloody murder every time I tried to pick him up. Only wanted his momma. I resented that. It's crazy, a baby and all, but I did, I resented it. 'How dare the little fucker?' You know? I wouldn't hardly have anything to do with him.

"When me and Clara split up a year later, she took Billy with her to her mom's. I was killing myself in the mine back then, running wild when I wasn't. Clara got her child support every month, and I'd stop by now and then with a toy or a box of Pampers, but, truthfully, I didn't feel nothing for the kid, and he didn't feel nothing for me. He'd rather watch cartoons than visit. Wouldn't say two words to me when I showed up.

"I moved to Louisville when I was twenty-one, and pretty soon it got down to birthday cards and a check at Christmas. Every year a school picture of Billy would come in the mail, and I'd take the old one out of my wallet and put in the new one. Didn't mean shit, but it did, you know?"

Taggert pauses again. The car seat creaks as he shifts his weight. Olivia's never seen him this deep in his past. He's telling the kinds of stories she's been prodding him for since they met, giving the details he's always claimed to have forgotten, swearing that he runs lean and mean when it comes to memories, tossing overboard any that might weigh him down.

"He called me once, when he was about twelve," he says. "Out of the blue, Sunday afternoon. I was living in San Diego. Clara got my number from my brother, told him it was an emergency.

"It started out as catching up. He was playing Pop Warner. His grades weren't too good, but he was going to summer school to bring them up. I asked if he had a girlfriend, and he said, 'Hell no!' Just like that: 'Hell no!'

"Then I heard his momma: 'Tell him. Tell him now.'

"Turned out he'd been arrested riding a stolen motorcycle. He didn't know it was stolen, of course, had borrowed it from a friend or some such horseshit, lying like a rug. I knew Clara wanted me to give him hell, do the daddy thing, but I was sitting there with a kilo of coke and two machine guns on the table in front of me. Cracked my ass up. That woman, man, she never did get it...."

His voice trails off once more. Olivia's still too frightened to raise her head, but she squeezes his leg and murmurs, "So what'd you say to him?"

"I said, 'Be more careful next time, son. Don't get caught.' "

"Really?"

Taggert drinks his beer, doesn't answer. The dogs are going crazy now. Must be a mountain lion prowling nearby.

"I was pissed Clara had tracked me down," Taggert says. "Thought I was being funny. That was the last time I ever heard from him. I got a newspaper article from my brother two years later. Billy'd shot himself in the head at a party, in front of all his friends. They think it might have been an accident because there was no note or anything. I hope it was."

Olivia looks up at him. He's gazing out at the barn with a haunted look.

"People claimed we had the same eyes," he says, "but I never saw it."

Olivia scrambles onto the car seat, throws her arms around him, and buries her face in his neck. Now's the time to be the good girlfriend, to hold him tight and tell him that all the bad shit that's happened to him isn't his fault. Her heart is as cold as the moonlight that's never warmed anyone, and Taggert knows it, but he's so tangled in his own web right now, he's not even thinking straight. All she has to do is mouth the words he wants to hear.

"You ever considered kids?" he says.

"I don't know," Olivia says. "Why?"

"Once I'm out of the game, I'd kind of like to give it another shot."

Olivia thinks about tomorrow, about all that money coming together. She keeps her face hidden so Taggert can't see her smile and whispers, "Oh, Bill, you're gonna get me crying again."

24

OLIVIA AND TAGGERT ARE STILL SITTING UNDER THE awning, side by side on the car seat, when T.K. and Spiller come up from the bunkhouse. The men pause briefly next to the van, looking it over, then glance up toward the house, confused.

"Well, well," T.K. says when he sees Olivia.

"Hey, boys," Olivia says.

"Obviously, she's back," Taggert says. "We've talked things out."

"And I want to tell you guys that I'm sorry," Olivia says. "I acted like a real idiot."

"You're sorry?" T.K. says, and Olivia doesn't like his tone. There's something disrespectful in it, something superior.

"You need something more than that?" Taggert says.

"Not if you don't," T.K. replies.

"I don't," Taggert says, putting his arm around Olivia.

A blast of wind rocks the house and tears something loose, sends it clattering across the yard.

"So let's get down to business," Spiller says, trying to ease the tension. "Figure out who's doing what tomorrow."

"You want a beer or something?" Taggert asks Spiller and T.K.

"I'm good," Spiller says.

T.K. grunts his refusal.

"Let's go over this once more," Taggert says. "The meet is set for noon. Spiller, you and me will take off around ten for Lanfair, the ghost town where we're doing the handover. T.K., you'll leave a couple hours earlier and go to the Nipton exit off the 15, where you'll wait for Mando and his partner. After you check them and their vehicle, you'll call us with the all clear. Then you can head back here. Got it?"

"I got it," T.K. says.

"Meanwhile, me and Spiller will be searched by their guy, then drive on to Lanfair, where we'll hand over the money and get the paper."

They go back and forth a little longer about directions and gas money and what's for dinner tonight, but Olivia already has everything she needs. She sits there staring at T.K. while they talk, getting off on the way he won't meet her gaze.

BOONE, CARL, AND Robo are drinking coffee at the Coco's in Baker when the call comes from Olivia. Boone jabs the button to answer, barking, "Hello! Hello!" as he hurries through the restaurant and out the front door.

"You there?" Olivia says.

"Of course," Boone replies.

"The town is called Lanfair," she says quietly, like she's afraid of being overheard. "They're meeting there at noon."

"Lanfair. In the Mojave Preserve."

"Yes."

"Noon tomorrow."

"Isn't that what I said?"

Boone closes his eyes, squeezes them shut. "How's Amy?" he asks.

"Missing you lots, so don't fuck up," Olivia replies.

"Seriously, Olivia—"

"Seriously, Jimmy. Good-bye."

The phone goes dead. Boone walks back into the restaurant, returns to the booth.

"We on?" Carl says.

"Yep," Boone replies. He unfolds the map of the preserve he bought at the gas station and moves his finger around on it until he finds Lanfair.

"And this is where we're headed," he says.

THEY ARRIVE IN Lanfair about six. The last thirty minutes of the trip is spent bouncing along a roughly graded dirt road, with a short stop to shoo a small herd of cattle out of the path of the truck.

Boone walks to a crumbling concrete foundation and steps up onto it to look over what remains of the town, a small settlement established by homesteaders in the early 1900s. They planted wheat and barley, built homes and businesses, but clashes with the big cattle concerns over land and water rights and the difficulty of coaxing a decent crop out of the desert soil eventually wore them down.

According to the tourist info on his map, most of the residents headed west, to L.A. or San Diego, in search of work. The post office and general store closed in 1926, and the town was left to the wind and the sand and the sun, the coyotes and the pack rats.

The Xterra is parked on what was once the main drag of the community. Eight weathered wood-and-corrugated-steel shacks lean at odd angles on both sides of the road, interspersed with a few brick and stone ruins. There's a dilapidated windmill, a water tank shot full of holes, and what's left of a small train depot, the tracks and ties long since hauled away by enterprising scavengers.

Carl and Robo are standing on the lee side of the Xterra, using the vehicle as a windbreak. Boone walks back over to join them.

"What do you think about hiding the truck in that thing?" he says, pointing at a skeletal wooden hulk that used to serve as a warehouse. It sits on a bluff above town and has a clear view of the main road in both directions.

"High ground's good," Carl says. "Just as long as the damn thing doesn't blow down tonight."

"It's lasted this long," Boone says.

They pile into the Xterra and drive up to the warehouse. The doors have fallen off their hinges, and Boone and Robo drag what's left of them out of the way. Their activity disturbs a flock of pigeons that has taken up residence in the building. The birds swoop down from the rafters and fly past the men to regroup outside and wheel in unison against the evening sky.

Carl backs the truck into the tottery structure, so that when it's time to move, all he has to do is give it gas. A rank odor hangs in the air, decaying wood and bird shit. Dusty shafts of sunlight beam down from holes in the tin roof, and missing planks in the walls allow for narrow glimpses of the desert outside.

The three men walk out of the warehouse and stand at the edge of the bluff to look down on the town.

"Being that we don't know exactly where they'll be stopping tomorrow, we should spread out, take up three different positions, and hope one of us winds up near their meeting place," Carl says.

"Maybe there," Boone says, pointing at the train depot.

"And by that water tank, and another man across the street, near the last building on that side."

Carl nods. "Get some triangulation going," he says.

"Wherever they stop, though, I'm the one who goes out for the money," Boone says.

"I ain't gonna argue with that," Robo says. " 'Bout time the white boy did the dirty work." A sneaky gust of wind unseats his black Dodgers cap. He manages to grab it before it leaves his head and tugs it low over his eyebrows.

Returning to the truck, the men unload their gear. Robo gathers rocks for a fire ring and stacks the wood he brought along beside it. He watches as Boone spreads a tarp on a flat, sandy spot and unrolls his sleeping bag on top of it.

"You're sleeping out here?" he asks, incredulously.

"Sure," Boone replies. "Why not?"

"Motherfuckin' scorpions is why not. Motherfuckin' snakes."

Carl carries his bag over and sets it next to Boone's.

"You dudes are crazy," Robo says. "I'll be in the truck. With the doors locked."

The sun has dropped behind the jagged range of mountains to the west by the time they get settled, but the desert still glows with the last of the daylight. Robo brings out the guns, and the men pass them around, drawing back bolts and inserting clips. Boone raises an M-16 to his shoulder and squints down the barrel. It's military issue, configured to fire three-round bursts.

"Remember how to use that?" Carl asks.

"Come on, bro. Sergeant Rivera beat that shit into us," Boone replies. "I bet I could still fieldstrip this thing blindfolded."

Robo hands Boone a nine-millimeter Ruger and says, "You want that or a Glock?"

"This'll do," Boone says and sticks the Ruger into the pocket of his hoodie.

They give the rifles back to Robo to store for the night.

Boone's restless, so he takes a walk, following his shadow into the scrub. He crosses a wash, then climbs onto a boulder to look around.

Pulling the Ruger from his pocket, he sights on a rusty can lying on the ground fifty feet away. Before he can stop himself, he's squeezing the trigger. His three quick shots send the can skittering across the hardpan like it's being kicked by a ghost.

"Hey!" Robo yells from camp.

"Sorry," Boone calls back, but he's not.

THE WIND DIES at dusk, and Robo starts a fire. Boone and Carl eat MREs—chili mac and meatballs—and Robo has tamales. After dinner they gather beside the fire. Robo brings out a bottle of Cazadores, and it makes the rounds.

Night has reduced the world to a flickering circle, and the men gaze silently at the flames. The only sound other than the pop and crackle of the fire is the soft cooing of the pigeons, which have returned to the warehouse to roost. Thoughts of Amy disrupt Boone's reverie. He worries that she's scared or in pain.

It's a relief when Robo belches and says, "Jimmy, can I ask you something?"

"Go ahead," Boone replies.

"You went to prison for almost beating some dude to death?"

"That's right."

"What the fuck did he do to you?"

A log shifts in the fire, sending up a swirl of sparks. Boone watches them rise and fade and says, "I thought he was molesting his daughter."

Robo's face crinkles in disgust. He's a little drunk. "Are you kidding, man?" he says. "Shit, I'd have used a gun."

"Good thing I didn't," Boone says. "Because I was probably wrong. Looks like it was just some crazy husband-wife bullshit."

"You were going on what you had," Carl interjects. "No shame in that."

Boone shrugs and takes a pull from the tequila.

"Okay, how about this," Robo says, stroking his chin and assuming a philosophical pose. "When's the first time you got laid?"

"Jesus," Carl exclaims. "What the fuck is this, a slumber party? You need to go to bed, man. We all do."

Robo raises his hands and says, "Okay, okay, but I got to tell you this first." He leans forward to show he means business. "If something happens to me tomorrow, you motherfuckers better make sure my share gets to my family."

"What do you think we are?" Carl snaps.

Robo raises a warning finger. "I'm serious. I will come back and hunt you down like Dracula."

"Don't even think like that," Boone says.

"Okay. Good," Robo says. "Now I got to piss." He struggles to his feet and lumbers off into the darkness.

"Me too," Carl says quietly, after he's gone.

"What?" Boone says.

"If this goes bad for me—Diana and the boys, see they get paid."

When Robo returns they douse the fire with bottled water and handfuls of sand. Robo walks into the warehouse to sleep in the Xterra, and Boone and Carl zip themselves into their sleeping bags.

The stars are woven into a glittering veil that stretches across the sky, and Boone gazes up at them long after Carl drifts off, so long that he eventually dreams he's floating among them, like some legendary lost soul.

THE SUN HAS been down for a while now, but Amy's not tired. She's spent the past few hours struggling against her bonds. Again and again she strains to free her hands from the headboard until the pantyhose tighten up and she has to stop and twist her wrists to restore the flow of blood to her fingers. The bedspread is damp with her sweat.

Virgil's footsteps on the stairs rise above the constant drone of the TV. Amy closes her eyes, feigns sleep. The door opens, and the room is flooded with light. Virgil lingers on the threshold for a second, then steps inside and closes the door.

He stands in the dark, breathing hard. "You want more pizza?" he says.

Why doesn't he turn on the lamp? Amy is suddenly uneasy. "I have to go to the bathroom," she says.

"Okay. Sure," he replies.

A thin strip of light under the door gives vague shape to objects in the room. Virgil walks over and sits on the bed. He stinks of booze and chemicals.

"Where's your sister?" Amy says.

"Fuck her," the kid slurs.

Amy's body jerks with raw revulsion when he reaches out and cups one of her breasts through her T-shirt.

"You're hot," he says.

Amy tries to keep her voice calm. "Untie me," she says. The

kid is so fucked up right now, if he cuts her loose, she's sure she can get the jump on him.

"Will you be nice?" he says.

"I'll be real nice."

Virgil hesitates a moment, confused, then squeezes her breast so tight it hurts.

"You think I'm that stupid?" he says.

"Get your fucking hand off me!" Amy screams. She yanks hard on the pantyhose, puts her whole body into it again and again, until the nylon cuts into the flesh of her wrists.

"Whoa," Virgil yelps, pulling his hand away. "Calm the fuck down."

"Get out of here!"

"I will," Virgil replies. "I will."

He doesn't though. He continues to sit on the bed beside her. Amy sees him wobble a bit, and a moment later he brings his legs up and curls into a ball with his back to her. A snore rips the silence. He has passed out. Amy can see the Glock, black against the bedspread, in the light seeping in under the door, the kid's fingers still curled around the grip. Two feet away. Might as well be a hundred miles.

25

Spiller and T.K. come up from the bunkhouse early Tuesday morning for a last powwow before the meet. T.K. makes a face when he enters the kitchen and sees Olivia frying bacon at the stove. Taggert tenses up. This is a bad time for one of his horses to be bucking. He motions for the men to join him at the table. Spiller sits, but T.K. remains standing. "I pulled something in my back," is his excuse, but Taggert knows it's all about defiance.

Olivia pours coffee for Taggert and Spiller. T.K. watches her with hooded, angry eyes, and waves her off when she lifts the pot in his direction.

"You about ready to go?" Taggert asks T.K.

"I've been thinking about the plan," he says.

"Yeah?"

T.K. glances at Olivia like he's uncomfortable saying what he wants to say in front of her. Fine, Taggert thinks. He'll send her out.

"Babe," he says to Olivia. "Could you give us a few minutes?" The request angers her, he can tell.

"Whatever," she snaps as she turns off the stove and bangs a few pans together.

When Taggert hears the bedroom door slam behind her, he turns back to T.K. and says, "Go on."

"Why do I have to be the one to wait to pat these fuckers down?" T.K. says.

"Because you're my first impression," Taggert says. "They see a big black badass like you, it'll get their heads right."

T.K. grunts and thrusts out his jaw. "Something don't sit well," he says.

"All of a sudden there's a problem?"

"And what about this no-guns bullshit?" T.K. continues. "That makes me nervous. Guns keep motherfuckers humble, get them thinking twice about any foolishness."

"It makes me nervous too," Taggert says. "But there's only so much I can do here. We went to them for this, they didn't come to us, and the first time you deal with anybody new, you bend over and hope you don't get fucked. I've known Benjy since he was a kid, done business with him many times. I'm going on that and on my gut feeling that these guys are looking for solid partners on this thing."

"And you trust your feelings these days, do you?" T.K. says.

"What the fuck's that mean?" Taggert replies. He sees a shadow on the wall in the hallway. Olivia is hiding there, eavesdropping. Back less than a day and already up to her old tricks. It's something he'll have to deal with, but first he needs to get T.K. in hand.

"Seems to me you been a little shaky lately," T.K. says.

Taggert squints up at him. "Oh, yeah?" he says. "Why don't you elaborate on that?"

T.K. starts to speak, then stops short, like his brain suddenly catches up to his mouth. "Well, well, I'm just saying," he stammers before picking up speed and committing himself. "This girl of yours puts you down in the dirt in front of your crew, sticks a gun in your face, wrecks your truck, and runs off with some motherfucker who, for all you know, came out here to do you harm, and not only is the bitch still breathing, but you let her back in your house."

Spiller looks askance at T.K., then says to Taggert, "He's only talking for himself, boss."

"That's right, you punk," T.K. says. "Only for myself."

Taggert reaches up and touches the scar on his throat. He shouldn't be taking this. Five years ago the guy would have been choking on his own blood at this point.

"Anything else?" Taggert asks.

Olivia is standing out in the open now, watching them.

"I want you to explain the sense of that to me, of keeping her around," T.K. says. "Because I was raised to deal with shit like that in a whole different way. Bitch acts up; bitch gets put down."

Before Taggert can respond, Olivia walks over and steps right to T.K.

"Call me a bitch again," she says.

T.K. turns to Taggert with a disgusted grimace and throws his hands in the air.

"Olivia," Taggert sighs wearily.

"Call me a bitch again," Olivia says.

She's pointing a gun at T.K.'s heart. Taggert recognizes it as the .38 he keeps in the nightstand.

"Whoa!" Spiller yelps. He hops out of his chair and backs across the room until he's up against the stove.

"Olivia!" Taggert shouts. The wind grabs the house and shakes it like it's trying to pull it down.

"Call me a bitch," Olivia says.

"Bitch," T.K. spits.

Olivia fires as he grabs for the gun. The .38 ends up in his hand, but he staggers backward, a trickling hole in his chest. He bares his teeth in a kind of snarl and makes a strange grunting noise.

Taggert springs to his feet, can't believe what he's seeing. Olivia stands her ground, cheeks flushed, as T.K. sinks to his knees. He aims the revolver at her but begins to spit up blood before he can get off a shot. A second later he pitches forward onto the worn linoleum with a fleshy smack.

Taggert surges toward Olivia and raises a hand to slap her silly. Her terrified eyes meet his, though, and he stops mid-swing. She's breathing hard, and the fingers she uses to wipe a splash of blood off her forehead tremble like a frightened child's.

"I just wanted to shut him up," she says.

"Aw, fuck," Spiller moans. "Jesus Christ."

"There's a tarp in the bed of the Dodge," Taggert says to him. "Bring it in."

Spiller hurries for the door like he's glad to be getting out.

Taggert crouches over T.K.'s body and slips the gun out of his hand. He feels no anger, no sorrow. He's always considered this a gift, that when things go haywire, his emotions shut down, and the situation, no matter how dire, becomes nothing more than a series of problems to be solved. It's why he's lasted so long in this dirty business, where every day has its disasters.

"Don't kill me, Bill," Olivia whispers. "Please don't kill me."

He should. Should put her down like he would a biting dog. She crumples to the floor, though, and looks so tiny sitting there moaning and shaking. He forgets how small she is sometimes, how delicate, because of that oversize attitude of hers, but, really, he can see why things that wouldn't scare him might scare her, make her lash out. How can he know what the world looks like through her eyes, what's a threat, what seems dangerous?

"Shhhh," he says, setting the gun on the counter next to the dish drainer. "You think crying's going to change anything?"

OLIVIA THOUGHT T.K. was going to hit her, so she pulled the trigger. Turns out he was only going for the gun. So many times it happens that way, because of a misunderstanding. All the killers she's known have had similar stories. But knowing why it happened doesn't make it any easier to watch a man die by your hand. That's something that changes you, even if she can't yet say how.

The bang of the door slamming shut behind Spiller makes her jump. His face glows pink, buffed by the wind, and he's carrying a folded sheet of clear plastic.

"Get up," Taggert says to her and holds out a hand to help her off the floor. He takes hold of one edge of the tarp, and he and Spiller spread it out and lift T.K.'s body onto it.

There's blood on the linoleum. Taggert scoops a stack of dish towels out of a drawer and passes them to Olivia.

"Get it all," he says. "Do a good job."

She's not sure she can handle this. Kneeling at the edge of the red slick, she presses a rag into it. The blood has a smell, animal and chemical combined, and she gags the first time she gets a good whiff. When the cloth is saturated, Taggert has her toss it onto the tarp, with the body.

He and Spiller lean against the counter while she works, Spiller puffing on a cigarette. She tries her best not to get blood on her hands, but by the time the floor is clean, gore is caked under her fingernails and in the folds of her knuckles.

Taggert and Spiller wrap the body and the rags in the tarp and carry the bundle out to the Dodge. Olivia is scrubbing her hands with dish soap and a Brillo pad in the kitchen sink when Taggert steps back inside.

"You better come along," he says.

"Where?" she asks.

"Have you not figured out yet that I don't like those kinds of questions?"

"Okay," she says quickly and grabs her jacket off a chair. Dread coils around her like a snake.

She and Taggert walk out to the truck together. She sits in the middle, between the two men, and has to swing her knees over when Taggert wants to shift gears. They drive down the main road a short distance, then turn off on a narrower, rougher track that leads up a slot canyon to a square hole in the ground, the entrance to an abandoned mine.

Taggert and Spiller get out, lift T.K.'s body from the truck bed, and drop it down the shaft. Watching them from the cab, Olivia can't sit still. She rocks back and forth on the squeaky seat. If Taggert has decided to get rid of her, this is the place he'll do it.

He and Spiller are talking at the lip of the mine now. Olivia extends a trembling finger to press the button on the glove box. Taggert keeps a gun in there; she's seen it. The compartment is empty though.

As the two men approach the truck, their feet stir up clouds of dust that are promptly whisked away by the wind. Olivia reaches up to hug herself. She'll fight, that's for sure. They'll have to drag her out, hold her down.

Spiller says something to Taggert that makes him stop to answer. There seems to be some disagreement between them. Taggert, Spiller, Taggert, then they start walking again.

Taggert opens the door and sticks his head in.

"You cold?" he asks Olivia.

"A little," she replies.

"Put your window up," he says to Spiller as Spiller slides in beside her. He starts the truck and turns it around, heads out of the canyon.

Olivia is relieved to be alive, but she's still on edge. She doesn't trust this new Taggert. What kind of rules does *he* expect her to follow?

"Today's going down a little different than we planned," Taggert says. He steers with one hand while grabbing his sunglasses off the dash with the other. "A lot different."

"I don't know why," Spiller mumbles, staring sullenly out his window. "We could use Miguel."

Taggert puts on his sunglasses and says, "I told you he's gone. Went to visit his family."

"Great," Spiller says. "So what are these guys gonna think now?"

"Who gives a fuck if we've got the money?" Taggert says. "That's all they care about. It's a one-man job anyway. I'm only taking someone else along because Mando's gonna have someone. Even-steven and all that."

A tumbleweed rolls out of the scrub and into the road. Taggert swerves to avoid it, fishtails a bit, then glances at Olivia and says, "You're coming to Lanfair with me."

"Really?" Olivia says. She has to act happy about it, after pestering him for so long, but this fucks everything up. She'd planned to head back to L.A. as soon as Taggert left for the meet, sit there drinking rum with Virgil while they waited for Boone to bring them their money. How's Boone going to react when he sees her in Lanfair? Worse yet, what if Taggert figures out what's going on? She's dead for sure then.

Right now, though, she's got to show some enthusiasm.

"It could actually be good in a way," she says. "I mean, how out there is it—how, like, random—to bring a chick along? These guys are gonna be like, 'Holy fucking shit, this dude's got superballs.' "

"Give me a break," Spiller groans.

"You give *me* a break," Olivia replies.

"Shut up, both of you," Taggert snaps.

A long silence follows, just the old truck's rattles and the wind whistling through a gap somewhere. The sun throbs red behind roiled dust, and gasoline fumes are making Olivia dizzy. She's scared and getting scareder. It's the same kind of cold panic that surged through her, that made her choke and flail, the first time she walked out into the ocean and realized that her feet weren't touching the bottom anymore.

BOONE IS AWAKENED by a tickle on his cheek and a gust of hot, sweet-smelling air. His pulse rate jumps immediately, instinctively, but he keeps still, lifts his eyelids a bit. The horse staring into his face exhales again, a grassy blast.

"Hey, buddy," Boone murmurs.

The horse, chocolate brown with a black mane and tail, starts, spooked by Boone's voice. Boone props himself on an elbow and watches as the animal and another scout that had been investigating the men's camp lope off to join twenty or so other wild horses that are already fleeing. The herd follows the road for a distance before galloping across the desert toward the mountains.

Carl sits up and says, "What was that? Thunder?"

The wind has returned, and heavy black rain clouds fill the sky, not even a faint glow marking the morning sun's position. Boone stands with his sleeping bag wrapped around his shoulders, and the wind billows it like a cape as he glares at the mess overhead. Eight a.m. Four hours until Taggert and the Mexicans arrive.

Robo wobbles out of the warehouse on stiff legs and pisses in the fire ring. A billow of steam rises from the still-warm coals.

"Toss more dirt on that," Boone says. "We don't need anybody seeing the smoke."

"Aye, aye, Captain Fuckface," Robo grumbles.

It's warm despite the clouds, humid. Boone puts on his hoodie and joins Carl and Robo at the entrance to the warehouse. They stand around stamping their feet and choking down PowerBars and tamales. Boone accepts a cup of the cold instant coffee Robo mixes up and carries it with him as he walks out to look over the town again.

Quick and dirty is how it should go. As soon as he's got everybody proned out and has collected the money, he'll send Carl up to the warehouse to retrieve the truck. The whole thing should take five minutes, tops.

Carl brings over three Spider-Man walkie-talkies, toys that he borrowed from his kids.

"Getting all high-tech on me, huh?" Boone says.

"Short notice," Carl says with a shrug. "They're supposed to have a range of up to a mile though."

Robo and Boone switch on their units. Robo presses his SEND button and says, "Do you read me? Over."

"I'm standing right here," Boone says.

"Copy that," Robo says. He's wearing a fleece vest that he can't zip shut over his belly.

The men break camp and load everything into the Xterra. Boone covers the truck's license plates with duct tape and passes out the ski masks. Robo hands him an M-16. The weapon's cold heft and oily tang do nothing to calm his nerves this morning. Maybe he should have gone to the police instead.

He inserts a thirty-round clip into the rifle and twists the firing mode switch from safety to semi to burst and back again. An extra clip goes into one pocket, the Ruger is in the other. What should he say when he steps out of hiding? He searches for exactly the right words to let Taggert and the others know that he's in control and they'd better do as they're ordered.

A raindrop explodes on the bridge of his nose and splashes into his eyes. He blinks, confused, then ducks his head as a violent downpour beats down on him. He and Robo and Carl take cover in the warehouse, where they dodge leaks and speculate on whether the deluge will let up before it's time to get into position.

Water flows from the sullen sky with such intensity that at times Boone can't see more than twenty feet through the torrent. The runoff pools quickly on the packed-earth floor of the warehouse and begins to flow in small, swift streams out the door and down the hill toward the town.

RAIN? YOU GOTTA be shitting me. Spiller stares glumly at the drops speckling the windshield of Taggert's old Dodge, then sticks his hand out the window to feel it for himself. He's been waiting at the Nipton exit for an hour. The Mexicans should be pulling up anytime now.

He lights a cigarette and picks at the scab on his neck from the tattoo-removal laser. The ground around the truck is pocked with muddy dimples, and farther south, where the actual meeting will take place, it's really coming down. Looks like a black blanket has been thrown over the desert out that way.

His toes curl inside his Nikes a few minutes later when a

gray Silverado leaves the freeway and glides up the ramp. The truck cruises slowly past, the driver and passenger eyeballing Spiller, before easing over onto the shoulder about twenty feet in front of the Dodge.

Spiller flips his cigarette out the window and gets his Hawg from the glove compartment. Olivia brought it back when she returned to the ranch, the only good thing to come of that. He slips the gun into his waistband and zips his jacket to hide it.

The rain is falling harder, riding the wind. Spiller steps out of the truck and strides down the shoulder toward the Silverado. The driver, a greaseball bodybuilder who's even bigger than T.K. was, gives him a hard look when he peers in his window, while the passenger, some beaner in a cowboy hat, stares straight ahead.

"*Hola, amigos,*" Spiller says, making the greeting sound like an insult. He nods at the driver. "You first."

Mr. Universe opens the door, slides out of the truck, and lifts his arms. Spiller runs his hands over the guy's torso and legs, has him turn all the way around.

"Wait up there," Spiller says when he's finished, directing the bodybuilder to the front of the truck.

Mr. Universe glances at the cowboy, who nods slightly. The big man moves off to stand about ten feet away.

"Next," Spiller says.

The cowboy gets out and walks around the truck to face Spiller, his stupid smile revealing a gold tooth. He reminds Spiller of a pool shark who once tried to stab him, so he does an extra-thorough job—goes up his leather coat to check under his arms, sticks his hand down inside his boots—before sending him to join his boy.

Turning his attention to the Silverado, he sweeps under the

seats, front and back, opens the glove compartment, pulls down the sun visors, even lifts the floor mats.

There are two duffel bags on the rear seat. He unzips the first one and whistles at the sight of all those phony hundreds, neatly stacked and banded just like the real thing. He slides his hand around and under the piles but doesn't find anything, and there's nothing but funny money in the other one either.

It's pouring by the time he finishes his inspection. Big fat drops pass through his thin hair to tap his scalp, and he wishes he'd worn a hat.

"Okay, amigos," he calls to the Mexicans, who are standing with their shoulders hunched, their backs to the wind and rain. "*Adios.*"

He trots to the pickup and scrambles inside, uses his sleeve to dry his face. Scooping up his phone from the dash, he calls Taggert.

They've worked out a code: "Everything's fine" means "The motherfuckers are holding a gun to my head and making me say this." "All clear," on the other hand, means "Proceed as planned."

"All clear," he says when Taggert answers. The Silverado's taillights come on, and it pulls back onto the pavement. "They're on their way to you now."

"Okay, bro. See you at the ranch," Taggert replies—"at the ranch" signifying that everything is okay on his end.

Spiller pats his pockets for his cigarettes and lighter. He notices that the Silverado has stopped and is now backing down the road toward him. Fucking morons probably need directions.

The Silverado stops alongside the pickup, and the cowboy motions for Spiller to roll down his window.

"*Hola, amigo,*" the cowboy says.

"Yeah?" Spiller replies.

The cowboy reaches up into a hidden stash box that's been added to the headliner of the cab and whips out a pistol. He thrusts it out the window until it's about a foot from Spiller's face and pulls the trigger.

You gotta be kidding me, Spiller thinks in the instant before a bullet destroys his left eye and slams into his brain. You gotta be fuck—

26

TAGGERT HANDS HIS PHONE TO OLIVIA, TELLS HER TO PUT it in the glove box. They passed through their checkpoint ten minutes ago, stood around in the rain while one of the bodybuilders from the Indian casino searched the truck for weapons, and, finding none, waved them on.

The wipers of T.K.'s Explorer are going full speed, and Taggert can still barely see through the windshield. There'd been talk of a summer storm, but it wasn't supposed to hit until Wednesday at the earliest. It's hot and muggy to boot, almost tropical. Taggert switches on the air conditioner and cracks his window.

"Slow down," Olivia says.

She's been quiet since they left the ranch, kind of pale and spooky. Maybe she's finally realizing what he's been trying to tell her all along, that she's not cut out for this life. Shooting T.K. was a good lesson for her. Some people can handle a thing like that; most can't.

He tries to remember how he felt the first time he killed a man. Well, not the first time, because that was in Nam, where greasing gooks got to be like shooting gophers for a bounty. No, no, his first civilian kill was in Louisville, some pimp who ended up on Big Donnie's bad side. Taggert walked up to him on his corner one night, put two in his dome, and went to a movie afterward, *Papillon,* with Steve McQueen. So he must not have been too busted up about it. Relieved the thing was over, probably. A little scared of getting caught. Hard to say. It was a long time ago.

He reaches out and squeezes Olivia's thigh, and she flinches like he burned her.

"Hey," he says. "Everything's cool."

She nods and gives him a sickly smile. He'd laugh if he wasn't certain it would set her off. She looks like she's going to puke. After hounding him for how long to let her come on a job? Good thing all she is is a warm body on this one. Imagine if he actually needed her for something.

He glances over his shoulder at all the money he has in the world, wrapped in a plastic grocery bag on the backseat, and smiles. He's almost giddy now that everything is in motion. This is when he feels most like the man he wants to be, the man he *is*. Tomorrow it'll be back to worrying about this and that, back to contemplating and deliberating and driving himself crazy with all the choices it takes to make it through a single goddamn day, but right now, what's going to happen is going to happen, and there's not a thing he or anybody else can do about it.

They come to the hamlet of Goffs, a windburned scatter of rickety wooden structures and mobile homes cowering miserable in the storm. The paved road makes a sharp right turn here, but Taggert keeps going straight, heading down a rutted asphalt track that soon peters out into graded dirt. He's forced to reduce his speed because of the many potholes that have already become muddy puddles.

At one point, a ten-foot-wide stream rushing across the road stops him completely. Not willing to risk a blind crossing, he gets out of the truck and walks to the edge of the flow to check its depth with a stick he picks up off the ground. Five inches, six. No problem.

He's soaked by the time he returns to the Explorer. Olivia leans back in her seat and braces herself as he releases the parking brake and creeps forward.

"Are we gonna make it?" she asks.

Taggert blinks the rain out of his eyes and says, "We better."

The truck easily fords the stream, and they continue on their way.

"This is crazy," Olivia says, the shadows of the drops on the windshield like tears on her face.

"Crazy's good," Taggert says. "Crazy means there's nobody out here but us lunatics."

Just then a crooked spear of lightning arcs out of a black cloud shot through with gray veins and slams into the ground somewhere beyond the horizon. Taggert feels the thunderclap deep in his chest and shouts, "Fuck yeah!"

BOONE SQUATS NEXT to the rusty water tank on the main street of Lanfair. Carl has taken up a position at the depot, and Robo is hidden in the remains of a cabin at the edge of town.

Rain is still falling, but Boone is relatively dry under the narrow wooden awning attached to the tank. He can see most of the town from here and has a clear view of the road. Wherever Taggert and the Mexicans decide to get down to business, he'll be able to keep an eye on them until he reveals himself.

He checks his watch—11:52—before turning around to make sure the Xterra, parked in the warehouse on the bluff behind him, won't be visible to anybody approaching the town from either direction.

The walkie-talkie in his pocket beeps, and Robo's voice crackles out of it, singing, "Raindrops keep falling on my head..."

"Let's keep the chatter to a minimum," Carl barks.

"Roger," Robo says. "Ten-four." Then, after a pause, "Kiss my ass."

Boone chuckles to himself. His glands are shooting all kinds of buzzy stuff into his system that makes him feel like a superhero. "I pity the fool," he chants quietly to himself. "I pity the fool. I pity the fool."

A flash to the north gets his attention. There's been some lightning this morning, but this is something else, lower to the ground. He peers through the binoculars Carl lent him, sees a truck splashing down the road toward town, headlights on.

"Vehicle approaching," he announces into the walkie-talkie. "A mile or so out."

The truck, a Silverado, slows to a crawl when it reaches Lanfair, rolling past the depot, the general store, and finally stopping in the middle of the road about twenty yards from the water tower. Its wheel wells are caked with mud. Boone can't see who's inside, but whoever it is doesn't seem to be in too much of a hurry to stand in the rain.

Another vehicle appears, this one coming from the south. An Explorer. Boone doesn't risk using the walkie-talkie this time because Robo and Carl would have to be blind not to see the truck as it drives into town.

The Explorer brakes, its taillights turning the rain to blood, and comes to a stop facing the Silverado. There the two vehicles sit, thirty feet apart, until Taggert finally steps out of the Explorer and raises his hand in greeting.

Then Boone sees something he can't be seeing. He presses

the binoculars to his eyes in the hope that a closer look will prove him wrong. Nope: that's Olivia in the passenger seat of the Explorer. Boone isn't sure what this means. If the plan has changed somehow, she would have called, wouldn't she? Best to stick to the program for now. He pulls the ski mask over his face and swings the M-16 into firing position.

Raindrops slither down inside Taggert's collar and make him squirm. He stands in the no-man's-land between the Explorer and the Silverado while Mando and his boy sit with mean grins on their faces, high and dry in their truck, and watch him take a soaking from the storm. Taggert clenches his fists and squishes one boot in the mud, then the other. Right now he could do both of those bastards with his bare hands.

The two men slide out of the Silverado, Mando in a white straw cowboy hat that shines like it's lit from within. They approach Taggert, carefully placing each step to avoid puddles. When they get close, Mando smiles at Taggert from under the dripping brim of his hat.

"Good afternoon," he says. He has to raise his voice to be heard above the rain.

"You piss somebody off?" Taggert asks with a nod at the seething sky.

"Not me, amigo," Mando replies. He squints at the Explorer. "Who you got in there, your sister?"

"I've got your money," Taggert says. "What do you have for me?"

"Everything you asked for."

"So then what?"

Mando motions to his partner, and the two of them start back to the Silverado. Taggert walks to the Explorer, goes to the passenger side and opens the rear door.

"What's happening?" Olivia asks. The glare of the dome light bleaches all the life out of her face.

"A few more minutes," Taggert says as he reaches for the grocery bag and opens it to look at his money one last time. He glances out the windshield and sees that Mando and his man are already returning, each carrying a bulging duffel bag. Everything is going like it's supposed to, except for the rain, and who could have foreseen that?

Taggert slams the door of the truck and walks out to meet Mando, the grocery bag clutched to his chest. There's an instant of hesitation when they come together again. Neither wants to make the first move. Taggert finally steps forward, holding out the bag of money to Mando with one hand and extending the other to take his duffel bag. The exchange completed, he reaches out with his free hand and accepts the other duffel from Mando's partner.

He hefts the bags a bit and says, "I'm gonna trust you on the count."

Mando opens the grocery bag just enough to confirm there's money inside, then wraps it up tight. He grins at Taggert and says, "Maybe I fuck your girl now, like you fucked mine."

Something almost like fear jolts Taggert. "I don't think so," he says.

"No?" Mando replies and whips out a pistol from under his coat.

Taggert lifts one of the duffel bags to protect himself. The first round passes through the bag and bores into his shoulder like a railroad spike. The second grazes the side of his head, zipping off a strip of scalp.

"You motherfucker," Taggert roars.

The duffel he was holding with his injured arm drops to the

ground. He swings the other up and flings it into Mando's face before running for the Explorer.

Mando jumps back, startled, and loses his grip on the grocery bag. It falls open, and stacks of rubber-banded bills plop into the mud at his feet. Regaining his composure, Mando fires again, and the bullet hits Taggert in the thigh as he reaches the truck.

Taggert yanks open the driver's-side door but slips climbing in and falls to his knees. Another round smacks into the door, which is now between him and Mando, protecting him from the waist up. If he can get inside before the pain registers, he'll be able to start the truck and run them down, or at least distract them enough that he and Olivia can escape.

"Oh my God," Olivia screeches. "Oh my God," and he wishes she'd shut the fuck up. What happened to me? he wonders. When did I forget everything I know?

THE MEXICANS ADVANCE on the Explorer, the one with the cowboy hat firing a pistol, the big one what looks like a MAC-10. Taggert is struggling to pull himself into the driver's seat, and Olivia leans over to grab his arm as the big guy sprays the Explorer, spiderwebbing the windshield.

Boone steps out into the street. He was about to order everyone to hit the dirt when the shooting started, but now his only thought is to keep Olivia alive long enough to find out where Amy is being held. He squeezes off two bursts into the mud in front of the Mexicans and shouts, "Drop your weapons."

The big guy whips the MAC around and sends a string of bullets his way. Boone drops to the ground and rolls behind an old concrete foundation. The sodden ski mask has twisted around to cover his eyes, so he tears it off.

The Mexicans run to the Silverado and scramble inside. The engine starts, but before they can get moving, there's more gunfire, and half a dozen rounds chew up the grille of the truck. The engine emits a shrill scream, then grinds to a stop.

Wind-driven rain is pounding down harder than ever, and Boone can barely make out Robo, who is advancing cautiously toward the two vehicles, covering both with his M-16.

"Jimmy, where are you?" Robo shouts.

Boone rises to his knees and waves. "Over here. What are you doing?"

"Coming to help. I thought they got you."

"Go back to cover. And no more shooting."

The Spider-Man walkie-talkie beeps incessantly. Boone takes it from his pocket, keys it, and says, "Yeah?"

"We got to go," Carl says.

Boone watches Robo waddle toward a cabin on the side of the road. Before he gets there, shots come from the Silverado, and he falls to the ground.

"Bring the truck," Boone yells into the walkie-talkie. "Wait for us by the depot."

WHEN OLIVIA MANAGES to haul Taggert into the Explorer, he slumps in the driver's seat, his breath coming in stuttering gasps. There's blood all over his face, and bright red gouts of it spurt from a hole in his thigh. He clamps a hand over the wound to stanch the flow.

"What do we do?" Olivia asks, shaken by his suffering.

Taggert looks past her out the passenger-side window. She follows his gaze and sees the fat man in the ski mask who just went down. His body lies in the road, ten feet from the Explorer.

"Get that guy's gun," Taggert hisses.

"I can't," Olivia wails.

He shoves her hard. "Do you wanna fucking die out here?"

Frightened into action, Olivia shoulders her door open and leaps out into the storm. Three long strides bring her to the body. The man is on his back in the mud. Olivia snatches up his rifle, then spots a pistol in the pocket of his fleece vest and takes that too.

A flash from the Silverado pulses in the corner of her eye, and bullets crack and whistle all around her. She half crawls, half runs back to the Explorer. More rounds ding into the truck, metal hitting metal. She and Taggert cower beneath the dash until the shooting stops.

"The M-16," Taggert says, reaching out the hand that isn't applying pressure to his leg.

"What?" Olivia says, confused.

"The fucking rifle."

She passes it to him, and he uses the stock to punch a hole in the shattered safety glass of the windshield, then releases his hold on his thigh long enough to draw back the bolt and fire at the Silverado.

"Take the keys out of my pocket," he says. "Put them into the ignition."

His voice is slurred, his tongue uncooperative. They killed him, Olivia marvels. She fishes in his pants with tears in her eyes. Her hand comes away coated in blood.

TAGGERT LETS LOOSE with another burst. Got to keep their heads down until he can start the truck. He's getting weaker, though, feels the juice draining out of him. The round in his thigh must have hit an artery. As soon as he and Olivia break out of here, he'll have her apply a tourniquet.

The girl fumbles with the keys. As she's pushing them into

the slot, her door pops open. It's the fat man who, just a second ago, appeared to be KIA. She screams and slides over the center console in an attempt to get away from him.

"Let me in," the fat man says. He's bleeding from a wound in his side, looks half crazy.

"Shoot him," Taggert snaps at Olivia.

She kicks the guy, catches him in the chest. He falls back into the mud.

"Shoot him," Taggert yells again.

She bobbles the Glock, gets it straight, and leans out the door to point it down at the motherfucker.

"Stop!" someone new shouts and knocks her arm sideways before she can pull the trigger. "He's with me."

Boone. The son of a bitch who came asking about Oscar crouches behind the door and fires at the Silverado with another M-16, like he's on their side.

"What are you doing here?" he asks Olivia.

"I...I don't know, I..." she stammers. "What do we do now?"

"Hey, it's your fucking plan," Boone says.

Everything becomes clear to Taggert then. Not the dirty details, but the gist of Olivia's betrayal is right there in front of him. She was fucking him over too, had something cooked up with this Boone, some sort of double cross that fell apart when the Mexicans started shooting. The little bitch has been playing him all along. He must have Alzheimer's or something, not to have seen this coming. He must have stroked out and not even realized it.

His vision is fading, and there's a chill in his guts. He's done for, no getting around that, but he'll be damned if these snakes will watch him die.

"Get out," he says to Olivia.

"Wait, Bill," she says.

He lifts his right hand from the hole in his leg, balls it into a bloody fist, and punches her repeatedly in the face and body.

"Get. The. Fuck. Out."

Olivia retreats under the hail of blows, backs awkwardly out of the truck. Taggert starts the Explorer and pops it into drive. He can't feel his right foot anymore, so he uses his left to jam the gas pedal to the floor.

The tires spin in the mud, then catch, and suddenly he's moving toward the Silverado, picking up speed. Mando and his partner fire wildly through their broken windshield—at him, at Olivia and the others, who are now pinned down with no cover.

Taggert grips the wheel in one hand, the rifle in the other. At least he got out of Kentucky. At least he got to be boss. He fires the M-16, peppering the Silverado with bullets. Mando and the big man duck, but not fast enough. Both take rounds, jerk, and slump. Taggert can barely keep his eyes open. He dreams he's back at the ranch, in bed with Olivia. What'd she say that day? "More good times than bad, baby, that's all we can ask for. More good times than bad."

THE MEXICAN IN the cowboy hat bails out of the Silverado an instant before the Explorer plows into it. A spark hits gas somewhere, and an explosion blooms, its fiery petals unfurling into the lowering sky. Boone throws himself on top of Robo as bits of jagged steel gouge the mud around them. When he lifts his head, both vehicles are burning, the conflagration mirrored in a thousand flickering puddles.

"You're squishing me," Robo says.

Boone rolls off him and rises into a crouch, his rifle trained on the crash. Thick black smoke rises up to join the clouds. There's no movement in the wreckage.

"How you doing?" Boone asks Robo.

"Great, 'cept for this hole in me," Robo replies.

He tries to sit up, but Boone puts a hand on his chest. "Hold it," he says. "Someone's still kicking."

The Mexican in the cowboy hat is lying next to the burning trucks. He raises his arms and yells, "Help me. *Por Dios*."

"Toss the gun away," Boone shouts at him.

A pistol arcs into the air and splashes down near the side of the road. First things first though. Boone looks around for Olivia. He spots her lying facedown in the mud and duckwalks to where she's sprawled and turns her over.

Her breathing is labored, and her eyes bulge with terror and pain. A glimpse of blue intestines and yellow fat makes Boone flinch. Something—a bullet, shrapnel from the explosion—has torn a hole in the girl's stomach. Boone wipes mud from her face and brushes back her matted hair. He'll have to work fast.

"Can you hear me?" he asks.

Olivia nods, white lips trembling.

"We're taking you to a hospital," he says. "But first you need to tell me where Amy is."

Olivia shakes her head. "Hospital," she grunts. "Now."

"Listen to me. Where is Amy?"

Olivia grimaces, shakes her head again.

Boone pulls the Ruger from his pocket and shows it to her. What he's about to do sickens him, but he can't think of any other way to go about it.

"You've got a hole in you the size of my fist," he says. "Tell me where Amy is, or I'm going to shove this gun in there and stir everything around until you do."

"Hospital," Olivia hisses.

Boone presses the pistol's barrel to the wound. Olivia gasps and arches her back. Boone takes the gun away, and she settles into the mud.

"Okay," she gasps.

"Tell me," Boone says.

"You love her, huh?"

"Tell me."

Olivia swallows hard and whispers an address, then says, "Hospital. Now!"

Boone stands and looks up at the warehouse. Carl eases the Xterra out of the ruin and starts down toward the depot.

"A few more minutes," Boone says to Olivia.

He slips the M-16's strap over his shoulder and covers the Mexican with his pistol as he approaches him. Both trucks are fully engulfed now, the flames like greedy, caressing fingers. Hot steel hisses under the steadily falling rain.

The Mexican lifts his head. "Help me, amigo," he says. "I got money, dope, whatever you want."

Looks like he's been hit in the chest, the legs, both arms. Hard to tell with all the blood. His hat lies beside him in the mud.

Boone hears splashing and turns to see that Robo has managed to get to his feet and is now staggering toward Taggert's grocery bag and the stacks of bills scattered around it. The big man lowers himself to the ground next to the money just as the Xterra's horn blows once, twice, again.

"The fuck's his problem," Robo says.

Carl is stopped on the bluff above town. He's standing on the running board of the truck, waving frantically. Boone lifts his arms in a "What?" gesture.

"Run!" Carl shouts.

A grinding, frothing roar rises above the din of wind and rain, and the ground shakes beneath Boone's feet. Thunder, he thinks. Or an earthquake. He looks to where Carl is pointing and sees a five-foot wall of brown water sluicing toward town down a previously dry wash. A flash flood triggered by the storm.

He takes a step backward, bewildered, agog, then sprints to where Robo is shoving soggy bundles of cash into his pockets. Water is swirling around their ankles when he jerks the big man to his feet.

"Whoa," Robo says, shaking off his hand. He's ready to fight until he spots the torrent bearing down on them. Frozen in place, he gapes at it, and Boone has to grab his T-shirt again to get him running toward the bluff.

They pass Olivia. Her eyes are closed, and she isn't moving. Boone considers dragging her along with them, but then Robo stumbles and almost goes down, and he's forced to turn his attention back to him.

They reach the rocky slope below the bluff and scramble up it as the flood slams into town and courses down the main road, sweeping away everything in its path. Robo is behind Boone, and the water quickly rises to his knees. The current sucks at him and threatens to yank him off his feet.

Boone grabs his arm with both hands and pulls, heels braced against a boulder. The pain from his injured ankle makes him yell, but, step by shaky step, Robo emerges from the maelstrom, until he collapses beside Boone and enthusiastically thanks sweet Jesus for saving his life.

Boone watches as the flood surges through the town. The vehicles have been pushed farther down the road and now lie wedged against the old stone post office, everything above the waterline still burning furiously.

Olivia is nowhere to be seen, borne away to a muddy grave.

The Mexican too. The counterfeit bills, what was left of Taggert's money, all of it gone.

Lightning flashes, followed by a heart-stopping peal of thunder. Carl appears above Boone and Robo at the top of the bluff and slides down to where they're lying.

"Y'all are some lucky motherfuckers," he yells over the noise of the storm and flood.

Boone wipes the mud off his face and watches a drowned cow float past. The water level is already dropping. The way these desert storms work, in an hour the torrent will be little more than a trickle. Nothing left but the scars.

27

Robo stretches out in the backseat of the Xterra and lifts his T-shirt so Boone can examine his injury. Looks like the bullet passed right through a roll of fat, missing any organs. There's not even much blood. Boone presses a bandanna to the wound and tells Robo to keep it there.

Carl barrels through a puddle that turns out to be deeper than it appeared. Muddy water splashes up onto the windows, and the tires lose traction briefly before digging in and lifting the truck out of the bog.

They're headed north, toward the 15. The map showed more pavement that way. Even with all the luck in the world, though, it'll still take at least three hours to get back to L.A. Boone settles into the passenger seat and adjusts the vent so that cool air blows in his face. He needs to ready himself for what's coming next. Rescuing Amy could prove to be hairier than what he just went through. Close quarters, no idea of the layout or how many people he's up against. A real learn-as-you-go situation.

He rips the dirty bandage off his forehead and crumples it in his fist. The windshield wipers scrape across dry glass. The storm has eased up, and a band of brilliant blue in the distance augurs its passing.

Robo is busy with the money he snatched from the mud.

He counts the bills three times before announcing, "There's almost forty grand here."

"That'll do," Carl says.

The money makes Boone feel better. At least Robo and Carl will get something for putting their asses on the line. He drops his head and grinds his palms into his eyes. "I want to apologize to you guys," he says. "I have no idea what happened out there."

Robo slaps him in the head with a stack of hundreds and says, "I'll tell you what happened: the strong survived, just like they're supposed to."

Strong? The shit some people sell themselves. It can break your heart and make you laugh all at the same time.

VIRGIL CHECKS HIS phone again, makes sure he's got a signal. Olivia should be calling any time now to tell him how things went. He's feeling a little muzzy today. Most of last night is a blur, but he knows that he ended up on Amy's bed. At five this morning he awoke there beside her and lay confused as hell for a while before running to the toilet to puke himself empty. He's pretty certain he didn't fuck her, but he can't be sure, and she's not talking. Not a word all day. And she won't eat either. He sure hopes he didn't fuck her.

He aims the remote at the TV and cycles through the channels. Nothing holds his interest for more than a few seconds, so he stands and walks to the front door. Tigger meows at him and leaps into the weeds when he steps outside. Olivia told him to bring in the mail every day while they're here, so nobody wonders what's up with Eton and decides to check on him. There's nothing in the box but coupons for a Mexican supermarket.

A silver Audi coupe pulls up to the curb in front of the house.

The guy who climbs out of it is one of those Hollywood dickheads with the blond highlights and the Bluetooth. His jeans look like something a chick would wear.

He stands on the cracked and stained sidewalk and says, "Eton around?"

Virgil gives him a hard look. "He's on vacation."

"Well, check it out"—the guy comes closer and lowers his voice—"you wouldn't know where I could get some weed, would you?"

Fucker could be a cop, but, no, not with those gay-ass sunglasses. Virgil decides that it ain't no sin to make a little easy money while he waits for Olivia.

"What do you need?" he asks Hollywood.

"Just a quarter."

"Wait out here."

Virgil runs upstairs to Eton's file cabinet, opens the top drawer, and sorts through his stash until he comes up with what looks to be a quarter ounce of marijuana sealed in a Ziploc bag. Hollywood is standing on the porch when Virgil returns, jumps when he opens the door.

"That'll be one fifty," Virgil says, waving the bag.

"Really?" the guy says. "Eton usually charges me one twenty."

"You see Eton anywhere?"

Hollywood frowns but reaches for his wallet.

When he drives off, Virgil decides to sneak upstairs to check on Amy. He's a little worried that she might be up to something. She's been acting awfully strange.

He turns the TV up to cover the sound of his approach and ascends the stairs slowly, pausing on each step to count to ten. Once in the hallway, he drops to his hands and knees.

A floorboard creaks beneath him. He waits, head down, but the only sounds that come to him are the TV and the wind outside.

The door to the bedroom is ajar. He eases forward and peeks in. Amy is lying on the bed just like he left her, hands and feet tied to the bed frame. Her eyes are closed. Nothing fishy at all.

He's thinking he ought to wake her up anyway, double-check her bonds just to be sure, when a rustling gets his attention. He rests his cheek on the floor and squints into the dark cavern beneath the bed. Dust bunnies as big as his fist, a dead woman's slippers, and a rat. A greasy black rat staring back at him.

Virgil scrabbles to his feet, all sneakiness forgotten. He races down the hall and takes the stairs two at a time back to the living room, where he falls onto the couch and lifts both feet off the floor. He's going to stay right here, smoking bowls and playing Call of Duty until Olivia shows up, and when she does, he's checking into a Motel 6.

BOONE WALKS PAST the house Olivia gave him the address to, the hood of his jacket up to hide his face. It's a dilapidated Craftsman foundering on an overgrown lot. Two stories, boarded-up windows, a blue tarp nailed to the roof to stop a leak.

Everything's shut up tight, as far as Boone can see. The place looks deserted. He wonders if, as a final fuck you, Olivia sent him panting to a long-abandoned firetrap. Only one way to find out.

He returns to the Olds, which is parked half a block away. He drove over as soon as Carl dropped him off at the bungalow. Carl offered to come with him, but Boone told him no, he'd already done enough, and someone had to pick Robo up from Doc Ock's. He slips into the car, reaches under the seat for the Ruger Robo lent him, and stows it in the pocket of his jacket.

A police car appears as he's walking back to the house. He keeps his head up, eyes straight ahead. One foot in front of the other, nice and easy. The cruiser rolls past, the cop behind the wheel too busy jabbering into her phone to notice him.

Boone steps through a breach in the broken-down picket fence and jogs to the corner of the house, one hand in his pocket to keep the pistol from bouncing out. Pressing his back to the wall, he listens for sounds from inside. That's a television, for sure.

He moves to a window and goes up on his toes to peer through it. Heavy drapes block most of the view, but a thin gap reveals Virgil lying on an overstuffed velvet sofa in the darkened living room, video-game controller in hand, a Glock on the coffee table. No sign of Amy.

Boone creeps farther along the side of the house. The next window he comes to is covered with plywood, and the next. When he reaches the backyard, he draws the Ruger and thumbs the safety.

Two steps lead up to the back door, which opens onto a cluttered utility room containing a washer, dryer, and water heater. The door is unlocked but held shut by a hook-and-eye fastener. Boone pulls the door open as far as it'll go, then slides the blade of his pocketknife into the space between the door and the jamb and lifts the hook out of the eye.

The door opens with a squeak. Boone pauses, alert for footsteps. Nothing but the sound of gunfire and explosions drifting out of the living room. The door between the utility room and the kitchen is wide open, and he steps through it.

The sink is full of crusty dishes, and a dried-out slice of pizza sits in a delivery box on the counter. Boone's shoes stick to the linoleum as he moves toward another door. He's careful to avoid a puddle of brown liquid that's leaked out of a trash bag slumped against the stove.

He holds the Ruger in a two-handed grip, elbows bent so that it's pointing at the ceiling. Sidestepping to the doorway, he leans over to peer through it, only his head exposed. The dining and living rooms flow together. Both are dark, cluttered with antique furniture and dusty knickknacks.

Virgil is sitting cross-legged on the sofa, wrapped up in the game he's playing. Boone pulls back into the kitchen to work through what comes next. There's no stealthy way to take the kid out. It's going to be all about speed and surprise. He picks up a can of SpaghettiOs off a shelf. He'll toss it into the room as a diversion, then charge in and do his thing.

He draws back the can, steps into the doorway, and comes face to face with Virgil, who is on his way into the kitchen. The kid yelps and drops the plastic cup he's carrying. Before Boone can grab him, Virgil turns and runs. He heads across the dining room to a staircase leading to the second floor instead of toward the Glock.

Boone is right on his tail, pounding up the stairs behind him. He gets a hold of the kid's Rays jersey as Virgil reaches the upstairs hallway. Yanking him to a stop, Boone brings his other hand around to slam the gun into the side of the kid's head. Virgil's legs go all loosey-goosey, and he drops to the floor.

Boone crouches next to him and swings the pistol from side

to side to cover the doors opening onto the hallway. No movement, no sound but his own breathing.

"Amy!" he shouts.

"Jimmy," comes the reply from the first door on the left.

Boone grabs Virgil's jersey again and drags the kid behind him down the hall. He opens the door, and there's Amy, tied to a bed.

"Is there anybody else in the house?" he asks.

"Just him," Amy says with a nod at Virgil.

The kid moans as he comes back to consciousness, tries to sit up. Boone puts a foot between his shoulder blades and presses him to the floor.

"Stay down," he barks, and Virgil goes limp.

Boone steps over to the bed and uses his knife to cut Amy loose. She sits up and rubs her wrists and ankles. Her hair is tangled, and dark circles ring her eyes.

Boone places a hand on her arm and says, "You all right?"

"Give me a second," she replies, and Boone can feel her shaking.

"Tell him I didn't hurt you," Virgil says from the floor.

"Shut up!" Boone snaps.

"You're by yourself?" Amy says. "No police?"

"No police," Boone replies.

"Should we call them?"

"No," Boone says.

Amy stares at him long and hard, then shakes her head, disappointed. She stands gingerly, one hand clutching the bed frame until she can trust her legs to hold her up.

"I have to go to the bathroom," she says, anger and disgust in her voice. She pushes past Boone and steps over Virgil on her way out.

I've lost her, Boone thinks.

As soon as he hears the bathroom door close, he pulls Virgil to his feet. The kid whimpers and brings up his arms to protect his head. "This was all Olivia's idea," he says.

Blood dribbles from a cut under his eye, and a lump is rising on his cheek. Boone contemplates slapping the piss out of him, giving him a beating he'll never forget, but knows he'll just regret it later. Instead, he pulls the kid close and hisses in his ear, "Time to go."

"Can I get my shit?"

"You've got about five seconds."

Boone follows him into a room across the hall and stands over him while he frantically stuffs clothes into a Nike gym bag. When he's finished, Boone takes hold of his jersey and pushes him downstairs.

"My shoes," Virgil says as they're passing through the living room.

Boone walks to the coffee table and uses his foot to push the Glock off and kick it under the couch. He hooks the laces of a pair of Adidas lying on the floor and carries the shoes to Virgil. The kid balances on one leg, starts to slip the left shoe on, but Boone pokes him with the barrel of the Ruger and says, "You can do that later." He unlocks the front door and pulls it open. Virgil steps out onto the porch, then turns to face him.

"What about Olivia?" he asks.

"She's dead," Boone replies.

Sudden tears shine in Virgil's eyes. "Was it you that did it?" he says, his voice hoarse.

"The men they went to meet in the desert fucked them over," Boone says. "Shot her and Taggert."

Virgil nods slowly, lost in thought, then wipes his eyes with the backs of his hands and walks off the porch and out to the street.

Boone closes the door and finds Amy watching from the bottom of the stairs. She glowers at him and walks to the dining room table to rifle through a purse sitting there.

"Everything in it?" Boone asks.

Amy pulls out a pair of sunglasses and a ring of keys. "What do you care?" she says. "You just let the guy who held me hostage walk away scot-free."

"We can talk about it now," Boone says. "But it's probably better if we get moving."

Amy puts on the glasses and rushes past him. He follows her out to the porch and closes the door behind them.

Amy pulls up short when she reaches the sidewalk, looks both ways on the street. Her knees begin to tremble, and a sob rolls through her body. Boone can't stop himself; he moves in and wraps his arms around her. She tries halfheartedly to shake him off, then stands with her head bowed, quietly weeping.

"My car," she says.

"They probably parked it close by," Boone says. "We'll find it."

He steers her to the Olds and helps her into the passenger seat. It's hot inside, so he rolls down the windows. Amy digs some Kleenex out of her purse and blows her nose. Boone decides to drive around the block, see what they can see.

Amy spots the Civic as soon as he turns the first corner, parked under a tree, covered with bird shit. She's out the door before Boone can say anything. He waits while she unlocks the car and slips inside.

"Want me to follow you?" he calls to her.

She doesn't respond, just drives off. Straight to the cops for all Boone knows. And how can he blame her?

NOT TO THE cops, though—home. Boone pulls up to the bungalows after stopping at the store for dog food and is relieved and grateful to see the Civic out front. He parks the Olds and walks up the steps. Amy's door is closed, her blinds down.

Joto barks and tries to leap into his arms when he enters his place. Boone cleans up the messes the dog made, then takes him for a quick walk. When they get back, he pulls a beer from the fridge and calls Carl, who tells him that it only took the doc an hour to patch up Robo's bullet hole and that the last he saw of him when he dropped him in the valley, he was fighting off his kids, who wanted to crawl all over their dad.

"I guess it went okay with you," Carl says.

"She's safe and sound," Boone replies.

"Ock cost us five hundred," Carl says. "I let Robo hold the rest of the money till we have a chance to sort things out. You think that's okay?"

"It's fine," Boone says. "We'll deal with it tomorrow or something."

He feeds Joto, grabs another beer, and is out cold on the couch before he's halfway through it. He dreams of floods and fire and Olivia's dying face until he pops awake about midnight, shaking all over. It's going to be rough for a while. You don't squeeze a thing like this into your old life. You have to tear down and start over, build a new one around it.

He takes a long, hot shower and puts clean dressings on his bites and other injuries. He's not hungry but knows he needs to eat, so he boils some spaghetti, pours half a jar of Prego over it, and wolfs it down.

He's asleep again by two and doesn't surface until the phone rings at eight. It's Amy. He sits up in bed, wide awake. She's at work. He can hear children in the background. There's a Starbucks in Los Feliz, and she wants to meet there when she gets off.

"I almost called the police ten times last night," she says. "But I'm going to be much cooler than I should and give you a chance to explain before I decide how to handle this."

"That's all I ask," Boone replies.

THE CAFÉ IS busy when he arrives. The line to order stretches out the front door. Amy is already there, grading papers at a table on the patio. She looks so tired, so fragile, and it kills Boone that he has anything to do with it.

"No coffee?" she says when he sits down across from her. "Guess you're doing better than I am."

"I can't believe you went to work this morning."

She sips from her cup and shrugs. "Trying to keep my mind occupied."

"I want to thank you for talking to me."

"I don't have a lot of time," Amy says, glancing at her watch.

"Sure, sure," Boone says. "So let me get right to it."

He starts with Robo being hired to find out what happened to Oscar, then tells her about visiting Maribel and the baby, and how he came to feel that if he got to the bottom of Oscar's death, it would somehow make up for what happened in Malibu, for the years he spent in prison, for ruining Carl's business.

Amy's face is blank as he describes the trip to Taggert's ranch and what happened there, and how he thought the whole thing was done when he threw Olivia and Virgil out of his bungalow, but it wasn't, and soon people were dead, and people were hurt, and she spent two days tied to a bed, fearing for her life.

"And now, after all that, I've got to ask you for a favor," he says. "If you feel you have to go to the police, I understand. But please, just one thing, please leave Carl and Robo out of it. It's my fault they're involved in this, and they don't deserve to have their lives messed up because of me.

"I'm way out of line, I know, but I'd be forever thankful. They've got wives and kids, and they're good men, really good men. If you do this for me, I don't know what I can ever do to pay you back, but whatever you think of, I'll make it happen."

Amy shuffles her papers and taps her pen on the table. A bus's brakes squeal like something being slaughtered, and Boone doesn't know where to look—at her, at the ground, at the sun festering in the dirty sky.

"Did it?" she finally says.

"Did what?" Boone replies.

"Did finding out what happened to Oscar make you feel any better?"

"After everything that went down, things getting out of hand like they did, no," Boone says. "In fact, I feel like even more of an asshole. I mean, sure I got to the bottom of it, sure there's a little more truth in the world, but at what cost?"

"Truth," Amy says, looking Boone in the eye. "Huh."

"Or something like that," Boone says.

Amy leans back in her chair and sighs. She reaches into her purse for a pack of American Spirits, pulls one out. "Remember when I told you about getting shot and leaving the force and all that?" she says.

"Of course," Boone replies.

"There's more to it than that."

"Okay."

"After the kid shot me, my partner shot him, in the leg," Amy says as she puts a match to her cigarette. "The kid went down, threw away his gun, and started yelling that he wanted a lawyer. My partner didn't listen though. He fired three more times, killing the boy.

"Then he came over and sat down beside me, put my head in his lap. 'Girl,' he said, 'good thing you were out cold and didn't see what just happened. That fuckhead was fixing to finish you off, and it's only by the grace of God that I was able to put his lights out first.'

"He gave me my story, and I stuck to it all through the investigation. Out cold, didn't see a thing. I didn't want to mess up his life. I also didn't want to be a cop anymore. So I quit."

She flicks the filter of her cigarette with her thumb and stares down at the ground. Boone wants to touch her, to offer some kind of comfort, but they're not like that anymore. Everything's already changed.

"Get out of here," she says.

"What do you mean?" Boone replies.

"I mean I'm done with this. I'm not going to call the police, but I also don't want to have any more to do with you. What happened that day with my partner was the last secret I ever wanted to keep, but now you've gone and saddled me with another, and I can't forgive you for that. I can't stand secrets. They're too close to lies."

Boone gropes for her hand, but she pulls it away. Everything comes loose inside him. He stands and clears his throat. "Thank you," he says.

She takes a deep drag off her cigarette, ignoring him, and there's nothing for him to do but walk away.

The light turns green, and traffic surges with a terrible roar.

He beats his way forward against a tide of smiling faces and extravagant gestures. A woman laughs as she passes by, a baby cries. Everybody's spouting nonsense, and everybody has a point. The bashing, crashing swirl of the city threatens to tear him to pieces, so he puts his head down, holds tight to a few hard truths, and lets the rest be swept away.

Epilogue

BOONE'S PAROLE OFFICER, DEEANDRA CUMMINGS, LEANS forward in her chair and plays with the rhinestone glued to her thumbnail. A skinny black woman with close-cropped salt-and-pepper hair, she's always immaculately turned out when Boone makes his twice-a-month visits and always seems like she'd rather be anywhere but behind her desk, talking to him or any other criminal.

"How's life treating you?" she asks, squinting at her nail.

"Good. Everything's good," Boone replies.

"You're all healed, finally."

Boone reaches up to touch the fresh scar on his forehead. "Close to it," he says.

"You men and that boxing. What's the fun in beating on each other?"

BOONE HOOKED UP with Robo and Carl at a Shakey's on Sunset a couple days after he met with Amy. Over a pitcher of beer, they discussed how to divide the money.

Robo needed two grand off the top to replace the M-16 and pistol that didn't make it back from the desert. Boone asked for five thousand dollars to pass on to Oscar's kid. Robo and Carl agreed to that, and Boone told them to split whatever was left between the two of them. They ordered a pizza and watched the end of a Dodgers game on the big screen, then walked out to the Xterra to cut up the cash.

Robo insisted that Boone accompany him when he drove down to Maribel's aunt's house. He wore his security uniform and Boone donned his sport coat. Their story was that Oscar's death remained a mystery, but his employer at the ranch had asked them to deliver Oscar's last paycheck.

Maribel accepted the money shyly, thanking them in a voice so low, they could barely make it out. Little Alex crawled happily around the cluttered house. There was a scab on his forehead from where he'd fallen on the porch the day before, trying to pet a cat that had wandered into the yard. He's so fast, Maribel's aunt said, like a little rabbit.

DANNY BERKSON CALLED one day.

"You got a dog living there?" he asked.

A tenant had complained to the owner of the property about Joto. Boone asked Berkson if there was anything he could do to get the owner to change the rules regarding pets.

"The guy *does* owe me," Berkson said, and a few hours later he called back to tell Boone he was free to keep Joto in the bungalow.

Boone called Loretta and asked her to take Joto off her Web site.

"I knew you'd come around," she said.

"Why are you crying then?" Boone asked.

"I'm just so happy."

Boone wondered if she was this overjoyed when she received the anonymous e-mail he sent the day after he got back from Lanfair, the one containing the address of Taggert's ranch and a suggestion that she might find a couple of abandoned pit bulls locked up in the barn there.

BOONE KEPT A close eye on the news and saw a small article in the paper about the discovery of two vehicles and two badly burned bodies in a remote section of the Mojave National Preserve. Investigators were trying to determine if there was a link between the as-yet unidentified corpses and another body, that of thirty-two-year-old Paul Spiller, found shot to death beside the 15 Freeway near the California-Nevada border. Physical evidence was hard to come by, though, because the area had recently been hit by a powerful storm.

Boone was tense for a few weeks after reading this and waited for a knock at the door. He assumed the worst when two detectives walked into the restaurant one day and flashed their badges, but it turned out they wanted to see Simon to warn him about a couple of robbers who were targeting boulevard businesses. June slipped past, July, and Boone was still a free man. He began to relax a bit, sleep better, and to think that maybe he was going to squeak by this time.

"STAYING OUT OF trouble?" DeeAndra asks as she reaches into her desk drawer for her nail file and starts doing a little cleanup work on her pinky.

"You know me," Boone replies. "Boring as hell."

"Boring's good," DeeAndra says. "We like boring. Still living in the same place?"

"Same place."

"And the job?"

DeeAndra's office is a windowless cell, and the air conditioner is struggling. Boone can smell the sweat of every nervous ex-con who's ever sat where he's sitting.

"It's good," he says.

"No unauthorized travel?"

"Nope."

"No drugs, no guns, no thugs?"

"No girlfriend, no money, no fun at all," Boone says.

DeeAndra smirks, then marks off a series of boxes on the form in front of her. She opens her desk drawer again and brings out a plastic cup.

"Fill this up on your way out," she says. "Officer Ito will accompany you to the restroom."

"My favorite part," Boone says as he takes the cup.

"Yeah, I know you," DeeAndra says with a smile. "You a kinky one, ain't you?"

AMY LEFT FOR a month as soon as school let out for the summer, slid her rent check under Boone's door in advance. He never learned where she went, but she seemed to be happier when she returned. He heard her laughing into the phone one evening and was filled with relief. They exchanged nods when they passed in the courtyard but didn't speak. He held out hope that one day the ice would thaw. They had something before, and they could have it again; he was sure of it.

But then she gave notice that she'd be moving out of her bungalow at the end of August. No reason in the letter, just the facts. Boone wanted to talk to her, to try to change her mind, but no matter how he spun the situation, he couldn't see where he had the right. So he just continued to smile and nod every time their paths crossed and worked seven days a week to keep his mind off her.

August flew by in a blur of shockingly hot afternoons and long, hectic nights at the restaurant. Then this morning he walked out to find a moving van parked at the curb and a team of short, burly Latinos carrying boxes out of Amy's place. He hurried off before he caught sight of her, and vowed to stay away until she was gone. Not a brave reaction, he knew, but maybe, finally, a smart one.

AFTER HIS PISS test Boone walks out of the CDCR building. He has a few hours to kill before work, so he decides to see a movie. He buys a paper from a sidewalk box and pages through it to find out what's playing where. A semi hauling ass down Alameda blows its horn, and he jumps back from the curb, spooked. Two shitbirds in jail ID wristbands snicker, then try to sell him a laptop neither of them knows how to turn on.

The theater is almost empty. Some spy film with lots of running, lots of gunning. They're in Russia, D.C., Vegas, fighting in a jungle somewhere. Boone can't follow it; his mind keeps wandering. After a while he gives up, decides to go into work early.

IT'S A MONDAY evening, superslow. The only customer at the bar is a tourist from London who's nursing a pint while his wife and kids shop for souvenirs.

Boone is checking inventory on the shelves, putting together a list of what to pull from the liquor locker, when a ragged figure enters the restaurant. His clothes are grimy, his hair and beard matted, and his eyes dart about in their sockets like nervous birds in twin cages. He hesitates for a second as if confused about where he is, then shuffles to the bar and slides onto a stool. Homeless, or damn close to it.

"Good evening, sir," Boone says. "Welcome to the Tick Tock. What can I get you?" This is Simon's latest stroke of promotional genius. He's decided to class the place up by having the staff greet every customer this way, and there's a five-dollar fine if you don't.

The homeless man licks his cracked lips and says, "Johnny Walker Black on the rocks."

Boone pours the drink and sets it in front of him, and the man reaches into the pocket of his filthy coat and pulls out a plastic bag filled with coins.

"What's that go for?" he asks.

"Nine dollars, sir," Boone replies.

The man begins to carefully count out and stack quarters on the bar.

Simon hisses and gestures from the waitress station, and Boone walks down to see what's bugging him.

"What the fuck did you serve that hobo for?" he whispers.

"Guy asks for a drink, guy has money..." Boone lets his voice trail off with a shrug.

"One and he's done," Simon says. "And what the fuck is Robo thinking, letting him in here in the first place?" He storms off to find out.

Simon doesn't irritate Boone as much as he used to, mainly because Boone knows he won't have to take his shit much longer. He's been talking to the owner of a new bar opening on Las Palmas, an exclusive speakeasy catering to the youngest, richest, and most famous of Hollywood's partying class. The owner comes in for a drink now and then, he and Boone hit it off, and last week he offered Boone a job. Nicer joint, bigger tips, and no rat-faced daddy's boy looking for any opportunity to bust his balls. Sounds like a dream come true.

He's feeling fat and sassy as he wipes up a puddle and snaps his towel at Gonzalo, who wings an ice cube at him. Boone ducks and comes up just in time to watch Amy walk in and sit at the bar. For a second he thinks he's mistaken, that it's merely a girl who resembles her, but, no, it's her all right. He walks over to greet her, not even trying to stop the smile spreading across his face.

"Hey," he says. "Hi there."

"Hello," she replies.

She looks great. Silky black blouse, tight jeans. Her hair is loose on her shoulders, the way it's prettiest, and the playful twinkle has returned to her eyes, the one he fell for the first time they met.

"What can I get you?" he asks.

"That's not really..." she starts, then stops and sighs. "How about an Absolut and tonic."

Boone hopes she doesn't notice how much his hands are shaking as he prepares the drink. She grins after her first sip and says, "Perfect." He's got a million questions but isn't sure he's allowed to ask them. They haven't spoken in almost three months.

They stare at each other for a few seconds, until Amy finally says, "I'm moving."

"I saw," Boone replies.

"To Montana."

"Open a used bookstore, marry a rich cowboy, right?"

Amy looks down at her drink, a little embarrassed, and stabs her ice cubes with her straw. "I don't know about that," she says. "I just want to do something different from what I've been doing, and Montana seems like a good place to do it."

Boone's smile is officially phony now. Hall-of-fame phony. "Supposed to be pretty there," he says.

"It really is," Amy says. "The mountains, the trees. I'm renting a little cabin by a river outside Bozeman."

Boone steps back from the bar and looks over at the homeless man as if he signaled for another drink. He wants to get away before Amy senses his disappointment. It's nothing she should have to deal with.

"Good luck out there," he says. "You deserve it."

She lifts her purse onto the bar and accidentally knocks over her drink. Boone is right there with a towel.

"I'm so nervous," she says.

"Me too," Boone replies.

She reaches into her purse for a folded-up sheet of paper, passes it to him. "Here's my e-mail address," she says, "and you already have my phone number. Keep in touch. Maybe you can visit sometime."

"Definitely," Boone says. He plays it cool, even though he's pretty sure you're only this happy a few times in your life.

"It's my birthday," the homeless man announces to nobody in particular.

"It's his birthday," Boone says to Amy. "Let me get you another drink."

She lays her hand on top of his, starts to say something, then stops herself. What comes out instead is, "That's okay. I'm leaving tonight, gonna try to make it as far as Vegas."

Without thinking, Boone leans forward and kisses her on the lips. When he pulls back, she says, "So, yeah, maybe you can come in the spring, after I'm settled in."

"I'm off parole in January," he says.

"Or maybe January," she says.

She squeezes his hand once more, then slides off the stool. On her way out she pauses next to the homeless man and says, "Happy birthday, dude."

"Hey! How'd you know?" he replies.

She turns to wave good-bye to Boone, then walks out the door.

"She's hot," Simon says from the waitress station where he's been lurking. "When she dumps you, give her my number."

Boone is feeling too good to get into it with him. A couple more customers come in, and he sets them up. The homeless guy finishes his drink and moves on to continue his celebration elsewhere.

When it's time for his break, Boone walks out front to see what's up with Robo. The fat man tells him a filthy joke and asks to borrow twenty dollars.

Most of the clubs are closed tonight, so there's not much traffic on the boulevard. A police car cruises past with two supremely bored cops inside. The sky is stained purple from all the neon, and it's still hot, ninety degrees at 10:00 p.m. An old Caddy rolls up to the valet stand. Robo steps over to open the passenger-side door, while a kid in a red vest attends to the driver, Mr. King. Boone smiles to see the respect the old man and his wife are shown.

He looks up at the full moon and imagines Amy driving alone across the desert tonight, the only bright thing in all that windy black. She'll be fine, he tells himself, she'll be fine, and heads inside to finish his shift.

Acknowledgments

Thank you to Asya Muchnick and Timothy Wager, for untangling the knots.

Thank you to everyone at Little, Brown, for all your hard work.

Thank you to the American Academy of Arts and Letters and the Rosenthal Family Foundation, for your generosity.

And thank you to Janet Fitch, Clayton Moore, Chris Offutt, and George Pelecanos, for your kindness.

RICHARD LANGE is the recipient of a 2009 Guggenheim Fellowship and the author of the highly acclaimed story collection *Dead Boys,* which received the Rosenthal Family Foundation Award from the American Academy of Arts and Letters. His fiction has appeared in *StoryQuarterly*, *The Sun*, *The Iowa Review,* and *The Best American Mystery Stories 2004*. He lives in Los Angeles. This is his first novel.